A DIST

A DISTANT DREAM

Margaret Graham

BANTAM BOOKS
TORONTO · NEW YORK · LONDON · SYDNEY · AUCKLAND

A DISTANT DREAM
A BANTAM BOOK: 0 553 40818 6

Originally published in Great Britain by Doubleday,
a division of Transworld Publishers Ltd

PRINTING HISTORY
Doubleday edition published 1995
Bantam edition published 1996

Set in 10/11pt Linotron New Baskerville by
Falcon Oast Graphic Art

Bantam Books are published by Transworld Publishers Ltd,
61–63 Uxbridge Road, London W5 5SA,
in Australia by Transworld Publishers (Australia) Pty Ltd,
15–25 Helles Avenue, Moorebank, NSW 2170,
and in New Zealand by Transworld Publishers (NZ) Ltd,
3 William Pickering Drive, Albany, Auckland.

Reproduced, printed and bound in Great Britain by
Cox & Wyman Ltd, Reading, Berks.

IN MEMORY OF

Daniel Joseph Buckley

Acknowledgements

Danny Buckley, owner of The Yeovil Bookshop, has been unstinting in his advice and help for this novel, though any mistakes are attributable to me. He told me of his father, Daniel Joseph Buckley, who served in the 1914–18 war with the British navy. He was wounded and taken by hospital ship to Dublin in 1916. He and his fellow injured were appalled to see the centre of Dublin looking like the ruined towns in Flanders and Northern France. One of the soldiers waiting on the quay to receive them warned them that a similar fate awaited the injured men if they messed the British about.

Daniel Joseph Buckley went home to Cork, completed his leave and returned to the Royal Navy, serving in submarines for the rest of the war but becoming an active republican on his return. He rejoined the Royal Navy in 1939 and died in 1942. Danny, his son, says, 'Most Irishmen of his generation respected and even admired England, though they didn't always like her. To them, the events of 1916 were as if a strict parent had suddenly turned into a tyrant. Their sense of outrage took a long time to diminish.' Danny has helped me in innumerable ways. My love and thanks to him. My thanks also to those I spoke to in Australia about the Catholic–Protestant situation as it then was in some sectors, and to my Australian friend over here, Hal Thomsett. And to

Charlie and Phyl Hine who once lived in Kalgoorlie.

As always, Bath Travel of Yeovil have borne with me, and helped me to sort out my travel arrangements in Ireland and Australia. I fell in love with Ireland and already love Australia. I was able to see the Group Settlers again, and refresh my memory for the later part of the novel. Sue Bramble and her staff of Martock Library were their usual brilliant selves, and Glenn Preedy's help was invaluable.

Chapter One

'Holy Mother of God, it's the Tans,' Cait breathed, hauling on the reins with one hand and brushing back her auburn hair with the other. The pony slowed, the cart lurched as the wheels nudged the ruts in the lane. The churn rattled behind her. It was 1920 and the Black and Tans were stretched across this track in County Limerick a hundred yards ahead, their mongrel uniforms etched dark against the early morning sunlight, and they had no right in her country.

'Steady,' she soothed the pony, but it was herself she was really calming. 'Steady, Tanzy, they're only British dregs trying to look like police. Sure, you'd have thought the Royal Irish Constabulary would have found proper uniforms for the men the British government sent across as police reinforcements, wouldn't you now? Steady.' She forced herself to concentrate on the Irish brogue that her voice was at last reacquiring after her childhood years in Manchester.

She heard whistling in the field to her left. It was Widow Murphy driving her cows out onto the road. There was dew still on the fields, and further back mist shrouded the thistles and hid the far-away hills.

'You're late this morning, Mrs Murphy.' Cait struggled to sound in control but knew that her pale skin was too flushed.

Mrs Murphy didn't break her stride, she just shrugged

towards the Tans. 'Sure, but we'll all be late at the creamery this morning, young Cait, and Manager Brennan will be dancing a jig and using too much air to tell how we've all put him out. We'll just have to tell him how there's others that have put us out.' She lifted the stick she carried and hurried the last of the cows in through the gate. 'It's a mortal sin, so it is.'

Cait called, 'Is the block to do with that firing last evening? Was it our Irish Volunteers?'

Mrs Murphy grabbed at the gate. 'Indeed it was. They were raiding a barracks for arms west of the lake, so I hear. The specials'll be searching for arms, or men. They found one lad late last night, your age, nineteen. Tied him to the back of their lorry, dragged him along the roads. Yes, it's a fine police force we've got now. Something to be admired.' Her tone was mocking then strained as she took the weight of the gate and lifted it onto the latch. 'They've done more than the executions after the Rising to bring us together. Look at them, they're beer-swilling scum who know no rules. They're supposed to be British ex-soldiers, but what does that say for the Army? No, I'll be betting that some of that lot were in jail themselves before answering the advertisements to police us. It's a disgrace they're here at all, earning their ten bob a day – but you know that more than most, young Cait.'

Cait clicked at the pony, narrowing her eyes which her mother had said were the colour of an Irish sky in the height of summer – but no, not her mother, not now, not here with the Tans down the road. 'They're covering the whole of the crossroads. I hate them, they're an obscenity. Why don't they clear out, go back to where they belong? Come on, gee up, girl.'

Mrs Murphy lifted her head and laughed. 'Because this is where they *think* they belong, and the British government with them. Our boys will show them different and before the year's out too, I hope, at long, long last. Should have been done centuries ago.'

'Honest to God, I wish I had a gun,' Cait ground out, then shook the reins. 'Gee up there I said,' she yelled at the pony. 'Don't you be too long, Mrs Murphy.'

'And don't you be barging into them because you've got your nose in a book as usual, relying on that pony to keep you on the straight and narrow, God bless her.'

The mare walked on, and Cait watched the smoke curling from the chimneys of the small town behind the roadblock, not the men who grew larger with every second.

But then the sound of them reached her – their rough English voices, the barking orders, the harsh laughter – and she could no longer look above and through them, as they held up the donkey and pony carts coming in from the right and left. Swaggering, they were, pushing their weight around. But didn't they always, and relish the doing of it?

She saw a Crossley tender to one side of the crossroads. So the Auxiliaries were in the area too, and now, as well as anger, came fear, because the Auxies were from England too; ex-officers, tough, merciless barbarians. And committed. And then came excitement, because it meant that the flying columns of the IRA really were operating here. At last the war had reached this small town in Limerick.

Now she was close, and a Tan raised his hand and shouted, 'You, stop.' He swaggered towards her, his khaki service tunic and green RIC trousers as out of place against the stone wall which guarded the lane as he was in her land.

His rifle hung from his shoulder. Seamus, in his donkey cart, was waved through from the left-hand track. The Tan was nearer, touching Cait's pony. He ran his hand along the mane. 'Pretty

11

hair,' he leered at her, lifting the mane, dropping it.

'You're attracted to ponies, are you?' she said. 'Now, tell me, why isn't that a surprise?'

'You bitch.' The Tan dropped his hand and came to the cart, calling over his shoulder, 'Come over 'ere, Ed, we've caught ourselves a smart one.'

Cait kept her eyes on his buttons, not his face. She wouldn't look in their faces, because she had last time and she would never again afford them the courtesy of considering them human beings.

His hand was on the side of the cart now, dirty with coarse hairs running down to his fingers. Hers were pale on the reins. She shifted her gaze to look ahead.

'I was going to wish you a good morning until . . .' The Tan shook the cart slightly.

She looked at his green cap, then at his black leather belt. 'Had you done so, sure I'd have wished you one full of excruciating pain.'

His hand came out and grabbed hers, his nails were cracked and dirty. She shook him off. 'Search the damned churn, you excuse for a policeman.'

He grabbed at the book on her lap instead, holding it up, shaking it out. 'So this is what you take to bed with you, is it? What do you do with it there? We all know the Micks can't read – all they can do is have Easter Risings, bleating for independence when the rest of us are in the bloody trenches.'

'And all you do is kill our leaders and anyone else you can get in your sights, like the fools you are.' She stretched out for the book. 'Get your filthy hands off my property.'

The other Tan was coming closer. Carts were being allowed through from the other roads. She heard the noise of their churns, of the carts on the hard-baked tracks, the barking of dogs in the distance. She half stood, the pony shifted her weight. 'Give me that book, you stupid ignorant pig.' She snatched at it. The Tan threw it to the other, who dropped it onto his foot and dribbled it along the ground. The pages fluttered loose. Coarse laughter erupted from the Tans.

She looked at their caps, belts, boots. 'Careful with those toes. You don't want to disturb the only brain cell you have between the two of you.'

The laughter stopped. The Tans turned to her. They unslung their rifles.

'Check that churn, Ed, now. And you, you silly bitch, get down here.' The Tan's hand was on her wrist, dragging her, the mare whinnied. Oh Holy Mother, what had she done? But at least she had done something this time.

She wrenched away, but he caught her again and now his nails were digging into her skin. She hit out at him, he caught that hand too, twisting it. She could hear her own breath, his grunts.

A voice spat through the chaos. 'That's enough, for God's sake. You, Jones, help check the churn, then take over on the Church road. Send Adams and Franklin over here.' She saw an Auxiliary striding across in his khaki uniform, pointing towards the queue of carts coming in from the right. The dogs were still barking, her breath was still loud. The Tan must have glared as he thrust her from him, but she didn't know, she still hadn't looked at his face.

She sat back in the cart, gripping her skirt to stop the shaking which had come from nowhere and which they mustn't see. She looked down at the pages of *Jane Eyre* which were fluttering and drifting in the breeze. The Auxiliary bent down and scooped them together, those that he could catch. He stuffed them between the covers of the book and returned it to her. 'They're only doing their duty.'

She looked at his tam-o'-shanter bonnet, with its

crowned harp, the emblem of the Royal Irish Constabulary. She looked at the bandolier across his chest, at his belt, bayonet and scabbard, his holster. 'As my dada, and ninety thousand other Irishmen did against the Germans, and now you fight us, stain our land with your presence, brutalize your way through our lanes, our towns, our villages, for whatever blood-money they pay you.'

She felt the weight of the ruined book in her lap. She had goaded them, she could not complain, but she must. He spoke. 'You have your book back.'

'I'd rather have my country a republic,' she shouted. She wouldn't touch the book, because then he would see how her hands shook.

'That's not my province, the book is all I can run to.'

Her hair blew in the heightening breeze. She let it be. 'I guess at the gaps, do I?' She nodded to the pages caught on the honeysuckle and the blackthorn.

The Tan was peering in the churn. He shook his head at the Auxiliary. 'Nothing here except milk.'

'Get on to the next cart then.'

The cart lurched as the Tan jumped to the ground. The Auxiliary indicated that she was to drive on. She snatched at the reins with hands that were steady now. He stepped back, then called out, 'Wait, I'll need your name.'

'Caithleen Healy.'

He hesitated. 'I keep hearing an English intonation to your voice?'

She looked him square in the face. 'Never.' His eyes were grey, his face thin, his brows arched, his mouth wide and full. 'I have lived there, but I'm not one of you, murdering your way through someone else's country.' Beyond him, she saw a donkey cart being waved forward. It was Mick O'Brian. He waved, grinned, but his blue eyes were wary, curious, anxious.

'Never English,' she repeated loudly. Mick smiled,

turned away, flicking at the reins, his shoulders flexing beneath his shirt. She had stroked milk on his bare back last week to soothe the burn of the sun when he and the neighbours had helped harvest her dada's wheat. It was the first time she had really seen him again since she and Dada had returned and she felt weak at the thought of him.

She looked at the Auxiliary now. 'Can I go?'

'Yes, Caithleen Healy, you can go before your hate curdles your milk, and you might like to know that there is a happy ending for your Jane Eyre, eventually. She gets her Rochester.' He pointed to the book on her lap.

'Nothing like spoiling the story, is there?'

Their eyes locked. He said, his lips barely moving, 'You should be more cautious, Miss Healy. Words can provoke.' He looked towards the Tans.

'You don't need an excuse, you make a virtue out of pain. It's not policing, it's destruction.' Her voice broke. She stopped. He stepped back. She clicked at the mare, they moved forward, the breeze lifted her hair. Again she did nothing to stop it.

Ben Williams, the Auxiliary, stood quite still, watching her leave, seeing her red hair lifting, just as the pages on the stone wall lifted. He pictured her delicate face again, the paleness of her skin, the fire in her eyes, the slightness of her body, and the sorrow which had spread into all of these, like the shadow the clouds were casting over the stubbled fields. What the hell was he, an Englishman, doing here, pretending to be a policeman? Earning his £1.00 a day, taking the equivalent rank of an RIC sergeant along with the other Auxiliaries, using thugs, being a thug, to subdue thugs, or were they?

It was bloody crazy. What did knowing the difference between a misdemeanour and a felony, and the policeman's power of arrest as taught to them when they arrived here have to do with guerrilla warfare?

What did sweating in trenches have to do with it either? What did beautiful girls who read *Jane Eyre* and sounded half English and half Irish have to do with anything?

He walked back to his Crossley tender. Thank God they'd had some bombing and firing practice, it looked as though they'd need it, especially as he'd been seconded with Tom, and four others, to the Tans in this area. How he wished he could have stayed with the other Auxies, and been used as the shock force they were intended to be. He looked after the cart. Yes, that would have been easier, somehow.

That evening, Caithleen Healy carried up a ewer of water from the rain-barrel, calling back down into the kitchen, 'Come on, Dada, hurry and finish your pipe. We'll be late for the dance.'

'You just keep yourself calm, there's time enough.' He rested his head back against the settle, his grey hair gleaming in the lamplight, his high cheek-bones burnt from the sun.

She hurried into her bedroom, poured water into the wash-basin. The water was cold and a relief after the heat of the day. She towelled dry, standing naked in front of the ancient, green-spotted mirror, then moved to the window. Owls hooted, though there was still light left. Would Mick be at the dance? She'd hoped to see him at the creamery, or returning down the lane, but she had not. She turned to the dresser and touched the rosary. Let him be there.

The dress Widow Murphy had given her last week was hanging on the wardrobe door. 'From America,' she'd said. 'I've no thoughts of needing it. Cut it down, or up, or inside out – make what you like of it.'

Cait shook it from the hanger, holding it against herself, waltzing around the room. Would he like it? Would Mick O'Brian like it, like her, hold her, kiss her, love her?

Before she dressed she stroked lavender water on her breasts, her belly, her thighs. Caithleen Healy, sweet nineteen and never been kissed, or not by Mick O'Brian, and not in Ireland. England didn't count, nor the kisses of the men there, though there were only two, and chaste ones at that.

She slipped the dress over her head, then again moved to the window, breathing in the scent of summer, tracing with her eyes the contours of the hills, sweeping the dew-drenched meadows, pouring over the harvested fields. Oh, those fields, the heat of Mick's skin beneath her hands, his smile at the roadblock.

She tore from the window, hurrying down the stairs into the kitchen. 'Oh Dada, you've not even started. It'll be a great night and we'll miss it.'

Her father smiled, groaned. 'It's a witch you are, Cait, giving your father not a wink of peace.' He tapped his pipe on the hearth, pushed back the glowing turf. His leggings caught the light, his side laces were loose. His dark brown eyes looked less tired.

Cait ran water into the sink for him. 'I'm off to put the hens away. You be ready now, when I get back.'

'Now, aren't those just going to be the most confused hens in the world? They'll be after thinking they're coming to the dance too. You'll put them off their laying.' He was unbuttoning his shirt. 'At least put your boots on, for heaven's sake.'

Cait looked down and laughed. She rushed across, kissed him, smelt the tobacco, and the whiskey he always had after the meal. 'I love you, Dada. I'm so glad we're back here. It's home.'

It was still warm in the yard, the hens were quiet. She closed the wire door. A dog barked in the distance, the mare shifted her weight in the shaft over by the yard entrance. 'Are you changed yet, Dada?'

His voice came down from his bedroom. 'I'm on

my way down and I should be sprinkling you with holy water, and telling you to behave, as your mother would have done.' There was the sound of his door shutting, his footsteps on the uncarpeted stairs, and then the flagstones of the kitchen. He stopped, called out, 'Are you expecting to dance in your boots then, or are you after taking your shoes?'

She laughed and met him by the cart. 'Maybe I'll just manage a jig in the boots to shake off the mud.'

'No daughter of mine will do such a thing and live to tell the tale.' Suddenly they both fell silent and neither moved as clouds drifted between the moon and the earth. Cait touched his arm. 'Then I'll be, doing no such thing, Dada.' Her voice was soft.

As they rode in the cart along the track Cait asked, 'Why did we stay away so long, Dada? And don't tell me it was because Manchester and account-clerking were so wonderful. You know you missed the farm.'

His profile was clear, his nose straight, his chin firm, his hat worn forward.

'Your grandfather was angry with me.'

'But he wasn't always. He just loved us to come back for holidays. He knew you needed to go away to find work. He told me that. He said the farm would only support one family. Was it because you fought for them, the British, in the war?'

The crossroads were in sight but there was no Tan presence. She relaxed and looked at her father again. 'Was it, Dada?'

He let the reins lie idly on the pony's back. There was just the creaking of the harness, the rattle of the wheels, the breeze through the blackthorn.

'No, not then. It wasn't everyone who hated the British then, it still isn't now, but it's getting on that way, with the Tans and the Auxies here. A lot of us felt it was our duty to fight and we hoped that we'd get

18

Home Rule any minute, once the war had finished.'
He fell silent again.

Cait shook her head. 'But Grandpa changed in
the war. I remember his letter to Mum telling us
we could never come back to the farm. Why did he
change? Was it the Rising? But what did that have to
do with you? Why couldn't we come back right after
the war? Why did we have to wait until this spring?'

They were past the crossroads now and entering
the town. Light seeped out of windows, men doffed
their caps. 'You're well, are you, Con?' her father
called to one.

'Will I be seeing you at Tooley's Bar, Paul?' asked
Con.

'I'll be there for a wee drink or two, then I'm
on to the dance to make sure Cait is behaving.' The
men laughed softly.

'Why, Dada?' she repeated as they passed the
draper's then the baker.

'Cait, you go on until I can hardly think. Why
are you on about this now?'

'I want to know, Dada. I need to know.' She waved
her hand to either side. 'So much is happening. I
should know what went on in my own family when
I'm trying to make my place here, trying to make
everyone forget I'm an outsider.'

He looked at her and it was as though he'd never
seen her before. 'Poor Cait. I forgot that you would
have to cope with that, especially now when there are
too many British here, in uniform, destroying us. It
was quite simple really, Cait, and in a way, it was the
Easter Rising, or the putting down of it, at least. I
came back just after it, let me see, it was May 1916,
the hay was almost ready for cutting.'

His voice became a monotone. 'I'd been injured at
the front. The hospital ship put in to Dun Laoghaire.
We were disembarked into lighters, taken along the
coast and up the Liffey to Dublin. As the lighters drew

nearer we saw a town that reminded us of the ruins of France and Belgium. There were British troops on the quay. We clambered out of the lighters. We couldn't speak. The British soldiers were embarrassed. There was silence, then Paddy O'Rourke said, "Holy Mother of God preserve us." A soldier looked at us and said, "This is what we'll do to the rest of your bloody country if you bloody Micks bugger us about again." ' Her father stopped, drew breath, began again.

'We were mustered on the quay, given travel and leave documents, then addressed by a young captain in the Rifle Brigade. He was pale, he limped. He'd been where we had been. I remember he carried a blackthorn stick.' Her father nodded towards the hedge they had passed. 'He was decent. He said, "You will be escorted to the appropriate railway stations for your final destinations. Those of you requiring further medical treatment will be taken to hospital here in Dublin. You are reminded that it is a court-martial offence to consort with any member of the so-called Fenians or Irish Volunteers. That is all. Carry on." "English Hun," someone shouted from the ranks. The captain ignored it.

'He was a decent man, as I said, and he knew that we were being treated like traitors when we had been fighting the same enemy and would be going back, when recovered, to do the same. And all the time our country was being punished like this, by the British.'

They were approaching the old billiards hall where the dance was to be held. Her father looked straight ahead. 'But how could you go back and fight for them?' she said, wanting to shake him. 'How?'

'That's what your grandfather couldn't understand. "Isn't it enough that blood has run under the door from the executions, that houses are searched without cause, that wholesale arrests have taken our boys, many unconnected to Sinn Fein, to prison in Britain?

Isn't it enough that you allow a soldier to speak to you as he did? You're serving a bloodstained master if you go back, and he should no longer be in control, let alone fighting a war to protect Belgium, a small state. What are we, but a small state? He should have gone long ago. We might as well be starving on blighted potatoes whilst corn is being exported if you go back." My, how he went on.'

'But, Dada,' she pulled at his sleeve, 'why go back?' Disbelief shredded her voice.

'For heaven's sake, Cait, d'you think I haven't asked myself that?' His voice was harsh, loud. He pulled from her. 'D'you think we didn't all ask that? But it was our duty, that's why. I'd left friends in the trenches. I had a job to do.' He was panting. 'I already had a bloody enemy, girl.'

'How could you be so stupid?'

He shouted at her, his lips thin, his eyes fierce, 'Hold your tongue. I won't have you calling me, or anyone, stupid.'

They were outside the billiards hall now. He reined in the mare. Girls were going up the steps, arms linked, heads close together, their giggles clear in the night air, and suddenly she couldn't bear that they should quarrel. They only had one another. She reached across and gripped his hand. It was hard and calloused after six months' work on the farm. 'I'm sorry, Dada.'

He lifted her hand to his cheek and spoke softly. 'We came back because you can't keep a feud on for ever, and he was dying, you know that. He needed us, he was lonely. So,' he paused, 'I wrote, asking him to forgive me. I couldn't do it before, too much pride, so stupid. So you were right, Caithleen Healy, I am stupid. We wasted a lot of time.' He squeezed her hand.

She said, 'I'm glad we came back and saw him. I know Mum wanted . . .' She couldn't go on.

A dark-haired girl stopped by the cart, her cheeks rosy, her smile wide. 'Are you coming in then, Cait? I want to see that dress you've been spinning us yarns about until we're aching with boredom. Tell me, Mr Healy, was she after shutting up the hens before or after she changed? Bridget and I have a wee shilling on it that it was after.'

Her father laughed aloud, giving Cait a push. 'Go on with you, go with Rose and show off your finery and', he dug in his pocket, 'you'd better be giving the girls this and be thankful you've remembered to change out of your boots. I'll be along shortly, after I've warmed up my insides, and don't let me find you getting out of hand, any of you.'

Rose laughed up at him, her chestnut hair falling out of her combs. 'There'll be not much fear of that, Mr Healy, not while Cait's still up there on the cart anyway.'

Cait hesitated. He grinned. 'Go on, tonight is for fun. The past is past.'

'I love you, Dada,' she whispered.

'I love you too. Now get along in. Isn't there a certain Mick O'Brian who might be along?' He laughed and she with him, excitement rising.

She straightened her dress.

'Get on with you, girl, or it'll all be over.'

Rose called up, 'That's right, Mr Healy, turf her out, there's a party waiting for us.'

In the hall, the walls barely reflected the lights. 'Could do with a splash of paint,' Cait said, holding Rose's arm and looking around, her smile fading. Mick wasn't there.

Rose dragged her towards the end where the other girls were grouped. 'Sure, it's too much to ask of the men that they paint over anything, they'd rather be in Tooley's Bar, which is where they are now, so slap that smile back on your face. They'll be in later.' She

22

nudged Cait. 'Though I expect they could all stay away, except for one. Am I right?'

The girls were leaning up against the wall, or sitting on chairs set out round the room. The accordionist was playing, but the fiddler was nowhere to be seen. Rose laughed. 'He'll be downing a wee bit of lubrication with your dada and mine, and everyone else's.' The girls straightened as Cait and Rose joined them, moving into a circle, fingering her dress.

Rose linked arms with Cait. 'Isn't it just great? Widow Murphy must be sick with rage to think she could have drifted in here tonight looking like Cait.'

Patricia, who lived on the Limerick road, groaned. 'No, never her legs on show, please.'

They were called across for ginger beer from the trestle-tables set up at the end.

'One cake now, girls,' Patricia's mother called. 'Another at the drink break. Nice to see you again this week, Cait. It's your third dance so you'll be on the cake roster soon.'

Cait looked at Rose and grinned. 'It'll be the first and last time I'm asked.'

'Sure, you'll not be getting out of it that easily, my girl. I'll lend you some recipes my aunt sent from America – you can borrow the magazine, but give it back.'

Mrs Malone called from the chair by the door, 'Will your father be after coming in later, Caithleen?'

'He'll be here, or so he said.'

Rose and the other girls walked back with her to the corner, whispering and laughing. 'It's grand to see your Dada looking better. He's got his spark back.'

Cait sipped her drink. It was warm, fizzy, nice. She nodded, looking over the top of her glass at Rose, whose eyes were such a pale blue that they seemed almost empty. 'Yes, he's better. It's just happened, really. Maybe it's because we've the first harvest in. I thought it would take a year to get over.'

Patricia looked up, her mousy hair pulled tight into a bun. She raised an eyebrow. 'Talking of harvest, did I see Mick O'Brian without his shirt?'

Rose butted in. 'Did you also see these hands, those very same ones that are holding that glass of ginger beer, stroke milk onto that perfect back?'

'Rose,' Cait protested.

Patricia laughed, looking over her shoulder. 'Well, you can keep that particular back. The one I'd stroke belongs to Niall, and he should be here tonight.'

Mary, the daughter of the blacksmith, shook her head. 'And that's from the rose-red lips of the girl who told Father O'Rourke she was going to be a nun, and got sweets for the saying of it.' They all laughed, swaying to the tune that was wheezing from the accordion.

Cait said, 'They did that at our convent near Manchester too.'

'They do that at all convents,' the girls chorused, linking arms now that their drinks were finished. Cait relaxed, feeling at one with them. It was happening. She was being accepted and now Rose dragged her off to dance a reel and Cait's skirts flew, and her hair, which she had rigged up into a pleat, fell loose about her shoulders, her pins scattering on the floor. 'Leave it,' Rose panted. 'Mick'll not recognize a neat and tidy Caithleen Healy anyway.'

When will they come from the bar? Cait wondered, looking towards the door, hot with impatience, but then they danced again, drank ginger beer again and Patricia held out a letter she had received that morning.

'From Maria. She's away in England and I don't know why she thought I'd be interested.'

Mary said, 'It's a shame. I liked her.'

Cait watched the door, then swung round as Rose

flared up. 'Liked her, she was a bloody policeman's daughter. She had no right here.'

'What's this?' Cait asked.

Rose had her hands on her hips. Patricia turned on Cait. 'Trust you not to know, tucked away in England, and not rushing back until you had a farm to your name.'

Silence fell on the chattering group. The accordion was playing a jig. No-one moved. Then Rose slapped at Patricia's arm. 'Don't be making such a scene. How can she hurry her dada? How could you hurry yours?' She swung round. 'Will you look, it's only a few steps from Tooley's to here, and they've still not made it.'

There was laughter again and Patricia shook her head. 'Sorry, Cait, I just can't stand the police.'

Cait had now remembered the boycotted RIC family, their lonely pew in church, the refusal of the baker and every other tradesman to serve the family. 'Can anyone stand them.' It wasn't a question. For a moment the group was serious.

Mary said, 'We grew up with her, with her father and mother. I liked them and I don't care what you say, Patricia Flannigan, so there.'

Patricia looked to left and right. 'What I say, Mary High and Mighty, is that I'm for joining the Cumann na MBan, you know, the Sinn Fein women's organization. Anyone else?'

Patricia glared at Mary, who looked at the floor. Cait was the first to nod. 'Will we fight?'

They all laughed, then looked at Mary again, but she was also nodding. Now Patricia shook her head at Cait. 'No, nothing like that, so my uncle tells me. You just take tea to them when they're hiding out in ditches and old barns.'

'Doilies, of course, and serviettes?' Cait blurted out. The girls laughed louder still.

Rose licked her lips. 'And first aid, all those brows

to soothe.' They pretended to swoon while Patricia nodded.

'Yes, first aid too,' she confirmed.

'And—' Cait began, but Rose was gripping her arm, looking across to the far end.

'Will you just look at all those brows ripe for the stroking, Caithleen Healy and Patricia Flannigan. Mine's the one in the middle.'

Mick was there, his wild, curly hair gleaming in the dim light, his face turned towards the group of girls, his blue eyes seeking – who? She hardly breathed. He found Cait, smiled, nodded. His eyes stayed with her. Her breath caught in her throat, and then he turned to a man who gripped his shoulder.

'Holy Mother,' whispered Rose. 'It's Des O'Brian.'

The fiddler had taken over from the accordionist. Her father was talking to Rose's uncle. Mick and the man called Des moved to the back of the group. Other men, strangers, took up positions at the door. Cait wanted Mick to move towards her, not away. 'For God's sake,' she murmured. 'What's he want to talk to men for, when I'm here? Oh Rose, does he like me?'

Rose was studying the group. 'That's not just men, that's Des O'Brian, his elder brother who was arrested after the Rising and interned in Britain with Michael Collins, the Big Fella, the commander of the IRA. He's not been seen here since then.' Her voice was low, the others were crowding in.

Bridget looked across then back at them. 'They say he's part of Collins's assassination squad in Dublin.'

Teresa shook her head. 'My dada was saying he's commanding a flying column.'

Patricia grabbed Cait's hand. 'I don't care who's here, Niall's just given me a look fit to melt me into the ground. And I saw the one Mick gave you, and Paddy just wants to eat you, Rose.'

The girls all looked now, pretending that they

weren't. Cait whispered, 'Tomorrow I learn to roll bandages. I already know how to stroke milk on sunburn.' They were giggling, laughing, and it was born of nervousness. They looked again at the men, who were by now deep in conversation, and so they danced with themselves. The music stopped at Mrs Hanney's announcement: 'Tea Break.'

The accordionist went across to Tooley's as well.

Rose moaned, 'Though why they need one so soon, when they've only just come is a mystery known only to them. And will they be bringing back the fiddler? And will he be sober? That Ryan is a terrible boozer when he gets a wind behind him.'

Patricia giggled. 'But sure, that won't matter, just as long as the boys come back. Just imagine, you might be walking out with a hero's brother.'

They couldn't eat or drink but kept on looking from the clock to the door and ached with impatience, then laughed with excitement and could think of nothing to talk of until Bridget told them of the woman who had had a ring driven into her bum by the IRA for consorting with a Tan, and another who had been cropped by her neighbours for kissing a soldier. They giggled. Rose flicked Cait's hair. 'Stick to kissing the IRA, darling.'

'Mick will do nicely,' Caithleen grinned, then saw the gramophone in the corner. She looked from it to Rose, who paused, then nodded. They hurried across and found a tango. 'Sent by a cousin from America. Can you do it?' Rose asked, her face glowing in the heat of the hall.

'Can I do it?' Cait asked in mock horror. 'There's no-one better.' She fingered the vinyl.

'I dare you,' Rose whispered, winding up the gramophone. Patricia, Mary and Bridget were with them now. 'Yes, why not be christening the dress?' Bridget urged.

Cait looked around the hall at the older women

who were busy heaving the table back against the wall, at the others sitting and standing round the room, at the closed door through which the men had gone.

'I'll need a partner.'

Rose shook her head. 'You're on your own, my darling.' She could scarcely speak for laughing.

'Put it on, stand back, and see how it's done,' Cait ordered. They did so, not believing she'd do it, but she would, because she'd been dared, and tonight she was part of it all. The gramophone crackled, the tinny sound of a piano began, took heart, the saxophones mingled, and now Cait danced, her hands clutching an imaginary partner, her hair falling around her face, and all she could hear was the music, her own breath, the laughter of her friends, their clapping hands, their warmth, and then she saw the men return, her father's face, the shock, then the amusement and she didn't stop, though Mrs Flannigan was open-mouthed with disapproval. The committee likewise.

Now Mick was there too, and he stood and watched, and ignored the touch of his brother's hand on his arm, and she danced for him, only for him, and as her eyes met his she knew that he understood this.

The music stopped and Rose, Patricia and Bridget, all the girls, drew around her, and in between them she saw that Mick still watched. Then Mrs Flannigan came, and the committee with her, and took the gramophone to the storeroom and the records too. Mick looked from her to the committee, then back to her again, and now he raised an eyebrow and smiled, and only then did he turn to his brother.

The fiddler began to play as sweetly as though no brew had passed his lips, and the girls moved back to their corner. Cait trembled and was glad of her friends' hands slapping her back, the laughter, the chatter, because she wondered whether her father was still amused, or had become as shocked as Mrs Flannigan.

She looked, seeking him out amongst the other men. He was waiting for her to do so, and there was still amusement and approval and exasperation and resignation.

'I thought I said, behave,' he mouthed.

'I will, I will,' she mouthed back, and they smiled at one another.

Behind him Des moved towards the door again, taking Niall and Mick with him. They stopped. Mick was shaking his head, and Niall too. Des stiffened, his eyes darkened. His lips, so like Mick's, thinned, but Mick was already turning, moving towards her across the room, and Niall followed, and Paddy. Cait moved, hearing the indrawn breath from Rose. 'Holy Mother, don't be so forward,' her friend warned.

But Cait was gone, meeting Mick in the centre, feeling his arms around her, holding her too close to his body in the waltz that the fiddler was playing. Her father's face grew sombre, and she withdrew and danced with space between them as the others were doing. Her father smiled.

Mick's voice was soft, his face was close, she smelt the beer on his breath, the tobacco on his clothes. 'I'm glad you're back, Cait. It's been a long time without you picking the apples off your grandfather's tree, and giving us both bellyache.'

'You didn't have to eat them, Mick O'Brian, and I seem to remember you did some picking yourself.'

'Oh, is that a fact? You can be very persuasive, very bold. Too bold.'

Her heart sank. She had gone too far, she shouldn't have walked towards him, she shouldn't have danced. She stiffened, her chin going up. He grinned down at her.

'You bristle quicker than my grandmother's broom, Caithleen Healy, as the Tans found out this morning.

29

As I said – too bold. Take care – things have changed since you last came home for the summer in 'fourteen. It's a different world here.'

The music was lapping around them, over them, his words 'take care' echoing inside her head, she basked in the admiration in his eyes, the feel of her hand in his, of his hand on her back, the heat of his body which she could feel though they weren't touching. 'I know it's different, we're different too. The last time I saw you we were fourteen, children.'

He bent his head towards hers, they touched. 'Oh Cait,' he murmured. 'Meet me by the river tomorrow. I thought you would become all English, all neat and proper, like their land.'

'I put milk on the heat of your sunburn, didn't I? Was that neat and proper?'

'I didn't know what it was, what it meant.'

His forehead was still against hers, their eyes were half shut, their bodies moved to the music. His lips were so close, other dancers were so close, his hand was so tight around hers. They were moving in time, as they had moved as children, coming together for the picking of apples, for the turning of hay, for the laughter of picnics. But they were not children any more and he was drawing her to him, and her breathing was quickening as was his.

But then Des shouted his name, his voice strident in its urgency, cutting across the music. The fiddler stopped. Des shouted again. 'Mick, come on, *now*.' Mick jerked upright, his face alert. She heard the lorries tearing down the street. Mick turned, forcing his way from her, shouldering through the dancers, and now there was roaring and revving down the main street, and shouting, and the sound of rifles firing.

Rose came to her, they held one another's hands as Paddy followed Mick.

'It's the Tans,' Mrs Flannigan shouted.

Des's voice was loud again. 'Start the bloody music. Fiddle, damn you.' Then he was gone, with Mick behind him, and others, but not her father. He was pushing his way through the men and women that were left. 'Dance,' he was shouting at them. 'Dance, until they come. We know nothing, you hear that, nothing. No-one's been here.'

'We know that, right enough,' Con shouted back. 'Everyone remember that.'

She forced a way through to him. 'You dance with me, Dada.' She grabbed his arms, feeling him shake with the same rage she had felt this morning. 'Dance with me, hold me, give me strength.' Though she knew it was he who needed her strength as he had every day since her mother had died. She looked again towards the entrance as rifle butts pounded on the front door, smashing the panel. Mrs Maloney pulled the door open. The Tans poured in, knocking her to one side.

Chapter Two

There was comfort in the never-ending ritual of the churn rattling in the cart, the mare swishing the flies with her tail, the reins in Cait's hands, the shadows moving across the fields, the blue of the sky between the clouds. Cait eased her back. She had not slept well the night before. The sound of the Tans' jeers, the spittle they gobbed, and the chairs they threw around the hall, played amongst the feel of Mick's hand on her back, his forehead against hers, his lips so close.

She looked up now and saw what she expected – the roadblock at the crossroads. They would all be asked again about Desmond O'Brian, and again they would deny all knowledge. She braced herself as she drew near.

'Take care,' Mick had said, and now she relaxed. 'Meet me at the river.' But when? He had gone before he could say. Her eyes searched beyond the block. He wasn't there.

The Tan stood in the middle of the track, his hand up. Another came to her. She looked ahead. He searched her cart and churn, whistling, grinning. 'This one's clear.'

She was waved on. 'Have a good journey to the creamery,' one called, laughing. She ignored him, not understanding the lack of abuse. She looked behind her. Still no Mick, but other carts were coming through, barely searched.

She clicked at the pony. 'Gee up.' The sooner she arrived, the sooner she would be back at the farm. She'd go down to the river. She touched her hair. Mick liked it loose, or so he had said when they were children.

Carts were coming towards her now. Was Mick amongst them? No. She looked ahead, but Seamus called to her when he was almost alongside. 'The bastards have wrecked the creamery – you just be taking that churn back to your daddy now and tell him we'll fix a lorry to one further north for tomorrow.' His face was set in a mask of fury, his knuckles were white as he gripped the edge of his cart.

Cait turned the cart, joined the queue, looked back, and noticed for the first time the smoke being carried on the wind. She too felt the fury, the hate, but she wouldn't show it. She wouldn't even glance at the Tans who were ahead of them again, laughing, lolling against their lorries while their companions still checked carts through from all sides, waiting for those that were returning. No, she wouldn't give them that satisfaction.

She was stopped, searched again, waved on, and nothing had flickered on her face. But then she was waved down again in the middle of the crossroads and it was the Auxie, his thin face shadowed, his voice hesitant. He came to her, close up to the cart, looking up into her face while she stared into his grey eyes, no rage showing. No, no emotion for these people.

His hand was reaching into his tunic, his back to the Tans. God Almighty, what was he doing? Holy Mother, he was like the rest, he was going to shoot her. She jerked backwards, dropping the reins, her hands outstretched. Why me? her mind screamed, though nothing came out. Please don't, Holy Mother, please don't. Oh Mama. Still no sound.

'Please,' he said, withdrawing his hand, holding

33

out a book. 'Please take this. I've spoilt the end for you, but you can at least fill in the gaps.'

She looked at the red-backed book, scuffed at the corners, at his fingers, long and slender, at his uniform, at the bonnet with its emblem, and felt trembling taking over her body, turning her legs to water and now the rage tumbled out, fed by the humiliation of fear and relief. '*Jane Eyre* – from you. I would rather die than even touch it.' She picked up her whip and lashed the mare.

The cart knocked Ben Williams to one side, the book fell, pages blew free. And she was glad, glad d'you hear, her mind roared, trotting Tanzy through the guffawing Tans. 'Got another book off her did you? We must have missed it.'

Back at the farm she and her father lugged the churn to the dairy, tipping the milk into shallow pans. 'I'll churn it tomorrow,' she said, not wanting to talk, just wanting Mick.

She hurried past the shallots, the gooseberry bushes, the currants, black and red, past the pond; and her father let her go because she had told him about the Auxie. The chores could wait for a while longer.

The honeysuckle flowered in the hedge and late cabbage roses flopped in the warmth. Her legs seemed to belong to someone else as she ran. She slowed, and was now in the shade of the laurels. 'I hate them,' she panted, and she was crying and at the river she sat and listened to the wind in the rushes, the curlews overhead. Oh God, oh God, he'd seen her fear. That Auxie had seen her fear and she'd promised herself they would never touch her again. Mick, where are you?

Ben Williams threw the book into the tender. 'Bloody bitch. She's just a Mick dragged out of the bog.' But as he repositioned his men he couldn't forget what he now recognized as her fear, and cursed himself for his stupidity. Why shouldn't she think he was going to kill her? It's the fear that everyone lived with now; the Tans and the Auxies, the RIC, the Army, the Irish. He looked across to the hills. And out of fear grew cruelty, and out of cruelty grew revenge and mayhem. And what the hell was he doing here? It wasn't the adventure he had thought it would be, the breathing space, the chance to earn clean money in a world where ex-servicemen were queuing for jobs.

Cait waited for Mick, lying back on the grass, watching the clouds turn into sheep, a hen, a rolling tide, and by lunch he hadn't come and so she walked back, through the thistles, the ragwort, the stubble of the cornfield denuded of the stooks she had helped to bind. In the afternoon she moved the chicken run, tipped the tea-leaves onto the rhubarb, then leaned against the wall of the stockyard with her father, nodding as he said, 'The ground's so hard we'll have to bring the cattle in and give them hay soon.'

In the late afternoon she walked into the town to the Cumann na MBan meeting. There was no longer a roadblock. She looked, always she looked for Mick. Surely he would come, if not today, tomorrow. Or should she go to his farm? Would he even be there? Was he with Des? Would he go with the column elsewhere? No, he mustn't.

She stopped outside the draper's, staring at the bales of cloth in the window, moving aside for the shawled women and capped men who passed either side of her. She'd go now, this minute, to his farm. She turned, but then stopped. Without the girls, the music, she had no courage.

In the backroom of the draper's, while thread and yards of material were being sold, she learned from Dr Quinn how to make field dressings and smiled with relief that Rose and Patricia had not seen Paddy and Niall today either. They packed safety pins, scissors, cleaning lotions, disinfectants, cotton wool and bandages; they drank tea; they applauded her for knocking a bloody Auxie out of the way, and put her on the list for taking tea after dusk to the column, who would be spending a second night in hiding. 'But not a word to anyone,' Mrs Flannigan said quietly to the group she had chosen. 'Someone must have informed on Des last night, because the Tans knew who they were looking for.' Rose caught Cait's eye, and they clasped arms as they left, excitement making their steps quick and light.

'At last we're doing something,' Cait murmured. 'So that Auxie can stick it in his Tan pipe and smoke it.'

She walked back along the track alone, as Rose turned left to her farm, basking in the richness of a harvest sun so large and heavy it seemed impossible that it still hung in the sky. Tonight she would see Mick. Tonight, as she stole through the fields with her flasks and scones, she would be one of the trusted few.

She baked the next day's bread as her father brought the cows in from the meadow. Together they milked them and drove them out again as the moon came up. They sat by the turf fire, watching the colours of the flickering flames, smelling the fresh bread, turning the pages of their books, though she read not a word of *Pride and Prejudice*. 'I feel I belong properly, Dada,' she said softly, as he closed his book, tapped his pipe and eased himself from the chair, not knowing of the task that she had been assigned.

'Yes, last night we all pulled together,' he agreed. 'I just wish your grandfather and . . .' He stopped, his face suddenly still.

'I know,' she said gently. 'But Mother knows, I'm sure she knows.'

He made his way towards the stairs then turned. 'Were seven masses enough? Should I have paid the Brothers for more? Perhaps I should. It means little to me any more, but it meant so much to her.'

She went to him, held him. 'No, that was enough. It would have been enough without. It was our love she had.'

'She had no time for the Act of Contrition. Did the masses give her peace?'

'Yes, now go to bed.'

She watched him go, then filled the ewer with water and took it to her own room. But where is our peace, Dada? she wanted to ask. She knew it could only come from action.

In the woods there was silence, except for the breathing of Rose beside her, and the steady sound of their feet on the dry leaf mulch. The flasks were heavy, the scones breaking up. The column was where they had been told it would be, the lookouts waved them through. Men sprawled against logs, or huddled in ditches, snatching at sleep. Neither Paddy nor Niall was there, nor Mick, and she felt the disappointment hard in her throat. The men were eager for the tea and cared nothing that the scones were in bits.

Des was over in the darkness of the rhododendrons. She whispered to Rose as they left, 'He'd have come out of the shadows for scones on doilies.' They both laughed.

A figure hissed from the darkness next to them, 'Hush up, and get home to your beds.' They didn't recognize him but there was a Dublin edge to his voice, as there was now to Des's. They stood taller as they walked, proud to be part of a struggle greater than themselves.

Drizzle was falling as Mick joined the group beneath

the trees the next morning after the churns had been delivered to the lorry. About twenty men from the village were there, crouching or sitting on logs, smoking, talking quietly. He made his way to Des who was checking the lookouts.

'Well done, Mick,' Des congratulated him.

'It's good men they are, I think.' Mick's collar was upturned against the damp. Water was dripping through the leaves of the oak beneath which they were standing.

Des shrugged. 'We'll soon find that out.' His face was cold, his voice terse.

Mick touched his arm. 'You need some sleep.'

'There'll be time for that when all this is over.'

'No,' Mick insisted. 'You need it now.' Des's face was gaunt, lined, tired. He looked fifty, not thirty.

Suddenly Des smiled and gripped his brother's shoulder and it was as though the sun had come out, and the brother who had chucked him onto the hay wain all those long summers before the Rising was back again. 'Jesus, Mick, you sound like an old mother hen, so you do. It'll help just having you here – just being back for a bit. Tell Daddy I'll be in for a wee bite this evening, Tans and Auxies, and the military, permitting.' He grinned, then turned towards the other men, shaking the wet from his almost black hair, which was too long. 'Let's be getting things straight then,' Des called softly.

Immediately the talking ceased, the men looked up, their shoulders still hunched against the damp, and perhaps against the step they might be going to take.

Des positioned himself so that he could see everyone, and be seen. 'It's great that you're here today but before you come closer to us, before you commit yourselves to anything, I want you to listen and listen good. I want you to know that once you're in, you're in. I want you to know why we're fighting, I want you

38

to know how we're fighting.' He stopped and looked around, studying their faces.

'And I want you to know I was informed on at the dance, and that the informer will be found, and dealt with.' For a moment no-one moved, not even Des, and there was only the dripping of rain through the branches until a twig cracked. Everyone started, then relaxed. It was a lookout, that was all.

Des sank his hands into his pockets. 'Why? Now that's a question. Why are we fighting? Why has the backing for the cause grown from the handful of us who rose against the British in 1916 to you, and you, and you?' His hand was out of his pocket, sweeping around the group, and out beyond the wood, to the town. Mick·thrilled to hear him, to see him, because the tiredness had been shrugged from his brother's body and his voice and eyes were alight.

'The Easter Rising failed and who of those amongst you cared? Why should you, dug deep into the trenches of the Somme as you were?' His smile was sympathetic. 'It was the wrong time, but as our leaders of that Rising were executed – then you cared. You cared when hundreds were transported, without trial, to prisons in Britain.' His finger stabbed the air. 'You cared when our oppressors demanded conscription of the Irish. "Oh yes, you Irish Micks. We execute you, we imprison you, but you *will* fight our war for us." At our protests conscription was dropped. We won that battle, just as we won the General Election at war's end. It was a majority vote for independence. The British ignored our democratic decision.'

Des fixed each man in turn with his gaze, then continued. 'We appealed to the Peace Conference who had made such loud noises about recognizing the rights of small states. But who in their right minds would offend the British Lion?'

He looked around. 'I repeat, who in their right minds? Who? Who? Who?' His voice was rising with every word. He was looking round now, his eyes boring into all those fixed upon him.

Mick shouted, 'We would.'

Des whirled round to him, then back to the others. 'We would and we are,' he shouted. They echoed him, nodding, grinning.

'Are you really ready?' he shouted.

'We are,' they yelled.

'Who is "we"?'

The men were standing now. 'Ourselves alone,' they roared.

'That's right,' Des waved them down, quietening them. 'Sinn Fein – ourselves alone.' The men were slapping one another's backs, and Mick shook his head. Jesus, but Des was brilliant.

Des was walking round the group now, eye to eye with each of the men, as he continued. 'So we know what we want – a Republic of all Ireland. No partition, no Northern Ireland with our Catholics trapped inside as the British and Ulster Protestants insist. But how are we to achieve this, gentlemen, how?'

He swung round and came back to Mick, facing him, his violet eyes so fierce, so strong, drilling into Mick's which would never be as fierce or as strong. God, but Des was great.

'How? By making Ireland ungovernable, by breaking down the administration. I called them stupid, and so they are, for they imprisoned hundreds of us together with Michael Collins. Jesus, what a man he is. The Big Fella, our military leader who turned us into an organized guerrilla force, who set up classes.' Des was walking round the group again. 'Who set up an intelligence network and taught military tactics, while those still free in Ireland worked up their own network.' Des was standing still now, looking across to the lookouts. 'All clear, still?'

The men nodded.

He continued. 'So how did we, and do we, make

Ireland ungovernable? We upset the police. We assassinate the intelligence agents. We disrupt, demoralize. We unite and we fight—'

A man interrupted. 'Were you one of Collins's assassins then, Des? The word is that you were.'

Des froze, and coldness radiated from him. The man shifted uneasily. At last Des said, 'No-one asks questions about who did, or does, what. This is a war. This is life and death. Just you, and everyone, remember that no Collins assassination is without a reason.' He smiled at the man, but it didn't reach his eyes, and to Mick it seemed as though the glade was even darker than before.

Des began to pace backwards and forwards. 'So how? Gentlemen, we destroy their tax offices. We put the police and the Tans in fear – boycott them, destroy their police posts. We attack them, and the Army. It is the only language that the Empire understands. Justice and truth and democracy are words they do not recognize. We've tried that.'

He came now, and stood next to Mick whose heart nearly burst with pride. Des put his hand on Mick's shoulder and shook him gently as he continued. 'If you doubt the contempt they feel for us, look at the towns and villages. See the blackened houses, the wrecked creameries. Think of the reprisals, the outrages, the lack of law from these "upholders of the law". They are the symbols of an empire which would keep us as slaves. But we won't be slaves, will we?'

The men moved forward. Des held them back with a gesture of his hand. 'Your role in the fight is to work your farms, keep to your jobs, but come with us when you're needed. I want you to be able to melt back into your haymaking, your shoe-mending, your blacksmithing. Now think about it, because once you're in you obey, you train, and you are mine until the end. Until we have our republic.'

The men waited for a moment, and then grouped together, talking, lighting up cigarettes. Mick did the same, passing one to Des, who cupped his hands around the flame of the match as he sucked in greedily, exhaling up into the air, his head back, exhaustion now in every movement.

'You were great, Des, so great.'

Des smiled at him. 'You listened well, did you, young Mick – really well?'

Mick nodded. The rain had stopped, the darkness was lifting.

Des caught his arm. 'Really well?' he insisted.

Mick didn't understand. 'Yes, every word.'

'Then you'll stay on the farm, with Daddy, except when I need you – like the others.' It was a statement.

Mick stepped back, hurling his cigarette to the ground. It hissed on the sodden leaves. 'Des, no, that part wasn't for me. I'm joining you. I brought the men in. No, I want to be with you.'

Des led him from the glade, away from the men who had stopped talking at the sound of Mick's shout. Mick tried to shrug him off. 'I'm in the fight, I tell you, Des. If I can't come in with you I'll go in with someone else.'

Des laughed. 'There is no-one else. Look, it has always been "I want" with you. You'll help me most this way. I can't be worrying about Daddy and the farm. This way I'll have an ear, a proper, honest ear, in the town. It's crucial I know what's happening, who's safe, who isn't.' They were pacing, in step, like soldiers, Mick thought, two brothers together. Des was wrong. They should be together.

He felt Des's grip tighten, felt the weight of his arm across his shoulder, heard his brother's voice close to his ear. 'I need you there. I need you beside me when we fight, not when we're running. That's your position. My right-hand man, at the front, and in the rear. You're the one watching my back, Mick.

No-one else can do it.'

Des felt his young brother straighten his shoulders, and smiled inwardly, relief shifting the tiredness for a moment, but only a moment. Mick must be safe, the boy who had tagged along after him all his life, and whom he loved more than anyone on earth, must be safe. He dropped his arm now. 'I must sort out the others. Come with me, watch and listen.'

But Mick held Des back. God, but he was so thin. He curbed his argument, and said instead, 'You need somewhere that's safe, Des, if you're operating here. You need somewhere to rest, somewhere to take your men if they're hurt. Bring them to the barn.'

'Can't do that. They'll be watching the farm and there's no cellar. But you're right, we need a safe house.' This time it was he who pulled cigarettes from his pocket. They both smoked silently, deep in thought until Des murmured, 'Ideally we need to neutralize the Tans so they give a particular place a miss. Impossible, of course, just can't be done. However, young Mick, we can't be expecting a miracle every day, now can we? This turnout is more than enough, and that's down to you, so thank you. Now, let's be getting on with it.'

Mick followed his brother back into the glade, his steps firm, his mind racing. It could be done. It could damn well be done, if Caithleen Healy agreed, and if they boxed awful clever about it.

Cait pushed down on the slane, slicing a sod from the black turf bank, watching the water squelch and ooze into the black bog puddle but thinking of last night and how she'd listened to the rain on the roof and the mice in the rafters. How she'd breathed in the scent of the flowers in the room and pictured the men she had left in the glade and ditches.

She straightened. The clouds were low, there was

rain on the hills though it had stopped there. She'd run the milk to the lorry but Mick hadn't been there with his cart. His father had come, nodding to her. So she'd gone to the river and heard the wind singing in the reeds, but he hadn't come. Perhaps he was there now? She strained to see past the trees. Maybe he was away, off with Des?

A curlew cried, the poplars shuddered. A shawled woman in a donkey and butt passed along the long straight track. Cait rested, then bent to the slane again, cutting the turf, heaving it up.

'Sure, but you'll make a fine navvy, Caithleen Healy.'

She spun round. It was Mick. He took the slane from her, and cut one sod, another, another, his muscles moving beneath his shirt and along his thighs. The sun gleamed on the golden skin of his arms. Words were trapped in her throat. He jerked his head towards the blackened patches of ground where she had boiled kettles for her father when they had worked here together. 'We'll not be having tea then?'

She shook her head and now her voice returned. 'If I'd known you were coming I'd have brought doilies, and the crown jewels.'

He cut another sod, another, and sweat ran down his neck and disappeared beneath his shirt. 'Then, Cait, I'd have been here at the crack of dawn.'

'It's my tea, and my jewels you're after then, is it? And I always thought it was my grandfather's apples.' The curlews were still crying.

He stood straight, eying the sods. 'Now, will your daddy be happy with that pile? Because if he will, you and I should take ourselves to the river, as we said.' He looked straight at her, and it was as though he had reached out and stroked her bare flesh.

She nodded, the words had fled again. Together they walked. The poplars still shuddered, there was still rain on the hills. He reached for her hand, holding it, but staring ahead. She stared ahead too, but saw nothing, just felt his hard calloused hand, smelt his pungent skin, heard his breathing.

He slid his arm around her waist and they walked in stride, thigh to thigh, and as they walked, she slipped her arm around his waist, and his heat fused with hers. The sun beat down, and now they were where the river lapped the bank, moving around and over and in between the large flat stones, and where the rushes sighed in the breeze. It was as though the sound of the curlews was all around as his lips found hers, and his body was hard against hers, and his arms were strong around her. His breath was in her mouth as he said, 'God, I've missed you, Caithleen. I've truly missed you.'

She clung to him as his lips became urgent, as his tongue flicked hers, as the heat poured through her body, melting her, stirring her, weakening her limbs. Her arms fell to her sides, he pulled her closer to him, kissing her neck, and she his, tasting the sweat that had trickled along and down, and with her tongue she traced its path.

He moaned, and ran his hands down her back, her buttocks, her thighs, pulling her to his hardness, moving against her, then kissing her mouth again and again, until slowly they drew breath, and slowly their eyes focused and they drew apart, seeing that there was still a sky above them, and the earth below them. Their fingers touched. 'God, I've missed you,' Mick repeated and they smiled, feeling shy suddenly.

Cait was trembling. She sat on the bank, wrapping her skirt around her legs. She leaned her head on her knees and watched the reeds, not Mick. Holy Mother, it was as though she'd been on fire, as though she had no sense of decency.

Mick walked to the river bank, crouched, cupped water, sluiced his face. He turned, offering her some.

45

She shook her head. She wanted the scent of him on her for longer.

His collar was damp as he came and sat beside her. He leaned his head against hers. 'It's not your jewels I like, so it must be your tea. Or at least, that's what the men in the woods liked.'

She started with surprise. 'You know I was there?'

He held her hand, running his fingers up and down hers. 'With a brother like mine, you learn a lot. He's an important man, Cait.' The pride in his voice made her smile.

He said, 'It's not funny, he's risking his life for us, for you.'

'I don't think it's funny. I was just smiling because you care for him. I like that.' She felt foolish, stupid. 'Please, I'm sorry.'

Mick kissed her hand. 'No, it's me that should be sorry. I just fly up in the air at the moment. God, Cait, it's so important. We've been servile so long, wallowing in our own squalor—'

She interrupted. 'No, that's not right, how can you say that about your own people, our people?' Now it was she that was angry and pulled from him.

He stared at her. 'Don't be so stupid, Cait – I'm talking of a squalor of the spirit. We've a great cultural legacy, we've a grand civilization, and for so long we've allowed ourselves to be the slaves of English masters. We've allowed them to plod all over us. Now, everyone must do the most they can. Everyone.' His voice was fierce, his eyes searched hers, and they were hard and cold, and she didn't know what he was looking for, and she didn't know where the closeness of before had gone.

She straightened, gripping her skirt. She watched the river eddying around the stones, and counted the ripples. 'I took tea to your brother's men. I've done something. I'll go on doing it.' Her voice was level, as cold as his eyes had become.

His hand stroked her hair. 'So many waves; red, rich waves. So Irish. Are you Irish, little girl from England? Does taking tea to a flying column make you Irish? Does hurling a book from an Auxie onto the road make you so? Will it be after making you belong?'

She turned on him, dragging his hand from her hair. 'Leave me alone, you pig. I do the same as the others, more. It was only Rose and I who took tea, not the others.' She struggled to her feet. He sprang up, reached out. She slapped his hand away, hitting him, again and again. 'How dare you? How dare you kiss me, and then say this?'

He fielded her blows but one struck home. He seized her wrists. 'The Tans killed your mother – is taking tea enough revenge for you?' She gasped. He had struck her as surely as if his fists had landed on her body.

He let her go. Her arms fell to her side. She shook her head, again and again, and now his eyes were warm, full of love and he held her, and she let him, because there was no strength in her, only grief, and rage and pain and confusion.

'You know taking tea will never be enough. I hate them, hate them,' she whispered.

'I know,' he crooned. 'I know, and that's why I've done this. I have a way forward for you. I have a way that will bring you revenge – you or your daddy should do something if you're to have any pride in yourselves and, as I say, I have a way forward, one that will make you a heroine to everyone around here. I'm choosing you, helping you, because I love you, and because I care what happens to you.'

Cait waited for her father by the wall as he drove the cows in for milking. His trousers were tucked into his leggings, his hat was set down against the low sun. She had spent the afternoon baking, then had plucked a chicken which was now roasting in the oven. It was his favourite meal. She brushed at her skirt. It was still dirty from the cellar. It would need to be cleaned, chairs taken down, blankets hidden behind casks.

'Is this a welcoming party then, Cait?' her father called, standing between two cows with a hand on each. They flicked their tails. Midges were dancing around her face.

'I just thought I'd help.' She opened the gate, leaning against it as the cows squelched through, then followed him to the milking shed. Milking first one, and then another, until all ten were done. Neither of them spoke until the cows had been driven back into the meadow, and the dairy cleaned. She said, as they crossed the yard, 'It's chicken tonight.'

Her father stopped, turned, looked. 'It's something else as well – there's enough buttering up going on to save churning for a week.' He slipped his arm through hers. 'What is it – a dress for the next dance? Then maybe Mrs Murphy will have another you can cut about?'

They kicked off their boots by the step, put on shoes. The smell of freshly baked cakes mingled with roast chicken. Her father washed at the sink, glancing around at the cakes and scones, then at her as she handed him the frayed towel. 'Maybe it's more than a dress?'

She nodded. 'It's important, Dada.'

He walked to the settle, took his pipe from the mantelpiece, put it to his mouth then stopped in mid-action. He had seen the cellar trapdoor flung open. He looked from it to Cait. 'Why have you been down there?' His voice was curious, that was all.

She busied herself laying the table, saying as she did so, 'Because our cellar is well hidden, because the flying column need a safe house, because I can make it safe.'

48

The sun was roaring red as it dropped beneath the horizon, a breeze swept in through the open door, the oil lamps flickered then settled. She shut the door against the moths that would swarm to the lamps.

Her father was absolutely still, and his voice was measured and cool and strange as he said, 'In what way can you make it safe, may I ask?'

She stood by the table. 'I can neutralize the Auxiliary at the roadblock.'

'My word, and have you swallowed a military dictionary, Caithleen? Or have you had one thrust down your throat?' His voice was no longer cool, but loud, and growing more so with each word. He stabbed the air with his pipe. 'Neutralize, explain it to me, or shall I go to that Mick O'Brian? Or is it Des we have to thank for this? Neutralize. Just tell me it's not what I think it is.' His voice was almost a bellow.

She leaned against the table. He stormed to the trapdoor and slammed it shut before facing her, his hands on his hips. His stomach strained against the buttons on his shirt. 'Well, Caithleen. Explain.'

She looked not at him but at the clock that was ticking on the wall. 'I strike up a . . . well, a friendship with the Auxiliary. He will then stand between us and a proper search. The cellar will be safe for any wounded, or any in need of safety.'

Her father nodded, his face grim and unsurprised. 'This friendship will mean that you kiss him, that you sell your body—'

'No, not that.'

'That you sell your body, or as good as. That you are ostracized by our neighbours.'

'But only until we've won.'

'Then you'll be the little heroine, is that how they've sold it to you? Is that why you're doing it? For God's sake, Cait. You're so stupid, so childish, so dramatic.

You could be cropped, hurt, shot. Either way, you'll be soiled.' He was ranting, coming towards her.

She put up her hands, screaming at him, 'No, it's not because of that. It's because they killed Mum. It's because I want to do something or I will burst with hate. One of us has got to do something. One of us.'

Her father stopped. 'But I already am. I'm part time with Des, I was recruited weeks ago.'

Cait was confused. 'Mick didn't tell me. He couldn't have known.'

'He knew, of course he knew.'

'But he said . . .' She rubbed her forehead. Had he said one of them should do something? She couldn't remember. Or had he said she was the only one who could do something, because she had the contact with the Auxie? Yes, that must have been it. Then he'd held her, and they'd talked of the dance that would be held when Independence was won, and the looks on the faces of the townspeople when they realized what she had done. And afterwards she would go to her mother's grave.

Her father moved to the fire. He pushed tobacco into his pipe with his hands that were rigid with rage. 'He said what?'

'He said I was the best one for the job. I had been in England, it was a point of contact with the Auxie, and I had already met him, and because of the books they know of a way for me to strike up an acquaintance without arousing suspicion. I'm the only one who can do it.'

'I forbid it.'

She shook her head. 'You will not forbid anything. I see now why you have your spark back. You must let me do something too. I will do it. I have to do it. I can do it. It must be done. I will go to confession if it makes you any happier, every day.'

'What's the point of that, if you are going to

go on repeating the sin.' He was shouting again. 'Besides, the priest supports the cause.'

'It's not a sin – it's to wipe out their sin against Mum. For God's sake, Dada, I cry every night for her. Say you'll back me, for I'll do it anyway. Say they can use the cellar, for I'll bring them anyway.' Her voice was louder than his.

Again and again their voices rose and fell, drowning one another, then falling silent, then rising again until at last he said, 'The Black and Tans have stripped civilians and flogged them with straps and whips to drag information out of them. They crop the heads of girls who are Sinn Fein supporters. The IRA crop the heads of girls who fall for policemen and Tans. Neighbours do the same. Don't do this, Cait.'

'They'll look after me. They've promised. I'll be careful, the Auxie will never know I'm using him.'

There was silence except for the ticking of the clock. The chicken was burning. The knives and forks gleamed.

When her father spoke his voice was low, and uncertain. 'I can do nothing to stop you, can I? Damn you, Cait, for being so stubborn. You're just like your grandfather. Well, they'd better look after you and I'll do what I can to keep you safe.' He held her to him, thinking of his wife, knowing it would not be what she wanted, but not knowing how to stop it, any of it.

'Mick will look after me,' she said softly. 'He promised.'

Chapter Three

'Why's October such a miserable month?' Cait grumbled as she hoisted herself onto the cart, pulling her shawl tighter against the lingering drizzle. Sodden leaves had been driven into the corners of the yard by last night's wind and rain, and the gutter was dripping. 'Get yourself on to the bottom field now, Dada, the fence won't wait for ever. The storm will have tipped it even more.' She added, 'And stop fretting.'

'Who's fretting? I'm just making sure you don't go out of here so fast you tip the churn over.'

She shook her head at him and grinned. 'I'm not that eager, Dada.' The smile hadn't reached her eyes, any more than it reached his when he waved. He called, 'Take care. There's still time to change your mind.'

They both knew that for her, this wasn't an option. She clicked at Tanzy, the cart wheels rumbled. The lane, when she reached it, was muddy and progress slow. She looked back at the farm. The apple trees were stark and bare but it had been a good harvest. She looked at the glistening fields, then up to the hills, but they were hidden behind the damp, and at last down at her lap. She could see the shape of the book, beneath her shawl – for word was the Auxie would be at the roadblock today.

Way back in August she'd fired herself up to

play her part but the next morning the Auxie had gone. 'To the North,' Des had told Mike. How did he know? 'We can wait,' he had said. 'He'll be back.' Her father had been glad. She'd been half relieved, half not.

Mick had come last night as he came every night. 'Des says the Auxie will be in place tomorrow.' He had kissed her in the front room which smelt of autumn damp. He had held her against him, and she had clung to him, her hand in his hair, his wild curling hair. And he had wound hers around his hand, imprisoning her, kissing her eyes, her mouth, her neck, slipping her blouse from her shoulder, kissing that, and then her breast – and she had moaned and sagged.

He had kissed her mouth. 'Shh,' he had breathed, still pinioning her by her hair, stroking her breast, her thigh, pulling her against him, touching her, lifting her skirt, finding her and again she moaned, and again he kissed her, and his mouth was hard on hers, his breathing quick, his eyes half closed, his body urgent. Then he had broken away. 'God, Cait, you're a fine woman, and you're mine. Never forget that. You're mine, not his, not that Auxie's. That's business, that's for the cause.'

Cait's hands were trembling now as she slowed the cart to let Mrs Murphy drive the last of her cows across the road.

Mrs Murphy raised her hand. 'I know, I'm late. I'll be after churning it myself today, but at least the drizzle's stopped.'

Cait hadn't noticed. She smiled, dropped the shawl from her shoulders and Mrs Murphy laughed. 'I see you've your book as usual.' She was lifting the gate onto the latch. 'God bless that mare of yours – she doesn't need any guiding.'

Cait searched the crossroads. Yes, the Crossley tender was there. How did Des know these things?

53

They'd all learned it was better not to ask. Just as the man who'd informed on him at the dance had learned it had been a mistake to do so. He'd been found shot between the eyes with a placard round his neck: *Informers and Spies Beware*.

Would her friends think she was an informer? Even if they did, Des would protect her, with Mick beside him. She glowed at the thought of Mick, fixing on him, nothing else. It was grand how well he was doing. He'd told her he was Des's right-hand man, though still based on his father's farm. Holy Mother, but he was just such a grand boy. Cait touched the book.

The cart was nearing the roadblock. The Auxie, wearing the new dark-blue uniform, was seeing to the carts coming in from the right. Damn. The Tans motioned for her to stop as they had done so often. There were more of them now than ever before. They were pouring into Ireland because of men like Des, and, maybe, women like her. It gave her courage as the Tan leered at her. 'I've got a good one for you today, Missy.'

Cait stared ahead.

'Oh yes, you'll appreciate this one. Now why d'you think you had the Famine in Ireland, Missy?'

Cait watched the Auxie out of the corner of her eye and ignored the Tan, as she always did.

He continued. 'Because the apes you call your forefathers forgot where they planted the potatoes.' The Tan guffawed, and his spittle reached her hand and now she could ignore him no longer.

'Get out of my way, you apology for a man. Go and dig latrines which is what you were made for, and which your forefathers did so well for years.' She was wiping her hand on her cape, again and again, clicking at the pony to move on. The Tan swore and lunged at the bridle. 'I haven't finished with you yet, you bitch.' Again his spittle reached her.

54

'Well, I'm done with you.' The Auxie was forgotten, everything was forgotten except getting this Tan off her mare's harness, getting him away from her, getting his spittle off her hand.

The Auxie's voice cut through her rage. 'That's enough. Yet again, that's enough from both of you. Get on over and take my post, Jones. And you.' Ben Williams shook his head. 'You, Caithleen Healy, don't you ever learn?'

'Try teaching the Tans some manners, but then they're not capable of learning anything, are they?' Her rage made her shout. 'And take your hands off my mare.'

The Auxie laughed and his face was transformed. He looked so young. 'Be on your way.'

Cait hesitated, wanting to go on but knowing that this was her chance, and he had made it easy by recognizing her. But now that the moment was here, fear and repugnance overwhelmed her. She couldn't do it. It was too much. She hated them. She'd tell Mick she couldn't do it. But the shame, the look in his eyes . . . She dredged up the picture of the dance at the end of it all, the heroine she would be, the husband she would have in Mick, because he would marry her, she was sure of it – they'd become so close, after just three months.

The Auxie was walking away. She called to him. 'Please, just a moment.' She picked up the book, not wanting others to see.

The Auxie stopped, turned, his eyes wary, ready for more battles. She smiled. 'Please, we . . . I mean, I, couldn't get *Jane Eyre*. But *Wuthering Heights* might suit you as well.' She pointed to the sky. 'It's reading weather now.' His eyes were still wary, but surprise was creeping in. She breathed deeply. 'I'm sorry I damaged your copy of *Jane Eyre*. It was wrong of me.' It's only words, she said to herself. Just words, not a real apology, just acting, just a game – for the cause.

He looked around. No-one was watching. He reached for the book, opened it, saw the convent stamp, raised his eyebrows, then roared with laughter. 'Get on with you. You'll have to go to confession, pinching it from the nuns.' He handed it back.

She was dismayed. He must take it. She saw Mick coming through the roadblock. He shook his head and mouthed, 'Be yourself.'

She flared up at the Auxie. 'Well, you deserve to be told the end then to think an honest Irish lass would steal – or was that something you thought I'd picked up in England? I was only going to lend it to you. Where do you live anyway?' Des had said to stress the English connection.

The Auxie eyed the book on her lap, then looked up at her, then round at the roadblock. There was another Auxie watching them, a smile on his face. It was his friend Tom. He'd never hear the end of this tonight, but he didn't care. She had spoken to him, not shouted. Her red hair was still the same, so too her blue eyes and that creamy skin a man could drown in.

'I was brought up in Chester, along Hough Green, the road into North Wales. A big high house with an orchard at the rear of the garden.'

Cait felt excitement stir. How right Des was, how clever. 'I know it. I lived in Manchester. You go through Saltney to Wales. Please, take the book, just don't tell me the end, because I haven't read it myself yet.' She handed it to him. He didn't move. 'Please. But I'll need to return it.' She forced a smile. 'To keep my conscience clear. Please take it. It's my way of making amends, that's all.'

But oh no, it isn't, not really. It's my way of getting even, you English idiot. He's taking the book. He's damn well taking the book, stuffing it in his jacket. Oh Holy Mother, Mick, I've done it. We're almost there.

The Auxie smiled at her. 'I'm a quick reader. I can return it next week. I can slip it to you at the roadblock.' He knew Tom had seen and would automatically cover his back, coming between him and the Tans.

Cait shrugged. 'Or I could show you our river but it's not as big as the Dee that runs through Chester. In fact, it's a tiddler. Be careful, don't be seen. I'll be there Friday morning, elevenish, even if it's cold and wet – it's the farm past the Murphys'. The river is down to the east of the turf bank, there are willows, one a weeper. Get inside. It's where I had my camp when we came to stay with Grandpa.'

She clicked at the mare and slapped the reins. The other Auxie was intercepting a Tan who was coming towards them. Ben Williams stepped back, clutching the book, not sure how any of this had happened, but glad, God damn it, so glad.

That evening Cait skimmed two buckets of milk and tipped the cream into a can. What did it matter that the milk would have a low fat content at the creamery next day? She baked apple pie.

'A treat?' her father queried.

'We deserve one,' she replied.

Mick came as they were reading by the lamplight. She recognized his knock. 'Come into the warm,' she said softly.

'No, I like the dark.'

She put on her shawl, dragged on her boots and stood with him in the shelter of the apple loft, breathing deeply, washing the Auxie away with the scent of apples, washing away his sparkling eyes, his smile which made him human, his voice which brought him alive. They were murderers, they were paid murderers. Mick's arms were around her, his lips on her neck. 'I can't stay,' he said into her hair.

'Are you on active service tonight?'

'Very, if you'll let me. I can achieve a lot in a short time.' His laughter lifted her hair. Then he sobered. 'You did well. It's Friday he's coming, isn't it? We'll be there, protecting you. You were like a professional, Caithleen Healy. Revenge is sweet.' He moved from her, touching an apple in the rack, stroking it, looking at her all the while. 'Your mother never got to eat these, back in the land which is hers. Your mother never got to see you wed. For you will wed, Caithleen, when all this is over.'

He held her again and no longer did she see the Auxie as a human being. All she saw was herself married to Mick.

On Friday Cait walked to the willow, carrying a few cakes in the basket, hearing the wind in the reeds, the curlews on the wing. She looked but could not see Mick's men. They'd be there though. She could see no movement from the willow, but the Auxie'd be there, skulking, her book in his hand.

There was a weak sun today but it must have been a miserable night for the column. This man, though, would have been cosy and warm in his barracks. She pushed aside the fronds. He was there, in his uniform, leaning against the trunk, holding two books. He straightened, removed his bonnet, stuffed it in his pocket and smiled hesitantly. There was a moment's silence. Neither knew what to say. She said, 'Did you . . . ?' at the same time that he began, 'Perhaps we . . .' They stopped. She said, 'You first.'

The Auxie smiled more firmly. He held out his hand. 'Perhaps we should introduce ourselves, pretend that we have never met before.'

'Never yelled before, you mean,' Cait quipped. It was easier than she thought it would be.

'I'm Ben Williams and I enjoyed the book enormously.'

'I'm Caithleen Healy, and I'm glad you enjoyed the book enormously.'

He laughed, then waved a hand around. 'This was your den, was it?'

She reached up to the branch above her. 'Oh yes, I always felt safe here. I'd bring picnics. Mum would put milk into a medicine bottle and boil an egg for sandwiches, and that was me for the rest of the day. Ambrosia it was, curdled warm milk and soggy sandwiches.'

He laughed, and she with him. Yes, it was so much easier.

'Tom's here, on watch for us.' His face was earnest, he brushed back his straight light brown hair. 'I wanted to make sure I didn't get you into any sort of trouble. I've heard about—'

She cut across him. 'Where is he?' She knew her voice was too sharp, but, for God's sake, the Volunteers were out there too, guarding her. If Tom saw them, she'd be exposed.

'He'll be dug down safe, don't you worry. He's an Australian who's been through Gallipoli, he knows all about keeping his head down. He'll not be found unless he wants to be.' Ben laughed softly.

Cait thought quickly. 'Well, I'm not having any poor colonial boy digging down safe to look after the likes of you and me unless he has something inside himself to keep warm.' Somehow she had to make sure that Mick's men knew he was there. She thrust the basket at Ben. 'Go on,' she insisted. 'Call him in, let him take a few back into his hole with him.'

Ben looked at those eyes, that skin, that hair, that glorious wonderful hair. She was kind as well as fiery, and he knew that he was sinking into love, when this was the last place on earth it should happen. He tore himself away from her, and pulled aside the fronds, whistling twice.

Cait stood behind him, scanning the fields, the

walls, the hedges, and there, over by the thistles was a flash of uniform. The Auxie rose to the left of the pile of moss-covered logs. She called and waved. 'Shh,' urged Ben. 'Just in case.'

Exactly, she thought. Now everyone knew where everyone was, or her side did, anyway.

Tom sped across the ground between them, crouching low, bursting into the den. 'Probs?' His voice was curt, crisp. His brown eyes sharp, darting, his lips thin, his pistol drawn.

Ben calmed him, showed him the cakes. Tom turned. 'Strewth, missis, they'll go down nicely.' His grin was wide, his face alive, freckles spattered across his nose.

'You're so young,' she blurted out.

'Naw, just look it. I'm twenty-two, like Ben here. Been mates since Ypres, ain't we, mate? Always watched one another's backs, always will.'

Ben was peering out, traversing the ground. Tom took four cakes and rammed a fifth into his mouth, nodding at her, unable to speak. She laughed. 'Go on with you.'

He was gone, then poked his head back in, swallowing hard. 'Just like back at home playing lookout at a two-up game. And I reckon there's no cheater here, mate.' He was gone again, back to the thistles and the logs.

Ben relaxed, moved to the centre. Dead leaves whispered beneath his boots. 'That was very good of you.'

'It's very good of him,' she replied, still seeing the fresh young face, and not wanting to. These thugs shouldn't have faces. 'Two-up?' she questioned.

Ben laughed gently. 'A sort of betting game like heads or tails. They play it with coins in Australia but it's illegal, so they meet – oh, out in the bush in Kalgoorlie where he's from, or anywhere they can. Bit like your poteen stills.'

'Cheater?'

Ben handed her the book he'd been holding all this time, and the other with it. '*Jane Eyre*. I put the pages back.'

'Cheater?' she insisted, her senses alert.

'They're players who used double headers.'

She looked at him, forcing herself to look affronted. 'Did you really think that of me?'

'We have to be careful.' He flushed with embarrassment and moved from foot to foot. 'But no, of course not, and if I did, I'm certain now.'

She opened *Jane Eyre* and read the bookplate stuck in the front: *Ben Williams. English Prize. King's School.* Her hands were trembling with relief, but he thought it was anger. She looked up at him. He was staring at her. She flicked her hair back over her shoulder. He looked away. 'I'm sorry to doubt you,' he murmured, desperate in case she sent him from her.

Cait shrugged. 'You're a soldier, it's your job.' Relief flooded through him. She continued, 'So why a soldier in this war?'

'It isn't a war, we're keeping the peace, or trying to.' He reached up and broke off a frond. He wound it round and round his finger.

'It's a war,' she said flatly.

'For God's sake, Caithleen, it's not.' His voice was sharp, the relief forgotten. 'There are some guerrilla forces disorganizing the place, or trying to. We're just containing it, trying to keep some sort of lid on it, make it governable. We're not all convicts and the dregs. I'm all right, so is Tom. The Tans have a few good ex-soldiers in them. Why can't you all just settle down and be part of the Empire? There's a lot to be said for it. Is this mayhem what you all want?'

She put the basket down and picked up a handful of weeds. 'Not all of us, but it soon will be. Do you know that in the famine people died of starvation, or poisoned themselves with the weeds they ate, whilst their English landlords exported the corn that could have saved them.'

'That was years ago.'

'Then you transported Presbyterians into the North to make you feel more comfortable, taking our land, dispossessing us. Then we voted after this war to rule ourselves. You took no notice. You never take any notice.'

Ben Williams was looking at the ground, shaking his head. He turned to go. 'This is pointless. I thought for a moment we'd meet as two people, not two sides. Keep the book. I don't want it back.' He pushed aside the fronds.

Oh God, what had she done? Why couldn't she keep her mouth shut? She rushed forwards, held him back, turned him round. 'Forgive me. Please. It's the uniform. You're right. We must meet as two people. I want that. I really want that. I'm not on any side. I just can't forget . . .' She paused, then pushed the basket towards him with her foot. 'And I baked these for us. You can't go without tasting just one.' He looked at her, his disappointment still visible. He ignored the basket.

She stooped, picked up a cake, brought it to him, held it close to his mouth and said, 'Tell me about *Wuthering Heights*. I flipped through some of it. Have you ever been to the moors?'

He looked at the cake, then at her, and laughed, and again, for Cait, it was as though the sun had come out here, in the darkness of the den, and nothing an Auxie did should light any gloom, and she was confused. 'If I bite into that *and* tell you about *Wuthering Heights* there'll be an interesting few minutes. Make up your mind, Caithleen Healy.'

He held her wrist, looking into her eyes, and the touch of her skin set him on fire. He took the cake, walking back with her to the centre and they talked of Heathcliff, and Cathy, and no, he hadn't been to the moors, but one day he would. 'Have you been to the Lake District?' he asked.

'Oh yes, often. We'd take a boat out on Windermere. It reminded my mother of Killarney. We'd have picnics.' She sat down and leaned against the trunk, patting the ground beside her. 'It's quite dry, you can brush your uniform off when you get up. How long have you got?'

He sat beside her, resting his arms on his raised knees, still fiddling with the frond, winding it round and round, then back again. He was nervous, she thought. Good heavens. She watched his fingers. They were so long. A pianist's hands, her mother would have said.

'On these picnics of yours – was the milk warm and the sandwiches soggy?' His face was quizzical. He raised his eyebrow in the same way as he had done when he had looked inside *Wuthering Heights* at the roadblock.

She laughed. 'Absolutely.'

'And does your mother still make such picnics?'

The laughter died. She dug her fingers into the dead leaves. 'No.' Her voice was cold. It shouldn't be. She should be warm, full of laughter, just as Des had decreed, as Mick wanted, as the cause needed. But she couldn't be.

He stopped twining the frond and looked closely at her, concern in his voice as he asked, 'What have I said? Whatever it is I'm sorry.'

She felt the trunk at her back, its hardness. She felt the leaves beneath her fingers, their crispness. 'It's too late for anyone to be sorry. She's dead. Is yours?'

She looked at him now, her eyes carefully empty. He said she was.

'Did she die in her bed?'

He said she did, watching her closely all the time, but she wouldn't let the hate show. No, she mustn't do that.

'My mother died in the road, mud in her mouth, her nose. She was flung from the cart bringing us to the farm at the end of March, after all those years away. She was shoved over the side by Tans. She was dragged along the road because an empty customs house had been burnt. They kicked Dada and me out as well, held us down. We couldn't stop them dragging her. She was all limp. Her neck had been broken when she hit the road. I still dream of it and taste the mud. I still hear them laughing. They were drunk, they thought it was funny. "Just like a bloody ragdoll," they said. They didn't know she was dead but neither did they care. No, I don't have any more soggy sandwiches.'

Damn it, her voice was breaking, her eyes were full. No, no more soggy sandwiches, Mum. She stared ahead. She mustn't blink, the tears mustn't fall, not here, with him.

He stirred. 'I'm so sorry. It's no good to say that, but I am. I'm just so sorry, Caithleen.' He handed her a handkerchief, crisp and white. She shook her head. She didn't want to touch anything personal of his. A book was different. He rose, dusted himself off. She brushed at her eyes while he did so, then stood up, forcing a smile, picking at the pieces of bark on the back of his tunic.

He said, 'Don't bother, just remember to return the book to the nuns. Keep mine. I had hoped to see you again, but I couldn't impose, not now, not knowing this. All I wonder is how you could bear to see me at all.' He held out his hand. 'Good luck, Caithleen.'

She shook his hand. 'Come again, next Friday. I'm a fast reader too. Who knows, maybe I'll have prised something else from the nuns for you. Take care not to be seen. It's risky for us both, you know.'

Des had said to play on his sense of honour, of the English admiration for bravery.

He still held her hand, and now his eyes were wary, and thoughts of double-headed coins were ebbing and flowing. 'But why, when we killed your mother? Why ask to see me again?'

She looked away from him, wanting to pull her hand free, not knowing what to say. It was the one question she should have been ready for, but was not, because she hadn't thought she would ever reveal her life to any of this scum.

'Why?' he repeated, conscious of this alien land, of his uniform, of hostile forces who melted into the community. Surely to God he hadn't been wrong? But why would she want to see him?

She looked at him. 'I don't know why. I just do.' There was a ring of truth in her voice, in her face, that even she recognized, and Ben nodded, satisfied.

That evening she read *Jane Eyre*, then basked in Mick's praise when he applauded her quick thinking concerning the Auxie guard as they held one another in the darkness of the yard. On Friday she went to confession, but was not explicit. On Sunday, after mass, she skimmed *Wuthering Heights*. On Tuesday she went to the draper's, and rolled more bandages, knitted more balaclavas and scarves, and longed to offer herself for tea duty, but Mick had told her she must not volunteer. 'If you were caught the plan would be finished. In fact, you shouldn't be with the Cumann at all. What if the draper's is raided? You'd be spotted, and the game not even begun.' But nothing would stop her going. She wanted to do everything and anything to help.

As they rolled the bandages she and Rose whispered and laughed and planned for next month's dance. 'Will your man be dancing a tango with you then?' Rose said, nudging her. 'Or is he dancing a sight too many already? Because my man certainly is. Oh isn't it all great, Cait? Just great.'

It was just great, all of it, and as she walked home, she stood tall.

She and the Auxie met only twice in October.

'He's not really engaged yet,' Des complained to Mick as the rain dripped through the branches of the trees around them in the gloom of the wood. 'It's going too slowly. We need to be sure of him. We're going to be needing that cellar, really needing it, as winter comes and the actions get tougher. We've got to plan something big to keep up the momentum. There'll be searches, perhaps casualties, and our last safe house was blown two days ago.'

Mick told Cait to hurry it along when he held her that evening. She shook her head. 'The Auxie must make the running. He's relaxing, trusting me, but still not sure. It mustn't be forced, or he'll suspect double-headed coins.' She leant back in his arms. Mick didn't understand and grew angry, because there must be no secret language between his woman and the enemy.

Cait tossed her hair and enjoyed his frustration, his jealousy, as she told him it was an old Australian saying.

October rolled mist-sodden into November. The column were trenching roads, ambushing patrols. The Tans were searching houses, barns, cellars. One day they came to Cait's house too, throwing furniture around, cursing, swearing.

'You've got to hurry it up, or we'll scrap the idea. We'll fix up something else,' raged Des to Cait in the yard, his men posted, who knew where, in the darkness.

Cait hissed, 'I can't do any more. He's busy. I'm Irish. He's cautious. Go somewhere else if you've all these complaints. Tell him, Mick.'

'There's no need to try anything else. She'll sort it out.' Mick gripped her arm tightly. She must. His idea must work.

That night, before he left, he kissed her, stroked her, talked of the life they would one day live, the love they shared, how grand their kids would be and how proud they'd be of their mother.

In the first week of November Ben was at the roadblock as Des had predicted. She passed him Jane Austen's *Pride and Prejudice*. 'It needs returning,' she said, her eyes locking with his.

'I don't know – what if you're seen? There's been a cropping in a village we went through last week.'

'I won't be. I miss you.' How could she say these words and hear that ring of truth again? 'Friday? I know it's cold by the river, but it would be so nice just to see you.'

He came, and she brought cakes for Tom as always, so that Mick's men could mark him. She and Ben stood out in the open as she wanted, but still hidden from the road by the willow, and discussed the water, and the sky, and Chester, and Manchester, and the Lakes, and then he leaned across and kissed her and his lips were disgusting on hers, his tunic, as it brushed her shoulders, was repulsive, and the feel of his body as she brought her arms up and round him made her want to scream, but Des wanted action, so Des would damn well have it.

There, was he watching? Was Mick? Was pride coursing through him, as disgust was coursing through her? She held Ben's face, drawing away from him, smiling, making sure the smile reached her eyes.

'Please,' he murmured. 'Please see me on Tuesday. I can't wait for Friday.' He bent his head, searching for her lips. She opened her mouth, her tongue stroking his lips, softly, gently, with distaste. Look at this, Mick. Is this fast enough for you? Is pride tinged with jealousy? Is this driving you wild? The wind whipped her clothes about her. His mouth was hard on hers. She shuddered.

He held her close, whispering, 'Yes, it's so cold. If only we didn't have to skulk, if only I could take you to a theatre, to dinner, show you off.' He stroked her hair, adoring her, admiring her. 'You're so brave, Caithleen. So very brave.'

The following week they met again, and she clung to him, and they talked very little of the book, but of her farm and of his family – his lawyer father, his loving mother, his brother who had been killed in the war, his parents who had died of influenza, but really a broken heart. They'd left nothing, even the house had been rented because his father had poured money into his practice to keep it afloat, hoping for better days.

He looked up at the sky. 'I'm going to Australia with Tom when this is over. He's got a stake in a small gold-mine at Kalgoorlie with his old Uncle Roy and we're going there. Tom didn't know if he wanted to go back to it when the war ended so he joined the Auxiliaries with me to give himself time to decide. There's talk of the Government giving assisted passages to ex-soldiers, particularly those who've served in Ireland, so I'll apply for one. Imagine the sun, Caithleen.' He touched her hair and kissed it. 'Do you like to be warm, Caithleen?'

'I love Ireland, Ben.' His name still sounded wrong in her mouth. She wanted to spit out the word 'Auxie'. What did it matter that his parents had died, that he was alone in the world, that he was too thin, that they liked the same books, laughed at the same things? It mattered not at all. This was work. This was the cause. He was an Auxie. Her mother was dead.

She moved away from the shelter of the willow. 'Careful,' Ben called. 'You can be seen.'

'Not with your trusty guard. He'll whistle, won't he?' And my own trusty guard, she thought, who'd practised his curlew cry until it was just right.

She looked out across the fields. Was Mick watching, pleased at progress, but angry too? Tonight would he kiss her, demand her love, insist that she was his as usual? Of course he would, and she would know she belonged, was wanted, desired. He would know she was Irish.

She looked out over the river, to the distant hills. 'It's clear today. You should go walking over the hills sometime, Ben. They're beautiful. Far more beautiful than all that sun or all the gold-mines in the world.'

He followed the line of her finger and asked, 'Will you show them to me? But no, of course you mustn't.' He stepped towards the basket. 'Let me pass you a cake.'

A movement from the lane caught her eye. A bike was approaching the farm. She froze. For God's sake, Tom, are you asleep? Mick, there'd been no curlew. She couldn't move, couldn't think. It was Rose, she could see her quite clearly. Move, hide.

Rose saw Cait. Stopped, waved. 'Get down,' hissed Cait to Ben who was behind her somewhere. 'For God's sake, get down.' She heard the thud as he hit the ground. 'Blessed Virgin, was it in time?' Cait watched Rose hesitate, her hand drop.

She stood motionless, as Cait now waved and called. Rose bent to the basket hanging on her handlebars, then shouted to Cait, 'I'll be back, I've forgotten the magazine.' She swung the bike round.

Cait saw a flicker of movement by the wall. It was Tom, flat on the ground, elbowing his way back to the thistles, well out of sight of Rose. Now Rose was bearing down on the pedals, her skirt flapping. Had she seen? She swung round to Ben. 'For God's sake. Did she see?'

Ben was crouching, beckoning her to him, his eyes darting from the diminishing figure on the bike to Tom, back to Cait. He stood, gathered her into his arms, cursing. 'Christ. What the hell's up with Tom? He should have warned us.'

'Did she see?' shouted Cait. 'For heaven's sake, did she see?' She pulled from him in panic, looking down the lane, then towards Mick. Tom was leaping across the grass.

'Strewth, Ben, I didn't see her. I heard something back behind me. I thought there was someone up there, behind the wall.' He was pointing to where she knew Mick was. 'I was working my way back.'

'You bloody idiot, you should have whistled.'

'I did.'

'Well, not bloody loud enough.'

Cait gripped Ben's arm, panic draining her strength. Oh God. Oh God. Mick had nearly had it. Rose might have seen them. What was Rose doing here? What the hell was she doing here?

Ben grabbed her as she shuddered, his arm strong around her. 'Get back, and keep your eyes open,' he ordered Tom.

Tom looked at Cait. 'I'm sorry. Just sorry.'

She shook her head. His young face was furrowed, anxious. 'No, Tom, it's not your fault.' She reached out, took his hand, squeezed it. 'You did the right thing. It'll be all right.' Tom backed away. 'It'll be all right,' she insisted, wanting to wipe the anxiety from his face.

Ben held her. 'I'll never forgive myself.' She felt safe in his arms, her face pressed against his chest, her strength returning. Then she focused, saw the uniform, and remembered who she was, and where she was, and who these scum were.

She eased from his grasp. 'It'll be all right,' she said firmly. Because it would. Mick would sort it out, or Des. 'Now tell me about these cosy new barracks you talked about when we last met. I want to know that you're going to be comfortable.'

Ben held her hands, searching the area, but coming back to her eyes, her wonderful eyes, seeing her concern for him, remembering her concern for Tom. How long it had been since anyone had cared whether he was all right. God he loved her.

She murmured, 'Go on, tell me, let me know you're going to be fine.' Des needed the details. 'Where is it? There are damp spots around, you know.'

He laughed gently. 'It's off the Limerick road, just the other side of the hill, or so they tell us. Is that going to be damp?' He kissed her hand.

She shook her head. 'No, that should be about perfect.'

'I don't know about that, but it'll give us a good base from which to operate, but enough of that now.' He gripped her hands, anxiety tugging at him again. How could they keep meeting like this? 'Let me take you away.' He swung her round. 'It's not safe. Let me get you far from here.'

She shook her head. 'I'll be all right. I know I will. She's my friend, we . . . I'll explain to her. Please. Forget it.' She kissed him. 'Just make sure you come more often. Please. You must see how much I care, or I wouldn't risk so much.'

In the woods that afternoon, Mick spun Des round. 'You can't just let her go to the Cumann meeting. I said we'd protect her. Rose saw them. I could see that from her face. It saved us. Cait told me at lunch that that bastard Auxie lookout was on his way to us. She's expecting us to make it all right. For God's sake, Des, she got us the information about the barracks from the Auxie. It's the peach we've been waiting for. We owe her. We must tell the Cumann or Rose at least.'

Des's hand was on his wrist, vicelike, lifting his hand from his arm. 'She knew the score. We can't interfere.

I said when you put it to us that you must understand that. You knew that at some point it would come out. She knew. We can't risk blowing it by bringing anyone else in on it. And watch yourself. I hear she thinks you're second in command. A loose tongue, Mick, and delusions of grandeur, can be dangerous. You'll never be that. You must not be. One of us must stay safe.'

Mick looked at his brother, feeling the pain of his grip, trying to wrench his arm free. He couldn't. The other members of the brigade were busy, making sure they didn't look, making sure they didn't listen. The woods were dripping. Didn't the rain ever stop? 'I might have said something, it was stupid. But look, she's going to the draper's. She's expecting us to have squared it with Rose. For God's sake, she could be cropped by this evening, not just ostracized.'

Des eased his grip, his eyes suddenly sharpening, then softening. 'Oh come on, Mick, just imagine if we told Rose. That stupid giggling fool would end up telling the world, and then what would happen to your Cait? The Auxie would find out. It would be more than a cropping then. Just think what they do to informers. Be more like a bullet in the guts.' His arm was round his brother now, his fist was gently kneading his arm. 'No, we've got to let it ride. That Cait of yours is a spirited girl, she'll cope, and it'll not come to cropping, though if it did, it would bring that Auxie round to her even more. The Brits love a sacrifice. But tell her that we'll be protecting her every day, every minute, from now on – well, from tonight anyway. I'll sort out a rota this evening.' He was impatient now. Mick could sense it.

'D'you give me your word on that?'

'I do. And remember it's for the cause. And tell her, Mick, she's done very well. We'll burn the barracks. It'll be a symbol. They've been burning too many of our Sinn Fein buildings. It'll be for her. Tell her that, and tell her, yes, it'll be before they occupy it, just like she asked.' Though it would have been anyway, he thought.

Mick nodded, breaking free of his brother. 'I'll get to her now – make sure she stays in until the protection's in place. I promised.'

Des called across to his second in command, 'You'll do that for the lad, won't you, Kevin? I want him to get off to O'Connor at the farm.'

Mick protested. Des snapped. 'Do as you're told. Do you want to heap trouble on the girl? You're my brother. We're trying to set up a safe house. She must be whiter than white. No-one must know you still see her in case the Tan hears. It would be far better if you didn't at all until this is over.'

'Well, that can go down the stinking drain. She's my girl. I want her to remember that. She's mine, d'you hear?' Mick was shouting, gripping Des's lapels. Kevin O'Higgins moved to stand beside Des. The other men stared at him, motionless and tense. The rain was still falling, the trees still dripping.

Des eased Mick's hands from his jacket. 'I think I heard that.' His eyes were steely, then he laughed. 'Fine, but see her after dark. Now get off to O'Connor's. Liam will brief you.'

Des watched as Mick trudged over to the fallen log. Des gestured to Liam, then turned to Kevin, leading him away from the group, his head close, his voice quiet, looking towards Mick, then away quickly, before his brother noticed.

Cait walked into town. Mick hadn't returned, so it must be all right. He'd said he would come right back if there was a problem. It was the end of market-day, there was straw and muck on the roads. She passed the colour-washed façades with their dim lights, the slaughterhouse, the public house, hearing the singing still going on. They'd been at the booze since before lunch, and would be at it when she left the meeting

73

in an hour. She felt relief lighten her stride. She didn't even mind the smell of dung which lingered in the damp, freezing gloom of early evening, or the torn paper which scuttered along the road catching against her leg as she walked. She kicked it free. I'm all right, I'm safe.

She drew her coat around her, tucking her hair inside her scarf. There were still carts around the market house. One had piglets squeaking in creels. She reached across and rubbed the snout of one, then hurried on, smelling the burned-out ironmonger's which the Tans had fired last week. They had even cut the fire hoses when the brigade had tried to save the building.

But my, how the barracks would burn – or she hoped they would. If only she could tell the girls that she had gleaned the information. But she couldn't, not yet – or maybe she could to Rose.

Two dogs were fighting in the street. She laughed and pushed open the door of the draper's, the bell jangled. Mrs Mullihan was measuring curtain material for her sister's friend. Cait hurried through, unbuttoning her coat, unknotting her scarf, feeling warm out of the wind. She pushed open the door into the back room. It was flooded with light and smelt of paraffin from the lamps. She sang out. 'I'm here. Sorry to be late.'

There was only silence to greet her. Silence and hatred in the faces of her friends, and Dr Quinn and Mrs Flannigan, who formed a semicircle facing her, their arms crossed. Cait froze, then backed as they came towards her. Rose detached herself from the group. There were tears in her eyes and anger and pain in the words which dropped from her mouth. 'Get out of here, you Auxie whore, you traitor. And don't send them here for us, we'll have gone.'

Cait put up her hand. 'You don't under . . .' she began.

'Auxie whore, Auxie whore,' they chanted, moving towards her. She backed away. Mick, Mick, you promised, her mind screamed. You promised. They were closer. She was in the corridor. She turned and ran, back out through the shop. God, was the door locked? She wrenched at the handle, the bell jangled. It wasn't. Mrs Mullihan's scissors flashed on the counter, surprise holding her motionless. Cait looked past her, to the back room, then she was out, and running down the street, her hair trailing, her scarf forgotten in her hand, her coat flapping, their chants still loud in her head. She threw a look over her shoulder. Were they following?

No. But still she ran. 'Mick, Mick,' she panted. 'Mick.' Past the pub. Would they come out, chase her, crop her, ring her, kill her? No, no-one burst from the doors, there was just the singing. Past the paint-washed houses, the lamps shining out on the drizzle-glazed road, overtaking the cart wending home, the piglets squealing.

She was out of the town now, running across the crossroads. A stitch seared her side, but she couldn't stop, wouldn't stop. 'Mick, Dada, Mum.' Her feet were pounding, mud splashed her legs, her raincoat, her skirt and dragged at her shoes. Her breath was sobbing in her throat, and now she heard what she had dreaded.

She flung a glance behind. There were men behind her. They must have been in the shadow of Widow Murphy's gate, or behind the blackthorn. She looked ahead, forcing herself into a faster run. Her heels were sore, she bunched her fists, her side was stabbing. They were gaining, she could hear their breath. Their feet. Their breath. Their feet. Hands grabbed her shoulders, swung her round, tossed her to the ground.

'Let me alone,' she gasped. 'For the love of God, let me alone.'

A voice rasped. 'There's been too much love, and sure, it hasn't been with God, Caithleen Healy.' They were masked. She struggled. They held her, threw her onto her front, her chin was in the mud, it was in her mouth. 'Mum.'

Hands were in her hair, pulling it tight, pulling her head up from the mud. Others held her still. A hand came under her chin. 'Sure, it's only your hair, not your life, you stupid girl.' It was the same rasping Dublin voice.

She lay still, hearing their breath, her own, and now the shears as they sliced, again, then again, and now her hair was no longer pulled tight, but thrown in the mud before her eyes. The hand beneath her chin was removed. Her head flopped to the ground, cushioned by her warm dry hair. But now the mud was seeping through and all she could hear was her heart beating, and the sound of their footsteps as they left.

She heaved herself up, pushing with her arms, forcing her legs to take her weight, swaying as she stood. 'You pigs,' she screamed after them. 'Just you wait. Just you damn well wait.'

She carried her hair carefully all the way home. She struggled into the kitchen. Her father was not there. Dinner was in the oven, the room was thick with the smell of potatoes, onions and cheese. Of course, she had prepared it before she left. It seemed so long ago. She moved as though her legs did not belong to her. At the sink she ran water and washed the hair that she held in her hands. Free, it had to be free of the mud. The water was running clear. She wound it round her hand, squeezed it again and again. She carried it to the fire, let it dangle, let it feel the heat. Steam rose.

The door opened. She turned. Her father came in carrying turf. He stopped, dropped the turf, and it was as though he had seen a sight fit to shock the patron saint of calmness, as her mother used to say. Yes, that's what her mother used to say.

'Oh Cait, oh Cait, baby.' He came and held her, tenderly, gently, squashing her hair between them. 'Kevin O'Higgins came. He said he'd try and catch up with you. He didn't say what it was. Has someone seen you with the Auxie?'

She eased away from him. 'Don't, Dada. Don't. It doesn't matter. I don't mind. Yes, they saw me. Mick must have sent Kevin. It was no-one's fault. One day they'll be sorry. One day I'll walk into the dance and they'll know what they've done, and my hair will have grown by then.' She clutched her hair tighter, winding it round her hand, as Ben Williams had wound the willow frond round his fingers.

She moved to the stairs. 'Just think, Dada, I can get up later every morning. It won't take so long to brush.' She climbed the stairs, and laid her hair in her drawer, on her mother's silk blouse, smoothing it, smoothing it.

Her father brought up water and poured it into the bowl on the washstand. 'I'm boiling more. The bath will be ready. It'll be by the fire.' He touched her face. His cheeks were tear streaked, and now she sobbed, and he held her and rocked her, and when she had bathed he tucked her into bed, and she slept.

When Mick came near midnight, her father roared at him and swore and crashed the furniture around the room, until Mick had to shake the facts out of him, and then he, too, wanted to rant, but instead he said, 'Oh God, oh no, we've set up a guard for every minute of every day starting now.'

'That's too late. It will end. I won't have any more of this,' her father said. 'You can't protect her. I'll send her away from Limerick, to a quieter area.'

Cait stood in the doorway, holding on to the door

jamb. She had been woken by the noise and listened and saw Mick and her father as though through a clouded mirror. She spoke, and she heard herself as though through a long-misted valley. 'We will have more of it. I was warned. It will make the Auxie guilty. It will bring him round even more.'

She was so very pale, Mick thought, so calm, so bruised, so like a child now that curls no longer fell down past her shoulder – who could resist her? His brother's words flashed through his mind – he'll come round to her even more – but no, Des wouldn't do that. Mick brushed the thought to one side, and moved towards her.

She turned from him, shaking her head, climbing back up the stairs. 'I'm tired. I want to sleep. Just let me sleep. Just let me be alone.'

Chapter Four

Mick eased his shoulders and crouched down next to Cait's father, just within the trees, but overlooking the road they had trenched. He checked his blisters in the moonlight. An owl flirted with the wind then disappeared into the branches. It was only two hours before dawn. He stared around, checking the men and Des, who was creeping back from the road, Kevin O'Higgins in his wake, their rifles glinting in the moonlight. He touched his own, running his hand along the barrel. At last they were doing something.

Des sank down beside him, patting Cait's father on the arm, elbowing Mick gently. 'Well, at least the Irish can be relied on to dig good trenches, isn't that what the English say? I should have let you go on and make a canal out of it. The navvy brigade, eh!' He spoke in a whisper, laughing silently. 'But we're running late.'

Mick brought out his cigarettes. His brother pushed them back. 'Not on an action, Mick, unless you want to get your stupid head shot off.' There was an edge to his voice, just as there had been when they were kids and there was a problem.

'All right, all right,' Mick rammed them back into his pocket. 'Are you off then?'

Des nodded. 'We'll be at the barracks in twenty minutes, fire it in fifteen, then back here. Now you all,' Des craned his neck, looking to the men on the left, and then on the right, 'you are here just as a back-up, part of your training. The trenching is in case a patrol comes along. It'll stall them. They'll be worried about an ambush. Maybe set them scuttling back. If they do come along, you,' he stabbed a finger at Niall, 'you, Niall, my lad, will come down that hill.' His finger stabbed towards the edge of the wood. 'Like a hare with a damn terrier after it, and warn us. The rest will do nothing, just fade.'

He was up in one easy movement, and the flying column with him. Up and away, through the trees, soundless, efficient, and Mick thought they were the grandest lads in the world. His eyes met Niall's. They nodded, grinned and settled themselves into the night.

Des led his men through the trees. No-one spoke. There was no need, they'd been briefed, they knew one another's thoughts, they'd lived together, killed together when they had to, some of their friends had died together. On down the hill, skidding on loose mulch. No-one cursed, they just froze, listened, then set off again. Out across flat terrain now.

Des led, feeling tiredness flooding through him. Even the surge of adrenalin didn't last long any more. Why was he fighting, burning, trying to stay alive in the lanes and fields he had played in as a kid? Wasn't there any other way? No. He shook his head. They wouldn't go unless they were kicked out and he cursed them, wanting his life back. Every time, during an action, he thought this now.

He flagged down his men, signing for them to fan out, not risking speech. It should be deserted, but you never knew. They crept forward steadily. It was an old police training barracks, extended, then deserted, out of fear, when the campaign began. The Tans were due to occupy it next week.

He stood still, watching as Paddy, Kevin and Liam found the paraffin they had buried earlier in the day.

Three others distributed the cans. The scouts reported back. 'All clear. It's deserted.'

'This'll teach the Tans to fire Sinn Fein halls,' Paddy breathed.

'Enough of that, keep your mind on the job,' Des snapped.

They lugged the paraffin into the building, down corridors, into dormitories, the hall, pouring it, smelling it. Des said to everyone he checked, 'Are your exits clear?' They were. He stationed himself outside, checking for Niall. It was all clear. 'Fire it,' he yelled. They did. He counted them out. All clear.

There were blasts of heat and light, the noise of wood cracking, glass breaking. It always surprised him. So loud, so light, so hot. They ran for the woods, and then they saw Niall, slithering and slipping down the lower slopes. At the same time, they heard a rifle fire. Niall ran to him. 'It's a Tan convoy. I think Mick might . . .'

Des cursed and ran, his men behind him, Niall last. 'God damn him,' Des groaned.

Mick felt the rifle buck. No Tan fell, damn it.

Paul Healy spun round, running back, slapping the rifle down. The barrel was warm. 'What the hell are you doing? Des said fade.'

The Tans were piling from the lorry, spreading out into the ditches.

'They were sitting ducks,' Mick protested, aiming again. The Tans were firing. Paul ducked. Mick fired again and again. Others were firing. A despatch rider was hit as he shoved his motor bike aside. He clutched his leg, crawled for a ditch. Tans shouted, some regrouped. A machine-gun rattled. Way beyond the trees the sky above the barracks was bright, and fierce with flames. God, but this was great.

Des burst through the trees, the column behind him. He threw himself to the ground, knocking the rifle from Mick's hands, punching him on the side of the head.

'You fool, you bloody, stupid fool.'

His men were knocking the part-timers out of the way. 'Kevin, take two, get across the road. They'll break through the woods. No-one's out there to stop them. They could flank us.'

Des took Mick's rifle, emptied it, flung it behind him, hissed at Paul Healy, 'Why didn't you stop the idiot?'

Paul shook his head. 'I didn't know.'

Des was firing the Hotchkiss light machine-gun. He said, not looking at Paul, 'I know, I'm sorry. He's only ever done what he damn well wants.' Bullets were flying. A man screamed to their left. Another to their right.

'We'll hold them. You all get back.' The part-timers hesitated. 'Get away,' Des ordered and waited until they left. 'Paul, you and Mick take the wounded. Use the cellar and don't let the others know where you're going. The less who know about the safe house the better. You'll need two of my men to help. Matt, take Mike and go with them. I'll get to you before dawn. All right with you, Paul?'

Paul nodded, shaken and confused. He backed away. Mick gripped Des's shoulder. 'Thank God I thought of using Cait. You said we'd need a safe house.'

Des was still firing. Another Tan fell. Another of Des's men fell. 'Go away,' Des shouted, 'and don't you ever go ahead with an action on your own. I've told you – no unnecessary loss of life. I won't have it. Now get away and think what's going to happen in the town tonight because of this.'

Cait hadn't been able to sleep. She'd been in and out of bed saying an aspiration as she had done after her mother died. It hadn't helped then either.

Before dawn she was standing at the window. Her father still hadn't returned. He hadn't even told her he was going. But that was part of it. The less she knew the better, the less anybody knew the better. But he must be back by dawn.

She looked towards the milking shed. She'd milk, but no, not take the churn to the creamery lorry. Her father had done it for the past three days. No-one had reviled him, rather they had pitied him. They knew he was a good man, that he couldn't be blamed for the daughter he had spawned – or so she imagined their minds were working. It was as hers would have done.

She ran her fingers down the glass, then pushed the window open, admitting the cold air. In the moonlight she saw the dew on the grass, on the hydrangea in the corner, on the blackthorn hedge, on the fields which were stroked by wisps of mist. She wished that she could walk into the mist and become it, without form or shape, or being, until all this was over.

She saw the glow in the sky and knew it must be the barracks. She smiled. At least she was useful, and now she stood straight. One day they'd know. One day it would all be over. She moved away, then heard firing echoing through the night and rushed back to the window, shaking her head. Oh no. Des had promised the barracks would only be fired if it was empty.

She banged on the sill with her fists. 'Damn you, Des.' She flung her clothes on and rushed downstairs and out into the yard, straining to see. Her father was out there, Mick too. Damn you, Des. The sooner Mick took over the column the better.

She waited in the kitchen, then out in the yard, then in the kitchen, unable to stand still. She brought in turf, sparked up the fire, boiled the kettle, cut slices from one of the flitches of bacon hanging from the ceiling. She cooked it. Why? She didn't know. Yes she did. It was something to do. Dawn broke, and then they came, straggling across the field.

She rushed to the cellar trapdoor, heaved it open, threw down cushions from the settle, and the blanket that hung along the back. She reached for iodine, bandages. The kettle was boiling. They were struggling across the yard. She could hear groans, then her father's voice. 'Come on, lad, not far now.'

They were in the kitchen. Her father's face was streaked with sweat, and so was Mick's. The man they eased down into the cellar was little more than a boy. His head rolled in pain. Des's men eased the other man onto the kitchen floor, checked him. 'Yes, he's dead, Mike,' the younger man said. Mike nodded, they hauled the body up between them. Mike looked at Cait, his face grim.

'All right, missis,' he said, his voice calm. 'You get down the cellar, fix Sean best you can. We'll take Rob out again.' Her father was climbing out of the cellar. 'You, Paul, get the cows in. Do just as you would normally. Get a few eggs on, missis. Be normal.'

Mick was climbing out now, brushing down his jacket. There was blood on his cheek. Cait gasped and rushed to him. Mike's voice cut across and its fierceness stopped her. 'And you, Michael, get on home. Get the cows in. Do something useful, something normal, sensible, if that's within your capabilities.'

Mick pushed past her, his mouth sulky.

'Mick,' she called.

Mike shouted at her as he turned to follow Mick, edging the body sideways through into the yard. 'Get on with it, the Tans'll be swarming round the place any minute. Des'll be here, bringing some of us with him.'

Her father was sluicing his face. She threw him the towel, pushing him to one side, pouring water into

84

a bowl, slopping it as she hurried down the ladder into the cellar. 'Put the rug over the trap, Dada, just in case.' She pulled the trapdoor shut.

Her father had lit the lamp when he'd left the boy down here. He was lying on the mattress, his lips white with the effort of suppressing his groans. She knelt beside him, grateful for the Cumann meetings, soothing him, tending him.

Three of Des's men, including Mike, stumbled down the steps ten minutes later, panting, carefully laying their weapons where they could reach them, hunching back against the wall. The boy had been shot in the shoulder. Cait had never seen a gunshot wound, never smelt fear such as this, or pain. Her hands shook.

Des hurried down the steps. The trapdoor slammed shut behind him. He exchanged a glance with Mike, then crouched near Cait, taking the bowl of water. His hands were steady, muddy. She poured iodine in the wound. Sean screamed. Des said, 'It's fine, Sean. You'll be fine.' She dabbed iodine on his cuts as well.

She glared at Des. 'He won't be. Not without a doctor,' she whispered. 'And you said the barracks would be empty.'

'It was. We had a spot of bother on the way back.' Des's face was white and drawn with strain, and something else. Was it anger? Well, any anger belonged to this boy.

Des gave her back the bowl. 'The Tans will be rushing around, tearing everything apart. We'll have to hope you've done your job properly, because we can't get the doctor to him yet. You get back up. We'll stay here with him. If we're found, we forced you, threatened to shoot you. Got it.'

She stumbled to her feet. 'What if they don't believe that?'

'With that hair, they'd be mad if they didn't. It should keep you safe.'

He was turning from her, brushing the boy's fair hair from his forehead. It was damp with sweat and grimy from the smoke. She touched her own. She hadn't thought of it as protection. Now she looked closely at Des, but he was talking to his men. He sluiced his hands with water and iodine, then worked on Sean, padding the wound, then bandaging. His long fingers were still steady. Hers trembled. Des said, without turning, 'If you're quick, perhaps there's time for some of that bacon that was in the pan, and tea, maybe eggs. But it must be quick. It's been a long night, and it'll be a longer day.'

She gathered her skirt, hurried up the steps, called back, 'Will there be others of you?'

'No, we don't ever put all our eggs in one basket. Obvious reasons.' His voice was crisp, dispassionate, but when he turned back to Sean, there was humanity and tenderness. She listened at the trapdoor, there was no sound. She pushed up, climbed out. It was no wonder she loved Mick. These O'Brian boys were the grandest of men.

Her father was milking, she heard his whistling through the open door. He only whistled when he was tense. She fried more bacon, some eggs, bread, made tea, delivered it and heard Des order, 'Put the light right down, Mike. I want no light showing up through the trapdoor.'

She washed the pots. She listened to the clank of pails from the milking shed, the soft mooing, the whistling. She listened for the lorries. Des was right, the Tans would be pouring in, searching, pushing, shoving. She scrubbed at the rust stain under the tap, again and again. It didn't shift, it never did. She fetched turf from the turf-house. It was dark in there, quiet. She banked them by the fire. She looked out of the door. Her father was driving the cows back into the lower field, sacking tied over his shoulders. It was drizzling. She swept the step. She listened.

They came before her father returned. They roared up in the lorry. Doors slammed on the track, whistles sounded. They clattered into the yard, shouting. They burst into the kitchen, their mongrel uniforms steaming in the heat, their presence fouling her house. They backed her against the dresser. The plates shook. One fell, broke. A Tan laughed. 'That's not all we'll smash.'

Others were in the yard, the milking shed, bayoneting the hay in the barn. 'Shall we fire it?' she heard.

'Maybe.'

Her father was running up through the field. The Tans waited, shoving aside the table, knocking over the chairs, smashing the crockery with their rifle butts. 'He's been taking the cows back out,' she shouted, rushing to the door.

A Tan came from the milking shed, milk was running from the doorway, staining the ground. 'Oh deary me, I seem to have knocked over the churn,' he yelled to his mate, who was carrying one of the hens by its feet. Its wings were flapping. It was squawking.

A hand was on her arm, dragging her back. The Tan leered and threw her back against the dresser. Where was Ben? Don't say he wasn't going to make it his business to come. There were more in the kitchen now, the stench of their damp uniforms filling the room, mud smeared the flagstones. Oaths and laughter rang in the air. Others had her father in the yard, driving him before them as though he were one of the cattle.

A Tan pulled down the bacon flitches and cursed as flypaper caught his hair, another swept his arm along the pantry shelves. Apple jelly, blackberry jam smashed to the floor.

'Find anything, Taffy?' bellowed the Tan who was pressing himself up to Cait, his hand at her throat.

'No IRA, but a nice bit of silver,' Taffy called from the front room.

'Get away from me,' Cait said, pushing at the Tan. 'Get away. Can't you see my hair? Can't you see whose side I'm on?'

The Tan looked properly and dropped back. She gripped her shorn head. 'This, because I chose an Auxie. And now you flood into my house, push us around.' There was a crash, the settle went over. A Tan was looking at the rug which covered the cellar trapdoor.

She pushed at the Tan again. 'My boyfriend will have something to say to you. He'll break your neck. Look at my house.' The Tan was confused. He half turned. She rushed past him, shoving at the Tan as he started to push the cellar rug with his boot. 'Get out of my way.'

That Tan lost his balance, teetered, fell, swore.

Taffy came through from the back. 'You little . . .' He lifted his arm. It was Jones from the crossroads. He recognized her, and laughed. 'Yes, you little—'

Ben's voice scythed through the chaos. 'Jones, stand back.'

Jones hesitated, stared past her, then back at her, and finally dropped his arm. She faced Ben, her face flushed, her breathing rapid, her hair so gloriously short. She watched the horror dawn as he and Tom, who stood behind him, saw it for the first time. More Auxies were in the yard, fanning out, checking with the Tans.

Ben dragged his gaze from her to the Tan who had pressed himself up against her. 'Where have you searched?'

The Tan raised his voice. 'Anyone been upstairs, Jones?'

Jones shook his head.

Ben nodded towards the door. 'Get out, all of you, except you, Rogers.' He stared at the Tan whose body she could still feel. 'You, come with me. Tom, you stay with her.' He spoke to Cait. 'I have to search, you understand that.' His eyes were on her hair, and horror still remained.

'Yes, I understand, but not him. Not a Tan in my bedroom.'

He agreed. 'He'll stay outside all the bedrooms, watching as I search.'

He climbed the stairs, the Tan treading heavily after him. 'Sorry, Sarge. Didn't know she was yours.'

Ben didn't answer. Her hair. Oh, how could he have put her in this situation? Was he mad? On the landing he pushed open doors, searched rooms which weren't hers, but were unused, damp, musty. Then her father's – square, plain, a photograph of his wife on the chest of drawers – and finally hers. He wanted to shut the door in the Tan's face, keep him from soiling the flowered wallpaper with his glance, the plant on the small table, the rosary on the dresser, the washstand, the tapestry chair, the knitting lying on it. There was an ancient doll on the window-sill, Jane Austen on the bedside table, the oil-lamp, the brass gleaming, but he could not.

He moved to the bed, and there was the scent of her. He touched the patchwork coverlet, knelt, checked beneath the bed, in the wardrobe. He must be seen to do his job. Nothing. Of course there was nothing. What Volunteer would trust her? They'd cropped her, hadn't they?

He moved to her chest of drawers. They had to be checked for documents, weapons. He started at the bottom. In the top one, was her hair, lying burnished against the white of her blouse. He touched it and looked up into the mirror, green-spotted with age. He was pale against the dark of his tam-o'-shanter, and his tunic. What was he doing here, tearing this girl's country apart along with these other thugs, causing hatred in the villages, and the towns? Was he mad? Was England mad?

He eased apart a strand, rolled it round his finger, put it in his pocket, shut the door. He couldn't stay here. He'd resign, leave Ireland, leave England. He didn't want any more to do with it.

When they'd gone, Caithleen climbed down the cellar steps. She was tired, so very, very tired.

'Get your father to fetch Quinn,' Des instructed, demanding fresh cool water to bathe Sean every half an hour until he came. 'You've done well, Caithleen. I want you to know you are brave and clever, and we are in your debt.'

She shook her head. 'No, we are all in yours. The Auxie wants me to meet him by the river this afternoon, but should I stay here, look after Sean?' She was kneeling by the mattress, holding the boy's hand. He was in too much pain to notice.

Des helped her up. 'No. Carry on just as you would normally, and meet him. Keep him sweet.'

Her father returned from the town. The Tans were rampaging. They'd burned the billiards hall, cut the hoses of the firemen, looted the pub in reprisal. It would be worse tonight when they'd more drink inside them.

Dr Quinn came, just as she left for the river. He dropped his glance as he came past her in the yard, then called softly as she walked away, 'I'm sorry, Caithleen. I didn't understand.'

She smiled to herself. One day they'd all say that. It would be the most glorious moment of her life.

The cold wind cut through her shawl. She drew it tighter round her head, crossing her arms, bending into the wind. She'd swept, wiped, dusted, polished from the minute the Tans left and only now did she feel her house was cleansed of their presence.

The ground was soggy beneath her boots, the hills were clear. She looked at them, long and hard. One day they'd belong to the Irish again. One day soon, please God.

Ben was by the willow, pacing, glancing towards the house, then towards Tom. 'I know, I know. I won't be long. She'll be here soon,' he called.

Tom was anxious. Ben gestured. 'I know,' he called. They had another three villages to scour. He wished he was with other Auxiliaries, being used as a shock force as they should have been, not scraping in the mud with the Tans. But then the Auxiliaries were out of control too, destroying, beating up. What a police force, what a bankrupt administration, what a way to behave. He was right to leave, but she must come. He couldn't leave her here.

Tom whistled and pointed to the slope. Ben swung round. It was Caithleen running towards him, her shawl streaming out behind her and her beauty took his breath away. He broke clear of the willow, and caught her in his arms, holding her close, pushing back the shawl from her head, kissing her hair, her eyes, her lips. He took her hands, kissed them. Stopped. They were stained with iodine. Her mind raced. She said, 'They opened an old cut on my dada's hand.' Her voice was unsteady with fear.

He shook his head and said nothing, just walked with her to the shelter of the trees. Had he believed her?

'I'm going to leave. I can't go on like this,' he blurted. 'I'm not an animal. I won't go on behaving like one. Is your father all right?'

Cait stiffened with shock. All this, for him to go. She could still feel his kisses on her; cold, clammy, disgusting. She tried to gather her thoughts. Should she weep? Should she plead with him to stay? She pressed her hand to her mouth. Think, try and think. What would Des say? What? She breathed deeply, her mind a blank. Then it came to her. Stay in character, that's what he'd say.

She pushed herself from him, turning, pushing her hands through her hair, making him look at it. 'That's right, run away, just when the going gets tough. Leave me to face the Shinners on my own. Well, go on. I can look after myself, even against Sinn Fein.' Her voice was strident, her chin up.

He put up his hands, pleading with her. 'No, you don't understand. I want you to come with me. I'm not one of them. Neither's Tom. I'm going to resign, so is he, when he's got some money together. We'll meet out in Australia. Come with me.' His hands were gripping her shoulders. 'It's too much of a risk for us to go on like this.'

'There's no risk,' she shouted, then stopped. He mustn't know that. She rushed on. 'They've done all they can, there's nothing more to risk.'

He pulled her to him, his uniform smelt as the Tan's had smelt. She wanted to jerk from him, tell him to leave her alone, stay away, go drown himself. She watched the heron fly over the river, looked across at Tom, at the farm.

Ben said into her hair, 'You say that, but what next? A bullet between the eyes, a placard round your neck. A girl was shot in the west for walking with a Tan. Caithleen, think about it.'

She walked from him to the river, standing on the bank, watching the water eddying round the stones. 'I can't leave Ireland. I'd miss it too much. It would be like running away. My father . . . I'm all he has.' Now she gambled. 'Go, if you must. But I'd miss you, Ben. I want you to stay.'

The river still eddied but the heron was gone. She looked across to the hills, waiting. She heard him come to her, but not touch her. Would he stay? Would she have to start again with someone else?

He stood close, and her words were still alive in his head. She'd miss him, she wanted him to stay, she was prepared to take the risk, she was wonderful. Out of this terrible mess there was this beauty, there was Caithleen Healy.

He kissed the nape of her neck. 'You are the most wonderful thing that has ever happened to me, and I can't leave you alone to face them.'

As she returned to the farm, her father was waiting in the yard, anxiety etched deeply, doubt in every movement of his body, anger in every word he uttered, speaking in a low voice, guiding her to the fire, turning her round, checking her. 'I should never have allowed it. That Mick's a menace. He opened fire. He's so stupid. How could a scheme he arrived at have any merit? Why did I let you near this Tan? What would your mother say?'

He had righted the settle. It had been too heavy for her. He made her sit down. She said, 'Dada, he's not a Tan, not like that. He wouldn't hurt me.' She was too tired for this. 'He's all right. I'm all right.' She stared into the fire, thinking of Sean. 'How is the lad?'

'He'll get through, no thanks to that Mick. I gave him a talking to, I can tell you. He nearly got us all killed. He always was a . . . oh, I don't know.'

She stared at her father. 'What d'you mean?'

'I mean he started the firing. He's a fool.'

Anger spurted. She fought to control it. She said, 'You just don't understand. There must have been a reason. Des wouldn't have made him second in command for no reason.'

Her father stared at her. 'I don't know where you got that from, and don't you raise your voice to me. He's a part-timer, like the rest of us, only he nearly killed us all tonight, instead of just a few of us.'

That night, as she nursed Sean and soothed his ravings, Des told her the lad was twenty – the same age as Mick. She was glad she was busy, too tired to think. And she was glad that Mick was not there.

Chapter Five

Through the rest of November she and Ben met weekly. The cold grew more bitter, the fighting more intense and as the month ended they carefully didn't speak of the fourteen British officers and officials who were killed in their beds in Dublin by the IRA.

Des said in the cellar that night as he darned his socks by the dim lamplight, 'They were brought over to boost British Intelligence. So now they won't. Any more than the twelve Irish men, women and children machine-gunned by the military and Auxies at the football match at Croke Park that same evening in reprisal will boost the crowd again, or the two men tortured and shot by the military in Dublin Castle the same night.'

'Mick told me he was your second in command,' Cait said.

Des shook his head, loyalty to his brother making him choose his words carefully. 'He'd never be that. Can't have two brothers in the firing line, but he is special, he's my back-up.' He paused. 'He's young, he's a good man. Just young.'

Relief filled her and she could barely wait for Mick that evening.

He appeared in the yard as she shut in the hens, his collar up, his cap pulled over. He kissed her, his eyelashes casting shadows on his cheek-bones in the bright moonlight. 'No training tonight,' he murmured, beer on his breath. 'Too much light.'

'I know,' she laughed. 'Your brother's exercising his fingers with a darning needle.'

Mick groaned, and opened his coat. She stood in close. He folded it around them both. 'It should be us in the cellar, then we could lie on the mattress and kiss in the warm.' He was seeking her mouth again. She clasped him tighter, tighter. 'And you could do my darning, especially if you're as nice as you are being tonight. It makes a change. I thought you'd gone cold on me.'

She pulled away, laughing, shaking him. 'Mick O'Brian, if you ever wait for me to do your darning for you, you'll be going round with holes like potatoes, and who wouldn't go cold in a winter like this?'

'Well, one day we'll lie in bed and you can keep me warm. Isn't that what wives are supposed to do? Later, you'd have a baby suckling at your breast.' He stroked hers lightly, kissed her throat, pushed his cold hands up her blouse, seeking her breasts, finding them, and the moan rose in her throat, and the future that would one day be theirs danced in her mind.

At the start of December she and her father carted hay daily to the bullocks huddled beneath frost-coated branches. They breathed on their hands, wrapped scarves around their necks, and Cait never left the farm.

In the cold night air the sound of fighting echoed and it was now as common as thunder, and the flames setting the darkness alight as unremarkable as lightning. Mick and his squad guarded her. Her father aided Des again that week, then melted back into his life, while flying columns and active-service units thrust against the British. The next day she met Ben, and the next and the next, and still they talked of anything but the struggle. Instead they explored, argued and laughed about the books they were reading. They talked of the Lake District, the clouds scudding across the sky, the distant hills. And still she baked scones for Tom who watched over them, and always he smiled.

Now she was glad of Ben's arms around her, protecting her from the bitter wind, and glad of the books, the Lake District, the clouds, because they kept reality and the ugliness of it all at a distance.

That evening she said, as Mick gripped her shoulders, glaring at her, cursing her for moving into the Auxie's arms so willingly, 'It's only because of the wind, that's all. You said use him. Well, I'm using him.' They laughed together and as he bent to kiss her mouth she saw for a moment Ben's thin face, felt for a moment his gentle lips, felt for a moment the hands which had held hers, hesitant, wanting more, but waiting, not forcing, and realized that you can get used to anything, even an enemy's kisses.

Before going to bed that night she took down tea for Des and three of his men, and asked him softly, 'How long did it take you to accept being a fighter, to accept being a killer?'

He held the mug between his hands, sipped it, the steam rising. He looked over the rim at her. 'You get used to anything, when you have to, Cait.' His look was steady, deep, gentle. 'Life isn't what we'd always choose but . . . well. We just do it, often without enjoyment. You've done well. We just have to hang on to the dream of how it will be, at the end.'

By mid-December many villages and towns in the south and west had been all but destroyed by fire as the British army and the Tans and the Auxies stepped up their campaign to catch the Irish gunmen. Irish snipers made it almost impossible for the security forces to use the roads. The cellar was being used every day, with another shift at night.

The City of Cork was burnt as a reprisal for the wounding of two Tans. At the roadblock, her father said, the Tans had danced for joy. A week later they were wearing burnt corks in their tam-o'-shanters because the Government denied any British involvement in the firing of the city. 'We want you Irish pigs to know who did it,' they told everyone who passed through the crossroads. 'We've had the best Christmas present ever. It's still smouldering – you should take a trip to see it. You can still warm your hands on it.'

Martial law was imposed in four southern counties, including Limerick. Ben held her, his gaze steady, calm, deep. 'There is a death sentence for aiding and abetting rebels now. It can be imposed like "that".' He released her, clicked his fingers. 'The penalty for being armed is death. If you know anyone like that, tell them.'

She clung to him, pressing her face into his tunic. He mustn't see the fear on her face. Did he know?

'What do you mean?' she asked.

He kissed the top of her head. 'Just that if your father was thinking of becoming involved, make him think again. It seems we're fighting our way through a country which is more and more behind the rebels, and who can blame them?' He looked down at his uniform. 'I know that you are torn. You love Ireland, but you spend time with me and suffer because of me. I want to repay you, if I can. So I'm warning you, tell your father to beware.'

She forced a laugh. 'My father's joints creak at the best of times. He'd give any patrol away.'

Ben kissed her, his lips so soft, his hands so gentle as he touched her face. Yes, you come to accept everything eventually, she thought as she opened her mouth beneath his lips, forgetting how once she had flinched with disgust, hate.

Just before Christmas, against the will of the vast majority of Irish people, Lloyd George proposed a scheme which would effectively divide the country into North and South, giving Northern Ireland a separate parliament, to appease the primarily Protestant Scottish settlers of the North-East.

'So what's new?' hissed Mick at Christmas in Cait's kitchen which was rich with the smell of roast goose. Holly gleamed on the sideboard and over the pictures. Mick told her the Volunteers had interrupted the dance last night – a dance now held at the other end of the village, well away from the blackened shell of the billiards hall – and asked for money. They were given it. 'They'll live to regret the mutilation of our land.'

She carved more breast for Des, Mick, Kevin, Liam and her father. 'How is the ammunition?' She glanced at the men keeping watch. One of them was Sean. He insisted he was better, but he was too pale. She carved more onto plates, carrying them to the oven to keep warm. Des wiped his mouth. 'We've something planned for the New Year.'

Mick leaned forward holding out his plate, shaking his head at Cait. 'Take some off, Cait, I've had some with Daddy. He doesn't know I'm here with Des.'

Des's lips thinned. 'You shouldn't be either. It's supposed to be over between you and Cait. You are her shadow, her guard, and not to be seen. Don't forget the curfew.'

'Aw, take a holiday, big brother. It's Christmas. What about the ammo?'

Her father was pushing the carrots towards Des. Cait heaped potatoes onto Mick's plate. 'Eat, fill your mouth. The more who know of Des's plans, the more risk he's in.' She heard the irritation in her voice. It seemed to echo in the silence that fell. She reached forward, held Mick's hand. 'I'm sorry, it's this slaving over a hot stove, cooking for everyone.' She sprang to her feet, wiping her hands on her apron, walking to the turf stacked by the hearth, putting one on the fire. What was the matter with her?

Mick slapped his brother's back. 'We're together in this. I'm no risk.' His voice was defiant.

Cait ran her hand along the mantel, then to the photograph of her mother, tucked behind which was the watch Ben had given her. It had been his mother's. She'd said no, pushing it back at him as he clutched the book Des had given her to give to him.

'Everyone's a risk.' Des's voice was flat. He changed the subject. 'Did our Christmas present of *Canterbury Tales* go down well with the Auxie?'

Cait spun round, plunging her hands into her apron, shrugging, as she sauntered back. 'Yes, very well.'

'Did he give you anything?' Mick's voice was fierce.

Cait picked up her knife and fork, sliced the goose. Her father had given her too many vegetables. She wasn't hungry. 'Just a Christmas kiss.'

Des laughed quietly. Mick glared, her father said, 'The less we hear about that Tan the better.' His voice was cold. 'I can't bear the thought of it.'

She slammed down her knife and fork. 'Do you think I can?' There was a silence again.

'Bloody cissy, spending all his time reading,' Mick grated out, then tore into a hunk of bread with his teeth. The crust hung from the corner. Cait swallowed her disgust.

Des said, 'He's not a cissy. I hear he's a good and fair fighter. He's not typical, nor is that Aussie friend of his. In another world, at another time, I'd like to talk to him, get to know him. D'you really think I'd have let you cook up this scheme for Cait if I hadn't checked him out?'

Mick pushed in the bread, looking from Cait to Des. 'I know that. And if you hadn't done, I would have.' His face was flushed, he wiped his lips with the back of his hand, then drank more Guinness.

I wonder, thought Cait. But no, she mustn't think like this. What was the matter with her?

Des and Liam changed places with the lookouts, and she brought their meals from the oven, giving Sean extra gravy, poured Guinness.

In January the wind bent the blackthorn hedges, and wet hens huddled in the farmyard, and mud splashed up onto her skirt and legs. Des said that the laying of ambushes was no longer so easy. 'A training school's been set up for the military. They're coping better with our tactics, moving out more and more into the country after the flying columns.'

Tension was rising at the farm. She heard low murmurs as she took food and drink into the cellar. Des grew thinner, if that were possible. Ben too. Mick defied the curfew to meet her in the yard, his kisses more demanding, his hands more urgent.

'Not now,' she said at last, as January became February. 'It's too cold, and it doesn't seem right, and you shouldn't take such risks coming here.'

'I don't mind if I'm caught. I can talk my way out of anything.'

'But what about me? What about the safe house? What if Ben realizes?' She flared. 'Why don't you grow up?'

He rubbed his forehead with his hand, then pulled her to him. 'Oh God, I'm such a fool. Oh Cait. How can you love an idiot like me? I try so hard, and I get it wrong.'

She remembered the boy who had fallen from the apple tree, over-reaching for the red one, which he was going to give her, and she melted, holding him. 'You'll learn, just as we're all having to.'

In the first week of February she felt as though the cold could snap the air around her and Ben. In the second week fifteen men were arrested and taken to a local centre for identification. Two were

Des's men. Would they betray her?

They did not. They were beaten though, her father said, because he had been picked up too, as he walked back from the draper's in the village, or what was left of it after the fire. They served from the back now. Her father also said, 'We can't beat them. There are too many of them, our supplies won't last.'

When she asked Des if he thought the same that night in the cellar, he said, 'We'll fight on, until Collins tells us to stop. I can't think of it as surrendering. There's outrage even in Britain about the Tans. There's a rumour that Lloyd George is pushing for a truce. Negotiations could lead to victory in the end, you know.' He gave her hope.

By the river Ben explained that they were just picking up people, trying to bag a gunman, trying to find out information, put troublemakers away. He had had her father released before he could be roughed up. She reached up, kissed him, held his face between her two hands, kissed his cheeks, his lips, his neck, and felt a surge of gratitude warm her, weaken her, make her want to weep.

It was a gratitude that didn't lessen as the next week arrived, and as March bloomed, the sky took on a blueness which Ben said matched her eyes. It was what her mother had said. There was warmth in their kisses, and in their hands as they touched, and in her voice as she talked to him, and now she wore the watch that had been his mother's. No-one else knew. He carried the snuffbox which she had bought in Windermere years ago. No-one else knew.

Mick came in the evenings, but only twice a week, and she was proud of him for his maturity, and her kisses for him were warm, but now was not the time or the place for lust, she murmured in his ear, as Very lights soared in the sky. She laughed with him as he kissed her breasts goodbye, though she could hardly bear his touch. It must just be tiredness.

In the second week of March, the rebels blocked roads, blew up bridges, cut telegraph poles, kept the pressure on, and her father was still back in time to take the churn to the creamery lorry, and for this she cooked extra large breakfasts and flung her arms around him while he ate it. 'I love you, Dada,' she told him.

In the third week, Widow Murphy's farm was burned. Des said, 'We'll help her rebuild, when all this is over.'

Cait went to see her, but Widow Murphy came out of the barn she was living in and threw water over her. 'Whore, to bring this disgrace upon your father.'

That evening Mick said that Rose and Mary had brought tea out to them in the glade, preening themselves as heroines. Cait tossed her head. 'One day, Mick . . .'

He nodded and she kissed him, opening her mouth, wanting hands on her body, but when he touched her it brought no comfort, only distaste.

She met Ben by the willows in the morning and gave scones to Tom, and a shawl. 'For heaven's sake, lad, lie on this, you'll be frozen to the ground otherwise.'

He grinned. 'I'll dream of Kalgoorlie, that'll warm me.'

She kissed his cheek. He blushed. 'You're a lovely man, Tom,' she said. 'And the only expression your face knows is a grin.'

She knew Mick would be watching from his hiding-place. Well, let him seethe. Ben led her to the river. It was misty today, there were no blue skies. They stood, shoulder to shoulder, watching the water swirl into and out of the bank. They didn't have to speak any more, they could just be.

She breathed in the scent of Ireland at the end of a long winter. Here, there was no smell of charred wood, of hate. Somehow the dampness of Ben's uniform bore no resemblance any longer to the damp odour of a Tan. Her hand lay calmly in his. As Des said that night so long ago – acceptance comes. It was as though she couldn't feel his skin, as though it had merged with hers.

She was doing her job well, the safe house was still in existence. Her father was not one of the hundreds swept off the streets and interned. Yes, she was doing her job well.

Ben lifted her hand to his mouth, kissed each finger. 'I'm going away.'

She spun round. She gripped his uniform. 'You can't.' His mother's watch glinted.

His hand covered hers. 'Shh. Only for a few weeks. It's leave. Tom's coming with me.'

Relief flooded her. 'I thought you meant for good.' She was laughing too loud, shaking her head. 'Don't scare me like that.'

His face was serious, his look deep and intense. 'I've asked you before. Come with me. Come away. I'll leave the force.'

'I've said before, I can't.' She turned back to the river, looking beyond it to the hills. 'This is my home. I'm needed here.' If only he knew how true that was.

Again there was silence between them, again her hand felt safe in his, but her mind was racing. A month without him. She wanted to press her hand to her belly, to still the panic. It seemed darker. 'You will definitely return?' she murmured.

'Oh yes, somehow. I'll insist I stay seconded, though whether or not we can swing it for Tom remains to be seen.'

She looked across to where Mick would be, then back to the house. She smiled, wanting to run up and down the slope as she had done on the first day back in Ireland every summer. He was coming back!

That night, Des asked if Ben had promised her any protection while he was away.

She said, 'He's thinking about it. He's coming briefly tomorrow.' She concentrated on the armhole of the sweater she was knitting, because it was only now that she realized that she hadn't thought of the safe house, only of Ben's absence. Had she covered quickly enough?

The next day she held Ben. 'Will the Tans come? Will they burn us while you're away? Will they haul my dada out of his cart at the roadblock?' The wind was lifting her hair which was just long enough to curl around her face. Soon it would be down to her collar.

His grip on her shoulders was harder than she had ever known, his voice fierce, when it had never been fierce before. 'The word is out. They'd be dead men, they know that. It's you who must be careful – of your own people. It is that that keeps me awake at night.'

There were dark smudges beneath his eyes, strain marks to the corners of his mouth, and her heart turned. She traced the darkness, the lines. 'I'll be careful. They're all too busy trying to cope. I'm safe.' She wanted him to sleep. He must stay alert, or he could be killed, and she couldn't bear that. She saw a flicker of movement out behind Tom. It was Mick, watching. She dropped her hand. After all, if he was killed, she would have to start again, that was all.

April seemed grey and gloomy. She wandered to the river, then home again. Des drifted in, and away, his face strained. Was Ben sleeping? Why should she care?

Des said, as she mixed hen food, 'Ammunition's low.'

She mashed the potato peelings. Her arm felt heavy and tired. 'Here, let me do that.' Des took over. She stared out of the window. There was none of the usual spring beauty, none of the usual freshness.

She heard nothing from Ben. She spring-cleaned the house, dug the garden, and the new potato patch, but still she didn't sleep. Mick came, but the evenings were getting lighter, and she said they shouldn't meet so often. She couldn't settle. She didn't want to talk, to kiss.

'What's wrong?' demanded Mick. 'Is it because lover boy's not here?'

'Of course it is, we're not properly protected, you could be picked up at any time. Oh, Holy Mother, it's a mess.'

'It's war,' he said, and they looked at one another and she wondered where the children they had once been had gone, and when the image of the struggle, and its glory had changed. They hugged, and she was glad of the comfort, but only for a moment.

In the last week of April Des came, dropping his cap on the table, checking his lookouts through the window, beckoning Mick in, bringing out two bottles of stout and asking Cait for three glasses, his voice strained, worn out. He slumped down opposite Cait's father who sat in the settle. The firelight danced on the bottles. 'You'll sup with us, won't you, Paul? Seems too nice an evening not to chew the cud, and we had to come along anyway.' He poured the stout. The froth was thick and creamy.

Cait made tea for herself, moving her knitting so that he could sit in the chair opposite her father's settle. The clock was ticking, and the farm cat stirred by the turf.

Her father said, knocking his pipe on the mantel, and raising his glass to Des, 'The talk is peace moves are being made under the surface. We're almost at the end of our run, aren't we?'

Mick sat at the table, tapping a matchbox. 'We mustn't give up – we swore allegiance to a republic, doesn't anyone remember that? And I can't see a republic here, now. Somehow we'll get more arms.' His voice was fierce.

Cait looked at Des, settling herself on the tapestry stool next to him, wrapping her skirt around her knees. He was still as thin. Was Ben? Des shook his head and defeat was etched on his face. 'We can only do so much. We'll have to leave it to Collins and de Valera. And don't be so bloody silly, Mick. How do we get more arms?'

'Attack another barracks.'

'That's just enough for a stop-gap. We can't bring them in from America, we can't get them through the British.' He was rolling his shoulders. Mick slouched further down in the chair he'd swung round from the table to face the fire.

'They'd better not sell us down the river. It's got to be all or nothing. We haven't fought like this for partition, or anything other than a republic. They'll not settle for less, will they, Des?' His voice sounded like that of a plaintive child. The fire crackled. 'Well, if they do, we'll fight on, won't we? On for a united republic.'

Nobody bothered to answer him.

Des looked up at Cait, then drew a letter out of his pocket. 'This is why I'm here.'

He tossed the letter to her. She caught it, turned it over. Could it be? It must be. Who else would write? She looked at the address. She'd never seen his writing. It was a bold hand.

Mick laughed, tapping his matches. 'He seems to have mixed you up with another Catherine. Got a bit funny, talking of running across the moors.'

Cait put the letter on her knee and turned to

him. 'You've read it? And how did you know it had come?' Rage was building. She turned to Des. 'For God's sake, have you put men in the Post Office just to spy on me?'

Des snapped at her. 'Don't you be so bloody silly. Of course we've put them in the Post Office but not just for you. They've been in place since this began. And just you remember, there's nothing private about the Auxie.'

'Or is there?' Mick asked as she dropped her glance to her lap.

She was really angry now, and held up the letter. 'How dare you? No, there's nothing private. Tell me what it says. I don't want to read his muck.'

She crunched it up, threw it in the bin near her father. He picked it out and dropped it on the fire. She watched it burn. They all watched it. She smiled. 'There, just like they've burned us, so often.'

She met Des's glance, and there was pity in his look.

'I'm sorry,' she said, reaching out to him. 'I should have realized you'd have people in place. I've made a fool of myself.'

The pity was gone, there was just the usual calm, deep look. 'You'd never make a fool of yourself,' Des said. 'Anyway, he's back in Ireland . . . He's fiddled his secondment. Tom's too, but it'll take a week or more to get back to Limerick. And, in case he asks, he went to Haworth, where the Brontës lived. He didn't run across the moors, he walked. And he thought of you as he did it.' His voice was non-committal, but his eyes were kind.

Her father said, 'It's as well she didn't read it. It would have made her vomit.'

Mick laughed.

Her father lit his pipe then talked again about the possibility of peace, and Mick argued with him and Des about the need to support their leaders' decision, if indeed peace was arrived at. Cait hunched over on the stool, hugging her legs, and her anger as she watched the letter shrivel and disappear. Damn the Auxie for making her feel even more of a fool – walking across the moors, thinking of her. Damn him.

Late that night, when the house was quiet and dark, she crept downstairs, lit a match from the box that Mick had been playing with, and searched for just a corner of the letter, but there was nothing, and she didn't know why she had come down at all.

In the second week of April her father returned from the morning milk-run. Cait was cleaning out the seed-boxes and stacking them near the new cross-shaft for the gate. Next week they'd get on with the sowing. This afternoon she'd plant the seed potatoes in the patch she had dug over during the past month.

Her father unharnessed the pony, and stomped over to the shed, dragging the reins in the mud. 'Oh Dada, careful.'

'Just mind what you're doing, and leave me to my business.' He was sharp as he scooped them up. He threw them into the shed.

She waited for him to re-emerge. What was the matter with them all? It was the uncertainty. It was all ending, and what would be the outcome of the devastation? Des was away in the west. There had been no 'guests' for several days. Perhaps her father was missing the evening talks.

'Come on, Dada, out with it. What's happening? Has someone had a go at you over me?' She unrolled her sleeves, suddenly remembering her watch.

He led Tanzy out into the field, saying over his shoulder, 'The Tan's back. Message at the roadblock for you to be at the willow at eleven. I hate it. I don't want you to do this any more. Me, a pimp for my daughter.'

She reeled with shock. 'Dada, don't say that. He's

not like that. I'm not. There's been nothing like that. He's too decent, I'm a good girl. Anyway, I've told you before, he's an Auxie.'

He walked on, not looking back, but shouting, 'No difference between the two, and no Tan's decent. Are you forgetting your mother? I hoped he'd never come back. It's been good with him gone.'

'I tell you, he is decent. He's saved you.'

But her father wasn't listening. He hadn't listened when she'd told him in the winter. He didn't want to owe his freedom to a Tan. Well, did anyone? But they'd be gone soon, and why was no-one grateful, if not to Ben, then to her? 'Damn you all,' she shouted to the wheeling crows.

She checked the time, hurried to the back door, heaved off her boots, throwing them to the side of the step, pushing her feet into shoes. She washed, looked down at her skirt, ran up the stairs, changed to the deep red one, her best. Her hands were trembling, she couldn't do up the button. There, that was it. She brushed her hair. It was growing, framing her face. There was more body than before. The colour was deeper. Whoever had cropped her had done her a favour. And she laughed.

She moved to the window, straining to see the willow, but of course she couldn't, it was below the slope. She could hardly breathe. She was nervous, that was all. Perhaps he had changed, no longer wanted to see her. She'd refuse to start again with anyone else. Des would understand, surely he would. It would be too difficult to set up, and why, when the talk was increasingly of peace?

She checked her watch again. Somehow, with him gone, she had taken to wearing it every day, all the time, hidden beneath her long sleeves. To remind herself how much she hated the Tans and loved Ireland, she repeated to herself, as she did every morning.

She rushed down the stairs. She'd be late.

'Your best skirt?' her father raged.

'I need to be seen to be pleased,' she answered, running round the edge of the yard, trying to keep her shoes clean. She heaved at the gate. He didn't help. Well, let him be like that. There, she was out through the gate into the field. The sun was shining, the sky was lighter than it had been all month. Where had the primroses appeared from?

She ran, dodging the thistles, leaping the ragwort. The trees were budding. The weather had been too gloomy for her to notice. The hedges were fresh green.

She ran on, over the hill, through the long grass. There'd be fine hay this year. She had baked no cakes. She slowed, then went on. Tom wouldn't mind, just this once. The willow was budding green. When had that happened?

She waved towards Tom's hiding-place. She couldn't see him – he was the best. Behind the wall would be Mick's squad. She slowed to a walk, panting. A heaviness settled again. But then she saw Ben, tall in his uniform, breaking cover from the willow. The river glistened, full and slow. The curlews rose and wheeled, and the clouds swept past the sun, and the day was light and warm again. She ran across the ground between them, into his arms.

His kisses were in her hair, on her eyes. Her arms were around him, they clung together. 'I've missed you,' she cried. 'And I've no cakes for Tom.'

She broke away, running through the long grass to the other side of the willow, calling out, 'Tom, forgive me, I have no cakes. Plenty next time.' There was no acknowledgement. She laughed, ran back towards Ben. 'I'll bring him extra tomorrow, that'll stop the sulk.' She stopped.

Ben was shaking his head, his lips were clamped together. His hands were bunched into fists. His eyes were sunken. He hadn't spoken yet, she realized. She pushed through the high grass, closing what distance was left between them. 'Fierce good pasture,' her father had said yesterday.

She didn't want to reach Ben. She didn't want to hear what he was going to say. If he didn't say the words it couldn't be true. The curlews were flying high, the wind was in the reeds, the river was teasing the bank.

She reached him. The wind was rustling the willow fronds, one caught on his uniform. She didn't pull it from him.

'He's not here, is he?' she asked.

Ben shook his head, his grey eyes were fixed on hers. They were filling with tears. He lifted up his head, gazing at the sky. Don't let them fall, he ordered himself. Men don't cry, soldiers don't grieve.

Cait took his fists in her hands, forcing herself on. 'He's hurt.'

It was a statement. It had to be true. It mustn't be anything more.

Ben tried to trace the shape of the clouds but they were blurred, formless, like the mist that so often shrouded this God-forsaken land and its terrible beauty.

He said, 'He's dead.' It must be his voice but it sounded so far away. 'He was shot in the face. He was always so cold here. "Kalgoorlie is so hot, Ben," he'd say. "We'll have such times together." '

Cait rocked with shock, though why? She'd known the minute she'd turned back to him. But it couldn't be true, it mustn't be. Ben's lips were clamped so tight that they were white, and now the tears were spilling down his cheeks, and he was shaking his head. 'I'm so sorry, stupid of me. I shouldn't.' His voice was so gentle, so broken, and she couldn't bear to hear his pain and now hers burgeoned, caught, held.

She drew him to her, holding him, rocking him,

unable to grasp that the world would never see the smiling face of Tom Fellowes again.

Ben's arms were around her, his head on hers and now the reality broke on her, and they wept together as the wind sighed, and the birds flew, until there were no more tears in them, for now, though they would come again, they both knew that. They clung together, like two children after a storm, exhausted and drained and slowly he talked of the life they had planned when all this was over; the travelling, the adventures, the small mine. 'He left me his share,' Ben said quietly. 'Come with me.'

She said, 'I can't. I'm Irish, you're a Tan. It would kill my father. I can't leave my own country.'

He knew that would be the answer. It always had been, but perhaps it would not always be so. He had to hope and, for now, he was alive, holding the woman he loved, as she held him, and together they were grieving and this was so much more than he had ever hoped for.

'I love you,' he murmured. 'I always will.'

Cait put her hand to his lips. 'Don't talk of always, don't think of anything but now, this minute. Just feel my fingers on your lips, my arm around you, yours around me. Don't think of tomorrow or the next day.'

He was bending to her mouth, kissing her and she was eager for his warmth, for his comfort, and she opened her mouth beneath his, welcoming his arms which drew her closer, and his body against hers, his hardness, and out of their grief grew a passion which drew them down into the long grass. Their kisses grew fierce, his hands were rough in her hair, and hers in his until that was no longer enough and now they looked deep into one another, a question in his, an answer in hers, and their kisses grew gentle, tender, slow, unhurried.

His hands touched her breasts and it was as though

she was merged into the wind, as though she had no form, except to rise and fall beneath the feel of him. Now those hands were beneath her blouse, so gentle, so kind, so firm, so slow and he played her, as though she were a song on the wind and their eyes were locked, their souls were joined. She slipped open his uniform. His skin was soft and warm, and her lips belonged in the crevice of his neck, and along the lines of his ribs, and the rise of his shoulder.

'I love you,' she murmured into his throat, and he said, 'I love you.' He kissed her lips. They looked deep into one another's eyes, and then lay quietly, in the warmth of the grass, the scent of it, the hush of it.

That night, as her father took the cows back out after milking, Mick came into the kitchen. Why didn't he knock? Did he own the whole world? He trod mud as he came to her chair by the fire. She bent to her darning. 'There's a mat,' she said.

'Stick this side of the damned tree,' he said, throwing his cap across the room.

'You didn't work your way round? Crawl on your belly?' Her voice was ugly, fierce. She didn't understand herself. This was Mick, the boy she had loved since she was five. Ben was a game, a necessity, which was easier to play, that was all. Today had been born out of grief, today was ... It was grief, that was all, damn it.

Mick flushed with anger. 'Of course we didn't. That damned Auxie was there, somewhere. I can never find the bugger.'

Her father was back in the yard. She heard the gate creak, the latch snap shut, his footsteps in the yard.

She fought to control her voice, to keep it neutral, uncaring. 'You won't find him ever again.' She wove the needle in and out, in and out. 'He's dead, shot in the face by the IRA.'

Mick guffawed. Her father said from the doorway, 'That's a blessing, one less of the devils to plague us.'

Still she wove, in and out, in and out, though she couldn't see the weave through the mist of anger and confusion.

The next morning she walked into the town, for the first time since the cropping. She bared her head to the world, refusing to pull the shawl up, and over. She marched into the Post Office, matching the stares of contempt and hatred, ignoring Mrs Maloney's spittle clinging to her shawl. It would wash, and what glory there would be at the party, at the end of all this, what red faces would surround her.

She wanted to scream at them that all this was for them, all this pain, confusion, acting. She belonged here, she'd earned her place. She'd take it, one day she'd take it, and by God, they'd know it.

She handed her letter through the grill. 'Give this to Desmond O'Brian.' She stared at the clerk. 'He goes through everything anyway, so don't pretend you don't know where he is, and don't read it, or the Auxie will have your guts for garters, or that's what you'd like to believe.'

She turned on her heel, and walked back to the farm, her head high. She couldn't wait until Des came again. She needed to reach him now to tell him that she'd not operate any longer with Mick as her protection. She couldn't work well, knowing he was there. Neither would she do any more unless Ben Williams was protected. At all costs, he must be protected. He must live, because she knew at last that she loved him.

Chapter Six

In May, a General Election was held, and Sinn Fein was almost unanimously supported in the Catholic states. Des said in Cait's kitchen, 'It's proof that our leaders have the support of the people, and the British can't ignore this.'

Mick raged. 'Forget that. The Ulster counties have voted to stay bloody British, so that's all the Brits'll see – it's a partition vote.'

Also in May the IRA launched their biggest Dublin operation. They burned the Customs House which was the centre of British Administration. The next day, by the river, Ben shook his head. 'They've shot themselves in the foot. We, the Auxiliaries and the other security forces, arrived as they were doing it. One hundred and twenty Volunteers surrendered.'

In June, Cait met Ben and sheltered in his arms, not from the weather, for it was a beautiful day, but from Mick's eyes, because Des had flatly refused to change the personnel of her guard. 'No way,' he had insisted at the farm the same night she had delivered the letter to the Post Office, his face drawn with tiredness. 'I can't take my men off their duties and train Mick up for proper active service.'

'Why the hell not?' she had raged in return.

Des had stormed from the yard. 'No, Cait. I can't change the plans now, but your Auxie will be safe, I'll make sure of that, I promise you.' And for her, that had been enough. Ben must be safe at all costs. She clung to him now, asking, 'What did you mean, shot themselves in the foot?'

He kissed her mouth gently, carefully, all round the edges, then her eyes, and finally her hair. 'I mean that Collins has now lost most of his Dublin arms and men. The nerve centre is almost dead. Soon, it must be over.' He laughed grimly. 'The countryside is still fighting nicely, though.'

They looked at one another. 'Come away with me?' he urged.

They both knew what her answer must be. She would never be able to choose between Ireland, her father and Ben.

That afternoon she skimmed all the cream off the shallow bowls that had been accumulating for the past two days. She gave the skim to the animals and churned the cream, resting when her arms ached, glad of the work, the repetition. Yes, it must soon be over. Ben thought the countryside was still strong, but if only he knew.

The tracks were so hard-baked that the Auxies, the Tans and the military were riding round the trenching, and the barricades of telegraph poles, and when Des's men's revolvers were emptied, they could no longer be reloaded.

She baked well into that evening because men were coming in to help with the haying the next day. 'I can help,' she'd offered, over supper.

Her father had said, 'Stay out of sight. I don't want you seen and insulted.'

'But not everyone feels that way. Some didn't glare when I went into town. Ben says quite a lot just get on with their lives and are not involved.'

Her father slammed down his mug of tea, it slopped. He rose from the settle, stabbed the air with his pipe shouting, 'Ben says, Ben says. If I thought for one minute you cared what that animal says. Just stay out of sight. And don't go near the river, don't go near that bloody man.'

'Dada, I started this for the cause, you know that. Why are you being so foul?' She packed his tea into a flask, his bread into the tin. His milk into a bottle. He looked at her, but didn't answer. Could he guess? she wondered, not meeting his gaze. 'I churned cream for you all to have with the scones. I'll leave them on the table, and stay in my room.' She carried the tins to the sink, wiping her fingers round the edges, eating the cake mixture, wanting to look normal.

Her father walked over to her, held her shoulders gently. 'I'm sorry, Cait. I just see you growing away from me, growing up, and I sometimes wonder what you do by the river, how you feel. But then I know you wouldn't, couldn't, not with a Tan, not after your mother.'

She wanted to scream – he's not a Tan, he's Ben. She said, 'I hate the Tans, you know that.' She leant back against him, and they both looked out across the yard, to the fields, and the hills beyond. 'I always will hate them.' It was the truth, she always would. But Ben was different, he was hers, a human being, the man she loved, the man she must lose. She shut her eyes.

She remained in her room the next day when the men came in for tea from the fields. Mick was among them, and Paddy and Niall. She heard their voices as clearly as though they were here. What were Rose and Patricia doing? Would they rub milk on their lovers' sun-burnt backs this evening as she had done to Mick after the wheat harvest last year? She leant against the window, breathing in the hay-scented air. Was it only a year ago? When Ben was gone would she forget him, love Mick again?

She put her head in her hands, then over her ears, not wanting to hear the sound of last year drifting up from below. Not wanting anything. Not wanting love or pain or laughter.

That evening Mick called her out into the yard when the others had returned home. He held her. He smelt of hay, of childhood, of light and easy days, and so she rubbed his shoulders with milk, and it was for the days which had gone, but perhaps it was also for the time which might come. 'You're a grand girl, Cait,' he laughed as he left. 'We're almost there – and just think of the party we'll be having any day now.'

Towards the end of June Ben waited for her, sitting by the river, chewing a grass stalk. It was almost over, thousands of Volunteers from all parts of the country, including some of the best, were in jails or internment camps, some awaiting execution. Anyone with any common sense could see that the rebels must be almost out of ammunition. Rumours of peace were everywhere. He'd be going soon. He'd been told of his posting to the counties of northern Ireland. He'd ask her again. She must come. How could he live without her?

Cait did not run down the slope, instead she walked slowly, breathing in the sight of him as he sat with his arms resting on his knees, a stalk between his lips. His hair lifted in the breeze as he looked across the river towards the purple hills. She stopped, not wanting to reach him, not wanting to hear what Des had already told her. She listened to the curlews and the wind in the reeds and knew that she would never come to this spot again after he had gone, finally gone.

He turned, saw her standing so still, and now it was he who barely breathed, he who traced every line of Caithleen Healy and recognized the love in her eyes, as the love also in his. She came to him then, sitting with him, neither touching.

He said, 'I'm being posted.'

'When?' Her voice was soft with acceptance. Des was right, acceptance came, in time.

'Any day.' He didn't look at her, just at the river, and the hills.

Clouds floated between the sun and the land, then swept on. She ran her hand over the shorn grass. The hay had been taken in, but its scent remained. Honeysuckle was clambering over Mick's wall, mingling with the fuchsias. Sweetbriar, thick fresh hedges, meadowsweet. Had the land ever been so beautiful?

Ben took the stalk from his mouth. 'I'll come back for you, before I leave entirely. I'm going to Tom's mine. We're going to Tom's mine.' His voice shook, he pressed his lips together.

She reached for his hand, brought it to her mouth, kissed every finger. She must remember everything about him; his grey eyes, thick brown hair, high cheek-bones, the lean strong body she hadn't had time to know, only to guess at.

'I can't,' she murmured against his palm.

'You won't,' he corrected.

'I can't. You are a Tan and I am my mother's daughter.'

'Time will change things for him. He'll forget. It *is* because of your father, isn't it?'

She laughed quietly. 'When have the Irish ever forgotten?' He looked at her now, taking his hand from her, cupping her face, kissing her. She said against his lips, 'Just as I will never forget you.'

There was no passion. They were too much in love, and in too much pain. They just sat, their hands entwined.

By the end of June King George V made a conciliatory speech in Belfast, providing Southern Ireland with a source of hope at the opening of the first Parliament of Northern Ireland. 'My guess is, we'll be negotiating soon and the terms will be close to what we want,' Des said, easing his shoulders as he sat in the cellar. 'Especially as they arrested one of our leaders, de Valera, the same night, and then released him – sounds as though they want to come to an accommodation. Can't come soon enough, as far as I'm concerned. We need a truce; our supplies have almost run out, we can't beat them. But I like to think they haven't beaten us, it's just logistics.' He shrugged, pulled a face, half laughed, but there was sadness underneath every gesture.

Cait looked at him. You and Ben would get on well, she thought, trying to picture a Tan here, in the village, growing wheat and hay, but it was absurd.

On 9 July the leaders of Sinn Fein and the IRA met British representatives and on 11 July as Cait, Des, Mick and her father sat around the kitchen table, while the sun reddened and lowered itself below the horizon, they heard from the radio that a truce had been declared, and that the rebels could keep their weapons.

'Thank God for that,' Mick grunted. 'And we'll damn well need them, if we don't get the terms we want in any Treaty Collins and de Valera hatch up. Sean, Paddy and I have been talking. We fought for a Republic and we won't settle for less – there's lots like us.'

Des met Cait's gaze and both recognized the other's fear and Cait was amazed, because she had never seen any sort of fear in Des before. It confused her, but only for a moment because Ben was leaving for the north in one hour, and he had sent a message that he would be by the river, one last time, but briefly.

She checked the clock. The weather was too hot to wear her sleeves down, and therefore his watch was upstairs. She wouldn't bother with a shawl. 'I'll come, watch over you,' Mick said, stuffing the remains of the apple tart in his mouth. 'Can I take your rifle, Des?' It stood in the corner.

Des shook his head. 'Sit down.'

Her father slammed his hand on the table. 'There's no need for Cait to go at all. There's a truce.'

Des said, as Cait hesitated, 'There's every need for her to go. Who knows how long the truce will last?' His voice was sharp, hard. 'We have things to discuss about the arms, storage and so on – let Cait keep the Tan away, one last time.' He turned his back to her, drawing pencil and paper from his pocket, but not before she had seen the encouragement in his eyes, and something she had seen before. It was pity.

The shadows were long by the river as Ben asked her one last time to come with him.

She refused. They kissed. The Crossley tender revved on the track and she watched love walk away from her, bruising the meadowsweet and the daisies in her father's fields. It was disguised in a tam-o'-shanter and a uniform – symbols of all that she hated – and she wondered how her life could go on.

She laughed and smiled through the days of summer because it was expected of her. Peace was here, her Tan was gone. Her father became expansive, his grief for her mother subsided. 'Because I've helped to rid the country of the Tans. They'll go soon, all of them,' he said. 'When the Treaty is signed they'll be off. Sooner perhaps.' Every time he said it, she nodded. Every time Mick gloated she agreed. Every time he said, 'We'll have that party,' she delayed.

And when night fell, and she could escape the world, she lay in her bed and lived again the times in Ben's arms. In her mind she stroked his thin face, his full lips. She kissed his eyes, his hands, his fingers, she heard his voice, replaying him again and again. She ached for him. She ran her own hands over her body, and wished that he had known her. She turned into her pillow. 'Ben, Ben.'

She flung aside the bedclothes and walked to

the window, glad that she couldn't see the willow, but straining to do so in the moonlight which lit the land she loved and the wheat which ripened daily. She pressed her hands to her belly, wishing she had felt him on her and in her. Wishing that he was still here, that he had done more than kiss her breasts, so tenderly, so gently. Wishing that they had drowned in one another, that all choice had been taken from her, that a child, his child, was growing inside her, deciding her future. Wishing that he had not been an Auxie, and that she had not lied and used him. Knowing that she deserved her loss, her pain.

'Perhaps I am a whore,' she murmured each morning as dawn broke.

Mick came to help with the harvesting. Sean and Niall and Paddy too. Des came on the last day. 'We'll have that party,' Mick panted as he heaved at the stooks, his bare back reddening in the sun. 'Niall and Paddy are tired of keeping the secret, and I'm tired of never dancing with you at parties.'

She handed her rake to Des. 'Time for tea.'

She walked to the shade of the oak through air thick with wheat dust and laden with its scent. Ben was in the north – so near, yet gone. She tore her straw hat from her head, wiping the sweat from her forehead, hearing the laughter of the boys in the field. 'He's gone,' she whispered. 'He's so near, yet he's gone.' She was under the shade of the tree. The baskets of food were stacked amongst the gnarled roots.

Des said, from just behind her, 'It's sorry I am.'

She stood stock still, then turned. He was standing just beyond the shade, light striking his hair, lightening his violet eyes. Neither said a word, just looked and he saw the misery, the heartache, and she saw his knowledge of them. 'I'm sorry,' he repeated. 'I should not have encouraged. I should not have given you the means. *Wuthering Heights*, wasn't it?'

Then Mick came swooping in from the field,

Niall and Paddy chasing him, Sean just behind, the scar on his shoulder livid even against his sunburn. She looked again at Des. There was no knowledge in his eyes any more. Had there ever been? She was hearing things, seeing things. What did it matter?

She unpacked the scones, sandwiches, unstopped the warm milk in the medicine bottle. She had never made Ben a proper picnic. She poured for the others, but not herself. She handed out scones. They ate but she did not.

'You're too thin,' her father said. 'Look at you, you're skin and bone. You hardly eat anything.'

'She's lonely,' Mick said, reaching for jam sandwiches, tossing one to Sean. 'We need that party. She needs to get back to normal, have fun.'

'No,' she shouted. 'He's still in Ireland.'

Her father looked at her over his mug, his eyes sharp. 'So what? It'd rub his nose in it if he heard.'

Mick laughed, brushing the crumbs from his belly which was running with sweat. 'I'd just love to see his face when he knows he's been used.'

She saw them all laughing at the image and wanted to dash their tea in their faces but she should be dashing it in her own. 'No—' she began.

Des interrupted. 'She's right. The Treaty isn't signed, there are Tans still in barracks. Who knows when they'll go? Who knows what would happen if he heard? Try thinking, all of you, and not leave it to Cait all the time.'

Her father nodded. 'You're right, she mustn't be exposed, mustn't be hurt.'

Mick leaned across and kissed her hand. 'One day then, soon.'

She looked at the crumbs his kiss had left. She deserved every hurt, every exposure. She wiped the crumbs from her hand. Did her disgust show? She walked to the river where she had promised herself she would never come, inviting pain, lying down, her arms outstretched where they had lain together, the sun burning into her, longing for memories of him to leave her, but dreading that they would.

That night the wind was strong, and rain beat against the panes and she heard Ben's voice as they huddled beneath the willow, and beneath her shawl when weather such as this raged about them. 'It's a wuthering wind,' he'd say, holding her tight. 'This is how it wuthered on the moors when I went to Haworth, beating and roaring at the window, as though it was trying to break in. It's like my love for you. It beat and wuthered and broke in, and now it can't escape. Is it the same for you?'

'Yes,' she said then, knowing that their time was getting shorter. 'Yes,' and his mouth had eaten the words as they left her lips, and their love had fused, and their bodies had clung, and they had no longer heard the wind, or felt the rain. 'But why didn't you strip my clothes from me, and drive into me? Why did you leave me no choice but to follow you?' she moaned now.

The next day she walked to the convent, through air which was fresh and damp and tranquil after the storm. The clang of the bell was loud, the face of the nun kind.

'The Library?' Cait murmured. The nun, her face tanned against the white of her wimple, nodded and pointed across the dark hall, closing the door behind Cait. The latch clicked shut. Cait's shoes squeaked on the waxed linoleum floor. She climbed the stairs. Dark wood panels lined the walls. Her hand was pale against the oak banister.

She walked along the landing. A door signed 'Library' was half open. She entered. Glass-fronted bookshelves lined the room, motes danced in the darkness. There was no-one else there and she was glad. She searched and there it was. Her hand trembled as she opened the glass door, trembled as she reached for and took down *Wuthering Heights*. She looked inside. Yes, it was the same one that she had given him so long ago. She gripped it, wanting him, hating herself. A voice said, 'Do you need any help?'

An elderly nun came across, her hand searching for the beads that hung within the folds of her habit. Her face was concerned. Cait said nothing, though words were there, jagged, disjointed, struggling between her thoughts and feelings as they had done, day and night, since love had come.

The nun peered at the book and Cait's white knuckles. Her beads clicked as she lifted her hand.

'I want this book,' Cait gasped, stepping back. 'I want it, to keep. I want it, because he's held it. I don't deserve it, but I want it. It's all I can have of him. I've taken too much from him already but I want it. Please, you must let me have it.' She backed away until a table stopped her. She eased herself along its length.

The nun let her hand drop to her side and stood quite still. 'Please, take it, Caithleen Healy. I heard your Auxiliary had left. I wondered if you could act love without a heart. And if you had a heart, whether acting would become reality. Desmond O'Brian thought you might come. He hoped you might come. "Sister Maria, be there for her," he said.'

The two women were alone in the world at that moment, in the silence, the darkness, the musty smell of books. It wasn't Ireland in here, it was peace and calm. It was her childhood, her life before death, duty, dishonour, betrayal, love. It was seeping into her body and Cait found words at last. Words and thoughts she had had to deny, to hide, to cloak for too long.

They were still jagged, disjointed but they were words that were the truth, words that she could not speak to anyone else, anywhere else. 'I love him. Don't deserve him. I deserve pain . . . Can't go to him. Should tell him . . . I used him. Choose, I can't choose . . .' Out they tumbled, in this place that was not the river, not the glade, or Mick, or Des, or her father, but rather the image of her old school, the church she had prayed in with her mother, it was the time before thunder was gunfire, lightning was flames, before love meant betrayal.

On and out the words swarmed until her throat was dry, and her face was wet with the tears that would not stop flowing, and her limbs were trembling with the exhaustion that had pulled at her for so long. 'There is only darkness,' she said. Then nothing more.

She felt the nun lead her to a chair behind the table. She watched her pull up another. Together they sat in the silence that fell. Her hands ached from the force with which she held the book. Motes still danced.

The nun said, 'Shall you think of going to confession?'

Cait shook her head, she had never been so tired. 'I should confess to Ben, anything else is too easy.' Her voice was muffled, unlike her own.

The nun folded her hands and nodded, her blue eyes serious. 'Then write and tell him.'

Cait shook her head. 'He would hate me. I can't. I want to know he loves me, even if he isn't here. I would have to tell him, not write. But I couldn't tell him. You see, I have to know his love still exists, and then I can exist.'

The nun sat silent, waiting.

Cait said, 'He need never know, if I never see him again, and so I will never see him again. My father hates him so I *can't* see him again. My life is here, in Ireland. All this', she gripped the book tighter, 'was for Ireland. I will be good. I will become the old Cait. I'll love Mick again. I'll have Irish children.'

The nun put out her hand. 'Then you don't still need the book?'

'Yes,' Cait whispered, 'I still need the book.'

'I will intercede for you,' the nun said, and though her lips did not move again, nor her eyes close, Cait knew, as she rose and walked to the door, that Sister Maria was praying for her soul.

Throughout September she worked hard, painting the outside of the house, helping her father to mend the fence, pushing Ben from her, sleeping with the watch he had given her beneath her pillow, and *Wuthering Heights* by her bed, but sleeping. At last she was sleeping.

Mick was working his father's farm. Niall and Paddy were working on theirs. Life was resuming its pattern. The leaves were falling as they always had, and always would. The fields were stubbled, mist hung like rags on the blackthorn and across the peat banks. She sliced the turf, she milked the cows. Her father took the churn to the creamery. She ate a little now, sometimes more than a little. She sewed by the fire and was glad that the days were drawing in, that there was not the restless light evening to live through. Des was away. She was glad. He knew too much.

In October Ben wrote. Her father watched her as she opened the letter, his eyes anxious, confused, angry.

She read her name, lingering over it. His hand had held the pen, his long fine, gentle hand. She knew what it would say, and so it did. She looked up at her father. 'The Tan is going back to his home, and then to Australia. We can have that party now.'

She placed the letter on the fire and watched it burn away the words that told of his love, words that begged her to come to him, that described his pain, and it was as though he was describing her pain. She stood, her hand on the mantelpiece, watching the flames devour all those words until only ashes remained. 'Yes, we can have that party now,' she repeated. She broke up the ashes with the poker.

Dr Quinn was to hold the party as October became November. 'We won't tell anyone why,' Mick explained to her as he helped her lock up the hens. 'They'll all be there and I'll take you. I'll walk in, tell them of my idea, of your part in it. It'll be a night to remember, Caithleen. It'll be what we've both been waiting for, it'll set us up, they'll see us for what we are. Did you like the material Des found you?'

She dusted off her hands and returned to the kitchen. 'It's grand.'

Her father was reading the paper by the fire, tension gone from him, peace soothing him. The burning of the letter had calmed him.

She began work on the dress the next day, using a pattern that Des had also brought. She turned the handle of the sewing-machine, watched the needle jab in and out. The seam was so straight, how clever she was, how nice the dress would look. Where was Ben now? But no, not any more. It was over, gone, burnt to ashes.

The dress was ready the next day. She washed her hair. It was long and thick, reaching almost to her shoulders. She looked at it in the green-spotted mirror, running her fingers through it, coiling it, tugging it. She looked at the scissors glinting on the dressing-table, picked them up, holding them to her hair, looking at the reflection of them against her hair. But no. Tonight was her return to her life. It had to be.

Music was playing as she and Mick approached, light was streaming from the bay window of Dr Quinn's impressive grey-stone house on the outskirts of town, and from every other window. There was a fiddler and an accordionist. There were carts in the drive, there were bikes, two cars.

Mick stopped the cart in the space by the front door. He turned to her, kissed her lightly, his face alive, his eyes excited. He smoothed his hair, the curls jumped straight up again. She laughed and it was something she hadn't done for so long.

Mick hugged her. 'Aw, Cait, I've missed you. I've missed doing this with you.' He waved at the house, then said shyly, looking down into her face, 'You look beautiful. Des chose the right green. Isn't he the grandest man?' He leapt from the cart, tied up the pony, came back to her, took her hand, steadied her as she jumped down, hugged her again. 'You deserve this moment.'

Don't talk about what we deserve, she thought.

Mick was leading her forward and up the steps. Coach lamps hung from the walls either side, beneath the portico. He knocked lightly. Dr Quinn opened the door himself, taking her hand, making her feel as though she was a queen.

Dr Quinn whispered, 'Everyone is in the drawing-room. They know something's afoot, but can't dream what it is to be. You've earned this, my dear.' His eyes behind his glasses were proud. Cait smoothed down her dress, her heart pumping.

Yes, she had been lonely. She had missed other people's houses. It seemed so light here, and the noise of laughter behind the doors drew her forward. She looked at Mick and his grin warmed her. She looked at Dr Quinn and there was respect in his glance. She straightened – there'd be some red faces soon, but indeed there would.

Mick opened one of the double doors. He turned, looked at her, winked. She laughed. Dr Quinn put his finger to his lips, then Mick was gone, the door was closed. She leant against it, and heard Des shout above the noise. 'Stop that row, Flannigan, for the love of God. Let the boy speak.' The accordion stopped, and so too did the laughter, and the talking.

She heard Mick's voice. 'This party is not just to celebrate the truce, or peace, because who knows if that will hold. It depends what they offer us.'

Groans greeted this and Des called, 'Do away with the politics, you republican hothead, and get on with it.'

Mick laughed amidst the clapping. 'Fine, I will get on with it. We've been through some difficult times, all of us. And for now it's over.' Groans again. He swept on. 'Times have been more difficult for some than others, we know that, don't we Des, Niall, Paddy and Paul Healy?' Cait heard the murmurs of confusion and imagined Rose and Patricia pulling at their lovers' sleeves, wanting to know what they knew. She realized how much she had missed them. 'There's someone who isn't here tonight. Someone who has been ostracized, cropped for consorting with an Auxie.' There was dead silence.

Cait leaned against the door, hardly breathing.

Mick began again. 'I devised a plan whereby we could secure a safe house, neutralize a Tan for added protection from searches. Cait agreed to take part, accepting that she would become an outsider, again. Working to my plan, she hooked him, played him, landed him, and with him a safe house, her house.' She was rubbing her forehead against the door. No, not played, not hooked, not landed, but loved.

The door was opening, Dr Quinn took her arm, led her in. Her eyes were misted, people were clapping, they were shamefaced, embarrassed, they thought her tears were for them, for the plan, but they were for the end of love. Because it must end. This was her life, this was all she was entitled to.

They were round her now, Rose, Patricia and the girls, hugging her, kissing her, apologizing, crying, laughing, and others too, including Widow Murphy who pushed her way through, grasped her in her arms. 'I'm sorry, I called you dreadful things.'

131

'I deserved them,' said Cait. 'I always will.' Widow Murphy looked puzzled.

Music was playing, and Mick was forcing his way through to her. He took her in his arms, and together they waltzed while the others formed a ring around them. He held her close, she caught her father's eye and he nodded approval, and people smiled, where before they glared, and as they danced around and around Mick kissed her hair. 'It's the same as it was, you're back.'

Rose was smiling in the crowd. Patricia too, then they were swept by Niall and Paddy onto the floor, Dr and Mrs Quinn joined them, Widow Murphy dragged Mick's father away from his Guinness and whirled him round and round, and they danced, all of them, until their feet were sore. Laughter burst from her as Niall, then Paddy, then Des whirled her round, and again laughter came as she and Rose and Patricia brushed their hair in the cloakroom, and whispered as they used to do, though awkwardness fell when Mary said, 'I just don't understand why you needed to woo a Tan to create a safe house? There were lots of other houses, you know.'

Cait looked at her in the mirror, her hand still on the brush. 'Were there?' She was confused, trying to think. Of course, there must have been. She never had the full squad in the cellar.

Rose turned on Mary. 'It's always you who drop in your twopennyworth, isn't it? For Des to have agreed the plan, there had to be a reason, and our Cait is a hero, and I'm ashamed. Holy Mother, so I am. And Cait, I just want you to know, I didn't know about the cropping. I'd never have done that to your hair, and I don't know anyone who knew anything about it.'

After they had eaten at the long table they drank Dr Quinn's champagne. 'To Peace,' they agreed, raising their glasses, and now the girls danced again, with one another, as they used to do, their arms linked, their hair in their faces, laughter brimming, and Cait was home, belonging again, looking across at the men, who stood, happier with their beer than champagne, drinking, talking, arguing.

Someone started the gramophone, and the girls danced a tango, calling Cait in. She joined them, danced, laughed, and the men came in and joined them, and her father too. They danced until their sides ached, and then they drank ginger beer, and the men drifted to the beer again, and the women raised their eyebrows and got to talking about the patterns in the books their relatives had sent from America and Australia and New Zealand, and they planned for next month's party, looking across at the men.

Rose nudged Cait. 'I'm glad we're back together. I've missed you.'

Cait saw Des detach himself from a group and ease himself out through the french windows. 'I'm going for some fresh air,' she whispered to Rose.

'Just picking up your man on the way?' Rose giggled, beckoning to Patricia, whispering to her.

'I'll come back for him. I need to cool down a little first, I'd set him on fire,' Cait quipped, sounding like her old self, though she'd never be that. She heard their laughter, as though from a distance.

She wove her way through the dancers and slipped out, into the November cold of the terrace, closing the door behind her, leaning back against it, watching Des turn, his cigarette glowing in the shadows.

She said, 'You're always in the shadows, Des.'

He looked out over the garden again, leaning on the balustrade. 'It's kept me alive so far, Caithleen.'

She walked into the darkness to be with him. He offered her a cigarette. She shook her head. 'Why did you crop my hair, Des?'

He put the packet back in his pocket, and drew

deeply on his cigarette. It glowed. She saw the cast of his eyelashes on his cheeks.

'I wondered when you would realize.'

'I think I've always known. But why?'

Des leaned forward, peering through the darkness, flicking his ash down onto the lawn, cupping his cigarette in his hand. 'For protection, Cait. I was concerned that if I didn't, someone else would, though more brutally. I also thought it would prove protection from the Tans who would take you as being on their side.' He paused. She waited. 'And, of course, because I felt it would hurry things up.' He threw the cigarette down onto the lawn.

She followed the arc of its passage and watched as it glowed then died. Des stood with his hands in his pockets. She could see his breath in the moonlight. The music still played in the room they had left, the light still spilled from the windows, not reaching them.

She said carefully, 'But why agree to the plan? There were other safe houses, it wasn't necessary. None of it was necessary, was it?' Rage and pain were in her voice.

Still he didn't look at her, but up at the stars now. 'It was necessary. It meant that Mick was kept out of the firing line if he had you to shadow. It kept him safe.' He turned to her now. 'I love him, I've always looked after him. He brought me his plan. He's a fool, as well as being my brother. I knew he would rush to meet death unless he could be kept occupied elsewhere. You just have to hear him now, talking of continuing the struggle if a republic isn't granted in the Treaty. God, can't he see that this could be the end of tension, fear, effort, anticipation of death.'

She gripped his lapel. 'So, to save your brother, you used me, just as I used Ben.'

His hand was over hers now, he was facing her, his head close, his eyes boring into hers. 'Forgive me.

I watched you fall in love, and I could do nothing. It was too late, we were committed, and it was working. Cait, get out while you have the chance. Follow him.'

Cait shook her head, and now she was resting her head on his. 'I can't. It's too difficult, but perhaps I can go on with my life. I was used, he was used. I can tell myself it cancels out and try to make myself believe it. Thank you for that, Des.' She pulled away, and the sadness that filled her was in his eyes too. 'There's nothing like a war to shed your childhood, is there, Des?'

He returned her smile. 'You've never spoken a truer word, Caithleen.'

Mick's roar of laughter reached them as he pushed open the french windows. 'Come in, join the party.' He waved his glass at Des. 'There's plenty more, boy.'

Des touched her elbow, and guided her towards the light. 'Can you accept this life?' he murmured.

'I must,' she replied. 'There can be nothing else.' She smiled at her father who came to meet her, and he looked as he had done when her mother was alive.

Des waited behind, lighting another cigarette. What was a man in his thirties doing, falling in love in the middle of a war with a girl whose eyes were the colour of an Irish summer sky, and whose hair was the colour of burnished copper? He leaned back against the balustrade, looking into the lighted room, seeing Cait whirl past in Mick's arms and he cursed himself for the unhappiness he had inflicted upon her.

Chapter Seven

Thoughts of the party lingered during the next week, as ploughing brought in the gulls from the sea, and her father sang as he urged the horses on. She found polish she had forgotten existed beneath the sink and worked until the furniture in the front room gleamed, and then the bedrooms. She forced open the windows of those that were unused. She worked in the kitchen until the copper pans shone on their hooks and soda bread and biscuits scented the air.

Mick called at four each day, and Cait drew her shawl around her and slipped from the house, waving to her father across the field, nodding as he called, 'Mind that wind.'

They walked, hand in hand, arm in arm, to the town, drifting amongst the shops. She wanted to reach out and run her fingers over the door handles, the stone walls, the windows, reclaiming all that had been denied to her for so long.

They ran down the track as dusk fell, her hair trailing in the damp wind, her voice singing louder than his, forcing memories from her of Ben, of love, drawing back Ireland.

Her nights were still long, filled with thoughts of him but he was gone from her. He could exist only between the pages of the book, in the tick of her watch, in her head, in the lines of her breasts that he had known, and each morning she grew stronger and the framework of her life grew more sharply etched.

The next week she saw, as though for the first time, the wind-bent hedge, the wet hens which huddled beneath it, she mashed the bran and meal for them, leaned her head against the cows' warmth as she milked, leaned into Mick's arms at the end of each evening, and brick by brick the wall was growing, closing her into her life.

November became December and on the Friday of the first week she danced at the party held in the hall at the end of town and it was almost as though she had never been away. Almost. There were still the nights.

The next day she, Rose and Patricia ate fancy cakes at Brannigan's tea shop and planned the dresses they would wear for the Christmas dance, then went back to Rose's where they ate scones by the turf fire and giggled when her mother said, 'Sure, and you'll be having to let those dresses out before ever you get into them, you three. What a Holy Trinity.'

Cait hugged her knees and leaned against Rose, welcoming the arm which came round her. 'The three of us together, we're unbeatable,' Rose said.

Niall, Paddy and Mick came and they ate supper round the kitchen table and the lamps flickered along with their laughter. They pushed the table back, and Rose's mother cranked the gramophone and they danced and talked of the spring, the haying that would follow and the farms they would one day have, and the children they would also have, who would play together, and after that would come their grandchildren.

Mick walked her home and ice cracked beneath their feet, and their breath puffed before them like the distant dreams they had conjured. His kiss was warm, his hands on her arms restless, they moved to her breasts. She said, 'No.'

He nodded. 'I can wait.'

She leaned back in his arms. 'We'll scrump Dada's apples next year.'

'You lead me into the ways of wickedness, Caithleen Healy, that you do.' He grimaced, his hair too long, as it always was. And he chased her round the yard, slipping and sliding as she was doing until their laughter turned to coughing in the chill air, and they hung on one another, as they had as children, slapping each other's backs.

She sewed in her own kitchen the next evening, with Rose, who smoked cigarettes though she choked when she tried to inhale, and hid them and flapped her hands to disperse the smoke as Cait's father came in from the yard. They collapsed laughing into one another's arms while her father stared and shook his head.

The next evening she and Rose made plum puddings for Christmas at Patricia's house, while Patricia's mother checked first one and then the other. 'More flour, Caithleen.'

'Get your arm behind the stirring, Rose. Don't be afraid of getting muscles. You'll be having to clip your man behind the ears enough times to give you bulges like oranges before you're forty.'

As they stirred they wished silently, their wooden spoons straining against the sticky solidity of the mixture. Cait's mind was empty. What could she wish? That last year had never happened? That she had never met Ben? That she could forget him? No. That the wall would grow so high it shut out all but the laughter in this room, the acceptance of her life as it was? Yes.

Mrs Flannigan said, as she stirred her own, 'I hope you all prayed for peace.'

None of them had, but none of them cared. The fighting was over, the rebuilding had begun, and they laughed and sang on their way to Patricia's back gate, and hugged one another, smelling of the spices they had used in the puddings.

On 6 December the Treaty was signed by Griffith and Collins in London. Her father rustled his newspaper as she cooked the bacon. 'We're to be a self-governing Irish Free State with twenty-six counties, excluding Ulster. There's to be a government elected by the people of the new State and responsible only to them,' he read aloud, then looked up and smiled. 'I suppose it's Dominion Status, but who cares? Soon there'll be no British troops in Ireland for the first time in seven hundred years and Collins and Griffith say it'll be a stepping-stone to a republic, and they're right. That Collins was always a realist. I just hope the stupid fool Mick won't follow de Valera, who's making noises like a disappointed bull. He's resigned as president of the Dail in protest, for heaven's sake.'

Cait turned the bacon. 'Will you be wanting any of this, Dada, or are you making do with indigestion from reading the paper before you've eaten? The fighting's over – just be thankful.'

'I'll make do with a bit of civility from you on this cold, crisp morning, madam.' He peered over his paper and laughed.

'Are you mending the fence behind the barn, Dada? One of the posts looks rotten.'

'I might just take a ride down into the town.'

She broke eggs into the pan. 'Now, why doesn't that surprise me? A meeting of great minds at Tooley's Bar, is it then?'

'Sure, and if it is or if it isn't you'll find something to say about it.'

'Why change the habits of a lifetime, Dada?'

They were both smiling as she brought the plates to the table. Today it was as it had been, before her mother died, and the struggle began, and Ben came into her life. Almost as it had been.

In the kitchen of his father's farm, Mick lunged at Des across the kitchen table, kicking away the chair. It rocked, fell. Des shielded himself with his arm. 'Sit down, you idiot. Just sit down. This is Daddy's farm, his kitchen. How dare you?'

His father stood up. 'Michael, I won't have this. Talk about it, don't fight.'

Mick came at Des again. 'The time for talking's done. Collins has sold us down the river, betrayed us – what about the republic we all swore to fight for?'

Des shoved him away, ran round the table, grabbed him, pinioned his arm up behind his back, saying quietly, fiercely, 'Are you going to pick up your chair, finish your breakfast and talk calmly about the Treaty? It's to be voted on by the people *we* voted into *our* Government or does democracy mean as little to you as it meant to the British in 1918? Think, Michael, for once in your life, think.'

Des felt his brother hesitate. Des hooked his foot over the fallen chair, scraped it along the ground, scooped it up with one hand. The other still held Mick. 'Are you going to sit down, Michael?' His voice was gentle, too gentle. His father was trembling. 'Sit down, Daddy. This is all going to blow over, isn't it, Michael?'

Mick still hesitated, then nodded. Des released him. Mick thrust away, shouldering Des to one side, grabbing his cap from the door hook. He turned at the door. 'I don't care what you say,' he shouted banging his fist against the door. 'It's an old man's compromise and we're not old men. For pity's sake, Des, have we been fighting just to stay part of the Empire, to give our oath to the King? I've already given my oath, and so have you, and it wasn't to the King and you should remember that, d'you hear me?'

'The whole of Ireland can damn well hear you.'

'For God's sake, Des, think of the woods, "ourselves

alone". It was all just words was it, the recruitment talks you gave? Well, you wait, there's some that will fight on and on.' He slammed the door behind him.

Des was on his feet, running out after him, through the yard, into the field, the frosted grass slippery beneath him. He caught him at the far gate, yanked him round, shook him. 'I should smash your head in for that but then you couldn't hear me. Listen, you fool, we don't have to give the oath, we declare our faithfulness to the King. The British say partition is temporary – it can be sorted out through the Boundary Commission.'

'And you believe that? Get your hands off me. You're not giving me orders now. I'm not listening to you any more – listening to you splitting hairs as you are. I'll never be your man again – skulking behind walls watching my girl spoon with an Auxie. Any brother who'd put me through that is not worth a farthing.'

Des saw the face of this boy whom he'd loved and protected screwed up in rage and hate and confusion and said slowly, 'Mick, now's the time to let the politicians get on with it. You're too good a man to go roaring off when we're on the way to something good.'

Mick struggled against him, his lips drawn back in anger. 'We nearly got there but then we gave in.'

Des shouted at him, 'Shut up and think.'

Mick punched him in the abdomen. Des doubled over. Mick head-butted him to the ground and ran as he fell. Des scrambled to his feet, chased after Mick, catching him through mists of pain, spinning him round, hurling him to the ground, holding him there. Mick looked up at the blood streaming from his brother's nose. He stopped struggling. 'Oh God, Des, I'm sorry.'

Des kept his brother on the ground, heedless of the blood. He panted, 'Wait, see if it's ratified by *our* Dail Eireann – a government that is at last recognized by the British. Don't get into anything. Promise me?'

As Des's blood dripped to the ground, Mick promised.

The Treaty was ratified two days later by a narrow majority.

Mick didn't come in until after midnight. Des was waiting, sitting by the fireside, his cigarette loose between his fingers, the smoke spiralling upwards. Mick stood in the doorway, looking at his brother who was still brown from the harvesting, though that had been over three months ago. He said, 'The vote was a sell-out. I can just imagine Collins – our high and mighty new Chairman of the Government – licking his chops.'

Des looked at him and when he spoke his voice was heavy with sarcasm. 'Voting is what is done in a democracy.'

Mick sneered. 'Collins and his followers are cowardly scum who back away from a fight.'

Des sat and stared at his cigarette. 'That's your opinion of me too then, is it?'

'If you're with Collins, then yes, it has to be.'

Des still watched the cigarette. The ash grew longer. Soon it would drop. 'You won't listen to the Dail, you won't take note of the ratification. You won't look around you at the burned-out houses, the new graves. You won't listen to me or Daddy, or anyone.'

The ash dropped, the cigarette burned his fingers. He threw it on the fire. His arm felt heavy, tiredness was dragging at him again, a tiredness born of despair. He looked up at Mick.

Mick held his gaze, then looked instead at the cap he was twisting in his hands. 'I'm not the only one. There's Sean and Liam, and over half of your men.

Most of the Limerick units are anti-Treaty, Des.'

Des shook his head. 'Mick, don't be one of them. Civil war is the most dreadful thing.'

'The Treaty is a dreadful thing. Come in with us.' His eyes were pleading.

Des shook his head. 'Don't make Collins have to fight you. Don't make me have to fight you, for that's what will happen if you take up arms. We are self-governing now, so we must govern, and we will, Mick. Never think that we won't.' There was such urgency in his voice, such anguish that Mick swallowed, trying to think.

It had seemed so clear at the meeting, so terribly clear. He'd wanted the new leaders dead and out of the way so he and the republicans could storm on to a proper victory. He looked at his brother, so thin, so tired, and loved him as he had never loved him before. He barged from the kitchen, back out into the cold night air.

He ran down the track, then across the fields, sensing the gaps, knowing them from the years he had run between his farm and Cait's. He careered through into the Home Field, into her yard. He knocked on the door, entered. She was still up, darning by the lamplight.

Her father called down. Cait said, 'It's only Mick.'

'Well, tell him to get to his bed. Doesn't dawn come at the same time for him as it does for the rest of the world?'

Cait walked towards Mick, her face questioning.

He held her arms as he panted, 'I can't agree. I can't. We're going to fight. Des won't join us. We'll be enemies.'

Cait shook her head, shock numbing her, then anger bringing her to life. 'You mustn't. Don't be a fool.'

He stared at her. 'Not you too? Doesn't anybody I love believe in justice.'

Cait clenched her hands. She must be clear, she must be calm. She must hold him back from this, somehow. 'It'll be brother fighting brother. Think of the hate it will leave. How will Ireland ever get over it? How will we look to the world? Irish idiots, that's what they'll think. Don't you have any idea how much Des loves you? Haven't you any idea how much he's fought to keep you safe, to get you this far?'

She was struggling to keep her voice low, to keep their words from her father. 'We – Des, your daddy, mine – think the Treaty is correct. We, Mick, we. Stay with us.'

Mick brushed his hand through his hair, anger, bewilderment, disappointment chasing one another across his face. 'Cait, I can't. It's in my heart, you see.' He rubbed his cheek and stared at her, then round the familiar kitchen. At last he said slowly, 'I must. I'll just have to be alone, outside all of you.' He looked the child he still was and suddenly, Cait knew, beyond all doubt, that the love which she felt for him was only that which they had shared as children. She had no love for him as a man.

He said, 'I'm going home now. I'm tired.' He seemed older, taller, as he stooped and kissed her cheek.

She sat up all night, sitting by the fire, listening to the wind, thinking of the Christmas pudding she had made, wondering who would eat it, wondering if she had been building a wall to enclose a world which was about to be torn and ripped apart.

As dawn broke she walked to the river, knowing that she could not tell Mick there was no love between them, not yet. Ice shone glossy between the reeds. 'Thank God you're safe, my love,' she called to Ben. 'Thank God.'

Des and Mick worked beside their father, repairing the barn, talking of that, and of nothing else. They repaired the fences, the dairy, and Des took the milk to the creamery and waved at Cait as she did the same, and each day he noted how the sky altered, how the wind strengthened, or weakened, how the nails hammered easily into the wood, or balked at a knot and it was as though he was seeing it for the last time.

He and Mick listed the repair jobs in the house. They replaced tiles, together. They replaced broken gutters. 'There, it won't leak for another ten years, Daddy,' Mick said.

'There, that gate'll see us all out,' Des smiled.

'There, turf to last a lifetime,' they both said and each knew what they were really saying, brother to brother, was goodbye.

Christmas came and went. They ate goose at Cait's and she carved, and they laughed and talked of the dance they had all attended, where there had been no talk of Collins the realist, or de Valera the republican. Just for once there had been no talk of that.

Cait hugged *Wuthering Heights* to her, as New Year's Eve became New Year's Day. Ben had not written, but it was as well. She wanted no re-awakening of the dilemma of choice.

By the end of January the Tans and Auxies were finally clearing out of their posts. The Military too. But the Irish Republican Army was breaking up into pro-Treaty and anti-Treaty factions, each taking over barracks evacuated by the British. The division reverberated throughout the country, in kitchens, pubs, churches, schools, tea houses. Lawlessness blossomed in the vacuum, old scores were settled, new ones discovered.

In February the jobs on the O'Brian farm were completed, and day by day the silence in the kitchen grew until 18 February when Commandant Thomas Malone OC Mid-Limerick Brigade published a proclamation repudiating the authority of General Headquarters and declaring Collins, the Chief of Staff, a traitor.

Des walked across to the Healys' farm and knocked on the kitchen window, startling Cait. 'Come in,' she called, opening the door. The cold came in with him. She took his hands and rubbed them.

He wanted to sink into her warmth, her beauty, her youth which had not seen the deeds he had performed, or the life he had lived. He said, 'Limerick City is about to be evacuated by the British. The antis will try something, I just know they will. Keep him with you, please.'

Cait still held his hands, still rubbed. She nodded as though she had known he would say that. 'He won't wait any longer then?'

'I don't think so. I think we've lost him to them. But it's not civil war, not yet.'

On 23 February pro-Treaty men in their role as the Free State Army took over the barracks to prevent an anti-Treaty occupation. Des was not amongst them. He was helping Mick to repair Caithleen's cart which she had deliberately tipped over in the ditch, and Des knew he would love her for this until he died, but then he had loved her that much since the day he had first seen her at the dance.

Then they heard that armed anti-Treaty men had surrounded the barracks in Limerick.

Des was called by telegram to report for duty, to support the Free State troops. He ignored the order. If he stayed, maybe Mick would also.

Within days an amicable settlement was reached in Limerick. Cait and Des relaxed.

But by March Mick had gone, joining Sean and Liam, and 70 per cent of Des's men, a close reflection of the split in the IRA. Within the week Des had taken his place in the Free State Army. He went to see Cait. 'I'll try to keep tabs on him, using our intelligence. Help me, Cait. Don't turn him away. Find out what you can.'

She could find out nothing in March because Mick

didn't come. Instead she listened to her father who swore and raged when anti-Treaty forces obstructed and prevented the explanation of the Treaty in the run-up to the summer election. 'They're breaking up newspaper offices and meetings. There's to be no free speech if it differs from theirs, is that it? It's to be Mick and his sort who decide what we should all think and say, is it? How are the ditherers going to know how to vote in the summer elections? How are the *people* going to be able to ratify it? All I wanted was the Tans to go and peace to come. This mob want to rule by the gun.' He glared at Cait. 'Don't you let me see you with that boy again.'

She said, 'I have to.'

Her father said, 'I forbid it.'

At the end of March the bank was robbed, a teller wounded. 'It's that boy and his sort,' her father said as he unloaded the empty churn.

In April a barracks which had been taken over from the British military by the Free State Army was raided for arms by more anti-Treaty forces, or so Rose told her as they met in the tea house. They met without Patricia. Her family were anti-Treaty and so were the Brannigans and half the town. Hatred and division were all around.

'Does she know where Mick is?' asked Cait.

'She'd rather know where Niall is. He's run off to America, doesn't want to be part of it. My Paddy would rather die than run away. You can never come back, if you desert.' Rose sighed. 'I'm missing the dances. You must be missing Mick.'

Cait nodded briefly. She couldn't say that their love was over, not now, not while this was going on. 'If you hear of him, tell me.'

She heard Des's anxiety mingling with the wind as she walked back from the town and as she walked through the Home Field she heard the curlew, again and again, and then the laughter. Mick was standing

147

by the Home Field wall, his hair blowing in the wind, his grin wide. She ran to him, holding him. 'Where have you been? Where are you going? You're thin. Come and eat.' She stopped. No, her father might be there. 'Wait here, I'll bring food.'

He gripped her arm. 'No, no time. Is Des all right?'

She nodded. 'He's not operating here.'

Mick looked over the track, towards the hill beyond which was his farm. 'And Daddy?'

'He's fine. You and Des left the farm well set up.'

'At least we did that. I love Daddy, tell him that.'

'And Des?' she asked.

Mick paused, his hands on her shoulders. 'I love him and I hate him.' Mick's voice was flat.

Cait wanted to shake him. 'He has only love for you. This is stupid.'

He ignored her. She repeated, 'I tell you this is stupid, evil. The people have yet to vote. How dare you be so arrogant as to decide for them?'

'The people don't know what's good for them. We've got to act, grasp what we *know* they should want. And we are grasping. Our Chief of Staff has set up our military headquarters in the Four Courts in Dublin and has Collins chucked us out? You bet he hasn't. He hasn't the guts.'

'But of course he has, and he will. It's his duty, you fool. We're a nation now.' Her voice was almost a scream.

He laughed and touched her cheek. She slapped his hand away. 'Forget all this.'

He stared at her, his eyes angry. 'I'd rather cut off my right arm.'

That evening her father said, 'When Collins goes in after the Four Courts men, it will start the war.'

Cait looked at the fire, tried not to think of the roof snipers firing on the barracks occupied by Collins's army and the bank raids which financed the

148

anti-Treaty forces and wanted her father to be quiet, and the mayhem to stop.

'It'll be anarchy,' her father groaned over the table the next evening. 'We've no police, no military.'

'Careful, Dada, you'll be wanting my Auxie back next.'

He spun round and slapped her. The sound rang out across the kitchen. Why had she said that? For God's sake, why had she said it? She silently screamed at herself.

'Go to your room,' he shouted. 'If it isn't enough that there's this mess, I have a daughter who's flaunted herself, not just with a Tan, but a rebel.'

'I have to pluck the hens for market.'

Her face stung. It was anger, disappointment, fear which made her say it. Because the life she had built her wall around was being destroyed more as each day passed and it made the choice she had made harder to bear. Don't push me away, Dada, she wanted to plead. Don't tempt me.

There were more raids on post offices, some clashes between groups. But Collins hadn't set his troops against the Four Courts. 'He must,' her father raged, 'or the British will be back to do it for him.'

Where was Mick? She could tell Des nothing when he wrote, so she told him instead of the sunset over the mountains, of the cake she had baked his father, though she wanted to tell him of the life which was disintegrating before her eyes, of the nights she drove her face into the pillow in an agony of loss for Ben.

In mid-June the election was at last held and the returns showed a majority in favour of the Treaty. 'Now Collins will act and there will be war again,' she breathed into the wind from the river.

Towards the end of June the Four Courts were bombarded by Collins's troops. Des was amongst them. 'It had to be done,' Des wrote.

Cait and her father turned the hay they had cut,

feeling the sun on their arms, clinging to that in the midst of chaos.

At night it was again the sound of thunder that was gunfire, lightning that was flames, and Mick came, whistling again, and she brought him cakes and bacon, and gave him iodine and bandages, and kissed him when her father called to her, 'Get away from that man. Get away.'

He was running up the slope towards the Home Field. She held on to Mick. 'Get out of it, Mick, or go away.'

Mick kissed her hands and laughed.

'Where are you going, Mick? Tell me where you're going,' she begged.

'To the coastguard station. Feel like a bonfire! Won't be back for a while, things to do.' He blew her a kiss and ran, his rifle in his hand.

Her father walked now, shaking his fist at Mick's departing back, shouting at her, 'For God's sake, girl, what are you? I don't understand you any more. A Tan and a rebel.'

She faced him, coldness flooding her limbs. His face was red, disgust was in every movement he made. She said, 'I'm trying to hold Des's family together, and it was all right for me to know a Tan for the cause, to keep you all safe. But it's not all right now, is that it? Well, I don't understand anything any more either. It's all moving too fast, it's leaving me nothing.'

He moved towards her. 'I'm sorry.'

She took his hand. 'Oh Dada.'

She cabled Des: *Mick's going to the coastguard station.*

The next day the road to market was trenched. They couldn't get their chickens through or their young pigs. 'They're interfering with the administration, making it impossible to govern,' Rose said, over fancy cakes.

Patricia couldn't sleep because her contempt for Niall vied with her love.

150

Her father couldn't eat when they heard that the Post Office had been raided. 'They're animals,' he said. 'I forbid the mention of that boy's name. It's over. I order that you never see him again.'

Cait shook her head. 'They're what everyone is in a war, they're what you were, what I was. We all degrade ourselves.'

'Get to your room.'

Every morning she looked for the post. Would Ben write? Why should he? Please write, I need something beyond this. Please write. But of course he mustn't. It would set her on fire again. It was pointless. Des wrote instead. Telling her of the sunset he had seen over the Liffey, the swallows diving against its backcloth.

He didn't tell her that he'd not tried to get to the coastguard station. How could he when he hadn't thought out a way to get Mick clear of all this? He was waiting for something, anything. He'd know what it was when it happened, but at least he now had Mick pin-pointed, at least he had his unit covered.

In July the anti-Treaty forces in the south were driven from Waterford and Limerick City. Attacks against their centre positions between these two points were launched by Collins's troops.

'Mick's side haven't the arms, the resources, the back-up of the Free Staters who're being supplied by the British. I never thought to be glad of anything they sent us,' her father said. 'Mick's finished. It's just a matter of time before his nose is rubbed in the dirt. And don't soil my land with his presence even when it's settled. Do you understand?'

She just looked at him, then asked, 'How can we build a country if there is to be no forgiveness, no reconciliation, when the battle's done?'

At the beginning of August Des read the letter which

had been intercepted and sent to him from his contact in Cait's Post Office. The minute he opened it, read it, and fingered the ticket, he knew that he had what he was waiting for. It was more than he'd hoped for. He could save Mick, get him out of the fighting. And he could give Cait back her happiness, force the choice upon her, take any alternative from her.

A week later Cait fingered Ben's letter, looking through the kitchen window, checking that her father was still at the lower field, listening to the wheat crack. The cornflowers and poppies were vivid against the ripening grain. The shadows were long as the day drew to a close. She held the envelope to her cheek, then her lips. Ben. Oh Ben. She must open it. But no. It was from Australia. Was he writing to tell her that their love was dead, that he was married? Or had he heard of her use of him? Was he searing the page with his hate? Or was he re-opening choice?

Her father was walking back to the house, then he stopped, leaned on the wall, touched the honeysuckle, sank his face into it, then rested, loving the land of his fathers. Cait watched and knew there was no choice. There could be no choice.

She turned the letter over and over. She should burn it. She couldn't. She tore it open, needing to read words which had come from those strong, thin hands, needing to know whether his love had gone.

She read of his need for her, of his love which had only increased, of his body that ached for her, of the gold-mine which was earning a bare living. Of Old Roy Fellowes, Tom's uncle, who had welcomed him in Tom's place and who promised better times. 'He feels it in his bones, and those bones have been around a good long time,' Ben wrote. 'There's a fall-off in work. The price of gold has slumped following the war, the big mines of Boulder and Kalgoorlie are laying off workers but we're surviving. There isn't much, we live in shacks and tents around the mine,

152

which is small. But there's peace. Please come. I send this ticket. Please get on the ship at Queenstown on 17 August. Come to me, leave the chaos. Come to me. Every minute of every day I wonder if you're safe. We should be together. We were made for one another.'

Inside the envelope was a first-class ticket. Her father was walking towards the house. She pushed the ticket, the letter and the envelope into her apron pocket, down, deep down. No. How could she? No, Ben. But her heart thrilled to know that she didn't love alone, that he had scraped together enough for a first-class ticket. She must send it back, but not yet.

Every day for more than a week she read it, kissed it, and though there was only strain between her father and her, she knew there was no choice. There would never be room for a Tan in their family.

On Monday of the next week her father walked from the field into the yard, calling, 'I'm off to Tooley's Bar. We all need to plan the harvest.'

'Of course you do, have one for me.' The wind was gentle on her face, in her hair. She touched Ben's letter which was still in her pocket. This time tomorrow it would be too late. The ship would have sailed. She would arrange to get his money back for him. Des would help.

'Don't you be letting that boy near.'

She ignored him. 'Just be careful, Dada, take the cart. If anyone holds you up, give them what they want.'

He shook his finger at her. 'I'll give them what they need, not what they want. Especially if it's that young Mick. He needs a bullet in his belly.'

'For the love of God, Father.'

'He's a traitor who'll be hounded until he's caught or killed. They've destroyed our land, they're tearing it apart.' He grabbed her wrist.

She wrenched away from him. 'We're all tearing

the land apart, and ourselves. Go to your drink and spend some time thinking of how we're all going to go on living side by side when this is over. There's no room for this hate.'

'Just you make sure you shut the door in that Mick's face.'

Cait looked at her father. 'I've told you that he hasn't been here, and he hasn't. I don't lie, Father.'

'You did though, didn't you? For months you lied to the Tan. Why change things now?'

Tiredness drenched her. 'Go to your drink, Father.'

He stomped from the yard. 'I'll walk. It'll clear my head, it'll calm me down. It'll . . . Oh, I don't know what it'll do.'

She brewed tea, drank it. She shut up the hens for the night, read the letter again and again. No, Ben. I can't. These are my people. There's been one feud in the family, there can't be another. All this will pass. She touched her mother's photograph. 'It's all right, I won't leave, Mum.'

She remembered the Tans who had laughed when her mother died, and hate surged, and when it did, she understood her father and remembered how much she loved him.

As the evening drew on and darkness fell the wind rattled the windows and she couldn't sit, couldn't sew, couldn't bake. She dragged her shawl around her shoulders and went out into the night, running through the Home Field, down the slope to the willow. She watched the moonlight on the water, the ripples round the stones and remembered the feel of him, the sight of him, and the sound of him. She couldn't go. Must not go.

She left the river, walked up the slope, letting her shawl fall open on this warm August evening. The cattle were lowing, coughing. A dog barked. It was quiet tonight. There was no sound of gunfire. Peace will come, Ben. We'll live our own lives. But we'll always remember and that will have to be enough.

She pushed open the gate into the yard. There was sound from the milking shed. A churn rattled. Someone groaned. She froze, her hand on the gate. Republicans? She stepped back. Quietly, quietly, for God's sake. If it was Mick he'd have called.

What would they do to her? She must get to the road, run to the town. Another step back. The gate creaked. She froze again. There was movement at the entrance to the milking shed. A voice called softly, 'Cait.'

It was Des. She held her hand to her mouth, relief making her laugh, high pitched, stupid, ugly. 'I wanted your help about a ticket.'

He doubled out of the door, pulled her into the darkness with him. 'Shut up. For God's sake, shut up.' He slapped her. The sound was like a shot, the pain was like cold water. His grip tightened. 'You're hurting,' she gasped.

'Help me, Cait. You've got to help me.'

He dragged her to the byre. There in the moonlight she saw a body, lying on the straw. She was confused. 'Who is it? Is he dead? Is he one of yours? But he's not wearing uniform.'

Des was on his knees by the man. Cait looked at him more closely. 'Neither are you, Des, what's happening?'

He rolled the man over gently, coaxing him. It was Mick. Blood oozed from a bandage around his shoulder. His shirt had been ripped from him. Des dragged him towards the door. 'I've harnessed Tanzy. They're after him. They're going to kill him. He's on our list.'

He was panting with the strain. Cait moved now, helping. 'What list? What're you talking about?'

'Shh,' Des grunted. 'Get his feet.'

They carried him to the barn where the mare was harnessed. 'Where are you going with him?'

Cait whispered as they heaved him into the cart.

Des jumped down, taking her shoulders, turning her to the moonlight. 'I'm not going anywhere with him. I'm going to stall them.'

'Stall who?'

'My own squad. They've lost the trail, but they'll find it again.' His face was close to her, his words clear but almost without sound. 'Cait, if you ever loved him, if you ever cared for him in any way, save him.'

Cait didn't understand. 'Me, how can I save him?'

'Look, a man I trust is at the crossroads. He'll make sure you get safely to Queenstown, safely onto the ship, and he'll give you drugs to keep him sedated on the ship until you reach Australia. He's been treated, the wound is clean. You know enough to keep it that way.'

She pulled away, aghast. 'What are you talking about?'

Des reached for her again, pulling her towards him. 'I'm talking about getting Mick away, out of all this, before the fool stops a bullet that kills him, not just wings him. Take him. I've arranged to change the first-class to two second-class. There's a cabin booked.'

'But I'm not going. You know I can't. And how did you know about the ticket? Oh God, you've had the Post Office in on it. Does Dada know too?'

Des's face was close to hers again. 'Cait, go. I'll send money. It's got to be Australia not America – we've a passage, remember. London isn't far enough. Cable me when you arrive. I'll send money when it's safe for him to return. I'll cover for him – he's on intelligence or something. There'll be no shame. You can go to Ben. Yes. I know it's over between you and Mick. I know you still love Ben. Go.'

'I can't, there's Dada.' She was struggling against him.

'Do you love Ben?' His voice was harsh, demanding.

He forced her head up, looked deep into her eyes. He saw the answer. 'Then go, and save Mick's life into the bargain. If you don't take him, you are as good as killing him.' He checked his watch. 'I've packed for you.'

She spun round and saw two cases in the cart. He was heaving her up, and then they froze. There were footsteps approaching, her father was singing.

Des sank into the shadows of the yard, moving swiftly. Thank God, it would finally remove all choice. It would bring her happiness because it would take her to Ben.

Paul Healy came round the corner. Des pounced, his hand gagging him, hauling him into the shelter of the barn, dragging his scarf from his pocket, forcing it between Paul's teeth, tying it with one hand and his teeth, seeing Cait watching, frozen with horror.

'Get going,' Des shouted. 'Get Mick away. Use the ticket the Tan sent.'

At that her father struggled, threw Des from him, staggered towards Cait, wrenching the gag from his mouth. 'What ticket? What damn ticket?'

Des had him again, restraining him. 'For Australia, Paul,' he said. 'She loves him, she always has, always will. Let her go.'

Her father went slack then reared up again, his face and voice ugly. 'You whore, you lying whore. Mick, the Tan. Get out of here. Get out, away from my sight. I can't bear even the thought of you.'

Des forced the gag in his mouth, tied him up. Cait sat numb, frozen. She couldn't move, couldn't think. 'Let him go.'

'No, he'll raise the alarm.'

Des jumped on the cart, swore at the pony, lashed her with the whip. 'There's no choice, there's no going back. Your dada knows now, so you've *no choice*,' Des cried as they lurched out of the yard. The wheels slipped. Cait moved, hung on. They were out on the track. 'Dada, Dada. What have you done, Des? What have you done to me?'

'It's too late to go back.' Des was thrusting the reins into her hand. His were over hers. 'I've given you your future, because you would never have taken it. Keep Mick quiet on board. Tell Ben the truth. He's a soldier. He'll understand. But *you must* tell him. Confess, start with a clean sheet. I'll send money to Mick. I'll write explaining everything to him.' He was panting. The cart rocked as the pony strained in the shafts.

She couldn't think, couldn't feel, couldn't follow any of it. 'But Dada?'

'I'll talk to him tonight. I'll explain. Make him understand. Trust me.'

They were careering down the lane, towards the crossroads. Des's hands were still on hers. He pulled on the reins. The pony stopped. A man waited in the shadows. Des jumped down, the other took his place in the cart. Des looked up at her. 'You're saving his life. I gave you no choice, remember that. I'll tell your father. He'll understand.'

Cait stood. 'Then I'll go back now.'

'If you do, Mick will die. You must get him on the ship, keep him on it at all the ports of call.'

There were sounds of shots coming from the west of her father's farm. The man on the cart took the reins from Cait. 'See you, Des.' It was a Dublin accent. It was the same man who had helped Des crop her.

'Take care, Cait.'

He was gone. The cart was moving, lurching, Mick groaned.

She watched Des run back towards the firing. She saw him as clear as day, standing in the open, way up the track, firing at the Free Staters, his own side, drawing them away from the cart, and then she knew the depth of his love for his brother.

'Oh no,' she whispered. 'He's signed his own death warrant.'

'Only if they get him. They don't know it's him. And don't worry, either way he'll get back to your father first,' the man growled. whipping the pony.

'That's not why.' There were tears streaming down her face.

Des ran across the open field, hearing the men behind him, hearing his breath pumping in and out, in and out. He had to reach the river. He had to get into the reeds, then he could get to the house, see Paul Healy, explain that his daughter was a good, brave woman. Explain about love, about the decency of Ben. about the plan he had hatched to save his brother, to force Cait to follow happiness. 'Look at your own marriage,' he'd say. 'Would you deny that to Cait? Would you deny my father the life of his young son, the boy who scrumped your apples? I'm too old, I've seen too much, done too much. Mick is still fresh, innocent. A fool, but he'll learn.'

He burst through the hedge. The thorns dragged at his clothes. Good, they were still following him, not them, not Mick, not Cait. Mick would be safe. Had he seen Des fire the rifle that tore open his shoulder? Would he understand why? His legs were tiring now. It had been such a long, long day. How often was it that anyone planned to shoot his brother, a brother who would otherwise leap towards his own death in some battle, for some ideal that Collins would procure anyway? No, his brother wasn't going to die for that.

Where the hell was the river? The clouds parted, moonlight streamed through. There it was ahead of him. He would write, tell Mick that he had to be safe, that he had to be sent from the country. That he had shot him out of love. That Cait had taken him, out of remembrance of love. Just as he, Des, had taken choice from her, out of love – though he would not tell anyone of that.

The river was there, at the bottom of the slope. He was sliding, slithering, slipping down through the grass. His breath was heaving, hurting. He was in the water. The men were over the ridge now, his men. He waded through the reeds, doubling over, keeping low. He would cut up by the willow, get to Paul. Tell him of the daughter he had, the daughter he should love, forgive, admire.

The reeds were in his face, cracking, creaking as he moved through them. Too noisy. He edged out into the river, swimming, his clothes dragging at him, but not at his gun, this he held out of the water. Be quiet. They were there, he could hear them. But where exactly? Behind, ahead, alongside? Was Cait safe? Was Mick?

He inched forward. There was the bank, the break in the reeds. He listened. Silence. Where were they? He had to get to the farm. He had to get to Paul. No sound. There was no sound. He threw a pebble across to the other side of the reeds. No sound, no movement. He should wait, but he must tell Paul. He'd promised. He'd keep him quiet, then he'd get money for Mick – rob a bank, everyone else was doing it.

He moved towards the shallows, feeling the ground firm beneath his feet, feeling for the stones, rising from the water, moving towards the bank, searching the darkness, his gun dry, ready. The river tugged at his trousers. It was running fast tonight. He cocked his gun. Could he use it on his men? Yes. He'd do anything for her.

He froze. The darkness rose in front of him. 'Stop, or we fire.' It was Kevin's voice.

They blocked his path to Paul. He felt the weight of the gun, heard the click of the rifles. He couldn't fire. He flung himself towards the reeds. But they fired and he was hurled back into the fast-running river. It dragged him back into the current, away from Paul, but not from the pain which pounded and tore at his chest, his gut. He struggled. He had to get back. He struggled but there was no strength in him, there was only the cold and the pain, and he tried again, and the darkness was deeper, and now the river pulled him deep down.

He fought it, struggling. His chest was bursting, his head was exploding, roaring. But then she came, smiling, her hair streaming out in the water, her eyes warming him as an Irish summer sky would, and she still smiled, and he followed her, relaxing into the current as he said, 'I'm sorry, Cait.'

Chapter Eight

The seas were roaring and breaking all around them as the ship drove through the Bay of Biscay, and Mick's groans were barely audible above the noise. Cait tended him, half crazy with shock, confusion, misery and happiness. She was going to Ben. In the end, there had been no option. Des would explain to her father. He would make him understand, as her letter, written in Queenstown before she sailed, would also help to do.

She held Mick's hand, soothing him, forcing aside the sickness, as the ship pitched down, then up, then rolled sideways. Sometimes she slept and when she did she saw Des, darkly etched in the moonlight, firing, running from them, saving not only Mick, but her. She knew that now, because the man from Dublin had told her when she had screamed, 'Why?'

'Because the deeds he has done for Ireland have denied him the right, in his eyes, to life and love. All he can do is give those he loves back their lives – and believe me, Caithleen Healy, he has a very great love for you, greater even than for Ireland.' He had flicked a glance into the back of the cart. 'And for that boy there, though, for me, Des is by far the finer man. It's a terrible sacrifice he's making. Terrible in its waste. Make sure you make it count.' The man spoke no more until they were coming into the outskirts of Queenstown.

Then he had issued orders. 'The pain will keep the boy disorientated, unaware. Could be for some weeks. But after that, give him these.' He thrust a package at her. 'These are safe, light sedatives. Use them as directed and no harm will come to him.'

As they left the Bay of Biscay and the seas calmed into sun-drenched days, and balmy nights she tended Mick's wounds and told him, as she had been instructed, that they were in a safe house, and he, in his mist of pain, smiled.

'Glorious Cait,' he'd murmured. 'Glorious. You'll be taking me into the orchard soon?'

'Yes, into the orchard soon.'

She ate food in the dining-room, telling of her 'brother'. 'Such a bad traveller. He had the vapours in his pram.' The others at her table laughed. The stewards glided around them, the cutlery glinted, but not as much as the chandeliers reflected in the huge mirrors. The grey-haired woman to her right laughed and patted her stomach. 'Perhaps it would serve me to be similarly afflicted?'

Not if you knew the truth of it, thought Cait wryly.

'Still, I have until Cape Town to be firm with myself. Are you travelling further?' Mrs Smith, the grey-haired woman asked.

'To the rest of my life,' Cait murmured, looking at the reflections of the chandeliers echoing endlessly.

'I beg your pardon?' the woman queried.

'To Fremantle, then to Kalgoorlie. I am to be married.'

'Oh, my dear, how enchanting.'

Cait smiled, placing her napkin carefully on the table, rising. 'Please excuse me. My brother, you know.'

She walked between the tables, onto the deck. The wind tugged at her hair, the stars were so low they could almost be touched. She leaned against the rail, breathing deeply. Des, be alive. Ben, listen to me, understand why I lied. Mick, understand why we've done it. There was no list. She knew that now, the Dublin man had told her. 'It was to make you go, to confuse you, to make you obey Des. The idiot boy would've died though, because he's a fool. He's the sort who wants a valiant death but forgets he won't be there to see the grieving.'

At Las Palmas they took on coal, and though the ship was steady in the harbour, Mick still groaned with pain. 'We mustn't miss the apples,' he breathed, struggling to sit, jogging his shoulder, crying out in pain.

'Shh, the Tans are around,' she murmured as the Dublin man had instructed.

She changed the bandage. Then when he slept she joined Mrs Smith on a deck crowded with passengers throwing money into the clear-water harbour for natives, watching them dive for it, then hauling up baskets spilling with fruit that the money had bought.

Beside her, Mrs Smith fussed in her purse and said, 'Quite right, that poor brother of yours must have fruit. People can die from sea-sickness, you know. What does the ship's doctor think? And he should walk, you know. He'll get too weak, just lying down.'

There was never any need to reply to Mrs Smith, Cait thought, laughing gently. She would talk to Ben of Las Palmas. It should be a shared memory. Just as the willow would be. Oh Ben, will you forgive me the lie? Mick, will you understand? Oh Des, are you alive? Dada, do you understand, now that you've seen Des?

She rationed the fruit in the cabin. Cape Town was hours, days, weeks away. As the wound healed she began to administer the sedatives. 'Keep him under until there is no disembarkation before Australia. Then he'll have to stay out there until Des sends him money. You'll both have to stay – but you must anyway. You must make your life work,' the Dublin man had said.

She asked, 'What if Des . . . can't send the money? What if he's . . . ?' She couldn't say the word 'killed'.

The Dublin man had shrugged. 'Then Mick'll have to work it out. He'll have a lifetime to do that, won't he?' She could still hear the bitterness.

They neared the Equator. The cabins were ovens. She bathed him, nursed him, and in spite of the sedatives he knew that she did things for him that only a wife should do and he struggled, asking for a man, 'Shh. The Tans,' she murmured.

Each evening in the cabin she heard the music of the ballroom and in her head it was she and Ben dancing. It was his arms around her, his thin face, his grey eyes looking into hers, his full mouth on hers, their bodies merging, blending in the heat, the music. Mick murmured, 'We'll dance again soon, when this is over.'

As he slept she murmured softly, 'We're not marrying. I love the Tan. But I love you too, as my brother. I always will.'

She stayed on board at Cape Town, waving to Mrs Smith. 'He'll be fine,' Cait mouthed. 'Just fine.'

The Indian Ocean was smooth. Flying fish speared the water. The porpoises played, and now she walked Mick up and down the cabin, and he no longer even winced and they were drawing closer to Australia and some days his confusion lifted as the sedatives began to run out and there were longer periods in between doses. When it did, he looked at her, smiled, then turned on his side.

A week away from Fremantle the sedatives ran out completely and that morning Mick pushed her from him, as she tried to feed him. He hauled himself up into a sitting position, swung his legs over the edge, looked round the cabin.

He had thought he was dreaming as the pain

had roared and raged. He had thought he was damn well dreaming that this room was not the cellar, that a solid farm cellar was rolling and pitching. He had thought . . . Well, what had he thought?

His head ached, his shoulder hurt. He touched the wound. Scar tissue. He looked at her. 'Perhaps you would like to tell me what sort of a safe house this is?' His voice was harsh and angry as fear and realization vied with one another.

Cait sat on her bunk, facing him, twisting and turning her hands. 'You were wounded. They've sent you away to fund-raise. They wanted to make sure you were useful, even though you were out of the fight, for now.' Yes, that's what the Dublin man had said. Keep him quiet, keep him unknowing for as long as you can.

Mick felt the fear subside, and the anger. 'An early honeymoon in America. We might see Widow Murphy's sister. Come here, Cait.'

She stood by him, feeling his arms holding her close, his head on her belly, and the tension seizing her shoulders. 'They think I'm that important, do they?'

'He thinks you're that important,' she said.

He was drifting now, back into sleep. 'Who?' he murmured as he released her, and lay down.

But he was asleep and she said nothing.

The next day he was stronger and ate the meal the steward brought on a tray.

'It's six days to Australia,' the steward said. Cait froze.

Mick didn't touch the knife and fork, just looked at her as the door shut. 'Australia? Why Australia?'

Cait smiled gently. 'There are enough men out in America.' Break it in stages, the Dublin man had said. You don't want a riot on your hands, on a ship full of British ex-servicemen on assisted passages to Australia. You don't want him rampaging. Keep him

166

calm. Make him understand. 'Now eat your meal.'

He did, but all the time he was frowning. Who did he know in Australia? It was someone. And why had they sent him here, such a long trip, such an expensive trip? And why with Cait? She was for Collins.

But he was weak, and he couldn't grip the thoughts that floated in and out of his throbbing head.

The next morning she walked him around the deck, and she smiled and nodded to all the passengers. Mrs Smith's friend, who was travelling on to Fremantle, was knitting in a deck-chair and held up her hand. Cait tried to walk on. Mick stopped. The woman said, 'So you must be Caithleen's brother. What a time you've had with this dreadful sickness. How nice to see you up.'

Cait tugged at his arm. 'He's still weak.'

Mick doffed his hat and allowed Cait to drag him on. 'Brother?' he asked.

He steered her to the rail. 'Brother?'

'It was for appearances,' she laughed. 'They'd be shocked if we weren't family.'

Something was nagging at him, something whispered and crawled round his head.

He looked down to the lower deck. 'Who are they?'

'Assisted passengers. They are emigrating and have reduced fares.'

He turned, leaned back against the rail, hooking his elbows over the top, staring at the deck-chairs, and the stewards, and now the fear was here again. 'The IRA couldn't afford these tickets.' It wasn't a question.

Cait swallowed, then walked on. Make it as close to the truth as possible, he'll believe it then. Drip the truth in, or he'll explode, go mad, not understand. If he ever does, the Dublin man had said.

She hurried to the cabin. He followed, slammed the door. 'Who paid for the tickets?'

She shrugged. 'A friend. Ireland has friends, you know.'

His brow was furrowed. 'Why are you here? Why would they pay for you?'

'I couldn't stay in Ireland with you gone.' It was true. Des had made sure she couldn't.

The next day Mick was quiet. He still couldn't sort out his thoughts. And the next, and the next. Now there were two days to go. She must tell him everything. But how?

That night as she lay on her bunk she heard the rustle of sheets, and footsteps, and his breathing as he drew close, the weight of his hand on her breast as he knelt on the floor beside her bed, his lips on her eyes, her mouth. He lifted the sheet and traced a line from her shoulder to her nipple. She feigned sleep, but now he was kissing her shoulder, her breast, slipping her chemise from her shoulder, and it was his lips on her skin, his tongue stroking her skin, and it should be Ben.

She whispered, 'No.'

'Cait, tell me why.' His voice was like silk. His hands were on her throat, caressing her. But then he was pushing her down, hurting her, and his voice had become fierce. 'Tell me why, you bitch? Why?' She broke his grasp. He laughed, then hit her.

The blow burst her lip. He spun off her, and to the lamp. Light flooded the cabin and in her shock she couldn't move. He leaned back against the door. He was waving a letter. Ben's letter.

Her eyes flashed to her drawer.

Mick drawled, his lips smiling but his eyes cold. 'The moral of the story is, never go fishing in your girlfriend's drawers.'

Cait's mouth stung, her lips were clumsy as she formed the words. 'That's a very bad joke.'

He laughed and the bitterness in the sound hung heavily between them. 'I've remembered who's in Australia. Now, I suggest you tell me what the hell is going on before I put my hands round your neck again and strangle the truth out of you.' He itched to beat her, hurt her, because he feared what she would say.

He leaned on the door and listened as she told him of his brother shooting him to save his life, of the Tan she loved, the ticket they had exchanged to transport him to safety.

Cait edged from the bed, and stood against the opposite wall. 'Des did it for love. You would die, because you were so profligate with your chances.'

Mick kept his eyes on hers, and there was rage building, though his voice was calm. 'So Des pointed a gun at me and fired. He took me from my country, made a deserter out of me, made me a runaway, an exile out of love. Why did you do the same? Not out of love, my dearest Caithleen.' His voice was hard, scathing. 'I hear now the whispering voice. "Our love is over, Mick." I hear it, Caithleen. I remember too, all that you did for me, and I let you. Things that only a wife should do. You have shamed me, lied to me, betrayed me. Both of you.' He was shouting. 'I'm no better than Niall who also fled.'

She put her hands out to him. 'No, never that. Des wanted you to live, and so did I. He's sending out money so that you can return. He's explaining that you were tricked, just so that you can come back.'

Mick laughed again and his bitterness clung to every particle of air in the cabin. 'He's laughing back with his scum of a squad. He's got rid of his brother. He's the big leader. He never wanted me at his side. He wanted all the glory for himself. He knows I can never go back, not now, not after running, no matter what he says. And you're a fool if you think he'll say anything.' He spoke slowly now. 'Watch my lips, Cait. He's my enemy. We're on opposite sides.'

'It's not like that. You're mad.'

He punched his hand into the wall. She flinched. He swung back to her.

'You're the one who's mad if you think I could bear travelling away from my fight at the expense of a Tan.'

'Listen to me, Mick. Hate me if you must, but not Des. Des loves you. You can go back. They'll understand. Don't you see he shot you so that you can. Everyone will blame him, not you. You were forced out of Ireland. He sacrificed himself, his name, everything he's ever done, for you. You can go back. He's given you a future.'

'He's given me nothing. He's a bastard.' He was prowling up and down. 'There are men back there, fighting. He had no right to ruin my life.'

'He was only trying to save it. Cable him. Take his money, go home. The fighting will be over by the time you get back . . .' Once the words were out, she realized what she had said.

'Shut up, Cait. Just shut up.' He shook the letter at her. 'So, all this time you loved a Tan. All this time, when you let me kiss you it was him you were longing for. All the time I protected you by the willow, you were laughing at me. Was he too, Cait?'

She shook her head. 'I wasn't laughing, I've never laughed at you. I do love you, but not like that. And he didn't know. He never knew about you. I didn't love him in the beginning. It just happened.'

He laughed again, and now there was victory alongside the bitterness and Cait wanted to grab her words back. He said, 'So, Cait, does he know about any of it? Does he know how you played him? Does he know how *we* laughed about *him*?'

Cait kept her voice steady, though her legs were too weak to hold her weight. She sat on the bed. 'I'm going to tell him. Des said he'd understand. He said Ben was a soldier. He'd understand when I told him.'

Mick almost screamed at her. 'Des says, Des says. I'm sick of what Des says. Soldiers – who cares about soldiers? For God's sake, I'm his brother and he won't let me be one. His is to be the only glory.'

Now Cait flared, pushing herself from the bed, launching herself at Mick. 'Shut up. You shut up. You're not worthy to tie your brother's bootlaces. You're a fool, you always were, always will be.' She mimicked him. ' "No bullet's going to get me." There you were, always showing off, flaunting yourself. You can't see the glory and the grief when you're dead, Mick. When you're dead, it's over. Because of Des, it won't be over and it's because of me, and Ben Williams too. Be grateful for it.'

He shoved her, she reeled. He shook her, then hurled her to the bed, throwing Ben's letter in her face. 'Go to hell, Caithleen Healy. You've ruined my life and now watch me ruin yours.'

He left the cabin. She followed, but he had disappeared. She traipsed the decks, asked those who were leaning on the rail, the wind in their hair. No-one had seen him. Desperation took hold. She must talk to him, explain, beg, for now she knew what he would do.

She was still searching as dawn rose and Australia came into view. 'Believe me when I explain, Ben,' she called into the wind. She must reach Ben before Mick did. She rushed to her cabin, threw her things into her bags, and waited on deck.

She stayed at her post as Immigration and Quarantine Officers came out from Fremantle. She must be first. She ignored those that stopped to talk, to exchange addresses, shaking off hands which clutched at her arms.

A tug came and finally they anchored. Still she waited, looking around. She must be first. Her eyes swept the wharf, searching for Ben, heedless that this was a new world, heedless of anything but Ben. She must find him, drag him from here, tell him. 'He'll believe you,' Des had said.

The hawsers were being thrown. There were dockers, sheds. No Ben.

'Customs first,' the man standing next to her said. 'The relatives will be the other side of the shed.'

Her heart was pounding. She gripped the rail. They were setting up the companionway. Hurry, for God's sake, hurry.

Someone touched her arm. 'Miss Healy? Please come with me to the Purser's Office. We have a message from a Mr Williams.'

She clutched the steward's arm. 'Is it real?'

He looked bemused. 'Is what real?'

'The message.' She looked around wildly. Was it a trick? Had Mick sent it? She couldn't leave her post.

The steward laughed. 'It was brought aboard by an Immigration Official. I saw him do it. I gather it's just about where to meet.' Relief flooded through her. She hurried along the deck, to the Purser's Office. There was a queue. She wanted to hurl them all out of the way. He'd written. He was there. She'd get straight to him, explain, get him away. She waited and waited until finally it was almost her turn.

She checked her watch; Ben's mother's watch. Come on, come on, it had been almost thirty minutes. They'd be disembarking now. Should she wait any longer? Mick would be there, on the wharf. But he might not be trying to find Ben. She mustn't be stupid. But if he was? She half turned. No. If he was she'd still be there first, because she'd know where he was.

It was her turn. 'Please, it's Caithleen Healy. You have a message from a Mr Ben Williams.'

The Purser looked through the pile of paper and shook his head. 'No, nothing here.'

She banged the counter. 'It came on with the Immigration Officer.'

He shook his head again. 'No, I remember those that did. There was nothing for you, Miss Healy.'

She ran back along the deck, pushing through people, staring at the wharf, her bags crashing into legs. Where was he? Oh Ben, don't listen to him.

Mick was through Customs. He listened to the address system which was repeating his message. 'Will Mr Ben Williams please meet a passenger outside Customs.'

Mick smiled. He wasn't lying, like everyone else had lied. He hadn't said Caithleen Healy was the passenger. He hadn't actually handed her the note which told her that Mr Williams had left a message for her. A greedy steward had done that. A greedy British steward.

He looked around. Ben Williams was hurrying through the crowds, his face searching for Caithleen. Mick's spirits roared with the thrill of vengeance. 'Over here, Ben,' he called. 'I've the finest piece of news to tell you.'

Caithleen heard the message as she came down the companionway. 'Oh no.' She rushed forward but was held up by Customs. They searched her luggage because she was so rude, so impatient. She tore from the shed when she was released, looking for them. Pushing to the left, searching in the milling crowds, tripping over cases, boxes, children. No, no-one there. She turned and ran along to the right and then she saw them.

She saw Mick slap Ben on the arm and laugh. She saw Ben's slack shoulders. He was shaking his head, then he shrugged Mick from him and pushed past him.

She ran after him. 'Ben, Ben. Don't listen. I was going to tell you.'

She saw him stop. But he didn't turn. He straightened though, and then walked on. She ran, dropping her bags, her hat falling, her eyes latched to him. 'Ben,' she screamed. 'Ben.'

She was grabbed, swung round, held. Mick said, his face close to hers, 'Now you have nothing either.' She tore from him. 'Ben, Ben.'

But there were only men, women, children.

Ben pushed blindly through the crowd. He brushed at his jacket where Mick had slapped him. He brushed and brushed, but he could still feel the pressure of the Irishman's hand, could still hear his words.

She was here. She'd used his ticket as he'd pleaded, but she'd brought out her fancy man, the man who had been behind the wall, looking at them, laughing at them in the cool of an Irish meadow. The man who'd cropped her hair to trick him. The scissors had flashed, he'd said. They'd flashed. Ben couldn't get the image of scissors out of his head, flashing, always flashing. Then they'd laughed, Mick O'Brian had said. They'd laughed and kissed and stroked and loved. And it had worked, he'd said.

Ben pushed on through the crowds, on into Fremantle, out across the road. A carter shouted at him. A constable caught him by the arm. 'You drunk or something? Get off the road.'

Ben thrust him away and barged on, knocking into people, kicking aside a crate. It had worked, yes it had worked. Nausea was rising, catching in his throat. He swung down a dark shadowed alley, clutching his belly, vomiting, again and again. He could still hear that damn voice.

'We laughed,' Mick had said. 'We laughed at you every night. We laughed when your Tan died. We laughed when you sent the ticket. Thanks for the free ride, mister. From us both. You should be proud you helped send out fund-raisers for the cause.' He'd slapped his arm. 'I've dumped her now. Found her playing around with the Purser.'

Ben leaned against the wall. He wiped his forehead on his sleeve. He rocked backwards and forwards. Oh

God, Oh God. He'd loved her. He'd really loved her. Jones the Tan had been right. They were scum. All scum. Oh God.

That night she lay on a stark bed, in the Immigrants' Home, taken by Mrs Smith's friend who had found her wandering the wharf, dazed, parched, in despair.

'I've lost him,' she had raved.

'Then you must find him,' Mrs Smith's friend had said, before leaving for Perth.

She lay exhausted in the heat, helpless against the mosquitoes, the fleas and the bugs, listening to crying children and mothers who soothed. But she was alone. In the morning, as the sun rose, the flies came. She paid, left, walked by the water, feeling the cooling breeze, gazing at the calm blue sea, the deep blue sky. 'I've lost him,' she murmured. She sat on the hot sand, her head on her knees.

She walked through Fremantle and the September heat was like nothing she had experienced. 'I've lost him,' her voice echoed in her head. Her lip was sore, flies buzzed at it, and around her head.

As evening came, she found the beach again and sat and watched the sun sink, and then it was dark, so suddenly. As dark as it had been when Des stood, sharply etched, and drew his men away from her. She slept on the beach, alone, but at least she slept, because this couldn't be the end. It mustn't be.

The train to Kalgoorlie left from Perth in the late afternoon. She had prowled the streets of Fremantle until then, searching for Mick, thinking she saw him a million times a day, but being mistaken; wanting him to understand his brother's actions, his brother's love. It was the least she could do, but it was for Des that she did it, not for the boy with whom she had scrumped apples. For him there was just searing rage.

She dozed as the train rattled and lurched, and

she ached with lost love, nearly died with the heat then gasped at the size of the land as they pounded through paddocks stacked with hay and huge trees. She gasped again as these gave way to flat, dry, scrub-covered land. Where was the greenness of Ireland? Long gone, the rattling wheels echoed.

As evening became night she held fast to the Dublin man's voice. 'Don't waste his sacrifice.' Dawn came and with it the heat but that became as nothing, and the flies too, and the tiredness which pulled at her, in the face of her fear that Ben would refuse to listen when she found him.

At nine o'clock, when her father would be returning from the morning milk run, the train climbed over the top of the hill at Summerville and she saw the poppet legs of the mines rearing from the red earth, and the smoking chimneys, and the buildings – so many. It was a huge town, no, two towns. There were beautiful buildings, and trappings of wealth.

A fellow passenger said, 'That's Kalgoorlie and there's Boulder. It's not what you expect when you think of a gold-mining area, is it? Quite a metropolis, isn't it? The hills are tailings, or waste, from the mines. They brought in a water pipeline twenty years ago. It's made it bloom.' She gazed at the barren searing hills, the dust which hung in the air, like the mist of Ireland about the hills, but no, so unlike the mist, and it was as though her heart was twisting and turning. Where, amongst all that, was Ben?

She walked from the station into the town and the heat beat at her, and the dust was in her mouth, her eyes. Trams clanked along the wide street, delivery carts passed, a motor bike roared, and above it all was the thump of the mine batteries and the throb of the compressors, and she thought she would suffocate amongst it all.

She asked in the Post Office, 'Do you know Ben Williams?' The man did not.

'But you must,' she insisted.

'Listen, lady, I know what I know.'

She said, 'I gave Kalgoorlie Post Office as my address in a letter I wrote to my father. My name is Caithleen Healy?'

The clerk checked a pile on the table at the back and shook his head.

'It's too soon, that's all,' she said. The clerk shrugged.

She walked along Hannan Street which was lined with huge solid buildings and on one corner she stopped, then slipped into the cool darkness of the Palace Hotel.

'Do you know Ben Williams?' she asked. No-one did.

She asked in the shops, on the trams, the buckboards and the cabs. She asked those who walked alongside, and stopped those coming the other way. No-one knew him.

She returned to the Palace, standing in its dark shade, dust covered, sweat streaked, her hair dishevelled. She asked for tea. The receptionist frowned at her as smart women walked in and out, accompanied by suited men.

The dining-room was dark, slow fans turned, affronted glances reached her from nearby tables. She sat straight at the corner table they had led her to and stared back. I'm used to being ostracized, despised, she wanted to shout. Nothing you can do hurt me.

The table-cloths were crisp, her serviette too. Her fingers stained it. Her cup clinked as she replaced it in the saucer. Her hands trembled. But Mick had done everything to hurt her. Just as she had hurt Ben. She dropped her gaze and wanted to weep. But no. That was too easy. She searched her memory. Who was the old man who had been in the letter?

She closed her eyes, swayed. Held onto the table.

Her fingers stained more of the cloth. What was his name? It was no good, it was gone.

She paid, rose. Her legs were shaking. She gripped her bags, stood in the lobby. The receptionist stared at her. Cait asked, 'Do you know the uncle of a boy called Tom? He has a small mine.'

This time, the receptionist nodded, his expression softening. 'Everyone knows Old Roy Fellowes and everyone misses Tom. He was killed in Ireland. I hear Irish in your voice.' His expression hardened again.

She said, 'I baked him cakes.'

He told her where the small mine was located.

She walked through the town, though the receptionist warned against the heat of midday. What did heat matter when Ben hated her, when Tom was dead? What did anything matter when there was hurt to be healed, love to be fought for? She must fight, he must listen, he must understand. Des had said a soldier would. Oh Des.

She passed bungalows with verandas and paling fences. There were gardens, yellow-flowering jasmine, and pansies, sweet williams, all bedraggled in the heat, nearly gone, nearly dead, but there.

She and Ben could have a home, she could grow marigolds, she could sit on the veranda and sew. She could bake cakes. He liked cakes. Yes, she could make him cakes, just as she had made Tom cakes. She looked over at the houses again, and the gardens.

Tom. How could she have lied to them both? How could there be flowers in this heat? Because there were, because she had. Now she must make him understand. But could she? She must.

She was out of the town, walking along the track and with each footstep the heat pounded her more, the dust coated her more, the flies hovered more, settled, clung to her. Her bags were so heavy. The horizon shimmered, fragmented, disappeared. A camel train

178

passed, carrying wood. The Afghan leading the camels shook his head at her, and pointed back towards town.

'I must go on,' she murmured. 'I have to talk to him.' She looked ahead, dust spurted with each step. She coughed. Her throat was dry and sore, her eyes too. The horizon danced and leapt. She looked down. Just one more step. Just one more and with each step she cloaked herself in the darkness and coolness of an Irish night, and the images of Des, sharply etched, as he gave her the gift of her future.

Her bags were so heavy, her hands so sore, her body so drenched, her mouth so parched; the flies so noisy as they clamoured at her cut lip. It was nothing. Two miles were nothing, nothing, do you hear? But she couldn't hear, not over the flies, not over the pounding which wasn't the batteries any more, but the heat.

On she walked. A horse-drawn cart passed. 'Hop on, love, shouldn't be out in this.'

She shook her head. She must walk. It was her penance. Are you listening, Holy Mother? This is my penance. Make him love me. Make him listen.

She turned off the track at the boulder, just as the receptionist had said.

There were ruts gouged in the hard-baked track, just as there had been in Ireland. She stumbled, dropped her bags, clothes spilled from them, into the dust. She sank to her knees, thrusting them back, then forcing herself to stand. Just another step. And another. Her shoes cut into swollen feet.

Listen to me, Ben, she pleaded silently. Listen to me. It was hate for Mick that kept her going, and hate for herself.

But now she heard voices, and lifted her head. There were mine workings ahead; a windlass, a waste heap, smoke from a fire. She walked towards them. There were four tents, a bough shelter. There was an ore heap, there was a billy hanging on a tripod over a camp-fire, there were three men standing in the shade of a shelter, rolling cigarettes. Ben wasn't one of them.

There were two men by the entrance to the mine. One was old, the other was Ben. She dropped her bags. The men in the shelter looked up. Ben too. His face was the same but so tanned. She walked towards him, her hands outstretched.

'Ben,' she called in a voice parched and cracked. 'Ben.'

He still looked, but it was as though he couldn't accept what he saw. Then he turned away, pushing past the old man, striding out behind the rocks. 'Get her away,' he shouted. 'Get the bitch away.'

She ran on feet that were bleeding. 'Ben.' It was a hoarse scream.

The old man walked towards her, stopping her. She tried to pull away. 'I must talk to him.' A fly was in her mouth. She spat it out. He still held her, the stupid old man still held her and now Ben was gone again.

She struggled. 'No, I must talk to him. I can't go back without talking to him.'

The old man shook her. 'Quiet, will you. Just be quiet.' His face was close to her, his whiskers white against the leather of his skin, his brown eyes deep, his eyebrows bushy.

'I won't be quiet. I won't go until I talk to him.'

The other three men were approaching, confusion on their faces. 'What's up, Roy?' one drawled. 'Is this the two-timing bitch?'

Roy shouted at him. 'Never mind who she is, get some water.' Old Roy turned his head now, looking towards the heap of rocks. 'And you, Ben, get back here. I know how you feel, but get it sorted. It's only right.'

She looked at the old man, and then beyond

him to the rocks. 'How does he feel?' she whispered. 'How does he feel? Does he know I love him? Does he know I was coming to tell him? Does he know the truth?'

The old man looked closely at her. She said, 'I'm sorry about Tom. I liked him. I baked him cakes.' His eyes were neutral.

He replied, 'I know you did. He wrote to me about you. He died a soldier's death, that's all you can say.'

She nodded. 'Des was a soldier. He said Ben would understand, any soldier would, but he said I had to tell the truth. Mick got to him first. I don't know what he told him.' Her voice was a whisper. Old Roy was holding a tin cup to her lips. The water stung her blistered and damaged lips.

'Drink some more.'

She shook her head.

'Drink it,' he shouted. His hand at the back of her head now, forcing her down to the mug.

There was blood in the water from her lip. 'Did you fall?' he asked.

She shook her head. 'Mick hit me.'

Ben's voice sliced across from her right. 'He said you'd say that. He said you'd say anything because he'd dumped you for playing about with another man and you'd come to me, begging to be taken on. He told me we'd both been duped. You and your cronies laughed at me, and Tom. Did you know that, Roy? She laughed at Tom. Laughed when his face was shot away.' She swung round, stumbled, steadied. Old Roy put his hand beneath her elbow.

Ben's face was hard, his eyes were bitter and quite without love.

She said, 'Please, Ben. Please let me talk to you.'

Ben shrugged and said, as though he was standing near filth, 'Talk to me then. I'm intrigued to hear what Irish blarney you trip out this time.'

She looked around her at the three other men and Old Roy. 'Please, alone.'

'No.'

Old Roy stirred then, shouting to the men, 'Come on, have a smoke later. Let's shift this ore.' He moved past her to the mine, pulling his hat down over his eyes. The other men followed, looking back at her, shrugging, slouching. One spat, his eyes hard and cold as he looked at her. They kicked up dust as she had done.

Ben stood quite still. Heat was surging up from the earth and down from the sky. She told him exactly what had happened, every detail. There was silence when she finished, but only hate was in his eyes.

She pleaded, 'He tricked me. I love you. I love everything about you. I missed you. Des made it possible for me to come.' Flies were about her face again, and about his. He waved them from his eyes. His fingers were hardened, but still so long and fine.

'I love you, Ben,' she repeated. 'I used you, but I grew to love you and I won't go from Kalgoorlie. I'll stay until you understand, until you love me again.'

He pulled his hat down further, wiped his mouth with his hand. He didn't look at her, but over her head at the heat-seared sky.

'You'll stay then, until you're as old as Methuselah and I'm long gone.'

'I'll follow.'

'You can go to hell, Caithleen Healy, or back to your purser, or your Irish fool, and take your lying heart with you. There's not enough gold here to make me worth your while.'

She rocked on her heels. He strode past her, snatching up his water bottle, heading for the workings. She watched him go. 'Ben,' she called but the noise was faint.

She picked up her bags and began to walk away

from the mine, out along the rutted track, stumbling, staggering. She reached the main track, and now she counted each step and the sun was an orb in the sky and the dust a blanket through which she could hardly breathe. 'Twenty-nine, thirty, thirty-one.'

She heard a cart behind her. She mustn't stop counting. If she did she would fall, and never rise. 'Thirty-six, thirty-seven.'

The cart stopped. 'Get up here, missis.'

'Forty, forty-one.'

'Get up here, missis,' Old Roy shouted again.

'Forty-three, forty-four.'

The old man was out of the cart, and standing in her way.

'Forty-five, forty-six,' she gasped, struggling against the arms that held her, lifted her onto the seat. 'Forty-seven, forty-eight.'

He was walking round the horses. The cart tilted as he climbed up. The horses moved. Still she counted as he drove on.

At the camp Ben stood watching the dust billowing behind and around the cart. Let Old Roy take her back if he must. He wanted nothing more to do with her. 'You lying . . .' He couldn't continue. He looked down at his hand. He was clutching the snuffbox she had given him when the curlews had cried and the wind in the reeds had sung to them.

He opened it, touched the lock of hair he had taken from her drawer, then looked up again at the dust which now hid the cart. He turned and hurled the snuffbox out into the bush.

Chapter Nine

Cait found a room for the night near the station. Mr Vincenzi showed her the bathroom at the end of the corridor. 'Water, we have water now in Kalgoorlie.' His voice was heavily accented, his tone pointed, his shrug expressive. She brushed her dress with her hands. Dust lay thick on them, in her hair, around her eyes.

'I've been exploring,' she explained.

He nodded, his swarthy face lined, his hair greying at the temples. 'You are in time for a meal, if you hurry. But, please . . .' He gestured to the bathroom.

She nodded. She would wash the dust off her, but not the memory of his face and voice, never that.

In her room she dragged out her second dress, holding it to her face. Des, I'm sorry. Ben, I'm sorry. Dada . . .

In the dining-room starched serviettes and silverware were set on crisp white table-cloths. Several others were eating. All but two were Italians, and she could understand nothing they said, but none of them was the smart disapproving people of The Palace tea room.

Mr Vincenzi brought lamb stewed with tomatoes and garlic. There were china trinkets on the shelves in the room and pictures of Venice. So much water. She left the table, shaking her head at the fruit and custard. I must have air, she thought. She said, 'I must have a short walk.'

Mr Vincenzi nodded towards the blinds which were pulled down. 'The blinds, they almost keep out the dust. They also keep out the air.' He smiled gently. She nearly wept. Don't be gentle, she whispered in her mind.

In the garden a breeze was stirring, dust-laden. It was cooler, the night sky was clear and the stars white and brilliant. There was no moon. She thought of the moon over the river behind her father's farm. A mopoke sang on the dead tree by the paling fence. She thought of the owls flirting with the breeze. She walked to the station, then away again. She walked past parks, gardens and vegetable plots and bungalows with families in them; laughing, fighting, light streaming out onto the back porch.

She returned to the boarding-house. There were roses either side of the path. The steps to the veranda creaked beneath her weight. A man sat in a chair which was tipped back on two legs. His cigarette glowed in the dark. She paused. Ben?

It was Mr Vincenzi who said, 'It is quieter in Kalgoorlie now. Some of the miners have gone. The price of gold has gone down, the cost of mining has increased. Some mines are laying off workers, to re-organize.' He shrugged. 'How long will you be staying in Kalgoorlie?' His face was curious.

She stood, her hand on the screen door. 'I don't know, Mr Vincenzi.'

She slept fitfully. In the morning she was wakened by the whistles from the mine, the stamping of the batteries, the roar of the traffic, and the mutter of people passing. She counted her money. There was very little left. At breakfast Mr Vincenzi dropped the milk. The porridge was lumpy. The Australian men said, 'C'mon, can't you get it right? All the way from Perth to check our shares and we get spilt milk.'

The Italians around them stiffened, glared.

Mr Vincenzi opened his hands. 'Forgive. My wife is in Perth – a sick friend.'

After breakfast she walked to the Post Office. There was no letter. She walked to the outskirts, passing wood-framed houses. Some were run down. One or two were deserted. She returned to Mr Vincenzi. He was dragging a table-cloth from one of the tables. She paid him for her night. He gave her back some. 'For the porridge.'

She said, 'You need me. I'll work for you until your wife returns.'

He looked surprised. She took the table-cloth. He snatched it back, his hands veined and gnarled, his voice wary.

'I cannot do that. You cannot stay here with me, alone. That is what you want, is it not? It would not be proper. You will have to find work elsewhere.'

She took back the cloth, shaking her head. 'I have found a bed elsewhere, so there can be no objections.' She had someone to repay. At least she must do that.

All morning she washed, her arms bared to the elbows, and the humidity rose in the tin-roofed kitchen until she thought she would die, but she could not do that until she had earned the money to refund the ticket. And she could not die until he listened to her again, until he knew that she had loved him and still did. And she could not die because she was in too much pain from all this love which had nowhere to go.

At midday she took bread and cheese from the Coolgardie safe and made sandwiches for Mr Vincenzi. Then she made beds, dusted, polished and the beeswax brought back her mother and Ireland and the embroidered chair and the . . . No, she must not think of Ireland, not here, in this heat, where there were no green fields or mist-shrouded hills. Would her father write?

She ironed using the large, heavy coal iron and the two little black Mother Potts irons which were heated on the stove. There was no air, no breeze. She opened the shutters. Red dust blew in, over the table-cloths. She slammed them shut and rushed to the cloths which had been crisp white. Mr Vincenzi came in. He shouted, '*Mamma mia!* What have you done?'

She turned to him. 'I have washed and ironed, and your damn red dust came in and soiled them. I have done nothing, do you hear?' She was shouting, shaking the cloth at him. 'I have done nothing but everybody says I have. Everybody says I have. Everybody—'

He was shaking her. 'Now, now . . .' He took the table-cloth from her. 'It is only a little dust.' He was shaking the cloth now. 'There you see, only a little dust. There is nothing to worry you. Nothing.' He was smiling apologetically. 'I do not understand women. My wife, she is better for that.'

Cait took back the cloth, laughing now. 'No-one understands women, Mr Vincenzi, let alone women.'

He made a pot of tea. They sat on the veranda and drank it from white cups looking at the pruned roses and the cabbages growing at the end. Beyond them, beyond the back alleys and the rows of bungalows, there were the tailing heaps. 'Why are you here, Miss Healy?'

She set down the cup. 'Because I have to be,' she said, and nothing more, but she looked up and down the road for Ben. Please come. But why should he?

She cooked stew for the two male guests and they thanked her. 'We're back to Perth tomorrow, then London. When are you back to Ireland? Fled the mess the Micks are making, have you?'

'I've fled no-one.'

When the dishes were washed she slipped past

the Italians playing bocce, and those gathered in front of the boarding-house, milling and talking. They stepped back to let her through. '*Mamma mia,*' a young man breathed, touching her hair. She ignored him. Her hair was Ben's. It had been cropped for him, hadn't it? But even that had been a lie. I didn't know that though, did I, Des?

She carried her bags up the track to a deserted house. The door hung off. She pushed it open and slept on the floor that night, waking early, creeping into Mr Vincenzi's boarding-house at dawn, washing herself, then preparing breakfast, and putting her clothes in with the other washing.

Each day for the next week she did this, and slipped out mid-morning to the Post Office. Had her father written? Had Mick cabled Des? Each afternoon, as the heat soared, she drank tea with Mr Vincenzi and never stopped looking down the road for Ben. At the end of the week she counted her wages.

Soon she could go to the camp, soon she would see him again, put money into his hand, touch him. Every two weeks she would go, and perhaps he would see the love in every movement she made. He might believe in her again.

By the end of the second week there was a letter from her father.

She read it on the veranda of the boarding-house.

Caithleen,
You must never write again. You are dead to me, just as Des is dead. He was washed up on Mrs Murphy's bank, dying from six bullet holes in him. He kept saying, 'Tell Caithleen I'm sorry.' So I'm telling you, for what good it does.

You say you were forced to the decision. What does it matter how you arrived at it? You love – not just a Protestant, but a Tan. All these months you have lied. You met that Tan on my land. Have you any idea of the sin you have committed — loving a member of the force that killed your mother? Dead, you are, just so long as you love that scum.

That night, on the floor of the shack, she hugged herself against the chill of the night, and the echoes of her life, and the darkness of grief cloaked her. Even when dawn came, and the sun burst roaring hot onto the landscape and its heat throbbed in the tin-roofed kitchen, it was sweat rolling down her cheeks, that was all. Just sweat.

Mr Vincenzi poured her tea on the veranda and still she looked for Ben, and still he didn't come. On Friday she counted her money and walked out to the camp before dawn, before the worst of the heat.

She heard the murmur of voices as she approached, she saw the windlass and its sharp shadows. She saw the shapes of the tents, the shack. Smoke rose from the fire, a pot hung on the tripod, soot-coated. Two men were lugging tools to the mine. Ben stood smoking, looking out across the bush. She drank him in, so lean, so tall, so still. 'Ben,' she called.

The men stopped. Ben swung round, throwing his cigarette away. He shook his head. 'Get her away. Just get her away.'

Old Roy came from beneath the bough shelter. He looked from Cait to Ben.

'Get her away,' Ben repeated, turning on his heel.

She ran after him. Old Roy caught her. 'Don't do this to yourself,' he said.

Cait looked at Old Roy. 'Give him this. It's the first repayment of the fare. There will be more, until it, too, is finished.' She pushed her pay into his hand, though her eyes were on Ben.

The walk back was long. She refused Old Roy's cart ride, screaming at him to leave her alone, seeing Des's face, not the shimmering track, hearing his voice, not the battery stamp and the shift whistles, as she entered

189

the town, knowing that his death was as much of a waste as the hills of barren tailings.

That night Old Roy came to the boarding-house, but Mr Vincenzi shook his head. 'She lives elsewhere.'

Old Roy found the shack. She was sitting on a box on the rear veranda, looking out at the parched pepper trees. But they were far away, behind the images of Des and Ben and Mick and her father, and the sounds of thunder that was fighting, and lightning that was fire, and cropping that wasn't cropping, and love that wasn't love, and life that wasn't life.

Old Roy shook her. She turned. He handed her a leather pouch. 'He says, take this and go home. It's gold,' Old Roy said. 'It's for your passage home.'

She dropped it onto the veranda floor and rose, walking into the shack, shutting the door. 'This is my home,' she said.

Old Roy picked up the gold and looked through the door. He saw her bags in the corner of the room, and the rags on which she slept.

At the end of the week Mrs Vincenzi returned, large and bustling, but young, so much younger than her husband. She came into the kitchen and kissed Caithleen on each cheek, her own cheeks rosy, her smile wide, her large dark eyes full of laughter and life. 'Ah, it is so beautiful that you help my Mario.' The Italian in her voice was thick and warm and lyrical. 'It is so beautiful, and we wish above all else that we could keep you, but we cannot.' Now distress pushed the laughter from her eyes and voice.

Cait wiped the soapsuds from her arms, dried herself on her apron before wordlessly untying it. She hung it carefully on the peg, took the money Mrs Vincenzi held out to her, and walked from the kitchen.

Mrs Vincenzi came after her. 'No, please. Eat with us first.'

Cait smiled, though the effort wore her out. 'I'm not hungry. But thank you. I must find work.'

There was no work, though there was kindness in the refusals. She walked out to the camp as the day ended, seeing well by the light of the stars.

Ben looked up from the cards he was dealing to Bluey, Stan and Frank. How had he known she was there, standing between the two tents. The men fell silent, the smoke rising from their cigarettes. Bluey looked from Ben to her, then down at his cards. He tapped the old bush table. 'We playing or just messing about?' he growled.

Ben dragged his gaze away from her. The cards stuck to his fingers. He dropped them, cursed. Bluey laughed. Stan said, 'Try again.'

Ben picked them up. His hands were trembling. He dealt them, not watching her, but knowing she was approaching, just as he had always sensed when she was coming to the willow. Then it had been love, now it was hate.

He threw the cards down again, and yelled at her, 'Why haven't you gone? I sent you money. Get out of my life, you whore.'

She stopped halfway to the fire. The flames flickered. Her face was too thin. Too god-damn thin, but what did it matter to him? The men looked at him, then down at the ground. Bluey shuffled uneasily and half rose.

Ben pulled him back down. 'You stay. She's going. She soils this camp.' He looked round the camp. Not much but it could have been wonderful. He swallowed and felt the grief well up in him again, and the rage, and the humiliation, and the pain. Good God, the pain.

Cait walked with her head up, her face proud. She reached the fire and laid the leather pouch carefully on the flat stone on which the pots stood. She said nothing to anyone, neither did she look at them. Her hand was too thin, too damn thin.

She straightened, staggered. Ben wanted to catch her. Bluey stretched out his hand. She ignored them, recovered, turned, walked off into the darkness. They all watched her. No-one spoke. Then Old Roy came out from the awning of the bough shack.

He said, 'I thought you wouldn't buy her off. She's not a whore, whatever you may think, and I don't care for that language to a lady in my camp. My Tom liked her. Think carefully, Ben. Remember it as it was, not as you've been told.'

Ben looked at Bluey and the boys. They were stretching out tobacco on their cigarette papers, studying that, not him. Ben pushed up his shirtsleeves. 'She's a lying bitch, and she might just as well have pulled the trigger on Tom. She laughed, Roy. She used us both, and don't you forget it.'

Old Roy pushed back his hat, and looked up at the sky, then back at Ben. 'Sent your gold back, didn't she though? Think on that.'

Cait walked back to the town. She had been so close to him, so close that she had seen the sun-etched lines around his eyes, the shadow of his eyelashes on his cheeks, so close that she could feel the hate. Well, she was no stranger to hate. She had known it every day when she had been the Tan's whore. She had known it churn inside her on her mother's death.

She looked down at the dust she was kicking up. The moonlight glinted on his mother's watch on her wrist. She should have given it back. And she would, when she finally left. But she would only leave when the debt was repaid, and when she was sure that his hate would never change.

She walked the streets of Boulder and Kalgoorlie for the next two days. Still there was no work, and now she was dirty so, of course, there was less chance of work. She crept into the boarding-house and washed at the sink, and took food from the safe, and ate it like an animal in her shack, and knew that the days were passing, and there was no money to take and leave by the fire.

She walked into the darkness of the Catholic Church, remembrance tugging in air rich with incense. She ignored the confessional. No penance would be enough. She stood beneath Our Lady and wanted to rest her head against the warmth of a mother's body. She reached out and touched her. She was hard and cold.

She said prayers for Des and left. She walked to the street where women sold their bodies. She was a whore, wasn't she? She must do penance, mustn't she? His mother's watch glinted on her wrist. She removed it, and placed it in her pocket.

One house took her, if she would start immediately. 'We usually take Japanese girls, but there's quite a call for redheads. The Irish are a challenge, some men think. You're used to it, are you? We'll have no trouble?' the madam asked, her rouged cheeks creased into a false smile. Dark red curtains hung along one side of the room, worn sofas lined the other three walls overhung with mirrors. Girls lounged, staring at her or their nails.

Cait shook her head. 'No trouble,' she whispered.

'Wash your hair, leave it loose. Use the bathroom at the back.'

She washed it, she sluiced her body under the shower, and listened to the raucous laughter. She wore the clothes the madam had left. She was too thin, they hung on her. The madam came into the bathroom and undid the buttons of the bodice, showing the rise of her breasts.

'Now you're clean you can eat, and then go out front. A new face brings in new custom. Might be mines closing, but not our legs.' She laughed, nicotine and beer were on her breath, lipstick was smeared across her teeth. 'The more customers, the bigger your cut. Use the compartments along the front of the house.'

Cait nodded, her head was so light she felt it would float away. She wasn't fresh. She had a soiled body, a soiled soul, and Des had died for nothing.

Old Roy harnessed the pony and called to the men, 'Come on then, let's be having you. Ben and Stan will have drunk the bar dry.'

He climbed into the cart and the other two clambered in behind. 'We got a good lot of gold from the ore today then?' Bluey called.

Old Roy nodded. 'It's a good drive we're working at the moment, Bluey, and not before time. The mine's bottomed out earlier than I thought. But now we're set for a good run, I reckon.'

'That's why Ben's gone in early then, is it? Can't wait to get a schooner down him. These poms know how to celebrate.'

Old Roy nodded, flicking the reins. 'Happen it is.' The pony plodded down the track, past the place where Old Roy had seen Ben go back out after the snuffbox and search until he found it. That had been the morning after she'd brought back the gold. Since then he'd cycled into town every night and drunk carefully and steadily, throwing away his money on cards, on beer, only leaving when he had barely been able to articulate his hatred for Caithleen Healy. But articulate it he had, mumbling it as he staggered back into the camp.

Roy pulled his hat down lower. If that was hate, then it wasn't gold that the battery had stamped out of this week's load for them. It was love. Love which had been stamped on, and trampled, but by whom? Surely it wasn't Caithleen, for in her eyes was the same pain. Old Roy mused again over Mick O'Brian.

*　*　*

The town was alight with life and light, even though the mines were running down. Bluey dropped off the side as they entered. 'He's off to see his lady friend,' Frank laughed.

Old Roy nodded. 'He'll have worked his way round the chambermaids of Australia by the time he's thirty.'

Frank clambered over from the back onto the seat beside Old Roy, as the cart rolled past the houses. 'I'd like a garden,' Frank said.

'Weren't none before the pipeline. Just a desert it was, dust and difficulty, typhoid and—'

'Gold,' interrupted Frank and laughed.

'That too,' Old Roy said. Tom had wanted a garden too. Bloody fool – why hadn't he come on home after the war? Why fight for money? He shrugged. It was the toss of the coin, but damn it, he missed him. It was sad, too sad. He shifted on the seat. Typhoid. Talk about the toss of a coin. He'd thought it would be him that got it, not his Maureen and he ached for her, he always would, just as Ben ached for his Irish girl, though he was too damn stupid to see it.

They were passing the streets where the women worked. He shot a look at Frank, his eyebrows raised. Frank shook his head. 'I'm after my beer, tonight.'

They glanced down. The women were out in the heat of the night, men were too. There was a group near the top end but instead of the usual laughter Old Roy heard angry shouting. He pulled up the pony. 'Someone not getting his oats,' he laughed.

Cait felt their hands in her hair. They were all around her, shouting. She had stood here, smiling, pointing the men towards the house, but this one had wanted her. He had pressed his hand to her breast. He had dropped coins down her dress. He had gripped her buttocks, holding her body against his. She had felt

195

his hardness, just as she had felt the Tan's in her kitchen.

'Inside,' she gasped, pushing him from her. 'Go inside to one of the rooms. There are girls there.'

'But I want you, girlie,' he said. 'I want you pinned under me, I want your hair in my face.'

She'd looked at him, heard and smelt his breath, so rapid and harsh, and at last the lightness had gone from her head. At last she could see and feel again. And what she felt were his lips on her neck, her mouth, his hands inside her bodice, hard against her skin. She tasted his thrusting tongue.

She couldn't shake him off. Others had gathered.

She fought, but he was too strong, and now her rage soared at him, at Mick, at her father, at Ben, and finally at herself. She kicked and punched. She bit him, cursed him, and herself, and now he slapped her again and again, and the men bayed, and she fought on, and there was the madam's voice screaming above the rest, and hands reaching for her, tearing her clothes. 'Bloody cheat. Bloody whore.'

'Yes, I'm a cheat, but I'm not a whore,' she screamed again and again, beating them off her. 'I'm not a whore. Tell Ben I'm not a whore. Tell my dada.'

Old Roy heard the voice above the shouting. He stood, craning forward. He saw the red hair. He reached for the pickaxe handle beneath the front seat. 'It's Ben's girl. Go and get him.'

He was out and over the side, running towards Caithleen, shouting at the men, wading into them, pulling them back, calling them off by name.

Frank whipped at the pony, forcing it faster and faster round corners and into the main street, down a back street, pulling the pony up outside their bar. He leaped down, pushed his way through the men and grabbed Ben's shoulder, spilling his beer, panting,

'It's your girl. She's in trouble. Pack of men. Old Roy's there.'

Stan shoved his glass back on the bar, wiping his mouth with his hand. 'Come on then.'

Frank followed him, then turned. Ben shook his head. 'She can go to hell. She's not mine. She was never mine.'

Old Roy carried Caithleen towards the cart while Frank and Stan held the men back with the pickaxe handle and fists. He heaved her into the back. She felt the hardness beneath her, she saw the stars above but they were spinning. She felt the ground lurch just as Mick must have felt the ship lurch. But she had lied. What else would she do but lie?

'I lied to the madam. I said I could do it,' she whispered to Old Roy, grabbing at his jacket.

He prised her fingers from his coat, climbed into the driving seat, looking for Ben. He turned. Frank and Stan were joking with the men now, forcing tempers to cool. Soon they'd get them to the bar. He slapped the reins, turned the cart around and headed back to camp. She called, 'Why did Mick do it? Why did he lie to Ben about me? We grew up together, we scrumped apples, I rubbed milk on his sunburn. How could he lie when we were trying to help him?' Then she fell silent.

Mick didn't cable Des in Fremantle. Instead he sauntered into an Irish bar, and used the money he had stolen from the steward's back pocket to buy schooner after schooner of beer. He drank it down, hugging the look on the Tan's face, hugging the sound of Cait's scream. Call him all you like, he gloated, he's gone from you. You're as alone as I am, and serve you right for bringing me here. Serve you right for acting as my brother's lackey. He tried to hold the sound of her scream. It slipped from him. He tried to drag it back. No, it was gone.

He pushed his glass down the bar. 'Would you be putting another in there, Paddy.' His voice was slurred. He shook his head. He wanted to hear her pain again.

As Paddy pushed another beer up the bar an old man slapped Mick on the back then leaned in against the bar, saying, 'Well, and there's the sound of old Ireland, if ever I heard it. Name's Brennan, Con Brennan, father's from Killarney.'

Mick grinned. He could smell the beer on the man's breath, but then it would be on his own. He gulped his beer, trying to think. He wiped his mouth. No-one must know he'd fled, because he damn well hadn't. He nodded to himself, looked at the old man and said, 'Sure, it is, all the way from County Limerick to make me fortune in a new country. Outgrew the old, so I did. Wanted a fresh start, away from the girls who're chasing me.' He felt almost sober again and he'd only tripped on 'fresh'.

Con guffawed. 'Know the feeling, but you're the wrong colour cloth to make any fortunes out in this God-forsaken land.' Con's eyes were hard now. He slammed his hand onto the bar. 'Let's have another beer, by all the saints, Paddy, and in a glass. I don't like drinking from the bottle.'

Mick eyed the schooner that was thrust down the bar to the old man, then turned to Con. 'What d'you mean, the wrong colour cloth?'

Con peered into his beer, and hooked out a fly which twitched on his finger. He squashed it and flicked it onto the floor before saying, 'What I mean is, don't be getting your hopes up as I did. Don't be forgetting that the British settled this land to house convicts – and who was amongst those? Go on. Who?'

Mick shrugged, lifting his glass to his lips. Holy

Mother, it was hot, the flies were droning. He wanted to be away from here, back where the river ran. He felt Con's hand on his arm. 'Who?' the man shouted. 'Who?'

Mick shook himself free. 'Mind me beer, and how the hell should I know?' His lips felt numb. He'd be totally drunk soon. Good.

'The likes of us, that's who. Irish patriots.'

Paddy the barman threw his tea towel over his shoulder. 'And a damn sight more besides who pinched the landlord's sheep. Don't forget those, you old fool. And give us all a bit of peace.' He raised his eyebrows to Mick. 'Grabs all the blokes off the ships, but it keeps him out of our hair.'

Con gripped the bar. 'Oh yes, and what about them who came later, with stomachs shrunk from the famine? Free settlers they was, come to the promised land. Only it was promised to the Proddies, wasn't it?'

Mick looked at the old man now, his attention caught. 'What d'you mean?' He felt alert, sharp.

Con straightened his shoulders, tugging down his jacket. 'What I mean is that by then the British had set it up, with themselves in control. But sure, isn't that what they always do?' He eyed his glass. 'Got such a thirst on me, so I have, and nothing left in me pockets.' He slapped his trouser legs. Paddy shook his head and laughed.

Mick sighed and threw down some money. 'Just one then, Paddy.'

He turned back to the bar and ran his finger round the glass. So they were here too. But of course they were, it stood to reason when you thought about it. The flies were buzzing, sweat poured down his neck, soaking his shirt. God, it was too hot to think. Too hot to remember. What had the old man been saying?

Beside him Con sipped the beer. 'Anyways. With more and more of us coming they got scared and set up Orange Lodges, so we got together too and then – honest to God – had the brass neck to take our kids out of their school system and bring 'em up as Catholics. They thought next thing it'd be a popish rebellion – and us just a quarter the number of them.' He laughed, his lips gleamed with saliva. He nudged Mick, spilling his beer. 'It's been bothering them from the start.'

'Steady.'

The old man took no notice, just continued. 'So, you just look around you as you storm this "new land", you poor sap. The Establishment is A-n-g-l-i-c-a-n.' He spelt it out. 'And don't worry, it's got its Loyalty Leagues to sort us out if we get out of hand like you've done in Ireland. And I've still got a thirst on me, so I have, and this beer's not lasted more'n a tinker's wink.'

Mick gripped his arm. 'What d'you mean – Loyalty Leagues?' Visions of the Black and Tans flashed before his eyes.

Con put his finger to his nose. 'Old soldiers who didn't like our stand against darned conscription in the war. Been hollering ever since how they're going to put any traitorous Catholics in their place if they get out of line, just like them Tans were after putting you in your place.'

Mick shook the old man. 'But they bloody didn't, did they? We showed them.' He shook the old man again and shouted, 'We showed them. If you'd been there you'd have seen. But no, you're out here, dunning drinks off anyone you can dribble all over.' He staggered, nearly fell. The old man stepped back. Mick followed. 'Come back here and say they put us in our place again. Come back and say that to a fighter who was there.'

Paddy dashed round the bar, grabbing them both by the elbow. 'Enough of that. Get out into the sun and take your mouths with you. Go on, out of it and have a look round at all the Australians out there, who've left this all behind.' He shoved them towards the door.

Mick stumbled into the harsh sunlight. God, it was too bright. He grabbed the wall, his head was swimming. 'We showed them,' he shouted. 'We'll go on showing them – we'll smash Collins.' He stopped, looked around. Where was this damn hot place? Oh God, what was he going to do?

He stayed in Fremantle for a month and drank steadily until his money was almost gone, but not at the Irish bar. He didn't want to talk to anyone, he didn't want to think, he just wanted the beer, the thickening head which blurred the harsh sunlight and the memory of soft mists, and wiped out stupid old men who thought the Tans had put them in their place.

It was in a pub that he heard of the saw mills in the south-west of the state. 'There's a lot of rain down there in winter,' the man said. 'Bit like your neck of the woods, if your brogue is anything to go by, or you could go to the gold-mines, but they're laying off men all the time.'

Mick's journey from Fremantle to Manjimup passed in a blur. He travelled by rail, absorbing the lurch of the train, waking with a jolt, hearing Cait's anguished calls for Ben, wanting a drink. His hands trembled as he scoured his newspaper for news of the Irish Civil War. God, he needed a drink. He swallowed. His mouth tasted foul.

He read that fighting was continuing. Damn you, Des. You were jealous of me. All along that was it. I should have been your second in command. You wouldn't allow it. So I struck out against you. You couldn't stand that.

He stared out at the vastness of the countryside and at the huge tracts of forests and felt the loneliness sweep over him. Was Niall as lonely in America?

Damn you, Cait. Damn you. Tossing me over for a Tan. Damn you.

He took a bullock cart from the siding and couldn't believe it when he came across the high plateau and entered the karri forest. He reached out and tried to touch the huge pink-and-ivory trunks. He looked up at the towering crowns and then sat back in the silence, breathing in the fragrance of the karri wattle. It was so different and there was no-one to share it with. Damn you all.

He joined the forest camp where the tree-fellers lived. He cooked his meal on the fire. He tried to sleep, wrapped up in his blanket, and longed for the farm and for his daddy, and for life as it had been and the glory that should have been his.

He touched his scar as dawn broke, and nurtured his hatred as he trekked into the forest with the others who knew nothing of the fighting, who knew nothing of the man he had been, and the man he could have been, if Des had not taken it all from him.

'You know nothing,' he'd murmured as the foreman cursed him for not putting his weight behind the cross-saw. 'But one day you'll know who you were yelling at. One day when I've made my mark, and paid them all back.'

Chapter Ten

Ben squatted by the camp-fire rolling his cigarette. He licked the paper, looking over at the tent. How dare Old Roy bring her back here? How bloody dare he? Thirty-six hours she'd been in there.

He looked at Stan and Bluey hammering in saplings to the left of the camp. A shower for her, for the bitch. It was crazy. Next to him, Frank picked up the billy. 'Tea up,' he called.

Old Roy came out of the tent. 'In a minute, you get on.' He ducked back inside.

Frank said, 'She was in a bad way.'

Ben stood, lit his cigarette. 'Serve her right,' he muttered, then walked to the bark shack, kicking at the ground. He heard the men tacking hessian walls to the shower. He heard the tent flap lift. Old Roy coughed. There was the sound of water splashing. Ben turned.

Old Roy was bending over, pouring water on his head.

'Why don't you use the shower, or is it for her exclusive use?' Ben's voice was hard. 'And when's she going?'

Old Roy straightened and smoothed his hair. Water dripped down his back. 'I'll have that tea now, Frank,' he said.

Frank poured it and dished up porridge. Old Roy called to Ben, 'Come and eat.'

'I'm not hungry.'

'Suit yourself.' Old Roy sat on the stool he'd made out of a kerosene box. Ben stalked over to the windlass and waited. Damn her, damn Roy, damn them all. He yelled, 'Will someone come and let me down the damn mine, or are you all too busy nursemaiding?'

Bluey came shambling across. 'Keep your shirt on.'

'Shut your mouth,' Ben snarled, stalking across to the mine shaft, clutching the pickaxe to him, and hanging on to the wire as Bluey lowered him down the shaft.

It was cold and dark. He lit the lamp on his helmet and crouched down, working his way along the drive, the dust catching in his throat. He shoved the trolley before him. The pickaxe clanged as the trolley lurched over a stone. He wouldn't think of her. He'd think of the ore he'd be pitching into, the gold he'd be heaving out, the dust he'd be swallowing, just as he'd swallowed the dust when he'd levered out the ore which had paid for her ticket.

He reached the face and stripped off his shirt, throwing it over the side of the trolley. He raised the pick and brought it down, again and again, but all he could see was her face, and hear her voice. He felt his muscles strain. He brought the pick down on an outcrop, his joints jarred. He dropped the pickaxe and took up the shovel, hurling the ore into the trolley.

What the hell was she doing down that street? He rubbed his fingers over the ore, examining it in the light from his lamp, tasting the dust, but seeing only Caithleen as she had emerged from the darkness with his money pouch, her head erect, her face so thin and pale. He cursed and picked up the pickaxe again.

As he brought it down he wondered how the safe world of Chester could disappear so thoroughly, how the pre-war world could evaporate. How he could be down a mine. How he'd thought Australia would bring a new life.

He wrenched the pickaxe, a large piece of ore dislodged. Dust showered. He waited, scarcely breathing, watching the roof, the pit-props. They creaked, settled. He brought the pickaxe down again, but let it stick, there, in the ore, as a sense of utter loneliness swept over him, and grief for the love he thought he had found, and the agony it had brought.

Cait moved, groaned. She smelt eucalyptus. The tent flap lifted. 'It's all right, darlin'. Here's a drink.'

'Dada,' she whispered. Then she remembered. She opened her eyes. It was Old Roy. It was daylight. This was a tent. It was hot, so hot. Old Roy put his arm behind her, lifted her up. 'Here, drink this.' The mug hurt her lips. She pulled away. 'Drink it.' His voice was stern. She drank, lay down, closed her eyes.

'I must go,' she murmured. 'You've been so kind. I remember now.'

He was bathing her face. The water felt cool. He'd bathed her face before, she remembered now. She opened her eyes again. 'You've never left me, have you?'

He shook his head. 'You needed me.'

She looked away from him. 'I was a fool.'

Old Roy nodded. 'Yep, you could say that.'

She struggled to rise. He pushed her down. 'You ain't going no place, till you're a mite better.'

She struggled to rise again, saying, 'I must. I need to earn money. No, not that way again. But I have to repay him.'

'He'll wait, I guess,' Old Roy said, pushing her back again. 'You breathe in the scent from them leaves. They'll help you get well.' She was lying on a bed of eucalyptus leaves. Her mother had rubbed her chest with something that smelt the same. No, she mustn't think of her mother. She was drifting, sleeping. Old Roy moved. She gripped his hand. 'Don't go, don't leave me alone.'

She slept, woke, slept. She heard the sound of hammering. Heard Ben's voice: 'Lower me again, Bluey.'

Heard Bluey's reply: 'Ain't you had enough?'

'No, I need to rebuild my savings. The ones I used on her.'

She heard Bluey say, 'Give it a rest, mate. She's doing her best.'

'In a whore-house?'

'She never got that far, you know that well enough, so shut your gob.'

She slept again and all the time Old Roy stayed. When the sun was at its height he opened the flap and she heard the sounds of the camp more clearly and tasted the dust brought in by the breeze.

He gave her more water, then Frank brought tea, stooping in the opening, handing the mug to Old Roy, glancing at her, flushing, looking away. 'Have you told her about the shower then, Roy?'

Roy told her and she turned her face to the canvas. 'You mustn't be kind,' she whispered.

Old Roy nodded to Frank, who withdrew.

'We killed your Tom,' she murmured when Frank had gone. Still she looked at the canvas. 'I loved that boy. I made him cakes, then he died. That's when I knew I loved Ben. I didn't love him until then. I didn't know that he was my whole life.'

She turned and looked at him now. 'I made your Tom cakes. He had such a smile on him, but we blew his face away.'

Old Roy bathed her face. The bruises and cuts were sore. 'You didn't. The fighting did. You did your job too but I don't know why. That's what I don't understand, missy. Why use him like that at all?'

She just lay there, and finally she slept until the heat of the day was past. Then she woke and gripped Old Roy's hand. 'I did it because I hated the Tans. They killed my mother. I did it because of that, and for the cause.' She told him about it all, just as she had told her father and when she had finished she tried to rise again. He pushed her down.

'But I must go,' she insisted. 'I must go now. I don't want to see disgust in your face too.' Her head swam, her cuts and bruises throbbed, her ribs ached, her legs too. Old Roy pushed her down again.

'You listen. There's jobs to be done here. We needs a cook. I'll teach you how to make damper. You can cook for us, you can wash. You can go to Bluey's mates' camp and wash for them. Take money for that. We've a spare tent. You can bed down in there.'

He left, dropping the tent flap. She heard him at the fire, she heard the pony whinny in the distance and a goat bleat. The flap lifted. It was Old Roy with a tin dish. 'Here's porridge. You should be able to stomach it, even if Bluey did cook it.' He smiled, squatting down, dipping the spoon into the porridge and holding it out to her mouth. 'Come on, eat. We need you strong.'

She ate and the porridge was lumpy and the goat's milk strong and she was tired again. Old Roy pushed her down, but she caught at his hand. 'Why are you doing this?'

'Because I believe you, and because it's a mess, and if a good man's died, and a fool of a brother's done damage, it's time to call it quits. And love is too good to throw down the dunny.'

'But Ben. He hates me.'

'That Ben doesn't know what he wants. He threw your snuffbox away then went right out and found it again. Don't you be so quick to give up on what that Des gave you, you hear me. You owe a soldier like him more than that.'

*　*　*

The men sat round the camp-fire that night and took a vote on whether Caithleen should stay. Only Ben voted against, hurling his mug into the sand, storming from the fire when the motion was carried. Frank raised his eyebrows at Roy. 'I'll talk to him,' Roy said.

Ben was by the pony, leaning against him, feeling his warmth.

'A woman's warmer, softer,' Old Roy said as he came up behind.

'I want her to go.'

Old Roy said, 'Well, it's a sad fact that we can't all have what we want, only what we need.'

Ben glared at him. 'What do you mean – need? I don't need her.'

Old Roy stopped, picked up a pebble, looked at it in the moonlight. 'Always think it just might be a nugget.' He threw it up into the air again and again. 'We need her though. We're sick of Frank and Bluey's cooking. We're sick of scrubbing our clothes on a Sunday when we could be fossicking and turning up our fortunes. She'd do it for nothing.'

Ben burst out, 'She's using you, like she used me.'

Old Roy tossed the pebble far out into the bush. The goat bleated, the wind rustled the salt bushes. 'Seems to me she's the one who got used and now she's paying for everyone's sins. Seems to me she's more than a strain of truth in her. Seems to me you should have come to help us fight them men off. Seems to me you're afraid of facing up to what you feel for her, in case you gets hurt again.'

Ben faced Old Roy. 'What I feel for her is a bitter hate.'

Old Roy put his hands in his pockets. 'If you say so,' he said, returning to the camp, boiling up the billy, wondering if Ben would still be at the camp in the morning, because if he truly hated Caithleen, he would be gone and there would be an end to it.

Cait rose at dawn. She was stiff and sore as she set up the cooking fire and carried water from the barrel in an old kerosene tin, boiling the billy on the iron tripod and cooking the porridge on two old sleepers on the second fire. She stirred it. She milked the goat and hobbled it in a new area. The men were stirring, groaning, coughing. The heat was rising as she returned to camp. Ben was not there. She mixed the milk in with the porridge, a terrible emptiness yawning.

The men were pulling forward the kerosene chairs, smoothing their hair, fumbling with their cigarettes. 'Just light them,' Old Roy grumbled as he walked out from the bough shade. 'She's not a witch, or your grandmother. She'll not turn you into stone if you act natural.'

'Don't be too sure of that.' It was Ben's voice. He emerged from behind the compressor. Cait gripped the ladle. Roy smiled to himself. So Ben was still here.

She dished up the porridge. The men ate, smiled, came back for more. Ben's fingers around his bowl were as thin and fine as they had always been. He was still here, still here. She looked up at Old Roy and matched his smile.

Old Roy stayed with her in the camp as the men headed for the mine. He showed her the shelves beneath the bough shade, the washing-up dish with wire handles, the boiler for the clothes, the washing troughs.

'All made from kerosene tins,' he explained.

He showed her how to make damper, frowning with concentration as he mixed the flour and water. 'Just a pinch of that baking powder, and a bit of salt, and not too many flies.'

She added them. 'Yep, that's good,' he said. 'Put it in the camp oven.'

She dropped the camp oven into the hole of ashes and coals. He squatted back on his heels and pushed up his hat. 'Saved me life a few times in the early days, damper did. When times were hard I used to divide it into sections, be stern with meself, only take a bit at a time.' He nodded towards the mine. 'You'd do well to think on that. Take it slow, there's scars that've got to heal.'

She worked all morning in spite of the heat, boiling the clothes over the fire. She rubbed them in the trough, hanging them on the bough shade to dry, cursing the red dust, dampening the floor of the tent to keep the dust down, making bread in another oven.

She kept the billy on to boil, then pinned up her skirt because the hem kept catching alight in the fire. She wrapped a bush turkey in brown paper and wet hessian. Old Roy called, 'Put the vegetables and pumpkin in the hessian with it.'

She unwrapped it and started again, then put it in another kerosene tin, and buried it in the ashes.

'Leave you to it now,' Roy said, and strolled across to the ore platform, checking the grades in the shade that had been rigged.

She stretched, checked that the men were busy and walked to the shower. She unpinned her hair, stripped, tipped water into the pierced kerosene tin, and hauled it up quickly by rope, opening her mouth beneath the water, feeling its coolness, doing it again and again, until her body, her hair and her spirit were cleansed.

At the end of the day Old Roy pushed wishbone-shaped poles into the ground of her tent, and strung up hessian between them. 'Better than leaves.'

Bluey and Frank went off into the bush with their guns. She heard shots and stiffened. She saw Ben do the same. He glanced at her. Their eyes held. He turned from her. The men came back with five rabbits slung over their shoulders, laughing, nudging one another, showing her. Old Roy said, 'I'll skin them for you.'

She shook her head. 'I'll do it. I'm a farmer's daughter, remember.'

But she was no longer anyone's daughter and her voice trailed into a whisper.

She unwrapped the turkey. As the steam and the smell rose, the men groaned. 'Oh Bluey, why did we put up with your messes for so long when we could have had food that smelt like this?'

She said, 'Sure, but Old Roy showed me, and a fine cook he is.'

'What a smooth Irish tongue you have,' Ben said, through clenched teeth. 'Kissed the Blarney stone, as well as all your men. Shame you don't know the difference between truth and—'

Frank interrupted. 'Put some turkey in your gob and give it something better to do, Pom.'

She dished up in the silence that fell, saying, as she handed a dish to Frank, 'He's right. I used him. I lied. He's right. But he's wrong about the men.'

The men looked not at her but at the fire and, as darkness fell, she left the fireside and lit the hurricane lamp beneath the bough canopy. She sat quite still while the dingoes prowled and howled.

The next day Frank showed her how to fossick, dollying the dirt, crushing it in the bowl. 'It's like a pestle and mortar,' she said.

Frank nodded. 'Now put some water over the dirt.'

She did so, and then watched as he swirled the water and dirt over the edge of the pan again and again until there was just a tail of gold in the bottom. 'You try.' He handed her the pan. She tried. He steadied her, placing his hands on hers. She felt his warmth, his youth, and it reminded her that she was still young.

She heard his breathing and his laughter. Had he ever scrumped apples? Had he a home? Had he walked from his brother and destroyed lives as Mick had done? Where was Mick? She looked up at Old Roy in despair, and instead saw Ben, walking away, his shoulders rigid.

He walked out into the bush, hearing the mopoke, and Frank's laughter, seeing her hands on the bowl, her hair catching on Frank's shirt, glistening as his mother's red gold watch had done. When he returned he looked at Cait's wrist. Where was the watch? She'd sold it, of course, and the bitterness rose again.

That night Bluey's mates, Chris and Mark, came. They tipped their hats at Cait. Old Roy gestured towards the cart which was backed up by the heap of ore they'd taken from the mine. 'You meet us at the track in the morning then. Ben and Frank will be doing the run. But you'll have some tucker now.' He raised his eyebrows at Cait. 'There's enough stew, isn't there?'

She smiled. He was trying to get her additional work. 'Enough? There's plenty.'

The older man, Chris, ate quickly, then mopped up the gravy with the bread she had baked, wagging it at her. 'Will you have time to come to us?' His voice was cultured, like Ben's. She grinned, they arranged rates.

As the evening wore on other men came, carrying kerosene tins full of ore, or only half full, or barely full at all. Old Roy nodded towards the heap. 'Put it down.' They didn't eat with them but drank tea. Each can was named. 'Same terms as usual,' Roy said, nodding towards the ore. 'Still happy with the assayer weighing up?'

The men nodded, drank tea, then left.

Cait asked, 'Why do they bring so little?'

Frank, Bluey and Stan laughed, even Ben smiled. Old Roy shrugged. 'It's all they can carry.'

'Carry?'

Stan blurted out. 'They work for the big mines. It's – what shall we say? – the perks of the job. Everyone does it. It makes up their pay. Take it out in the crib tins, down their boots, under their hats, in the dunny tin. You name it, it's been done. They need it crushed though, so we put it in with ours. Weigh it first, weigh our ore, then weigh the gold we get out of it all, then divi it up. You should see that trans-continental train, snorting across the Nullarbor with all the miners who've got rich quick. Sometimes they can bring out raw gold, you know, nuggets. The perks are the reason why there's no real trouble in Kalgoorlie – everyone's satisfied.'

Ben said, 'I'd like to go East one day.' His voice was soft, thoughtful. 'Maybe I should get a job in one of those mines.' He slapped his legs. 'Get a fair few nuggets down these.'

The men laughed, and so did Cait. Old Roy said, 'You'll get as much from this mine, and with a bit of fossicking we should do more than all right. Cait's given us more time for that.'

Ben's face closed again. But as she slept last night, she hugged the sound of his laughter to her.

In the morning she helped to load the cart with ore. 'We stamp it at Ron's place. He bought up an old battery when he bought his mine. He was a tributor but got sick of the royalties the mine charged for processing the ore.'

'Tributor?' she panted, shovelling the ore.

Frank called, 'Companies are closing their mines then leasing drives to miners, but they charge for it, and it's dangerous because they're not maintained properly.'

Old Roy chipped in, not altering his shovelling rhythm at all. 'Needn't have shut the mines, if they'd modernized.'

'Oh yeah, oh yeah,' the men groaned in unison, as they shovelled.

Cait asked, 'So do you have to pay this Ron?'

Old Roy grunted. 'Don't pay nobody nothing if I can help it. I part own it, take a share of everyone else's crushing, along with Ron and two others. I believe in making my money work for me, making it grow.'

She rested a minute. 'So Frank, Stan, Bluey and Ben have that part share too, in with their share of the mine?'

Old Roy looked at her, taking off his hat, wiping his brow. 'Nope, but maybe they should. Just hadn't got around to thinking about that.'

The men were resting too now. They looked at one another, grinning. All except for Ben, who pulled his hat farther down, and resumed shovelling.

Old Roy told her as he eased his back, 'We allow an ounce of gold for expenses, everything above that is profit, split between us. Hey, hang on, Ben.' He hurried to the heap of ore. 'That looks like mullock, no point carting non-paying dirt. We got to check it more carefully.'

She shovelled the ore into the cart as Old Roy checked it. She was slow, and the sweat ran down her back, and blisters formed, and she knew that Ben's impatient eyes were on her. She tried to hurry but could not. The sun was hot, her throat was dry, her blisters burst, each shovelful was agony. Old Roy shouted across, 'Go and take a breather.'

She shook her head. 'No, I'm used to hard work.'

She shovelled, heaved, the dust caught in her throat. Shovel, heave, forget the pain. Shovel, heave, and now it was Ben's hands on her shovel, wrenching it from her. 'For Christ's sake, go and put the billy on, you're holding us up.'

She staggered, caught at the tailboard. Her hair was

in her eyes, she brushed it aside. 'And put something on those hands,' Ben shouted.

She looked down, they were bleeding. She looked at him, he was shovelling the ore, looking at the cart, not at her. Did he care?

Ben and Frank carted the load, meeting up with two more carts on the track. Ben pulled his hat down over his eyes, shading them from the glare, flicking the reins, glad to be away from the camp, away from her. He turned. Good, he couldn't even see the camp and he tried to push away the image of her wild red hair, her skirt pinned up, her golden legs, her small hands so blistered and sore, her straining body heaving at the ore.

For God's sake, she was too weak. It was too much for her, her bruises were too new. He looked up at the sky. No, her eyes were not the colour of this heat-hazed sky, they were the colour of that rain-drenched God-forsaken country where she had betrayed him. He must remember that.

The cart journey was slow, with the pony straining under the weight of the tons in the back. Ben and Frank travelled and breathed their own dust. They drank tea she had made. She'd be washing his clothes now. In Ireland, as they'd lain amongst the uncut hay, he'd dreamed that one day she'd wash and bake while he worked. That they'd love while the Australian sun smiled down on them. That she'd embroider footstools, that her firm soft breast would feed his children.

God damn her. All that was over. She'd spoilt it.

Frank talked of the races and of the two-up game. Ben dredged himself from thoughts of what might have been.

They arrived and all day, in the heat which seemed greater than it had ever been, they stood while the noise pounded around them. They rubbed the plates at regular intervals, smearing the right quantities of quicksilver over them, glad of the cessation of sound. It should be Tom doing this with him. It was her country that had killed him. He must remember that, it helped to keep the anger burning.

After the last stone had been crushed, the cleaning up began. They would camp beside the battery tonight, away from her. Away from the sound of her turning in the night, away from the sound of the shower water sluicing her body, her beautiful body, away from her singing as she washed and baked, her golden arms flour-powdered, her lips glistening.

The amalgam was retrieved. Ron told them to get off and take it easy in their camp. 'No point in you putting in more hours than necessary.'

Frank and Ben shook their heads. 'Can't – this is the best bit of the week.'

They relished the excitement as the amalgam was squeezed, retorted and at last smelted. They felt their mouths watering as they waited and waited.

'Gold is the most beautiful sight in the world,' Frank muttered as they watched it being poured into its mould.

Ben slapped him on the shoulder, pushing the image of Cait's golden skin from him. 'Yes,' he agreed. 'It most certainly is.'

His voice was so fierce that Frank laughed. 'Strewth, is this a case of love, or what?'

By eleven at night Ron was weighing the gold bar in his office, picking it up as though it were a baby, dropping it gently on the scales. He dropped one weight, then another. 'Let's check against the ore weight. You've made a note of the small buckets, haven't you? All right, that's forty ounces of gold to fourteen tons of ore, lads. So you just tell Old Roy he's still the luckiest devil. All the big ones are clawing back but he just keeps driving on.'

Ben and Frank sat round the camp-fire with the

other cart drivers and loaders. They ate the eggs
they had fried, and the bread and cheese, and neither
looked at the other, because they were missing a stew
back at camp, they were missing her voice singing
in the background. 'Bloody peaceful,' grunted Ben,
heading for his tent, lying awake for too long.

Cait headed off to Chris's and Mark's camp before
the cart returned. She left rabbit stew cooking in the
camp oven, and brownies to eat at tea-break, and
scones.

'All this, for us?' Old Roy had said, smiling.

'Of course, who else?' she'd retorted. They both
knew.

The track seemed long, and willy-willies danced in
the distance. She didn't stop to watch the whirls
of sand, she was already used to them. It was as though
she had never lived anywhere else. It was as though
Ireland had never been. Almost.

The camp was at least half a mile away. When
she arrived she found two tents, two bough shades,
a windlass and compressor. The men were working,
though Chris broke off to come to her, pointing out
the clothes and the stores. She worked all morning,
scrubbing, boiling, drying, cooking.

She cleaned the Coolgardie safe and put fresh
water in the trough. 'You must keep it damp,' she
told them at lunch. 'You must, or everything will be
rotten or rancid. You'll be ill.'

They nodded, chewing on the meat and potatoes.

'You must keep the tents clean too. No old mugs
left lying about, no old plates of food. By St Teresa,
is it not too much to ask that you wash up a few
old mugs?' She flapped at the flies. 'You might
just as well send them out an invitation – ". . . and
bring your dysentery with you". You'll be ill. And you
need to change these clothes more often.'
She pointed to the trousers and shirts. 'Holy Mother,

they almost walked to me, begging for the boiler.'

The men nodded, looked at one another, then laughed. Chris said, 'Just think how Old Roy will suffer when he gets his cough this year, or if it doesn't come back on its own, he'll bring it back for the pleasure of being tongue-lashed by an Irish colleen.'

She flushed. 'Am I so very Irish?'

Chris leaned back, crossed his legs. 'When I was teaching, way back in time, a million years ago, in Oxford, I had an Irish student. It was as though the Irish mist floated into the room whenever she spoke. My dear, you clear this sun away, you conjure up agreeable green meadows, deep lakes and gentle mountains.'

She said, 'There's little agreeable about Ireland at this minute. It's writhing in its own pain and dragging us all in with it.'

Chris said, 'But not you any more. You escaped.'

She nodded. Yes, she'd escaped and she had just decided she wanted to wipe every mark of it from her, then the loss of it all would die.

She cooked for them in the afternoon, leaving a hotpot in the ashes, leaving brownies in a tin, scrubbing out all the kerosene tins, damping all the floors in the tents, turfing out the old eucalyptus leaves, and replacing them with new.

She boiled the billy and added tea, letting it settle. She called to the men.

Chris waved. 'Down in a tic, I'm just about to wind Mark up the shaft.'

She looked up at the sun. Four o'clock. She must go. Chris was hauling on the windlass, straining on the handle, helping Mark out of the shaft. They dusted themselves off then ambled across. She nodded towards the kerosene tin full of water. 'It's a grand idea to wash off dirt and not be eating it.'

They grimaced and sluiced themselves. Only then

did she pour tea, adding dried milk. 'You should have a goat,' she said, drinking her tea.

Chris and Mark exchanged looks and laughed again. 'We should have found you before Old Roy did. We're partial to being nagged out of existence, especially by an Irish brogue.'

Cait shook her head firmly. 'I'm not nagging, I'm advising.'

Her mother had said that. She shut her mind, and hugged her mug in her hands, sipping the tea, telling them to dig out the oven, and wash it when they'd finished.

'Or we'll be ill,' they echoed.

She laughed, and poured boiling water into the washing-up tin, sluicing her mug, tucking up the strands of hair which had fallen. Chris dug into his pocket and came out with her wages, handing them over to her. She gave him a shilling back.

He looked at it, then her. 'But we agreed a rate.'

'I know, but you're a teacher. Will you give me a shilling's worth of elocution? I want to talk like you. I don't want to bring Irish mists into every room I enter. That can't be me any more.'

There was a silence. Mark washed the mugs, then walked back to the mine. Chris tossed the shilling into the air, caught it, looked at it. 'Heads, though even if it had been tails I wouldn't do it. Why change yourself, Caithleen Healy?'

He tossed the coin at her. She threw it back.

'Because I want to. Because Ireland has rejected me. Because that part of my life is over. Because I want to talk like you.' Because you talk like Ben, she also thought, but wouldn't say. And because I don't want to come to him as the woman who betrayed him. I want to be what he wants.

All that evening she sat in her tent while the men murmured by the fire, drinking to the gold percentage. She read by the flickering candle light the list of words Chris had written down. 'Zavier, not Xavier. S'nt not Saint.' She used her lips, tongue and teeth. She read from *Wuthering Heights* which Des had packed for her, trying to imagine her voice as Chris had insisted.

Again and again she read the same paragraph, until it sounded different, less Irish Catholic, more British Protestant, because that was what Ben was, and therefore that was what she must be.

She heard Old Roy scratching on the tent flap. He called, 'What's that you're doing?'

'Just reading.'

'Is it a story? I like stories. Never had time to learn to read. Come on out, I want to hear it. The boys read me Tom's letters.'

She carried the book to the fire. The others were leaving for town. 'Celebrating,' Old Roy said, rolling a cigarette, settling himself into the chair, gazing into the embers.

Disappointment shafted.

Old Roy said, 'C'mon, get on with it.'

She began to read from *Wuthering Heights*, turning page after page until her eyelids drooped. Old Roy then rubbed mutton fat on her blistered hands and heels, and as he did so he said, 'You don't sound the same.'

She said, 'I'm glad. Chris is teaching me to speak as he and Ben do.'

Old Roy tied the greased paper back onto the fat and handed it to her, his face grim, though he said nothing.

She put the fat into the Coolgardie, washed and lay in her tent, and only then did she call to him. 'And my name is K-A-T-E now, not Caithleen.'

He grunted.

She called, 'You see, I'm in Australia where there's peace and hope. I want to be a new person.'

He merely grunted again.

All the next week, and the next, she worked and cooked and, as October rolled on, the thermometer climbed. 'Holy Mother, can it get any hotter?' she gasped to Chris, who made her say it properly.

She did: 'Heavens, it can't get any hotter.'

'Better.'

Back at Old Roy's camp she took turns on the windlass, winding the gear, hauling up ore, tipping it onto the heap. He showed her how to sort the mullock from the ore. In the evenings she fossicked with him and Frank and laughed when Frank lifted her in the air, and whirled her round when she found a nugget.

After that she fossicked every spare moment, and now she knew why those she passed on the track or the back alleys when she had completed her shopping kept their eyes on the ground. It was in case they missed a nugget.

Every Friday she left her pile of coins, her tails of gold dust, her tiny nuggets, just inside Ben's tent in the morning. Every Friday he nodded at her, his eyes bleak and Old Roy saw the disappointment in every movement she made until he could stand it no longer and told Maureen so, when he visited her grave, and gazed at Kalgoorlie, which had changed so much in the twenty years since her death.

'You'd not know it, pet. Gardens, flowers, not so much dust now there's water. But enough, still enough.' Then he fell silent. Years without love were bleak when there was no alternative. When there was an alternative it was madness.

On the last Friday in October Old Roy sent Stan to town, and he and Frank carted the ore. Cait watched as Ben argued with him, shouting at last, 'No, let me go. Frank can stay and work the mine with that woman.'

Old Roy climbed on the cart. 'What are you

afraid of? She's good and strong, she can winch up your ore for you – or is it something more than that?'

Ben stormed back to the mine. Old Roy called, 'We need more fuel for the compressor. Keep an eye on it. I'll get hold of Michael Flannigan, get him to get his team over here. If it runs out, you, Ben, get out of that mine – there won't be enough good air.'

Ben strode on, not answering. Old Roy called to Cait, 'Remind him not to use gelignite unless the compressor's got a full head of steam. The drives won't be ventilated enough without the air being pumped down.'

She nodded, waved, then looked back at Ben who was standing by the mine shaft. 'Don't just stand there then,' he bellowed. 'Winch me down.'

She ran across, lifting her skirts. He turned his back to her as she drew near. She wanted to reach out and touch him. He clambered into the bucket. She let him down gently, bracing herself against the speed his weight would bring. He shouted up to her, 'I'll push the trolley back to the shaft. You haul it up. It'll be in buckets by then. Get the cooking and washing done in between times, and keep your eyes peeled for those bloody Micks with the wood.'

'Yes sir, no sir, three damn bags full, sir,' she yelled down the shaft. There was no answer.

She scrubbed the clothes, and those that Frank's mates had brought in, to be collected tomorrow when they'd also pick up some brownies they'd ordered. She went to the shaft when she heard his bellow and winched up the buckets, tipping the ore onto the heaps.

She checked the compressor's boiler. The fuel was low. She stood on the heap and looked out across the country. The wood-carters should be here. Why weren't they? There was not even any dust to say they were coming. Oh God, they would have to be

Irish too. Why were so many of the carters Irish?

She'd said the same thing to Old Roy. 'It's just the way things pad out. The Irish and the Italians are the wood-carters. Even down the big mines you get like working with like. Just think of coming to a strange place – you'd seek out your own kind, and it grows from that. So now it's not likely you'll get an Irish Catholic foreman giving a job to a Protestant pom, or a Proddy pom giving it to a Mick. Any more than you'd get a Slav giving a job to an Irishman. They work in their own areas of the mine.'

He'd seen her fear. 'Calm it, it's not Ireland again. We know why we're here – to work, make money. We know that we get as much out of the mines as the bosses, in our own way. Think. Have you seen any trouble here? We all just rub along.'

She hadn't, and now, as she stood in the sun, she was again grateful that she was here, away from all that. And it was Ben's ticket, and his love, which had brought her, and it was his love she had abused.

She boiled the billy for tea and cut bread, then lifted the butter from the hole she had dug near the Coolgardie. She unwrapped the damp hessian which kept it cooler than the Coolgardie safe. She hauled up another bucket load of ore, and called down, 'There's bread and cheese, and tea.'

He looked up, his face grey from the dust. 'Lower the billy – I'll have it down here. You can't haul me up on your own. Old Roy didn't think of that, did he?'

She lowered it, checked the boiler. It was almost out.

She came back to the shaft. The trolley was gone from the bottom. She called down, 'Remember, don't use gelignite. The boiler's almost out. You should come up. You can help by levering against the sides while I pull.'

He didn't answer.

223

She checked the boiler. It was out. The compressor slowed. Stopped.

She rushed to the shaft. 'Ben, you must come up, and you mustn't light any charges.'

There was no answer.

'Ben, for the love of God, come out. Don't light the charges.' It was so dark down there, but quiet, thank heavens it was quiet. But then there was a thump and dust whirled up from the shaft, and the pressure of the air took the breath from her. She hung over. 'Ben, Ben, come out. It won't clear, you damn fool.'

She heard him coughing, heard the screech of the trolley. 'Leave the trolley. Just leave it and get out. Let it settle, let it clear.'

She was unpegging the windlass handle. Oh God, if he was hurt how would she get him up alone?

She peered over the edge. He was coughing, stumbling, and dust filled the shaft. She could just make him out, climbing into the bucket. 'Use your hands on the side,' she shouted, putting her weight against the handle, straining to turn it, opening up her blisters again, heaving, pressing. Damn Roy. She couldn't do it. Damn Ben, why didn't he listen?

She could only turn it slowly, so slowly, pulling, pushing. Her arms hurt, her back ached, her shoulders felt as though they would break, but he was coming up.

She was shaking, she mustn't stop. She pushed, pulled, and his coughing was louder, nearer. It was easier. He was helping. She turned just once more. Go on, just once more, and again, and there he was, hauling himself out of the bucket, clambering out of the shaft, lying on the ground, coughing, choking.

She pegged the handle and ran down for water, lifting her skirts, running back, kneeling by him, supporting his head on her lap, holding the mug to his mouth. He punched it out of her hand. The water splashed him, and her. He threw himself from her. 'Get away from me.'

He lurched from her, struggled to his feet and stumbled on across the camp, coughing, gasping, stopping midway, then stumbling on again to the water barrel, plunging in his hands, bringing water to his mouth, gulping. He grabbed a kerosene tin, dipped it in, poured water over his head, washing the feel of her hands from his face, her thighs from beneath his head, the look in her eyes from his mind.

That wasn't love. She didn't know what love was. He couldn't let himself see it. He couldn't erase the past or suffer the hurt all over again. But as he kicked the kerosene tin clear over the camp-site he knew that the hurt had never eased since that day in Fremantle.

Cait watched from the head of the shaft, still kneeling, and now she was too weak to rise, her arms were numb, trembling. The water had soaked through to her skin and she couldn't bear to remember the weight of him on her legs, the feel of his face beneath her fingers. Because for a moment, just for a moment, they had touched, but then he had punched the mug from her, and hate had shone from him, pure and strong.

She watched him sit on Old Roy's chair, staring into the mug he had taken from the hook. At last he drank. He sat like that until the dust no longer rose from the shaft. Still she knelt by the windlass, and there was no sound, not even a breeze. It was as though life was suspended.

He called without looking, 'Is the dust clear?'

She looked. 'Almost.'

He returned to the mine. She stood now, reaching for the pickaxe handle which stood near the handle. 'You're not going back down.' She stood between him and the shaft. 'You'll have to break my back, if you want to go down. There's not enough air. You heard Old Roy.'

He stared at her. 'Get out of my way.'

She shook her head.

'Get out of my way, you Irish troublemaker.'

'I'm not Irish any more. My voice is going to be English. My name is going to be K-A-T-E, and I'm not a troublemaker. I loved you. I really loved you. You never let me explain. You won't let me tell you I still love you.'

He moved towards the shaft. She lifted the pickaxe. 'You'll never get past me. I'll knock you out, break your arm, anything. You're not going back down.'

He stood in front of her, his grey eyes so close to hers, his mouth so still. He said, 'How do you explain kisses born out of lies? How do you explain your body next to mine, in high grass with your boyfriend looking on? How do you explain laughing about me afterwards, accepting my mother's watch when you have no right to it?'

Her hold on the handle weakened, then she gripped it tightly again, forcing her voice to stay steady. 'I did it for Ireland, and out of hatred of the Tans. That still exists, but I fell in love with you.'

He shook his head impatiently. 'Yes, yes, that's what Old Roy told me, but you see – I don't know what the truth is with you, Caithleen. How the hell am I to know? Now let me pass, let me get on with my work.'

She raised the handle. 'Keep away. If you want to go down again, you'll have to come near me, even touch me. Think of the horror of that.' She stared at him defiantly.

He looked at her. 'Anything but that,' he agreed in a voice like ice. He walked back to the camp. He sat in the shade. He smoked, read, walked to the track and back, but still she stayed, sitting against the windlass, the sun beating down, burning her face, because her hat lay where it had fallen, over by the water barrel.

Her tongue swelled, her lips blistered, her head throbbed. Ben drank but brought her no water. She stayed until Old Roy returned with a load of wood because the Irish Micks had trouble with their cart. She stayed until Stan lifted her upright because she couldn't move, and then she vomited from the heat.

Ben turned away and walked into town, drinking schooner after schooner of beer in the bar, but he couldn't drown the disgust and he swore it was at her. All he could hear was her voice, no longer Irish, and all he could see was her red hair, and her eyes like an Irish summer, and her face as she told him her name was Kate, and her limp body in Stan's arms.

The night was dark, and the lamplight was gentle as she sat beneath the bough shelter reading quietly to Old Roy. They heard him come back into camp. She didn't stop reading, though she heard Frank say to Ben in the darkness, by the shower, 'You two should be quits. She saved your life today, twice. She got you out. She stopped you going back.'

Ben said nothing. He entered his tent. Still she read until the book was finished. Heathcliff was dead, gone to join his Cathy. She finished, closed the book. 'Love brings great cruelty,' she whispered. 'But it *is* love that spawns it, isn't it, Roy? It isn't hate?'

Old Roy shook his head. 'No, it's not hate.' But he was beginning to think that, for Ben, it might be.

They heard Ben leave his tent and walk out of the shadows towards the fire. He came to her and held out a book. 'For tomorrow night,' he said.

It was *Jane Eyre*. She opened it. The label was still there. *Ben Williams. English Prize. King's School.* The pages were stuck in as they had been what seemed so long ago. He walked back to his tent. She called, 'Thank you,' and heard the curlews over the river, and the breeze in the reeds. Old Roy smiled. Frank and Stan and Bluey grinned.

Mick plodded through the jarrah forest. The trees weren't as big as karris but the wood was harder. His billy hung from his belt, along with his crib in a handkerchief. He was late, but what the hell? Today was party day. He'd heard that Collins was dead, shot to hell near Cork. With Griffiths gone, the Free State was losing its leaders. He came to the brook and waded through it, then climbed up the bank on the other side.

He could hear sawing, hacking, men shouting. It was his turn in the pit today. What did that matter when Des's side was hurting?

'C'mon, you lazy layabout.' Fred Parsons stood in the clearing with his hands on his hips. 'You're down in the depths today, where you belong.' He was laughing.

Mick laughed with him, but wanted to smash the smile off his pommy foreman face. He dropped down beneath the jarrah, taking the other end of the saw, his sweat soon turning the sawdust into glue. He felt the ants crawling up his legs. Each thrust jarred his shoulder but nothing could dampen his elation. Nothing could wipe away the thought of Des's fury at Collins's death. It was as though he, Mick O'Brian, was winning after all.

But then he paused, wiped his face. What if this bumped Des up in the hierarchy? What if it meant he was Mr Wonderful? He pushed and pulled on the saw with a vigour born of anger. What if Des got into the Cabinet? Oh yes, that'd be right. Oh yes, that would just about put the lid on it. Here he was, stuck out in the sticks, while his brother rose up, smelling of violets.

Just don't let anyone tell him Des had got rid of him to save his wee brother's life. Just don't let them even breathe it or he'd throw up. He'd done it so the path was clear. Sawdust was falling faster now. He had to get out of here. He had to get East, had to make something out of himself. He had to show Des and that bitch Caithleen that though they might have flung him in the mud he could get out, and when he did, just let them watch out.

Chapter Eleven

As 1 January 1923 blazed in, Cait knitted in the shelter for Lucia Vincenzi's daughter, Maria, born on Christmas Day, then washed and ironed for her ever-increasing customers. In the evening she read from *Jane Eyre*, and ignored Old Roy's comments about the loss of her Irish burr.

She was Kate; this was Australia, a long way from Ireland and the thunder that was firing, and the lightning that was burning, and the Tans, and the willow by the river. Here there was just the heat that Tom had loved, the friends she had made, and Ben.

But what did Ben feel about her? Nothing. It was as though she was any old washerwoman, any old skivvy, but at least he was here, where she could watch the shadows of his eyelashes on his cheek-bones, the sun-bleached hair which flopped across his forehead; and at night she would dream that one day he would hold her, love her.

In March St Patrick's Day was celebrated in the two mining towns and Kate waited back at camp, tense and subdued, because Ben was in Kalgoorlie and what would he say when he returned? He said nothing to her, just talked to Frank and Stan, and kidded Bluey about his two-up losses. He said nothing, not even snarled as she had feared he would when Roy's friend Jed had reminded them of the anti-conscription mob, back in the World War, who had blocked Hannan Street outside the newspaper offices.

'Lordy Lord, what a to do,' Jed had said as he sat by the camp-fire, rubbing his hands gleefully. 'Better than fireworks it was.' Then Jed's face had changed. 'Wasn't bloody funny really though, was it? Australian government was Labor then, see, girlie.' He'd nodded at Kate who had smiled, but didn't see.

Roy had called, 'Shut your noise, we don't want to hear all this again.'

Kate had said, 'Roy, don't be rude. Carry on, Jed. Explain it to me.'

Roy had said, 'You don't want to hear it. He talks too much and it's all rubbish.'

Kate had been shocked. 'Roy, please.'

Roy had shrugged at her and glared at Jed, who'd ignored him and continued. 'Hughes was the leader – he came up through the Trade Union side where the good 'uns came from – none of the popish rabble who rightly got no higher than the ranks.' He'd wiped his nose, and it took a minute for Kate to absorb his words. When she did she had been hardly able to breathe and wanted to stop him, wanted Roy to stop him, anyone to stop him. But no, she had insisted he speak. Oh God.

Jed had continued, 'Anyway, this Hughes proposed conscription for our Australian lads to help the Empire, but would the Catholics and Commies in the Labor Party agree? Would they hell? Forced Hughes out, and his followers – or they just up and left.'

Old Roy had pushed a cup of tea at him. 'Drink that up, and stop blathering on.'

Jed had taken the mug, looked at it, then up at them. Please stop, Kate had prayed silently. He had not. 'Either way, they were good men who'd rather sing out for the Empire than stick with a bunch of bloody rebels. All fired up, them Catholics were, over the squashing of the Easter Rising. And the Commies thought the rich should have their money conscripted if the poor were having their bodies taken, or some such bloody rubbish. So now the Labor Party's just the Commies and the Catholics.' He had nodded towards the fire. 'And that means a heap of trouble for the rest of us, cos they'll do us down when they can, you see if they don't.'

She'd said, speaking at last with a voice too loud and too fierce, 'Thousands of Irish fought in that war.'

A branch of burning wood had snapped.

Roy had said, 'Jed knows that damn well, and thousands of Irish did from here too. They just didn't want to be ordered to do it, and there was lots of others felt the same. The old windbag just happens to be forgetting that.' He was jabbing his finger at Jed. 'And if I remember right, it was because Hughes wanted a referendum when the Government wouldn't roll over with their legs in the air and support him that the rank and file in the party smacked him in the mouth. It weren't right, going over the top of them like that. Try talking sense, man, and anyway, just remember it ended up with two referendums and the result was – no conscription. So it wasn't just the Catholics, or the Commies, it was everyone.' He had avoided looking at Ben or Kate.

When Jed had gone she drew closer to Roy. 'I thought this was a new country. I thought you said there were no tensions here. I thought you said there'd be no hate.' Her voice was tense, her words rapid.

Roy held her hand, and there was comfort in the gesture, but it was not enough to push away Ben's eyes, which had flickered to her as she had shouted, and there was nothing but contempt in his gaze before he walked away, into town with the boys.

'Now, now, missy,' Roy said as they sat and watched

232

them disappear into the darkness. 'The Irish come out here and find things have already been set up by their old rulers and so the old hates are in place on both sides. Yes, there've been problems, in some places, but only some. And yes, you don't get over those like that.' He clicked his fingers. 'But before the war it was almost all forgotten. The war's gone now. People are learning to let go again, they're too busy getting on with their lives: being Australians. There'll always be your hotheads, but you avoid those. Just like we all try and avoid that crusty old fool, Jed, and then some darn fool of a girl goes and gives him an open invitation.' He kissed her forehead. 'Darn me if he isn't always grizzling about something.'

She shivered in spite of the heat from the fire. 'What hope is there for Ben and me?' she whispered.

'None, if you give up.' His tone was fierce. 'And don't be a fool. Pay attention. I said the war is over. Everything's settling, and I was right when I told you there's not that sort of trouble in Kalgoorlie and it's here you live.'

In the last week of March Old Roy led the boys down the shaft, leaving Stan up top. As Stan hauled up the ore, he called to Kate, shaking his head, 'He's right – that ore from the new drive's good. That old devil's got a nose like a foxhound.'

She laughed at the baffled expression on Stan's face. She raised her head from the dough she was making and called to Stan, 'Tell them it's tea-up. I want Roy to have a break. He's coughing so badly he shouldn't be down there.'

They came, their faces grey from the dust. She heard his cough before she saw him. She made him sit, gave him tea. 'Have you thought about what I said the other day?' she asked. 'There are plenty of empty houses in town just right for boarding-houses. You could set on a housekeeper to run it and live a life of genteel luxury.' She grinned and raised her eyebrows at the men, then grew serious. 'Please, Roy. You can afford it. This dust cakes your lungs. Think about it.'

'I'll think about tanning you.' His voice was sharp.

She gave the men their tea. Her eyes met Ben's. He nodded. 'She's right. You're sounding like a prime case of miner's lung. Come on, you don't want to put all your eggs in one basket. It would be a good hedge for retirement to start something else at this stage.'

She looked at him in amazement. The men glanced at one another. Old Roy slopped his tea, and looked from Ben to Kate. 'Ganging up, eh?'

Ben shrugged. 'Look at it how you like. Seems a good line to be in from where I'm sitting.'

He handed her back the mug, not looking at her. He walked to the mine. She looked at the dough and called, 'I was going to wrap the dough round sticks. You can bake them. I've jam to spread on them.'

He didn't stop walking, just shook his head.

He reached the woodpile and began to stoke the compressor boiler. Frank said, 'I'll have his.'

Everyone laughed, but then Roy coughed until he could barely get his breath, and for the moment Kate forgot that Ben had sided with her. But only for a moment. When Roy stopped coughing he smiled and said, 'Once every six months there's to be progress, is there?' He pushed himself up from the chair. 'Got to get on.'

She tried to push him back. 'Sit down, rest a while.'

He shook his head. 'There's work to be done, Kate, or Caithleen, or whoever you've engineered yourself into being.' He was smiling, but as he limped across the camp-site towards the ore table he said, 'I miss you, Caithleen Healy.'

She said, 'I don't miss myself. I'm glad I've gone.'

Old Roy walked from her to the ore-sorting bench,

muttering, 'I admired those who stood against conscription in Hannan Street, whether they were Catholic or socialist. They weren't going to be ordered around. They were who they were.'

She ignored him, and cleared the jam and the dough, and took up the bodice of the dress she was making for Lucia's daughter, and sat for a moment in a chair beneath the shade of the bough shelter. It was the chair that Bluey had made her for Christmas. The gold nugget on the bracelet that Roy had given her jangled. Ben had given her nothing. But she deserved nothing.

She had given him a shirt she had sewn, just as she had given one to each of the men, but Ben's had been worked with love.

She stretched her neck, listening to the sounds of the men as they wound up the ore, and called to one another. The goat bleated. The hens she had brought from Lucia scratched in the earth. Old Roy tossed mullock from the sorting tray. She pushed the needle through again. She heard a clatter as Frank pegged the windlass handle. The noise pierced the stillness with too much clarity.

She looked up and groaned. There was a stillness in the air, a silence. Another sand storm. She ran to her tent and threw the dress inside. She slapped shut the flaps on all the tents, and pegged down the Coolgardie safe and the food cupboard.

She shaded her eyes and found the small speck on the horizon. She watched as it grew into a red dot, then a ribbon, like those she had tied around the bush she had pretended was a fir tree at Christmas. That had been pink. This dot was livid red. The trees were tossing on the horizon. She looked across to the men. The trees hadn't done that before.

'Roy,' she called. He was the other side of the woodpile.

There was a faint roar now. She took the billy

235

from the fire, and looked again. The red ribbon filled the whole horizon, the roar was louder. It was coming closer. She called louder. 'Roy, Stan, Ben.'

They couldn't hear above the compressor.

It was closer, much closer, and now the roar was louder and louder. She looked in the direction of Chris's camp. Loose iron danced high up in the air. She ran towards the men but Roy was already shouting at the others. 'Winch up, Bluey, it's a blow. Get a move on.' The others turned the handle faster.

The peppercorns were stirring, their fronds whipping the air. Chris's camp was blanked out by surging red dust which swept ever nearer. She could hear the noise of the tin crashing and clanking within it. She ran towards the fowls, her hair whipping across her face. She locked them into the coop as the wind plucked at her skirt and the noise buffeted her. It was louder, so much louder.

Roy ran towards her. 'Take cover.'

'Where?' she yelled above the noise. 'Where?'

Ben was running towards her. 'Get in the shelter.'

But the sand was on them, roaring and raging round her, at her, pushing her, stinging her. She couldn't see, couldn't breathe. She clung to the hen coop. The wind tore it from her, bowling it along the ground. She stumbled after it, her hands to her eyes. The wind caught her, hurled her to the ground.

There was only noise, dust. She couldn't breathe. She scrambled to her knees. The wind tore at her again. She heard the crash and clatter all around, and there, above her, in the sand, was the water barrel. She screamed.

And now Ben was throwing her to the ground. 'Get down. Get down, damn you.' He threw himself half over her, pressing her into the ground, hurting her, but it didn't matter. He was here. It was his arm flung over her, his voice saying, 'Just keep down, protect your mouth, keep your eyes shut.'

'But my chooks,' she wailed.

'Damn your chooks,' he shouted, then coughed. 'You're an impossible, stupid woman, Kate.'

The sand stung and clogged, the wind roared, the Coolgardie whipped past them but then it was gone. His arm tightened, the roar grew louder, but it didn't matter because he was close, he was touching her, his body was covering hers, his chest was heaving against her. The sound was decreasing, the wind was no longer tearing at her, the sand wasn't stinging as it had done. She lay still, and now it was over and a deep silence fell over the camp. Ben pushed himself off her, scrambling to his feet, pulling her up, looking at her. He reached out and ran his finger down her cheek. 'You need a good polish.'

Thunder roared. Rain came, large heavy cooling drops, damping the dust and trees, and the wreckage that had been her hut, and the men's tents. And there was the overpowering scent of the leaves of the peppercorns, and now Ben turned away, and joined the men who were already clearing, cursing and swearing as they did so. But still she felt his finger on her cheek, and saw the confusion in his grey eyes, his grey clear eyes, and thought she would die of love, and hope.

Then the thunder roared again and the rain grew heavier. She laughed and lifted up her head to it, letting the rain wash over her. Old Roy called out, 'What the hell are you doing?'

She said, 'It's only thunder, it's not firing.'

Old Roy shook his head, and looked across at Ben. Ben was nodding. Yes, it was only thunder, not firing. He knew what she meant. After all, they'd been through it together. But then he looked down at the broken windlass strut he held. No, not together – that had been the lie.

He remembered the body he had just lain on and the face which had been so close to his, the face he had once kissed. How could anyone so corrupt look so innocent and feel so good? He threw the strut onto the timber pile, then looked at Kate again. But was she corrupt? Or was it Mick?

He shoved his hand through his hair, the light glinted on his watch. He pushed doubt aside, wanting proof of his need to hate. Hate didn't leave you vulnerable. He rubbed the strap. Where was his mother's watch if she was innocent? She must have sold it. That's how little she thought of him. That's how she turned everything to her own advantage.

Old Roy left for town with the cart the moment the rain ceased. Ben ran after him. 'Hey, I'm coming. We'll need to repair and replace practically everything. You can't bring it back on your own.'

Roy shouted back, 'Stay with Kate. She needs help.'

Ben called, 'She'll just take what she needs, don't you worry.'

Kate heard. The canvas she carried rasped her hands, but she hardly noticed. The moment between them was over. But it didn't matter what he said because it had happened, she could still feel the touch of his fingers, and see his grey eyes.

She helped the men recover what they could from the bush and searched for the coop, but it was broken into a hundred pieces. As the men tore down the remains of the camp and sorted out usable material she put personal belongings into piles. They were dust covered, ripped. Many were ruined.

'Could do with a cuppa,' Stan called. 'I'll put the billy on.'

She found Ben's copy of *Jane Eyre*, or what was left of it. Some of the pages must have drifted clear into Boulder by now, she thought. She brought out her copy of *Wuthering Heights* from her bag and placed it between his clothes.

The men were moving slowly, coughing on the dust

238

they had swallowed. The water tank was recovered. She laid the fire, put on the billy. Everything seemed so quiet, so unreal. The billy boiled. She made damper, putting it in the camp oven which had survived unscathed. Why did some things remain untouched in life, and others were destroyed?

Stan kicked out at the mangle, which was still standing. 'Should have our heads examined, sticking here. Old Roy in particular. This'll set off his cough worse than ever.'

Bluey shook his head as he held up the hurricane lamp with its shattered glass. 'There's been worse blows. Old Roy'll get some stuff back from town by nightfall.'

They collected round the fire and drank tea. The biscuits were crunchy with sand. 'Better get off and check Chris and Mark. Saw enough of their gear flying over us to furnish a store.'

But the men stayed for a while longer, rolling their cigarettes. Red dust from their fingers stained the paper as they licked and sealed them. Bluey handed one to her. 'Go on, you need one too. It'll set you up to argue with the boss. He's got to get into town, and out of here, you know – what was that about a boarding-house? Think on that. You're the only one who could swing it, we've been trying for the past two years.'

She put the cigarette in her mouth. He lit it. She sucked, choked, spat it out. A bit of the paper stuck to her lip. The men laughed. 'Never sounded so like Old Roy in your life,' Bluey guffawed, leaning forward and picking the paper off her lip.

Stan said, as he ground out her cigarette beneath his boot, 'He's heading for his fever again. The doc said he should get into a cushy billet last time. He's gone sixty, you know, and he looks a lot frailer than last year. This blow won't have done any good either.'

She nodded.

'I reckon Ben was on the right track with that miner's lung,' Bluey said, pouring himself more tea and holding a refill up to her.

She shook her head. 'I've got to find those chooks.'

Frank brushed his trousers off as he also rose. 'Glad to see Ben found you. Seems to me we should have a blow a bit more often.' The men were grinning slyly. Then, as she shook her head at them, they walked away whistling 'The Wedding March'.

She found three of the chooks, and helped Bluey to bang together a small coop, and it was while they were doing this that they heard the cart and helped unload as the sun died and the darkness fell. They erected tents by the light of the new hurricane lamps that Roy had bought.

'Boulder and Kalgoorlie missed it, so no-one's dusting there, not any more than usual anyway. That damn wind just loves taking apart the camps, bloody nuisance,' Roy said as he pegged down her tent. 'This'll do for you now.'

She touched his arm. 'Go to bed, Roy, please.'

'There's lots to do yet.'

She called to the men who had almost finished erecting their tents, and Ben, who was putting together the shelves. 'Tell him, will you, that we're not kids, we can sort this out.'

None of the men answered, they just came across and carried him bodily to his tent. Roy squirmed and protested as they dumped him on the hessian bed. She poked her head through the flap after the men filed out. 'If you go on making a fuss, I'll get them to hold you down while I undress you.'

Old Roy shook his fist at her. 'Chris is right, you're nothing but a shrew.'

In the morning he slept until the heat of the day woke him. Kate was putting clothes through the mangle, watching Ben at the windlass, repairing the struts. He had said nothing about *Wuthering Heights* but she barely thought of that. All she thought about was how pale Old Roy was, how he had coughed through the night, how his chest rattled.

She hung up the washing on the line Bluey had restrung for her. This morning the blacks had come selling pegs. Old Roy stomped to the fire. He poured tea and slurped it. His hair stuck up on end, his trousers sagged and ruffled about his ankles. He scratched his head. She fetched his hat and smiled. He grimaced, looked into his mug and threw the tea away.

She turned the mangle – a shirt folded into the basket, lifeless.

He came across and took hold of the mangle. 'I'll do it.'

She nodded and wiped her hands. 'Good. I need to go to town.'

He looked surprised. She said, 'I must replenish our stores.'

His cheeks were flushed, his shoulders shook as he coughed again.

She strode to the cart and harnessed up the pony. He was restless. She soothed him, and climbed into the cart. Ben stopped hammering. Bluey nudged Stan. She ignored them and trotted the pony from the camp.

In town she ignored the stores also and hitched up the pony outside Vincenzis'. She jumped down and hurried in through the front door, down the darkened hall and into the kitchen. Mario and Lucia were there, preparing lunch. They kissed her, gave her brownies, gave her Maria to hold. Kate gazed down at the olive-skinned child and then up at Mario. She cut across his pleasantries.

'Do you know who owns the broken-down house where I camped?'

Mario stopped in mid-sentence and looked at Lucia. Lucia frowned. 'My dear Kate. But let me think.'

Maria began to cry. Kate rocked her. Mario rubbed his chin, then smiled. 'Yes, now I remember. It's Sidney, the father of Lawrence Bailey who has taken his family to the East – Melbourne I think. But why?'

Kate handed Maria to him, saying, 'I'll tell you when I've sorted things out.'

She hurried through the yard and ran to Sidney Bailey who lived behind the ironmonger's. She clambered up the broken veranda steps and knocked on the fly door.

Sidney Bailey called, 'Get in, whoever it is, and shut the door quick. Don't want them damn flies in here.'

She hurried into the rancid gloom. Sidney sat in an old chair in front of the stove. He looked at her in surprise. 'Well, if it isn't Old Roy's little girl. So, what can I do for you?'

She told him. He studied her face, and then his nails. He said, as he poked at the cuticles, 'Hear tell he's crook. That anything to do with you asking to buy a broken-down house my son bunked off from? That Old Roy won't just give up, you know, and sit and do nothing.'

Cait nodded. 'I know, but the boys say he's much worse than last year. He needs to get out of the mine dust, needs to do less heaving about. The boys want to mine it for him, give him his share. I've already talked about building up a boarding-house business in town. Well, sort of talked about it.'

Sidney threw back his head and laughed. 'He can't cook and clean.'

She ran her finger along the grain of his table, feeling the grease. 'But I can. He can handle the business side and still make plans for the mine. If you sell it to me for a reasonable price, I'll come in here and cook and clean for you, free. But you'll have to accept stage payments. You'll have to wait until we get boarders for the first one.' Her voice was hard. If Ben thought she took what she wanted, then in this case, she would. She had to.

'Get him to stump up.'

She shook her head. 'He doesn't know anything about it. I want to sort it out. It won't be easy for him to refuse then, if he thinks it will help me. He's such a good man.'

Sidney's clawlike hands gripped the arms of his chair. His nails were too long and were yellowed from nicotine. He said, 'What makes you think I'd sell it to the likes of you?'

She interlaced her fingers. 'What do you mean, the likes of me?'

'You killed his Tom.' He sat back. The antimacassar behind his head was grubby. An old fly paper hung from the ceiling. The mantelpiece was thick with dust, the mirror too.

She whispered, 'No, I didn't kill his Tom. It was war that did that. I just betrayed Ben Williams. That's more than sufficient guilt, Mr Bailey, and none of your business.'

She sat quite still. She could hear the batteries thudding, the trams whining and clanking. Somewhere a boy whistled. A train hooted.

Mr Bailey stirred. 'Put that there kettle on, and have some biscuits, for Pete's sake. You can have the house. No repayments. Just give me fifty per cent of the value when you sell it. Might as well be used by you. No-one else'll take it on. No more families coming in these days. Still a few singles needing bed and board. Meals needed too, you should think of that. But you'll never get him there, believe me.'

Kate rose, feeling as though she had won a race. Just for once, she had won. 'We'll have to see about that.' She stooped and kissed Sidney Bailey on the cheek. 'You're a good man, and I'll make your house beautiful, and we'll sell it for a fortune when Kalgoorlie picks up, as Old Roy says it will. He's never wrong, you know.'

He flapped his hand at her. 'Get on with you. And yes, I know he's never wrong. Why d'you think I've let you have the house? Wouldn't, if he hadn't taken you in.'

She hurried back for the pony, and let it drink from the trough before returning to camp, her mind working. Old Roy came to meet her. He peered into the cart. 'Where's the goods?'

She jumped down, unharnessed the pony, the leather was hot and malleable from the sun. She stroked the pony, led it to its shelter, heaving hay into its trough. Old Roy watched her. She walked back to the camp and put the billy on to boil.

He followed her. She looked around at Stan and Frank, laughing as they put the finishing touches to the shower. She watched Bluey saw through a length of wood and toss it across to Ben. She touched the mangle and moved across to the clothes on the line. They smelt fresh and clean. The chooks were scratching. Holy Mother, she'd miss it.

She looked at Ben and her heart sank, her anger forgotten. If she hadn't been here when the sand storm came she would not have felt his arm around her. If she hadn't been here reading to Old Roy he would never have brought across *Jane Eyre*. She could never have stopped him going back down the mine when the compressor died. Holy Mother, how could she leave? No, no. Good heavens, how could she leave? she corrected herself.

She looked round the camp once again. Old Roy still stood by the fire. Again he coughed. She walked to him, and took his arm. 'Roy, I need you to do something for me.'

He nodded, his hand to his mouth as he coughed again. 'Anything, darlin'. You know that.'

She asked him then to live with her in the house she had just bought from Sidney Bailey. 'I can't stay here any more. There's talk in the town. Lucia told me again today.' It was a lie, but then that's what everyone thought was the core of her being.

He said, 'I've never heard that. This is your home. You love it here.' He coughed again and nodded in Ben's direction.

Kate could see that Stan had stopped work and was listening. 'Please come with me. I know the men need you, but you can work out the new drives at the house. I can bring you back here to sort out the mullock. In town you'll be in out of the worst of the dust, you'll be in out of the cold when the nights chill down. My reputation is bad enough. I need a man, someone the town respects. Please, Roy, I need you.'

Roy looked again from her to Ben. He kicked at the ash of the fire, then removed his hat. He smoothed the rim, replaced it. He looked at Ben again, then said to Kate, 'You'd leave him, to make sure I'm where you and the boys want me?'

He turned and looked round the camp. He walked away from her to the edge of the camp, gazing out across the peppercorns, and up at the sheer sky. In the spring there were wild flowers, and always the whisper of the breeze. His Maureen had loved it, but she'd loved him more. 'Come the old years we'll be out of here,' she'd said.

There hadn't been any old years for Maureen. 'It'll get your chest,' his Maureen had said. 'I couldn't bear that, so we'll move into shelter then.' Her eyes had been hazel, not violet as Kate's were, but the anxiety had been the same. He sighed and returned to Kate.

'I call that right fine of you, Caithleen Healy, and my Tom would be proud of you, and my Maureen would tell me how I couldn't refuse. So we'll just get the house sorted out so we's not sleeping on the floor, like you was.'

She was torn between relief and regret.

Mick travelled across the Nullarbor on the train, seeing the blacks camped along the tracks, seeing the nothingness of the desert. He looked again at the newspaper. So the Free Staters had won. Well, well, wouldn't the dear elder brother be just cock-a-hoop? And would the idiot still be thinking they'd get a Republic?

He touched his black eye. It still hurt but at least he'd given the Proddy devil of a foreman at the saw mill more than that. No-one was going to call him a bog-Irish Mick and be getting away with it. No-one was going to say that the Catholics wouldn't fight in the war, they'd only fight each other after it; that they wouldn't be conscripted in Australia because they were cowards and rebels. He wiped his mouth with his hand. God, he could still hear the sound of the loudmouth's nose breaking under his fist.

He smiled, flexing his fingers. The fool had done him a favour though, cursing and swearing about the Irish Catholics in Australia who'd have cheered if the Empire had gone down in the war. It had reminded him of all that the old man had said in the Irish bar in Fremantle.

But he'd gone on, the pommy foreman, struggling and fighting, yelling about the splitting of the Labor Party and the Catholics who now filled its ranks, and about the Loyalty Leagues. 'We're on top – we'll stay that way. My brother's back East in amongst them bright ones that knows best when the rest forget. That's where the Proddies'll make sure you bloody behave and stay in your place.'

Mick had shoved him to the ground, kneeled over him, hit him again, saying, '*You're* not on top now though, are you? So here's one for the Loyalty League and your damn brother.'

Now, as the wheels drummed, he looked out of

the window at the distant horizon. Well, he was off to Sydney. Off to where all this action was, in the Labor Party, his own kind and then let's be seeing what Des thought of him, when he was king pin, when he was bringing the Labor Party behind him, and dragging Australia towards a republic, and sod the Empire.

Chapter Twelve

Kate walked round the house. It was built of weatherboard and iron, with four main rooms and a lattice-front veranda overlooking a parched, neglected square of lawn. At the rear the veranda was partly shaded by a peppercorn tree growing beside the small washhouse. At the bottom of the yard was the lavatory, set against the picket fence.

Old Roy stood with her on the veranda, jerking his head towards the sagging rear door. 'I'll mend that when I come back tonight. Do the steps too.' He toed the broken wood of the second step. He touched his hat and slouched down the steps and through the yard.

She began in the kitchen where there was still a dusty black kettle on the iron stove, but there there were also inches of red dust. She swept, coughed, swept again. She damped down with water, swept again. She scrubbed, wiped down walls and cupboards.

There was a table, four chairs, and a dresser with crockery and cutlery. 'Have it,' Sidney had said. 'They took what they wanted when they left. You'll see that they didn't take me.'

She scrubbed until the sweat ran down her back, and drenched her hair.

She cleaned out the stove and polished it. She cleared a patch in the yard for the chooks which Roy would bring tonight. Were her father's sheltering in the hedge, wet and bedraggled? She dragged her bed out onto the veranda, and then threw the image from her mind.

She would sleep out here tonight, in the scent of the oily peppercorns. She dragged out the table and chairs too, for this is where they would eat. She laid several places, for the men had said they would make the trip to the house rather than cook for themselves ever again, or let Frank near the pots, more to the point. Would Ben come?

She swept out the living-room, and the two bed-rooms, sprinkling water as she went, and her eyes were sore from the dust, and her throat also. She shook out Roy's blankets and beat the mattress out in the yard. Would he sleep in the house or the veranda? It was his decision. The whistles blew for the end of shifts, and she fried up the sausages and the steak and boiled the vegetables. Would Ben come?

She checked the clock on the shelf above the stove that Old Roy had lent her. It was covered with a film of red dust already. She glanced down at her wrist. One day she must return to the whore-house. She knew she must, for Ben's mother's watch was still there in the pocket of her dress. She had written to say she would collect it, but she could not yet bear the thought of even looking down the street.

She stripped and washed at the sink, and wore her best dress. Surely he'd come. She brushed her hair, and let it fall loose on her shoulders.

She walked out into the balmy evening and touched the table. One day she would buy table-cloths with the money she'd earn by taking in extra washing. She would sell cut lunches, and buy serviettes and nice bed linen with the money. She looked across the yard. She missed the wide clear sky, the sense of space. She missed Ben.

She walked through the house again. Tomorrow

she would clean the other rooms properly. They could put two men to a room. She could take one end of the veranda as a sleep-out, and Roy the other. She checked the sausages. They were ready. She heard the cart coming up the back alley. She heard their voices. They walked through the yard, carrying the chooks.

'I'll bang you up a run later,' Bluey said, throwing his tools on the step. She looked beyond him. Ben hadn't come.

Old Roy slapped his hat against his trousers, then sat heavily on the chair. 'Old bones, old bones,' he wheezed.

'Where is he?' she whispered, disappointment tearing at her.

'He's running scared,' Old Roy said, coughing. She lifted the beaded gauze from the jug and poured water. He took it with a trembling hand. She felt the heat of his skin.

Bluey raised his eyebrows. 'He's getting the fever.'

Old Roy drank and scowled over the glass. All thoughts of Ben were chased from Kate at the sight of her old friend. He growled, 'You'll be getting a good tanning, if you go on.'

They ate, and she gave a dish to Bluey to take to Sidney Bailey. 'Tell him to come and eat whenever he likes, he's lonely,' she told Bluey.

When he'd gone she asked Old Roy, 'Let me call the doctor? You're so hot.'

Roy fiddled with his belt. 'I'm not seeing things I don't want to see yet, like your boy Ben. I'm not remembering things I don't want to remember, like that fool who wouldn't come here to eat. He's putting up a good fight against you, but I reckon we'll haul him in. Your Ben, that is, not the doctor to me.' His smile was forced, and then he coughed, and it was fierce and wracking, and he clutched at the post for support.

She put her arm round him, taking his weight, calling to Stan and Frank who were by the cart. 'Give me a hand to get him to his room.'

They ran back through the yard. Roy said, 'I don't want to be shut in.'

She pointed to her bed. 'On there then.'

She dragged the table out of the way as the men led him to the bed beneath the branch of the peppercorn.

She nursed him all night, and together she and Roy breathed in the oily scent. In the morning Bluey came back with eucalyptus leaves which she spread beneath the bed. She sent him for the doctor but when he came Roy would take no medicine, he would only allow Kate to bind his chest with red flannel spread with mutton fat. 'Like Maureen used to,' he panted.

The doctor said, 'Keep his fever down, but it's the same old thing, isn't it, you stubborn old mule? You should have come out of the mine last year. Thank heavens you've a tough lass keeping you in order this time. Those boys should have sorted it out before.'

Old Roy raised himself. 'Nag, nag, the pair of you.'

She pushed him gently down onto the pillows, smiling, but frightened at his panting.

Lucia came, bringing flowers to welcome Kate to Kalgoorlie. She pushed them into a jar in the kitchen, then put them on the table on the veranda. She came to stand by Kate who was bathing Roy's face. She said, '*Mamma mia*, he is so sick. I shall stay.'

Kate shook her head. 'You'll do no such thing. You have a child to care for and I'm not tired.'

'Then I will pray for him and light a candle.' Lucia's look was stern. 'Since you have done neither, have you?'

'Yes, I have prayed but I don't need a church for that. Those days are over.'

'Once a Catholic, always a Catholic.'

'I am nothing any more. I am just Kate Healy.

I don't want to belong to anything. I don't want to take sides. I am just me.'

'You are mistaken.' Lucia shook with anger.

'Please, Lucia, I am me. Anything else is too confusing.'

Lucia smiled suddenly. 'One day, my dear Caithleen, you will return to us.'

Kate replied, 'But I've never left *you*.'

Lucia lifted her hands in mock horror. 'I will go, you cannot be talked to, but I love you just the same.'

The men came for tea that day, bringing a tot of rum for Old Roy. Ben was not with them. They ate in the kitchen and whispered because Roy was worse, and when she had dished up she left them and sat with him. He called her Maureen and searched for her hand, and kissed it, and wept because he had missed her so, and the loss in his voice was dark and deep. Is this how her dada felt? Only about his wife, not his daughter, and sadness dragged at her. Is this how Mr O'Brian felt about Des and Mick?

She barely noticed the men leaving or coming the next day. She had prepared food for them, but hadn't washed the clothes that Chris and Mark had sent.

The next evening she did so while Bluey sat by Roy's bed. In the morning Frank came and then she ironed. In the afternoon it was Stan who sat, taking drags on his cigarette and blowing the smoke out over the yard, well away from Roy, he assured Kate, when she returned from Sidney Bailey and saw the butts on the ground.

They ate with her, but Ben still did not come. They stayed as she sat by Roy's side and forced him to take a little water and bathed his face, arms and hands. Bluey came with fresh water. She whispered, 'Is this what it's been like before?'

He nodded. 'Sort of, but this is worse. You've had the doc?'

'Should we get him again?' Frank called.

Roy gripped her wrist. She dropped the flannel. He said, 'Don't want that quack fussing round. It's nothing. He's a waste of money.'

'Shall I?' she mouthed to Bluey.

Bluey squatted, then they all turned at the sound of footsteps coming through the yard. It was Ben. He climbed the steps and stood there, looking at Kate. 'It's my turn to sit with him.'

Kate just looked. Bluey grunted, 'About bloody time. Now what about the doc?'

Roy whispered, 'I said no.' His voice was hoarse.

Kate hesitated. Ben said, 'Let's leave it for a while. I'll stay all night. If two of us are here, then it's easier to fetch the doc if need be. Bluey, you and the others get off now.'

His voice was neutral, his eyes empty, as he looked from Roy to her, then out to the yard. 'Don't you put your chooks to bed any more?'

They were clucking around the yard. She hurried down the steps, scooting them into the coop. How could he stay away from his old friend for so long? Bluey was right. About bloody time. She shut the coop. The boys waved as they clicked the gate shut. The stars were low and bright. She could hear laughter from the lane.

She walked back to the veranda. He was sitting on the steps, smoking, looking past her, at the coop. About bloody time. Her skirt brushed his shoulder as she passed. He said, 'The coop looks as good as new.'

She said, 'Things can be rebuilt.'

'Only sometimes,' he murmured.

She sat by Roy until he slept. Ben still sat on the step. She wanted to sit beside him. She wanted to feel his shoulder close to hers. She wanted to feel his arms

253

around her. She wanted to sink into his warmth, but she also wanted to hit him for ignoring his friend.

He said, jerking his head towards the chooks, 'Do they roost happily here? They don't feel as though they're being pressed in by the fences, the houses, after all the space of the bush? Do you think they feel trapped?'

She put down her sewing. A distant dog barked, traffic rumbled. A child cried, unable to sleep in the heat. 'They seem happy enough. Is that how you feel when you're in town – hemmed in, trapped?'

There was a silence. He threw his cigarette away. It arced through the night. 'I don't know what I feel. I wish to God I did,' he said shortly.

She barely breathed as she watched the set of his shoulders, his arms resting on his knees, his fingers clasped together. It's how he had sat at the river, his dark blue uniform clear against the reeds, and beyond them the hills.

Old Roy coughed, choked. She sat him up. Ben came. 'Water,' she snapped. He handed her the glass. She said, 'Come on now, Roy, drink this, just a little, just for me.'

He did, and looked up at her. 'I love you, Maureen. We've got a daughter now. Such a fine daughter. Should be married.'

Kate eased him back onto the pillows, and returned the glass to Ben. Their fingers touched. It took her breath from her. She looked at him. His eyes were dark and deep, and it was as though he had also stopped breathing.

Roy coughed again, falling off his pillows. She swung round and caught him. He seemed on fire. 'He's so hot, he's so damn hot. He's getting worse.'

Ben reached past her and touched the old man's forehead. 'Shall I fetch the doc again?'

'I don't know, I just don't know. He hates the idea.' They looked at one another, and their sense of uncertainty was shared. Ben wiped his hand across his mouth. He remembered his mother at his bedside, her warmth, her gentle touch, the scent of rose-water on her skin, the cool glass she had held against his lips when his own chest roared and ached.

Kate said, 'We must. We're being stupid. Will you go?' She held the glass to Roy's lips. Her voice was soft, her hair hung loose on her shoulder and breast. There was love in her voice, as there had been at the river. He looked at her. Yes, there was love, as she said to Roy, 'Come along, my dear. Try to drink.'

Ben felt a sense of peace, even though there was an old man whose breath was rasping in his chest, an old man whom he loved, and whom he had forced himself to stay away from because he couldn't bear to be near her. Dare he believe there had been love in her for him, after all?

She swung round. 'Please, Ben. Hurry.' He reached out and touched her shoulder. 'Hurry, for God's sake hurry, Ben.' She tried to sit Roy up as Ben ran through the yard, but the old man moaned at her touch. She poured water onto the flannel and sponged him. He coughed again and again.

She ran into the house and took her dresses from the case, bringing them back out to the veranda, stuffing them gently beneath his pillows, raising him that way. The coughing eased. She knelt, never taking her eyes off him. 'Hurry, please hurry,' she breathed, and only now did it occur to her that Ben had touched her.

Ben ran back in the yard, up the veranda, stepping over her, squatting. 'He's right behind me. How is he?' he whispered, panting. The same fear that she felt was in his voice.

She said, 'I'm frightened he'll die. I couldn't bear that.' There were tears streaking down her face. She wiped them away fiercely. 'He mustn't die. I won't have it. Do you hear me, Roy? I won't have you dying.'

255

Ben took her hands. 'I won't let him die either. Neither of us will let him die.' His voice was loud, strong.

Old Roy coughed again, and the doctor said, as he climbed the veranda steps, 'Neither of you will have anything to do with it. It's up to the old coot, and he damn well knows it.' His stethoscope was round his neck, he was flapping his hands at Ben. 'Get out of my way.'

Ben dropped her hands. She rose too. The doctor said, 'No, I'll need you to keep the old fool in order.'

She stayed while he examined and treated Roy. He handed her a linctus to give him every four hours. 'He'll come to a crisis within the next twenty-four hours,' he said to Kate and Ben, peering over his glasses at them. 'The lass can't do it on her own. She'll need someone with her?'

Ben nodded. 'There'll be someone here.' He stayed all that night, sitting on the steps, while she sat on the chair next to Roy's bed, and now she wondered if she had dreamt his touch.

In the morning he and Bluey put up shade around the veranda where the peppercorn branches didn't reach. Ben went back to the mine at midday and Bluey sat with Roy while Kate pleated the sheeting that Lucia had brought and tacked it along a length of board. Bluey hung it from the stay across the roof of the veranda. One or other of them pulled the punkah fan all afternoon and when Ben returned he pulled it until the sun lowered and heat went from the day.

She and Ben sat alone again as the evening wore on, she on the chair, he on the steps, and then Old Roy became hotter and sicker, and now they sat together on chairs that they had pulled up to the bed, breathing in the oily scent of the peppercorns, willing him to live, aching with tiredness, but never sleeping, always watching.

Ben checked his watch. It glinted in the light from the lamp. 'It must break soon.'

Roy's moans grew louder, his hands threshed, he tossed and turned. They sponged him. Again and again they sponged him and held water to his lips, and then squeezed moisture from a flannel and dripped it in his tormented mouth.

Ben checked his watch again. 'It's more than twenty-four hours,' he groaned.

She said, 'He's still with us.' Her voice was firm and calm, as his mother's had always been, and the Irishness was quite gone from it. He pictured her leaving the leather pouch on the stone by the fire. He pictured her running down the slope towards the river, and the look in her eyes had been that of love. Yes, he knew now that she had loved. He knew that she still did.

But then his glance fell to her wrist. No watch. No damn watch. She'd sold it. How could someone sell a gift like that, and then return a pouch of money? For effect, that's how.

He turned away from her, and now Roy was breathing easily, and there were no moans. He lay still. 'It's broken,' she murmured, turning to him, her face alight. She gripped his hand. He pulled away from her and his face was like stone.

He said, 'Is my mother's watch broken, or did you sell it? You came into the camp as though you had nothing. You returned my money as though you were a martyr. Living on lies again, Caithleen Healy?'

Kate sagged in her chair, looking at his face which was almost that of a stranger's, then rage tumbled up and out. She brought up her hand and slapped him. The sound rang out across the night.

'You bloody Auxie bastard,' she raged. 'You damned fool. You can dare to think of things like that when the man we love is lying there exhausted. We should be celebrating that he's come

257

through, and what do you do? You think of yourself. You, Ben Williams, are not worth the small finger on that old man's hand.'

She flung the flannel at him. The doctor called from the yard. 'Gather everything's back to normal from the sound of things. You two at one another's throats, and Old Roy in the middle as usual.'

Kate pushed past Ben. 'Just stop making wisecracks and get up here, and look after your patient. You, Ben Williams, come here.' She grabbed his arm, holding on as he tried to shake her off. 'No, you come with me.'

She wrenched him forward. 'If you want your watch, then you shall have your damn watch.'

She stormed ahead of him, checking that he was following her. He was.

She lifted her skirts and ran, calling back, 'Come on, you damn Tan. Come on.' Her hair was streaming out behind her, her chin was lifted. He ran faster but she was still ahead. His face stung. Anger tore at him. The Irish bitch. He ran faster. She was still ahead.

She swung down a street which was fully lit. Men milled around. She walked now, gasping for breath, a stitch slicing into her with every step. She walked into her whore-house. Ben followed. Japanese girls giggled. A man grabbed her. Kate slapped him away. The madam came towards them, her red dress shiny in the soft light, her breasts glistening in the heat. There was a heavy smell of stale perfume and sweat.

'You, Healy. Get out of here.' Her mouth was an ugly red slash. Lipstick had smeared onto her teeth, again.

Ben looked on as Kate stood her ground. His face still stung, his anger still raged.

Kate shouted, 'I want my watch. It was in the pocket of the dress I left here.'

The madam put her hands on her hips, threw back her head and laughed. 'You left a watch? Now what makes you think I'd remember that?' She leered at Ben who pushed away a girl who had sidled up. 'Lies, all lies,' the madam sneered.

'It always is,' Ben said.

Kate spun round. 'Shut up.' She swung back to the madam. 'Lies, is that what you want? Well, I'll go right out and tell them to the police unless you get me my watch. I'll give them such a pack of lies that they'll shut you down overnight. Rape, pillage. You name it, I'll lie about it.'

The madam stopped smiling. The girls stopped giggling. A man who was being led into a back room turned and slurred, 'What's going on?'

Kate shouted at him, 'Well, not a lot's coming off, unless I get my watch.'

The madam stormed over to the desk and unlocked a drawer. She brought out a cash box and took the watch from it, throwing it on the table. 'There's your damn watch, and I hope it's more good than you were. You never let anyone lay a finger on you, did you? Useless.'

Kate strode across to the desk, picked up the watch and slapped it into Ben's hand. 'Take it. How could you dream I'd sell it? But I don't care what you think any more. You're a fool, a selfish fool.'

She swept out.

At the house she told Old Roy what had happened, and she would not cry. She tended him, cared for him, brewed chicken broth, cooled water in the Coolgardie safe. She sat up on the veranda at night, though there was no need any more.

'I can't sleep, and I'd rather be with you,' she whispered.

'The man's a fool,' Old Roy said.

'Yes. And I more so because I still love him, Roy.' Roy sighed. 'I know, darlin'.'

Back at the camp Ben paced until Bluey swore at

him. Frank said, 'Strewth, go and talk to her, go and do something, you're driving us mad.'

Ben dug his hands deep into his pockets. How could he talk to her after all the things he had said? After all the things she had done? How could he love a woman who had used him? How the hell could he? How could they build a life together after everything that had passed between them? How could he ever trust her?

He went over the scenes again and again, until the madam blurred with the violet eyes which had looked with love on Roy, and on him by the river, and he could hear her shouting at the Tans, as she had shouted at him, he could see her red hair flying, her eyes flashing. He heard her voice reading to Roy and becoming English, and now he stood still. She had done that for him. She had become K-a-t-e for him.

She had not been a whore. She had not sold his mother's watch. She had worked to repay him. Had she loved Mick? She said that once she had. But now she did not. He rubbed his eyes with his hands. Damn it, damn it.

On the third evening of Roy's recovery Ben arrived in the yard. He wore a dark suit and carried a box beneath his arm. He gave it to her. 'For you.' His voice was soft. 'Perhaps you would be ready in half an hour. I need to apologize. Bluey is coming to look after the old coot.' He raised his voice as he said these last words.

Roy snorted in his bed. 'Just because you held my hand when I was weak and defenceless doesn't mean you can give me cheek every day of the week.'

Kate fingered the box. She looked at Roy. He nodded. She couldn't look at Ben because yet again she did not know what anything meant. She went into the kitchen and, by the light of the lamp, opened the box and held up a blue silk dress. There were shoes too. They were the right size.

Ben drew up a chair and sat with Roy. He ran his finger round his stiff white collar. 'This isn't every day of the week.'

Roy lay back on his pillows and smiled. 'This is special, is it?'

Ben nodded. 'Yes, you could say this is special.' They exchanged a look, and Old Roy's smile deepened.

He said, 'Learned something about yourself, have you?'

Ben rubbed his finger round his collar again. 'I've learned how little I've missed a damn collar.'

Roy lifted his hand and pointed at Ben. 'You've learned how much you've missed someone else too, I reckon.' He let his hand drop back onto the sheet again. Strewth, he had so little strength.

Ben slipped a flask of rum under Roy's pillow. 'You reckon too much, that's your problem.' Old Roy grabbed his hand. 'I need to thank you. You and her. You pulled me through.'

Ben returned Roy's clasp. 'An old coot pulls himself through.'

Roy whispered, 'You've got to mean it, if you say you love her. You can't hurt her. There's been enough of that between the two of you.'

'I don't know what I'm going to say. I don't know what she's going to say. Do you?'

'I've a pretty good idea,' Roy said.

The dress fitted perfectly. It was deep blue, the colour of her eyes, and as they walked into The Palace Hotel she stared at the receptionist and then grinned. He recognized her, inclined his head, and smiled.

She and Ben sat in the dining-room, beneath the swirling fans, and still she could not believe that she

261

was here with him. She looked at the wineglasses, at the flowers on the table, at the waiters drifting from table to table, at the other diners, so smart. She looked anywhere but at him. Why was she here?

She held up the leather-bound menu and chose her food. Ben ordered. Then silence fell.

The waiter brought wine. Ben tasted it. Nodded. The waiter poured for her, then Ben. He lifted his glass. 'To Roy's recovery.'

'To Roy's recovery,' she echoed. His eyes were so grey, his skin so tanned against his collar, his wrists so strong against his cuffs. I love you, I love you, she longed to say. All this has got to be resolved. One way or another, it must be resolved.

Instead she said nothing. The wine was cold, dry. She looked up at the pressed metal ceilings.

Ben replaced his wineglass. He ran his finger round the top. He said, 'Their billiards room is second to none. Before the pipeline it was the only green sward in Kalgoorlie.' They laughed.

'How did you know my size?'

'I went back and asked the madam.'

She dropped her fork. He laughed. She laughed.

As she ate, the knife glinted, and the conversations of the other diners ebbed and flowed around them, though their own stuttered and died.

I love you, I love you, Ben thought. But can I trust you? Her hand around the glass was small and tanned and calloused, when it should be white and soft. Her face was drawn with tiredness, when it should be pale and young and fresh. God, what a mess.

She drank another glass of wine. He said, 'Most of the people here tonight are mine managers.'

She turned, the room shifted. She clutched the table. She felt too hot. She said, 'I must . . .'

A waiter was pulling out her chair. Ben held her elbow. She leaned against him as they walked. Her head was swimming. 'I'm so sorry,' she said. 'So very sorry. I'm just not used to wine.'

As they went out, past the receptionist, she repeated, 'I'm sorry, so very sorry. So hot.'

As they stood in the cool of the evening and traffic passed down the wide street she said, 'I'm so sorry.'

He said, 'Don't be. I'm glad you're not used to drinking.' He steadied her.

She clutched him, her head was swimming. There were people passing. They were making her dizzy. 'No,' she said. 'It's me. I lied, I used you, but I suffered too because I loved you. I've paid now, Ben. I can only tell you once more that I'm sorry. It can't go on. Not even for Des's sake, can it go on. Not even for ours.'

Her head was spinning. She could still taste the wine. Her thoughts were like wisps of mist, slipping through her fingers. She looked around. She reached out. Ben took her hand. He was looking at her. Was there love in his eyes?

He looked at her lips which Mick had burst, at the face which had blistered when she had kept him from the mine after the compressor died. Did he trust her? He must, because he couldn't live without her.

He said, 'Loved, you said "loved"?'

His face was so close, his eyes so searching. She murmured, 'Love, I meant love.'

He was pulling her close, so close. His eyes were so grey, his mouth was so near, and now she felt his lips on hers, soft, gentle. People were jogging them, laughing, tutting. They mustn't; not here. She tried to pull away, but his arms were round her, holding her, and it was what she wanted, what she had always wanted, yearned for, would have died for. And now there were no people near them, there was only the wind in the reeds, and the curlews in the sky.

There were only his lips on her eyes, her cheeks,

her neck, her mouth. There was only his voice, 'I love you, I love you', against her lips.

A man said, 'Strewth.'

'The people,' she gasped.

'Damn the people,' he said, taking her hand, running her along the street until the breath caught in her throat, dodging down an alley, pulling her to him again.

'Marry me.'

His lips were on her neck, on her hands, her fingers. He held her face, looked deep into her. 'I love you. Marry me. Share *Wuthering Heights* with me.' He was laughing again, and she was too, and his lips were searching for hers again, and his kisses were no longer gentle, but fierce, impatient, and his body was hard against her, and his hands were running up and down her back, and she couldn't think, she couldn't speak. She wanted to tell him she was his, always had been, always would be, and she wanted him, needed him. But his lips were drawing her words away. They were forming, fragmenting, disappearing.

All she knew was that his hands were moving up and down the front of her dress, those long fine hands, and she wanted them against her skin. Now he was sliding the dress from her shoulders and his fingers were hot on her skin. He was kissing her shoulders, and her head was thrown back, and it was everything she'd ever dreamed.

'I love you, I always will,' she gasped, but he was kissing the words away again, and now she stroked his face, gripped his hair. She kissed him, her lips searching for the lines to his mouth, for the fine cheek-bones, for his mouth. But then a car hooted in the distance, and a dog barked. Ben opened his eyes, his hands became still. 'I love you. We've lost so much time.'

He gave her his mother's watch. 'I never want

it back, because I will never stop loving you. Please marry me.'

She looked at his fingers on her wrist and had never known such perfect happiness.

They married a month later, at a civil ceremony, and Lucia wept as she drank to the bride and groom and took Kate aside. 'But without the blessing of the Church it is not a marriage at all. It is not valid in the Church's eyes. He is a Protestant. What have you done?'

Kate kissed her and dragged Old Roy across with her eyes, while she said to Lucia, 'It is a marriage. It is my marriage. It is truly blessed.' She left Lucia with Roy and brushed the words from her happiness.

'I love you,' she told Ben as he opened the door to their room in The Palace Hotel. He lifted her in his arms, and carried her over the threshold. 'Are you sure?' he asked.

'You are my life.'

He put her down, and they held one another. 'I heard Lucia. She's right. It would have been easier for you to have married a Catholic. To have married Mick.'

She froze at his words, then walked to the window, staring out across at Hannan Street, at the figures who were hurrying either side of the street. She hadn't thought of Mick for weeks, and now he was here, in this room, between them.

She put her hand on the glass, spread her fingers and said carefully, into the silence that had wiped happiness from the room, 'It would have been impossible for me to marry Mick because I love you. Our marriage is legal in law. Do you wish it to be dissolved already? I told you. This must stop.' She closed her fingers and opened them again, and now he was here, turning her to him, holding her.

'Forgive me,' he said. 'Forgive me. I just love you so much.' The love was there in his eyes, strong and clear.

'Trust me,' she said. 'You must trust me.'

'I do,' he said against her mouth. 'I will. I do.'

He lifted her and carried her to the bed, and the light from the street cast his face into shadow. For a moment she was frightened because he was so close, and his fingers were in her hair and there had been fingers in her hair on the lane, before it had been sliced from her head. But then she remembered that it had only been Des protecting her. It had been him who had sent her to Ben.

She pulled Ben down to her, opening her mouth to his kisses, relaxing beneath his hands, which were undoing her clothes, and his own, and in the soft light his beauty took her breath away, as he stood beside the bed, running his hand over her shoulder, her breast, her belly, her loins, his eyes holding hers.

'I love you, Kate,' he said.

'I love you.' He kissed her throat and his body was lean and hard as he lay beside her, and it was the body she had only been able to guess at for too long. His hands were light on her breast, his mouth too now, his hair soft beneath her hands, and now he was kissing her mouth, and his tongue was stroking her lips, running down her throat, her breast, her belly, and she was drowning in love, and this wasn't enough.

She cried out, moaned, and her arms were round his neck, his body, and his hands were beneath her, along her, they were now on her belly, her thighs, and his eyelashes cast long shadows on his cheeks. His knee was between hers, working up and down, his skin harsh against hers, strong and harsh, and now his eyes were open, but they were clouded, and his breathing matched hers, and his hand was between her legs, and his fingers were searching, and now she

stiffened. He withdrew, held her gently, soothed her.
'I'm frightened,' she said.

'I know. Trust me.'

She did, and he was gentle, and slow, and she surged to the heights with him, and now he was in her, gentle, slow, and this beautiful man whom she had loved for so long was hers. They moved together and she belonged to him, loved him, and merged with him, soared with him, clung to him, and he to her until they could bear it no longer and both cried out.

Even when they rested they still clung, and explored one another's minds and bodies, and Ben knew almost beyond doubt that he could trust her love. Almost.

Chapter Thirteen

Just two days later, Kate, Roy and Ben sat around the table in the kitchen of the house Ben had bought the day after he had proposed. It was next to the Sidney Bailey house.

'I can't live in a house that I haven't contributed to. Do you understand?' Ben had said, as he held her in the Palace Hotel room on their wedding night, his face concerned. She had then insisted that he must accept as a wedding present her share of the Sidney Bailey house. 'To finally settle my debt.'

'No, that's no longer necessary.'

'For Mick's ticket,' she insisted.

He had accepted.

Now, in the kitchen, Ben watched her face in the flickering lamplight, hearing the rain falling on the corrugated-iron roof, smelling the kerosene lamp. God, how he loved her, how he'd always loved her. He put his hand on her shoulder and she turned to him, and her smile was gentle and vibrant, as their loving had been these past two nights.

He touched her hair, wanting to bury his face in it. He dropped his hand and leaned back in his chair, as Old Roy talked to her of the fine net she had bought to put up at the windows to keep out the flies. He listened to her measured reply, the voice which no longer had the wild surging Irish rage, the voice which she had changed, for him. He felt passion and he wanted to carry her through to the bedroom, remove her clothes, lie naked with her, with the woman she had become.

Now thunder roared. She jumped, laughed, and his laughter joined hers. 'No firing,' he whispered to her. She nodded.

Old Roy said, 'The chooks will be fussing.'

Kate said, 'They'll just be happy to be in out of the dry. Heavens, they could still be out in the bush with their coop in pieces where the sand storm blew it. That must have made their feathers curl.'

'That was nothing. Wait till you see a cyclone.' Old Roy paused, raised an eyebrow. 'On the other hand, darlin', just imagine it, don't feel you have to go and find one.'

They all laughed.

Old Roy asked Ben, 'When are you going back to the mine?'

Ben grinned. 'Worrying about things, are you? Well, tomorrow probably but we need to talk about your idea of building across the back of both your yards to make a series of rooms for lodgers.'

He leaned across and kissed Kate. 'Since you insist you can manage both houses.' She stroked his face. He gripped her hand, and the thrill of his touch set her alight and she saw from his eyes that he too longed for her. They smiled, their eyes locked. He said, 'And what do you think we should do?'

They both laughed for they both knew what they wanted to do, but that must wait for the darkness of the bedroom. Now there was a question to be answered, and their future to be planned, because they had talked all day, knowing that the mine wouldn't last for ever, and they wanted to set up as many boarding-houses as they could while property was cheap. They intended to use the income from the boarders to buy more, then sell up when prices rose. It would give them enough capital to start them in whatever venture they settled upon.

He sat close to her, his thigh against hers. He noted down figures. 'If we build on the boarding shed we could take in six extra men that way, at least. Everyone agreed?' He looked first at Old Roy, who nodded, and then at Kate, who hesitated, then shook her head.

'If we build, we'll have to put up money this minute. Also, if we build the shed, then when the gold market picks up and families start pouring in, we're restricting our appeal to ordinary house buyers. No, I think we need to concentrate on keeping the houses as houses, and selling them as such.'

Ben and Old Roy exchanged a look, and grimaced. Ben squeezed her thigh. 'Damn the woman. Why is she always right?' he groaned. 'So you think we should buy another house now, Kate, do you?'

'If you're going into partnership I think before you do anything else you two need to decide how much capital you are going to put up and how much that capital needs to earn while you're waiting to make the killing. And you need to decide how sure you are that there is going to be a killing before you decide on any of the other.'

Ben shook his head slightly. 'How do you know about business?'

She shrugged. 'Any woman knows about business. We have to run you lot.'

Old Roy stood up, bowed. 'Well, my Maureen would agree with that.'

Kate smiled and said, 'So I think we should knock this living-room and kitchen into one. Make a large dining-room. We can always put the wall back in if need be. We should offer cheap food to passing trade as well — as Sidney Bailey suggested — so we're not just relying on the boarders. But we'll only make a killing if the market picks up.' She leaned forward.

'Roy, how sure are you that things will pick up, that buyers will eventually flood in, that lodgers will fill our rooms until then? Don't forget, we're gambling on that nose of yours.'

Old Roy stared at the floor, then walked to the window. The storm was over, the dust would be settled. He opened the window, and breathed in the air. His Maureen had loved Kalgoorlie just after the rain fell. He breathed deeply again, coughing a little, but there it was again, that certainty that Kalgoorlie would bloom. He was as certain as he'd ever been about gold, or two-up, or life. He'd known the new drive would peter out, that the ore wasn't of such high grade. He had the best nose in the business.

He listened to the murmur of the voices behind him and frowned, anxiety gnawing at him. Yes, he was certain about the boom, but he didn't have that same certainty about the two people who sat round the table, and whom he loved. One had given too much, had changed to someone she wasn't, and the other still didn't understand or appreciate it.

'Come on, Roy,' Kate reminded him gently. 'How's the nose?'

He turned. 'Twitching,' he said. 'It's distant, but it will come.'

The next day while Ben was at the mine, Old Roy and Kate sat on the veranda and made a list of the changes that needed to be made to both houses.

'The boys are going to dismantle the wall between the kitchen and living-room first. Bluey said he'd be up for tea to talk about it. We can cut them in with a percentage of profits – work something out.'

Old Roy chuckled. 'They said they'd do it for the food, and for a sight of you. They miss you.' He hesitated. 'Caithleen—'

'Kate,' she interrupted, smiling gently.

271

He scratched his head. 'Stupid old coot, I've for-gotten what I was going to say.' But he hadn't, he had simply realized that he must leave well alone.

Kate said, ticking the list, 'So, let me get this straight: we're putting the lodgers in your house too and putting up partitions to split each room into two.'

Old Roy held up his hand. 'Remember I'll sleep on the veranda in the summer, so that's an extra room, and I'll be dossing out at the mine from time to time.'

Kate's voice was sharp. 'Now, Roy, you might have said that, but I said you should stay here. The doctor said you should stay here. You mustn't go down that mine again. The dust's too bad.'

'You see, you leap in, nag, nag. Wait on, darlin', I'm not going back down the mine. There's lots to be done on the surface, and the boys need me. I might be old, but I know a lot.' He was stabbing the table with his finger. 'And I'm used to lying on eucalyptus leaves, and seeing the moonlight through the canvas. Shouldn't leave what you're used to behind. It's what made you. You should remember that.'

Kate stood up. 'You're a stubborn old man, and I don't want to remember.' She flung her pencil down. It rolled across the table and dropped to the floor. She was shouting, her hands were shaking. 'Now I'm going to Lucia. I want her to know we're not trying to steal her trade by setting ourselves up.'

She swept past Roy. He grabbed her dress, stopped her, hauled her back, put his hands on her waist and pulled her round. 'We love you, all of us. Forgive my meddling.'

'Ben and I are happy. We understand one another, and the past. It's all behind us, now stop worrying.' She kissed the top of his head.

He let her go. 'Get on with you, and while you're out supping tea and cooing at Maria I'll be the one ticking off this list. Easier sloggin' at the mine,' he grumbled, taking the list from her and a pencil from behind his ear. He began to check the windows, mumbling to himself as she left.

Kate and Lucia pushed Maria in her pram towards the cemetery, then turned towards the station.

'She just loves the, um, how do you say ... ?' Lucia waved her hand as though trying to pluck the word from the air.

Kate shook her head. 'I don't know.' She laughed at the child. 'What do you like, sweetheart?'

Lucia slapped Kate's arm lightly. 'The movement, but that is not quite right.'

They were at the station now, and all around was the hiss of steam, the clank of carriages, the sound of engines in the yard, the smell of steam. Maria beamed. Lucia lifted her from the pram and handed her to Kate. The child was warm and soft, and untouched by life. Her little fingers reached out and grasped Kate's hair. 'Ouch.'

Together, they walked towards the railway lines. 'One day soon, it will be your own child pulling your hair,' Lucia said.

Kate looked at Maria's dark curling hair, her brown eyes. Would Ben's child have his grey eyes or her blue ones? His, she hoped, as she kissed the child. 'There is nothing I want more,' she called to Lucia who was peering down the track. The lines were quivering. A train was coming. The lines seemed to sink as the noise grew greater. Kate walked the child away, crooning to her, longing for her own.

Lucia made Kate push the pram as they followed the stream of passengers into the street. 'It is right that you practise,' Lucia laughed. They strolled past the banks, the shops, the hotels, the tea houses, the assayer's office, the share-dealers. They smelt the brewery, they talked above the noise of the stampers and compressors. 'Each month there are fewer mines operating,' Lucia said. They counted out the chimneys to Maria.

They turned off the main street and were now amongst bungalows whose gardens were clean and tidy, and full of sweet-smelling flowers. Kate groped for the right words to tell Lucia that she was also taking boarders.

Lucia talked of the sweets that she had made after the breakfasts had been cleared. 'But, my dear Kate, it is so difficult to find the peace. Everything must be right, the syrup has to be just the right heat. It is when I am interrupted that the sweets go pooff.'

'I'd like to see that,' Kate murmured, grinning.

'It is not funny, my dear Kate. They are for the bazaar, the church bazaar, but of course you would not know that.' Lucia clicked her tongue in reproof.

Kate shook her head in protest. 'Enough, enough, but I do want to confess something to you.' Her grin was wry.

Lucia put her hand on the pram. 'What have you done, my Kate?'

Kate told her then of their plan to take in boarders, of her concern that Lucia and Mario would think they were setting up in competition, and of her worry that she would lose her friend. Her words ran on, and now Lucia was shaking her head.

'Oh, you are so silly, so very silly. Do you go round with your eyes in the blinkers they put on the horses over there?' She pointed at the race course Tote Tower to the right. 'Of course you will not take boarders that might otherwise come to us. Hear my voice, dear Kate. It is that of an Italian.' She took over the pushing of the pram, rocking it slightly as Maria woke and started to cry. The baby slept again. 'It is Italian, so the Italian miners come to us. Yes, we had two visitors who were not, when you were helping, but they were outside visitors. You will have the English, for that is what you are – now. Is that not correct.' Her look was penetrating. Kate ignored it.

Bluey, Frank and Stan came every evening and helped to knock the dining-room through and build the partitions, while Kate set out small flower-beds and planted the rose that Lucia and Mario had given them, and pansies, sweet william and pin cushions. She grew nasturtiums over the trellis that Old Roy had made either side of the gate that now connected his backyard to hers.

She pinned up fine wire at all the windows and hung muslin too, to keep out the dust. She polished Roy's black stove, and hers. She hung bellows and a pair of tongs. She made pickles, she cleaned. She showed Ben where to place the large stones on the ground near the veranda. 'They'll keep the dust down.'

'And the pain in my back up,' he moaned.

'I'll kiss it better.'

'I'll keep you to that.'

In the evenings she embroidered cushion covers and knitted for Maria. At night she and Ben lay naked, their bodies entwined, their passion surging, ebbing, surging again until they lay satiated, and then they both talked of their love, and their trust, and their hopes, but never of the past.

By June she was three months pregnant, and Ben had never known such joy. He took her to the dance being held in the banqueting hall and held her in his arms as the music soared. He wanted to shout to the world, and to Mick, and to all those Irish peasants who had laughed behind his back, She's mine, really mine now.

Two months later he touched her belly, and she

was right, the baby was moving, and he kissed her swollen abdomen, her breasts, her mouth. 'I love you,' he murmured.

In September they had eight boarders, and the miners sat over their tea and listened to the young man from Scotland who worked at the School of Mines talking of the need for a better way to extract gold from ore. 'The field's struggling to survive. We must get up to date, we're working on a flotation process. It'll improve production and cut down dust.'

She joined Old Roy on the veranda, and while she rocked in the chair the boys had made her she asked him, 'Is your nose still twitching? Things are getting worse, aren't they?' She touched her belly. Were they wrong to put out money on another house as they were intending?

Old Roy sucked on the pipe he had changed to after the doctor had said he'd strangle him with his stethoscope if he kept on puffing 'those weeds' between coughs. 'It's twitching, there's work. And don't forget, we're doing well enough in the meantime. Keep calm.'

The heat was soaring by October, but still men came for meals to the cut-price restaurant, and still Kate took in washing from Chris and Mark, and the boarders, and anyone else prepared to pay.

'You must not become too tired,' Lucia warned.

Ben stroked her belly at night and kissed her gently. 'You are too tired.'

But she must work, because Old Roy had told her that as his mine was bottoming the ore was becoming poorer – soon it must close. The boys must try and get jobs in the big mines, but the flotation process was not yet in production, and in the big mines Ben would breathe in the dust. She wished they hadn't ploughed back their profits into a third house, then maybe they could have put up with the poorer grade ore. The next week she took in the washing of Sidney Bailey's friends, and still cleaned his house.

In November she fainted and Ben carried her from the wash-house and laid her on the bed, and that night Bluey cooked for the boarders, while Kate floated in the night sky, up amongst the stars, and rested as she had not done since she was a child, and when Ben came to her in bed, she clung to him. 'I'm not earning enough.'

He kissed her. 'You're going to be earning less. I have taken on Ma Smith's daughter. And we've chipped in to buy Sidney Bailey out, so he can pay Ma Smith's daughter if he wants a skivvy.'

She struggled out of his arms. 'But we can't. I can work. Our mine's closing. You'll go down one of the big ones. We'll have debts.'

He pulled her back to him, aching with love for her. 'Shh. There's just enough. We're in this with Roy, remember. You're outvoted. I'll go as a trucker, they breathe in less dust. Shh. It's all arranged. Roy knows the foreman. Do you think I would let you work, whilst I did not?' He kissed her, and she thought she would die for love of him.

In December the pains began as she made Christmas decorations on the veranda.

Ben ran for Lucia. Lucia laughed as he almost dragged her through the Italians on the pavement. 'Get out of the way,' he yelled at them.

'Hush, hush, it will be hours yet, poor Kate. The things we women do for you men.'

Ben shouldered his way through the remaining Italians. 'Can't they see this is a pavement? Can't they see, for God's sake? Why do they always hang about so others have to walk in the roadway?'

Lucia pulled him back, no longer laughing. 'It is our way. We move for you when asked. But no, it is your way to shoulder through. Which is best?'

Ben stopped and wanted to shout and swear, but

this woman was Kate's friend, this woman was helping. Why the hell couldn't Kate choose their own
kind, his own kind? He swallowed and said, 'I'm sorry,
Mrs Vincenzi.'

He and Old Roy sat on the veranda, while Bluey,
Frank and Stan set up a game of two-up in the yard of
Roy's house. 'Keep it quiet,' Old Roy growled. 'Don't
want the cops round.'

But no-one could concentrate and even the boarders were waiting. They might be placing their bets
with Bluey, who had taken the ring, but they were
waiting.

In the bedroom Kate rested between contractions.
Dawn was breaking.

'Soon, let it be soon,' she begged. There was
another pain, deep and long, too long. 'Holy Mother,'
she groaned. 'Oh, Mum, Mum, help me.' She felt her
mother's hands holding hers. 'Oh Mum.' But it
wasn't her mother, it was Lucia, and now the doctor
was here, and the pains were running one into the
other.

'Holy Mary, Mother of God. Holy Mary,' she
repeated again and again, and now the wind was
in the reeds, and the curlews were crying, and the
water was lapping at the bank, and the scent of sweet
hay rose into the night sky, and the darkness became
a nave, and incense floated down the nave, and the
priest knelt before the altar, and his silver-and-gold
cloak glinted, and her knees hurt from kneeling, and
the benediction was all around, lapping at her.

The water was lapping at the bank, her father
was calling, 'Caithleen'. She was walking away, and
she wouldn't turn, even when the Tans dragged her
mother. Then it was Ben dragging her, hurting
her, pushing her, and Mick too, and she screamed.
'Mum, Mum, I want to come home. Ben, Des, Mum,
Dada, I want to come home.'

But the pains went on and on, and still she called until her voice was a whisper and exhaustion tugged at her, and the heat baked, and then, at last, it finished, and there was the sound of a baby crying. Lucia passed her baby to her, laughing and crying, saying, 'It's over, she's here, your blessed baby is here.'

Kate caught at her sleeve, whispering, through her exhaustion, 'Could Ben hear me?'

Lucia looked across at the doctor, who shook his head, and mouthed, 'Tell her – no.'

Lucia kissed Kate's hand. 'Hear what, my dear? You said nothing.'

She rested her head on her baby's red-brown hair, and touched the tiny fingers, and Ben was coming, kneeling by the bed.

He touched his daughter and felt skin so soft, and heard a cry so faint, that it was like the breeze. He laid his finger on her hand. She gripped it, and her skin was pink against the tan of his. You're mine, he thought, you are both mine, you're not theirs, you don't belong to the past any more, and he fought down the rage and fear that her cries had brought. You're mine. I love you – this is your home, he willed her silently. He turned his back on Lucia, Kate's Catholic friend, wanting her, and all her sort, away from here, away from his wife, out of their lives, leaving them safe.

He said, 'What shall we call her?'

'Rose,' Kate murmured.

Ben smiled. 'You are so perfect. How could you know that my mother's name was Rosemary?'

She hadn't known, but now she made herself believe that she had, and that her daughter was named for his mother, not her Irish friend.

By June of 1924 Old Roy's mine had shut and the boys were in Perseverance, not Golden Horshoe, because that was mainly the preserve of the Catholics, and not Lake View which was mainly the preserve of the Italians.

In August Ben and Roy bought up a neighbouring house and, as the cooler months came, Old Roy helped Kate to set it up. This time Bluey, Frank and Stan took rooms, and supper was served in shifts at the main house.

Ben took her to more dances. 'I can show you off, and we can meet people who might be able to help.' They had thought that, one day, they would open a hotel in Kalgoorlie with the profits from the sale of the properties – 'If Roy's nose is right,' they muttered each time, but the uncertainty had its own excitement, for they were together, and what else mattered?

For each dance he bought her a new dress, and in December, on Rose's first birthday, just before the Christmas Ball he kissed her neck in the bedroom and slipped a necklace around it, doing up the clasp. Kate fingered it. 'It's gold,' she whispered.

'What else for my darling?'

'But can we afford it?'

'It's made from nuggets I've fossicked.' He was speaking into her hair. 'One day I will buy you emeralds to set off your hair, or shall I make it sapphires, to match your eyes?'

'If Roy's nose is right,' they said together, and laughed.

But then he sobered. 'This is also to thank you for our daughter.'

They danced only with one another that night, not caring about business contacts, and had eyes only for one another, and words only for one another, and they left early, walking home, refusing the calls of the hansom cabbies, and once they had passed The Palace he pulled her down the same alley where he had kissed her so long ago, and the same joy was in them, and the same excitement, but now there was a deeper love and Ben was relaxing because Kate was too busy to see much of Lucia.

In 1925 they bought two more houses and employed two more girls, and now Rose was talking and walking, and the house was full of laughter, and the evenings on the veranda full of contentment as Old Roy sat in the rocker with Rose on his lap, telling her stories of the stars while Bluey carved ships and Stan strummed his guitar, and Frank talked of the girl he had met at the bazaar Kate had dragged him to, carrying the sweets she had made, and Ben worked on his accounts and his plans and his dreams, and Kate sewed and planned the menu for tomorrow, and calculated the cut lunches she would prepare in the morning, and thanked God, her own God, for all he had given her, as she told Lucia on one of their rare meetings.

Lucia raised her eyes. 'We both work so hard, perhaps too hard. We don't seem to have time for one another any more. We should make time, it would be good for our children.'

In 1926 they bought two more houses in the same street, and the price was lower still because times were even harder in the two towns. Kate and Ben didn't laugh quite so loud when they talked of Roy's nose twitching and as the end of the year approached she said, as Bluey pulled the punkah rope on the veranda, 'It would help if we could widen our net, go beyond the ordinary boarders, and hook those who come to visit the country. After all, some do. Or tempt Perth people out here for their holidays. Kalgoorlie people go to *them*, after all. We could get Roy to take them round his mine, show them how to fossick. We need to sell them the idea of widening their knowledge of their land, their heritage.'

Roy nodded slowly, Rose asleep in his arms. 'Could

be good. That would set up some sort of a lead into the hotel, if we ever swing that one.'

Kate said, 'Maybe we could bring in Lucia, I see so much more of her these days. We could print some in Italian, some in English, they could share the cost, we could have a bigger spread then.'

Ben tensed, then rolled up his shirtsleeves. 'Leave the Eyeties to look after themselves. It all gets too complicated.'

Bluey stopped pulling the rope. 'Too right, jabbering away in the mines. We've got two with us now, it's dangerous, they can't understand orders, for hell's sake. They shouldn't be allowed down. They're taking Australian jobs, you know.'

Frank called, 'There's talk about setting up a quota.'

Old Roy said, 'There's always been that sort of talk, especially when times have got tight. A lot of things happen when times get tight. Leave them be. There'll be enough for everyone soon.'

'Not your nose, again,' Stan groaned. Everyone laughed, except for Kate, because she had listened to their anger, and it was so like the anger of the Tans, so like the anger of the Catholics, the Protestants, so like the anger of the anti- and the pro-Treaty men, and it was bursting out above ground now, and worse, it had reached Ben.

Old Roy saw her face. 'Time this little lass was in her bunk.' He struggled to his feet and took Rose through, knowing that Kate would come.

She did, tucking in her daughter, kissing her cheek, looking down on her. Roy touched her arm. 'It's only men's talk. It's fear for their jobs, it's grumbling. Let me ask you again, have you ever seen trouble up top?'

She shook her head. 'But why do differences have to matter?' And she felt fear clutch at her again and knew that she must always be on her guard, she must never lose control, she must never let Caithleen come back.

In early 1927 she and Ben travelled to Perth. At the hotel on their first night, they gazed out onto the city, and it was quiet after Kalgoorlie and so clean. Where was the dust? Ben said, 'We'll use the introductions that Seth Adams gave me at the races, starting with Smith, the manager of this hotel.' He kissed her hair. 'Oh Kate, it'll be good to get out of that mine. If only my father could see me at the end of a shift, he'd wonder if the world had gone mad.'

She wouldn't think of her father, because he didn't think she'd gone mad, he thought she'd gone to hell.

Ben's arms tightened round her. 'I'm going to talk Smith into leaving our leaflets in his lobbies and discuss a rake-off for him if he encourages his guests to come on to us. I'll build it into the price.'

He began to pace. 'Then we'll talk to the boarding-houses, and then the shipping lines. Same deal.' He came across and took her hands. 'If we get too many wanting a room, who cares? We'll buy another house, and another, and then the hotel. Roy will do the tours you suggested, show them the mine and so on. He's sorting it out while we're here.'

She was in his arms now. 'You're wonderful, Kate, and you deserve a holiday, so while I traipse round, you can get to the shops. Think about The Palace, look around this place. See how they do things. We'll need to set up two bungalows properly. Lots of smart hotel-type furnishings.'

She shook her head. 'Ben, Ben. Let me think.'

She looked out onto the city again, and around the room at the flock wallpaper, the tapestry curtains, the thick carpet. 'Look, my darling, we can't compete with this. There's The Palace if people want that.' Now she was pacing. 'No, what we have to do is sell the Kalgoorlie ethic, if you like. We must sell them the idea of a weatherboard house, and cart rides out to the mine. We must sell them fossicking, camping out under the stars. But in the boarding-houses we must have good food, clean table-cloths, flowers on the table. We must have miners' tools scattered around. We must have a price which includes everything, but also one which doesn't, so they can, if they prefer, do as they want.'

Ben was frowning. She stopped pacing. 'Oh, no. I'm quite wrong. You were right. Just tell me what you want me to do.'

He wasn't listening. She touched his arm. His hand closed over hers.

'No, I'm just thinking; and you're right, you're absolutely right.' He pulled her to him. 'We do make a good team, you and I, don't we?' His eyes were intense.

She kissed his mouth. Then she pulled away again. 'Yes. But what makes you think Smith will agree?'

Ben said carefully, 'We're from the same side of the tracks. He's English – our sort. We can trust him.'

She leaned against him and asked nothing else.

For three days he talked to other contacts while she bought table-cloths, vases, cutlery, enamel cups and saucers – just as the miners might have used. She made lists of the condensed-milk tins she must convert to mugs for the camp, of the tents they must buy. But these they could get from Kalgoorlie, and they could have bought the table-cloths there too, she thought ruefully, as she looked at the pile mounting in the corner of the bedroom.

That afternoon she walked by the Swan River instead of the shops, and then sought sanctuary from the heat in the Art Gallery, and stood before Hans Heysen's landscape, 'Droving into the Light', and wondered at the skill of the man, but all the time she missed Rose and Roy and Lucia.

In the evening they spent sixpence each and visited the carnival by the river, and heard the screams of those on the roller-coaster and watched pipe bands and Punch and Judy – but she couldn't bear it when Punch beat the policeman because she could see her mother in the mud, and Bluey swearing at the Slavs and Italians, and the Volunteers firing at the British.

Ben said, as she tucked her arm into his and they looked out across the river, that Smith was talking about going across to the East, to Sydney. He added, 'Might be an idea to think of that ourselves, once we've got the cash in our hands. We've already talked of an hotel, so why not make it in Sydney.'

He touched her face, traced her lips with his finger, kissed her, and she felt her body respond, but her mind was still with his words because she knew from Old Roy that in Sydney there were Protestant suburbs and Catholic suburbs. But she was being stupid. There might be differences, but they were contained as they were in Kalgoorlie.

She murmured, 'I want to go home. There's so much to do, and I miss Rose, and Roy – and Lucia.'

Mick felt the wind from the harbour trying to take the hat from his head. He jammed it on harder and looked across at Sydney, then at the harbour gate. He landed on the wharf at Manly and walked up the street, feeling the heat. He slung his jacket over his shoulder. He must keep moving. He had to keep moving. He felt the newspaper heavy in his jacket pocket. Damn them. Damn the Free Staters. Damn Des.

He bought lemonade at a restaurant, downed it in one. He strode out into the light, and there was the Pacific, storming and tumbling onto the yellow sand, like no sea that he had known in Ireland. Its rollers matched his anger, smashing and crashing onto the beach. He could stand still no longer.

He took a tram to somewhere, anywhere. He stayed on it, clenching and unclenching his hands, watching his whitening knuckles. Damn the Free State Government. They'd done a deal with the British government. Ireland would not be united. They'd had their debts to the British wiped out in return.

You bastards. Damn you, Des. Damn you. And where's your republic? Dead, like Collins, while you, you're still there, the cat that got the cream.

He jumped off the tram at the next stop, onto a wide sandy road. He walked past a small bungalow, past a small tin-roofed shop. Flies were in his mouth, round his eyes. He walked until his shoes rubbed. On and on, toiling up a ridge of sand which rose before him, slipping, digging in, like his life. One step forward, two back. The wind snatched at his hat as he crested it. There was the sea again, pounding, rolling.

He turned his back to it and looked across the huge hinterland, with its scrub and peeling gum trees, its shimmering sands, its emptiness. Yes, Des, you're back there, selling us down the river, like you sold me. You're there, the bloody hero, sitting round Daddy's table, with a roof repaired by me, looking at a barn repaired by me. And who's with you? Caithleen. She must be, because there's no-one here for her.

Was that it all along, Des? Were you sweet on her? Sweet enough to get me out here, leave me to rot. The sea was rolling, pounding. The heat was scorching him through his shirt.

'Is she rubbing milk on your shoulders now, Des? Is that it? Did you want her devious little hands on your body, just as you have your devious great mitts on my land?' He was shouting aloud, but who cared. No-one cared, not for him.

He walked back to the tram, caught it to Manly, caught the ferry to the city. He walked to the pub, throwing his newspaper on the bar, slapping down his money, drinking a schooner down, then another.

Listening to the men who worked in the same sportswear factory as he did, for the same Irish boss. Did they know how they'd been betrayed?

He told them, shouting down the bar, 'They have, you know. They've sold us down the river. Well, my lads'll not stop fighting. Sent me to raise funds, so they tried to tell me. Well, I'll bloody raise funds.'

He slammed his glass on the bar. The men laughed. Hughie, who shared his room in King's Cross, called, 'Go easy, Mick, or the leprechauns'll be after getting you.'

He roared, 'Damn the leprechauns. It'll be us who get the Proddies.'

The machinist drinking stout called from the end of the beer-stained bar, 'Get your hand around another glass, and then your mouth around it too, and give us some peace.'

A navvy called to the barman, 'Give him another, will you, mate.'

The barman did. Mick drank, gulping it down. He bought another, and all the time the anger was building. He shouted to the machinist, 'Come on then, let's get some money out of you, for the cause.'

The men around him laughed. Hughie called, 'Get it into your thick skull, we're Aussies. Which of us's going to pay out money to Ireland now? I'm not, I'm telling you. Strewth, right load of idiots you made us look, turning your guns on one another.'

The navvy said, 'I marched for you, in the war, so I did. I marched through the streets of Sydney to support the cause. I marched against conscription. No-one was telling me to fight for buggers who were shooting our leaders, imprisoning our relatives. So what do you do? You win, you send the Tans packing, then you kill one another. The Proddies in the banks, the commerce houses, in their bloody Sydney suburbs are splitting their sides at you idiots.'

'You watch your mouth,' Mick said, slamming his glass down.

'Go home to bed, Mick. Just go home.'

Mick felt hands on him, pushing him from one to another, until he was out into the heat of the evening. He felt the world tip. He grabbed at the tiled wall, steadied himself. 'Don't you worry,' he shouted. 'Don't you worry, Mick O'Brian's going into politics. Mick O'Brian's going to be someone. I haven't got taken on yet, but I will.' He fell, and rolled into the gutter. 'I'm going to be someone, d'you hear? I just need a bit more time.' Someone stepped over him. He heard laughter. 'Cait,' he murmured. 'Cait, why did you let Des do this to me?'

Chapter Fourteen

The shopping bags were heavy, and Kate eased her shoulders. There had been little sign of Christmas in the shops, fewer toys than ever to choose from, and fewer stampers and compressors slamming and banging. It was almost 1928, and what would the New Year bring? Was the up-turn round the corner?

She walked on past churches and halls that needed reroofing, painted shop signs that were peeling. Eric the butcher had closed up and gone, and there were no longer any rich warm scents oozing from the deserted bakery. The gold industry had almost collapsed, but Ben and Kate had bought up three more properties, two of which they had filled with boarders, so they were afloat and, what's more, saving a little, too.

She worked one day a week in Joe's Hotel while Roy minded Rose. She made beds, cooked, ordered food, took what bookings there were, and watched and learned as Ben had asked. She explained everything to Ben in the evening, after his mine shift, although she could scarcely see from tiredness but then neither could he after a day in the mine. And each night they slept in one another's arms – and she had never been happier, because they were in this together.

She walked on past more empty houses. They would fill their empty house with the tour guests who would be arriving in February.

She ran through the arrangements again in her

head, but the weight of the bags intruded. She set them down in the dust, and now she heard Old Roy calling from behind. 'Strewth, woman, you go like a hurricane. Lucia's taken Rose off for a walk, so just wait on, and I'll take some.'

She wiped her forehead and smiled as he hurried up.

'You take two, I'll take two,' he panted. 'And I hope you found something real nice to put round the tree for me, and something real nice for you to wear for the party.'

She laughed. 'You'll just have to wait and see, but I found Rose another colouring-book. Just remember not to fill it all in for her this time, for heaven's sake.'

Old Roy shook his head. 'I'll be too busy showing these pretend fossickers around.'

'Will it work?' she asked.

'Have faith,' he replied. 'There's no gold industry to collapse in Perth, so they've still got money in their pockets.'

He took the bags from her. She stopped him. 'Joe's Hotel is up for sale. Ben's still on about extending into that area. It would make everything perfect if we could stay here.' Her smile faded. 'He talked of the East again last night. I don't want to go and leave everyone. I don't want to move Rose. She's only four, and so happy here. You try and talk to him about buying Joe's too, will you, please Roy? With both of us at it, how can he refuse?' She was grinning but her eyes were serious.

Roy walked on beside her. 'The trouble with you women is that you always have to have something to worry about. He can't leave here while property has no value, so stop worrying. It's Christmas, you've a party to prepare, and I've got to put up another shack for the tourists to ogle.' But Old Roy's mind wasn't on his words, it was on the thought of life without Kate and Rose and Ben, and his eyes were serious too.

That evening Frank played his accordion at the boarding-house but he drank too many schooners of beer and made too many mistakes, and the guests, including Mario and Lucia, booed him, and everyone collapsed into one another's arms and laughed too much for him to continue.

'It's too hot, anyway,' Old Roy complained, flopping onto the veranda steps.

'Poor Frank,' Rose said, hugging Frank's knee. 'Nasty people.'

Kate scooped her up, kissing her face, looking into her blue eyes, similar to her own, but paler. She stroked the curly auburn hair. 'You are right, we're nasty, and Frank is going to cry.'

Frank couldn't cry, he could only laugh and take Rose from Kate. He threw her up into the air, and her shrieks of delight rang out, and then he blew on her stomach, and she giggled, but pushed him away. 'Your mouth's all wet. You *are* nasty.' Now Frank cried loud pretend sobs, but Rose hit him. 'You're only playing.'

He chased her round the yard, and Maria too. Bluey caught them both, and ran away down the side of the house with them. Kate watched all this, with Old Roy, and felt his arm go round her. 'Enjoy, darlin'. Enjoy every minute. Take every day as it comes. I've been talking to Ben. He's made a decision, and it should please you.'

Ben came down the steps behind them. 'Spooning, are you? You should be ashamed of yourselves.'

He watched Mario take the schooner of beer from Stan, while Lucia and Kate handed out sandwiches and cakes to the men, and to Stan's girlfriend, who was talking to Bluey's latest conquest. He ran his finger round his collar, feeling stifled. He hated to see Lucia and Mario here, on his property. He hated to see the exchanged glances between Lucia and Kate, the laughter, the friendship. They *must* move

East, be with people who were safe; but Roy was right: the time wasn't yet right, damn it.

He led Kate away from the dance and said, 'Roy and I have been thinking about the hotel. You know it so well. It would be like stepping into well-worn shoes, and it would be the ideal place to house extra tour guests. It would also be a good place to actually get in and learn the business thoroughly before moving East just as soon as things pick up. Let's try and buy it. We can put aside the tour money, even take a loan. Joe'll haggle over the price, so we'll stall him until we can buy him out. What do you think?'

His arms were round her, his mouth close, so close, and now his lips were on hers. 'I think you're so good to me,' she murmured against his lips, pushing his words about the East away.

On 31 December they toasted 1928 and knew it would be a good year. In January she cooked for Maria's school bazaar, though she would not go. 'No,' she said to Lucia. 'I've told you before, Ben wouldn't like it.'

'But, Kate,' Lucia protested, 'you should bring Rose, she would get to know the pupils, it would be less of a step for her. The first day of school is, oh, so difficult, though she and Maria can go together. She could meet the Sisters. Father O'Flannigan will be there.'

Kate brushed back a strand of hair, looking up at the punkah fans. 'Pull harder, Tim,' she called to the boy who was earning sixpence today. 'Pass me the flour please, Lucia.'

Lucia passed it. Kate said, 'For the last time, she's not going to the Catholic school, Lucia. She is going to the public school.' Her voice was crisp, her mind closed.

Lucia put her hand to her mouth. 'But, Kate, I felt sure you would reconsider. You cannot do this. Those schools are secular. They are not based on religion, there will be no mention of the Catholic faith. You cannot.'

Kate floured the board, and rolled out the pastry, sweat dripping down her back. 'I can, just as I can bake tarts for you, when it is already as hot as hell in here.'

Lucia gasped, 'Kate, please.'

Kate leaned on the rolling-pin. 'No, Lucia, please get it into your head that I am part of Ben. He is my life. I am not a Catholic any longer.'

'Then you are a Protestant.'

'No, I am nothing, or everything, whichever way you choose to look at it. This is the last time we must talk of it. We are friends, but I have chosen my life.'

Lucia said nothing for a moment, and then Kate heard her walk to the door. 'I must go,' Lucia said.

Kate spun round. 'No, don't go. I know we can't agree, but we can stay friends.'

Lucia fingered the fly door, her back to Kate. She said, 'You owe it to your daughter, you are denying her her roots, her faith.'

Kate said, 'Please, just let us live our lives as we see fit, as I see fit. Just leave it alone.'

Lucia looked back at Kate. 'But you swim in a wider sea. You are not alone. It is important that as Catholics we have our schools, that we keep our faith and our identity. We are apart, the only true faith. It is this you deny yourself, and your daughter.'

Kate gestured sharply. 'But that's what is so wrong. We should mix, forget all this.'

Lucia shook her head sadly. 'We must not, can't you understand that?'

She left, and Kate watched her leave the yard and turn into the alley. Then she threw the rolling-pin across the dining-room, breaking a mug. 'Damn it,' she shouted.

Tim called, 'Everything all right, missis?'

She brushed the flour from her hands. 'Yes, Tim, everything's fine.' And it was. She had her family, Roy's cough was better, they were buying an hotel in Kalgoorlie, and that was enough.

But that night she tossed and turned, twisting the sheets around her legs, dragging them from Ben who woke, reached out, and mumbled, 'What's wrong?'

'It's Lucia. We've rowed. I think I've lost her as a friend.'

Ben pulled her to him and his kisses were fierce. 'You have me. That is enough, isn't it?' And his passion surprised her and when it was spent she stroked his hair.

'Yes, you are my life. That's what I told her.'

Ben smiled, and in the morning he whistled as he shaved, and talked of a Kalgoorlie hotel with impatience, and shrugged when she mentioned the East.

'There's no hurry now.'

She stood at the bathroom door watching as he ran the razor through the frothing soap.

'Now?' She didn't understand.

He caught her eye. 'Well, it's like Roy said. It's not the right time.'

That day she walked round to Lucia's but Mario wiped his hands on his cooking apron and said that his wife was out. As Kate left, she saw the curtains of the bedroom twitch and knew that Lucia was there.

The next week she pedalled to Roy's mine, taking out the mugs, plates, cutlery, sheets and blankets in a cart she dragged behind her. In the searing heat she cleaned up the old meat safe, set up the Coolgardie. She brewed tea while Old Roy whistled, and made a new clothes boiler out of a kerosene tin.

'Be showing them how you did all the washing, will you then?' Roy said, as she called him for tea.

She laughed and shook her head. 'That is the last thing I'll do. I'll tell them though.'

'So, we'll bring them out in the horse and cart, give them a tour of the site. Take them on to Chris's mine if they want to go down a working one. Get 'em fossicking if they're happy with that. Chris says he'll bring the goat back for as long as we want it, and he'll nip across and hobble it during the week. Will you come every time?'

She shrugged, squinting against the sun, her skirt hitched up out of the ash. 'Whenever I can. That young Tim will come with you when I can't. He can't find work, so he's glad of a bit of cash, and so's his mother.'

Old Roy took out his pipe and banged it on the stones around the fire. 'Will you show them how to make damper?'

She wasn't listening, she was thinking of Lucia, and how she missed her, because the Italian woman hadn't been to see her, and when Kate had called again, Mario had still insisted she was out. 'So often,' Kate had said. Mario had shrugged.

'Hey, we've got to get this sorted out,' Roy chimed in.

She stared at him.

He repeated himself. She nodded. 'Oh the damper – is that all? You or I can do it.'

Roy looked at her. 'No, not just the damper.'

In February it was hotter still, but their first tour was fully booked and would arrive on the fifteenth. Ben sat in his rolled-up sleeves and worked out figures. He shook his head in exasperation at Kate. 'That old Joe, he won't come to a final figure for the hotel, you know, and we've enough for a down payment. You've got to work harder on him.'

She smiled. 'I'll try.' But what more could she do? As it was she staggered down the corridors with dirty linen and scrubbed pots in the sink until her hands were raw, and then she had to sit down and sort out the accounts and wages, with Joe peering over her shoulder and talking to her as though she were an idiot.

It was she who had to smile at the few customers that arrived and listen to their complaints about the food, and to Joe's about the money Ben was offering. 'Downright robbery, it is,' he would say, tipping another load of dishes into the sink, splashing her as he did so. Every time he did that – one day she'd hit him with the dishcloth.

'Make sure you do try,' Ben snapped.

'Three bags full,' she snapped back.

They looked at one another and laughed. She said, 'He's a difficult man, but perhaps we should give him what he wants. It's still a very low price.'

Ben touched her face with his finger. 'You don't understand. We can get him down further. Trust me. Nothing can go wrong.'

She wanted to say, but it already has. Lucia won't see me. And she didn't know why she didn't.

The next day she ironed on the veranda while Rose played with the ship Stan had carved, floating it in the old kerosene tin Kate had filled with water that morning. Old Roy whittled tent pegs on the steps and whistled between his teeth. She loved the fresh clean smell of the linen, and the beeswax which she rubbed on the base of the iron to make the table-cloths stiff and smooth. She had brought home Joe's ironing to keep him sweet. She looked across at the chooks, then at the wood Bluey had carted in for the laundry copper.

'Do you really think I should show them how I washed out in the bush?' she called to Roy, holding a table-cloth beneath her chin as she folded it. There was no answer. She looked up. Roy had called Rose to him and was sitting, his head up, his eyes searching the sky, but for what?

She picked up the iron again, holding it close to her cheek. It was too cool. She'd go round to Lucia's again today.

Roy called, 'There's a hush.' His voice was tense.

She listened. Yes, she could hear the stamping, the pounding, but almost too clearly. She came to the veranda steps. 'Oh not another blow?' She started to gather up her ironing.

Roy pulled himself to his feet, looking all around. 'More than a blow. It's a damn cyclone,' he murmured, throwing his knife to one side.

She clutched at him. 'Where? What do we do? Roy, what do we do?' She reached for Rose.

Roy looked at her, panic on his face where she had never seen anything but certainty. 'Get under the bungalow,' he said at last. 'Just get under it.' He was dragging them down the steps, pushing Rose beneath the veranda.

Kate could feel the wind now and hear the noise, the roaring noise, and she'd heard it before but this time it was louder, much louder, and the wind was tearing at them, sand was blinding them.

Roy was pushing her to the ground. 'Cyclone – get under.' The wind was screaming now. Rose was screaming. The fury of the wind knocked Kate back, over, rolling her away from Rose. She dug her head and feet down, and clawed her way back beneath the noise. Roy was on his knees, grabbing for her. Sand lashed into her face and eyes and there was no Ben to come for her. She caught Roy's hands, together they belly-crawled, their faces down, hearing Rose's screams, driven on by them until they reached her.

They fought their way to the veranda, the sand choking the breath in their throats and chests. The wind caught them, forcing them back again, across the yard. They fought, won, crawled beneath the veranda, clasping Rose to them. The noise was less, but not much, the wind and the sand caught them here, and the fear. Oh my God, the fear.

She pulled Rose between them, and they lay with their arms over her, and saw the hen coop lift and smash into the wash-house, and saw the wash-house tin roof take off, and the fence, and there were shapes in the air, but they didn't know what, the sand was too dense and it was dark, so dark. There were crashes and bangs, and a wrenching noise from above them, and then a great heave, and a tearing.

Kate screamed as the veranda floor creaked. She looked up. It was falling. It stopped an inch above her. Rose clung to her. Roy, who was crawling forward, pulling forward, pulled himself on his elbows.

'Don't leave us,' she shouted. She held Rose to her.

'Mummy, Mummy,' Rose screamed.

'It's all right, darlin'.' Roy gestured. 'I'll hold it up. You come.'

Kate inched forward. There was a crack, the veranda dropped, touched her back. Stopped. Roy turned, then drove on desperately. 'I'll lift it. Get out. Get Rose out.'

He was out from under, but then he was snatched by the wind, rolled across the yard, swept away in the dust. There was another crack. The veranda dropped, dug into her spine, took the breath from her. She arched her back, holding its weight. She must get Rose to the side, by the house supports. 'Rose, get right over, to the other side, where it's still upright.' She could hardly speak from the strain of holding all that weight. Rose clung to her, her face wet with tears. Kate screamed at her, 'Get to the other side. Get away to the other side. Now.'

It was killing her, cutting her. Had a wall fallen on it? Rose wasn't moving, her eyes wide in fear. 'Go on. For all the saints, go on. Now, now,' Kate screamed again as the veranda lurched and cracked again, tearing deeper into her back. She dropped her head, forced her arms beneath her, levered herself up again.

At last Rose moved, whimpering and crawling over to the uprights in the corner. 'Enough, enough. Don't go out,' Kate shouted.

'Mummy, Mummy,' Rose called, lying on her stomach, her sand-coated face tear streaked, reaching out to her.

Kate eased down, trying to move to join her. She couldn't. The weight was pressing her into the ground, she was eating the dirt, as she had eaten the mud in the Irish lane, as her mother had. She moved her lips in prayer. Purgatory would cleanse her for God. Or would it be for hell? Her lips moved. She could not make her act of contrition. Not here, with no priest. Had Des? Poor Des. The noise was all around, still all around, the weight was pressing deeper, her back was hurting.

'Father, forgive me, for I have sinned,' she murmured again and again.

Then the weight was easing. She saw Old Roy's legs, his hands on the edge of the veranda floor. She moved, her elbows digging into the ground as she used them to pull herself forward, and out. Roy pulled her to her feet. The veranda and the wall which had collapsed onto it crashed to the ground. They rushed round, and pulled out Rose. She was unhurt, and silent now in her shock. They could stand against the wind. 'It's easing,' he called. But still the words were snatched from his lips, still the fury was hurling and pushing and pulling.

Behind them, there was a roar and a crash, and now the whole house collapsed, and they saw that its roof had blown away and smashed into Roy's house, which was demolished. Debris was still rushing past them, the fence was in the air, so much was in the air.

They cowered on the ground, not knowing what else to do, and Old Roy's arms were round them, and he wanted to be the one to die, if anyone had to, because Kate was the daughter he had never had, and Rose his grandchild, and for another minute the wind plucked at them, hurled sand and debris at them, and the noise bombarded them, and their terror overwhelmed them.

Then it lessened even more and suddenly died. Thunder rolled, rain fell, but only a little, and still they lay there, because they could not believe any of it: the destruction and now their safety.

In Perseverance, over in Boulder, Ben froze. The electricity had been cut, the lifts weren't working – why?

'Out, get out,' the foreman called.

'How?' Bluey shouted, in the chaos.

'Climb, bloody climb,' the foreman yelled. 'Cyclone up above. Get up and see to your families.'

Ben rushed with the other men, climbing hand over hand, struggling for the surface, struggling against tearing and aching muscles. Hand over hand, foot over foot. Sweat streamed through the dust on his face. God, let them be safe. Oh God, please let them be safe.

His hands were raw, his arms trembling. Bluey was behind. 'Keep going, mate,' Bluey urged. 'Keep going.'

They did, they all did, clambering out into the daylight, seeing the three chimneys which had toppled and cut off electricity to the engine rooms. They drew breath. They took in the devastation. They grabbed bikes, anything, heading for Kalgoorlie, all of them, lifting their bikes over the tin sheets, water barrels, tanks and dead chooks which covered the roads.

The Tote Tower was down, houses, shops, hotels. Joe's Hotel, smashed, ruined. People, dazed, confused, weeping, swearing, clearing up, already they were clearing up.

They tore up their own street, hurling the bikes to one side, running on, leaping the debris. Roy's house was ruined. They stopped at Ben's. 'Kate,

Kate,' he screamed, rushing in, pulling at the pack of cards which it now was. He tore until his hands bled, pushing off the hands that pulled at him, until Bluey knocked him off his feet.

'You stupid bugger, they're all right.' Bluey's face was alight with relief. He was pointing down the road where Roy and Kate and Rose were standing with others in the street, their shoulders slumped with exhaustion.

He ran to them, scooping up Rose, holding Kate to him, his eyes meeting Roy's.

Kate clung to him. He was safe. Thank God. It was all she had been able to think of, all she had been able to talk of. He was safe, and his arms were around her, holding her so tightly that she could hardly breathe. Rose cried out and pushed her father away. 'You're hurting Mummy, Daddy.'

They laughed, and Ben put her down, and ran his fingers through his hair before turning to look again at the street and the devastation.

'It's all right, it'll be all right,' Kate murmured. Old Roy patted her and joined Ben, walking back towards the houses. Four of the six were ruined. The tour was due within days. Kate looked down at her hands, then at Rose and smiled. 'It'll be all right, darling,' Kate said, kneeling in the dust beside her daughter. 'We'll camp tonight.'

But Rose did not have to, because Lucia came then, to take her back to the hotel, and promised Kate, as they stood apart from the others, that they would rebuild their friendship, just as Kate and Ben would rebuild their houses. 'We will not speak of schools, or religion,' she murmured, stroking back Kate's hair, brushing the dust from her cheeks. 'You have made your decision, and I love you too much to lose you. Now I will take your Rose and prepare a meal for you all tonight. Come, Rose.'

Kate watched them leave, and then looked across

the rubble of the house to Ben, who was staring after Lucia. He dropped his head and kicked at the rubble. He said, 'It's hopeless. It's all hopeless.'

She looked again at Lucia and Rose, walking hand in hand. She called to him, 'It can be rebuilt. Anything can be rebuilt. We'll reduce the rent until things are back to normal. We'll all eat at Lucia's tonight. Do them good to mingle with the Italians. Do us all good.'

Ben's shoulders were hunched, his hands were deep in his pockets. She heard Bluey and Frank laugh over by the back lane. They had grabbed the table-cloth she had been ironing, and Bluey was the matador, Frank the bull.

She shrugged the tiredness from her, and now she felt the pain in her back, but that was nothing. There was a lot to be done.

She dragged at a corrugated-iron sheet, heaving it to one side. Ben looked at her. 'For God's sake, woman, what are you doing? Listen to me. It's useless. Even Joe's Hotel is ruined. Everything's gone wrong, in just a few bloody minutes. It's all gone wrong.' He looked at his child again, walking hand in hand with Lucia, he looked at his houses. Was everything going to be taken from him again? He spun round. 'Kate, Kate.'

She was pulling at the iron sheet, asking Roy, 'Is that nose still twitching?' She sounded so English. Was she really? Was she his?

Roy came to take the other corner. 'Certainly the nose is twitching.'

'Then', she panted, 'I'm clearing up, damn it, Ben, so that we can rebuild. And while we're at it, we can buy in extra materials and build on the plots that have now been cleared of empty houses. We'll buy enough material so that we can sell corrugated iron and wood on to people who want to build when things pick up.' She was shouting at him. 'And don't you dare give up. We're in this together, you and I.'

Bluey and Frank charged past him, the table-cloth flapping. He wanted to snatch it from them. He wanted to clear his head and think.

Kate shouted, 'Look, my darling, if you think I'm going to live back at the mine, in a tent, you can think again. Rose and I need a home. She can't go trotting off to school from way out in the bush. Miss Parish wouldn't approve.'

He walked towards her. 'Miss Parish?'

She dropped the corner of the corrugated sheeting. 'Oh, come on, Ben, this is too heavy for Roy. Are you going to help or not? Miss Parish is the public school teacher.'

He looked down the road. Lucia and Rose were turning the corner.

Kate called, her hands on her hips, 'You can put in an offer to Joe and build a smart new hotel, and for heaven's sake sort out that matador. He could chase the chooks instead.'

Roy dropped his end of the metal sheet. It clanged as it hit the ground. The dust billowed. Kate choked, flapped her hands. 'But first, cable Perth. Put back the tour for a month. They might want to see a cyclone-hit area – that's part of their heritage too.'

They worked all afternoon, and hope spurred them on. That night Joe told them that he was staying. He would not sell the hotel. Somehow he would rebuild, as everyone else was doing. Somehow he would open again. He had no option. Where would he go with the money he would get for a ruin?

Kate worked harder and wouldn't contemplate the future, because by the end of the next week, a week during which they had taken all their meals with Lucia, Ben had decided that they must definitely look to the East. He wouldn't risk the possibility of another cyclone, he told her as they walked back to their half-built house. His voice had been terse.

In 1929 the world depression exploded, but tourists still came to visit the mines on the tours they had set up, and Kate and Roy took it in turns to cook damper, and she knew by heart Roy's tales of sinking his first mining shaft, the hard ground, the slow progress, the gravel, the dry blowing when he came to the wash to assess the likelihood of gold.

Here she would interrupt and hand out dishes, and show them how to blow off a dish of dirt, holding one dish above the other, letting the wash run slowly into the empty dish, repeating it until the dust was blown away, leaving the gold, for often there was a tail of gold left. The tourists were as pleased as if it had been a twenty-ounce nugget and handed out tips to them all.

By the end of 1929 Kalgoorlie was blossoming in the face of the world's poverty because of the lower production costs, and Ben sat up until late at night, working out figures, selling on building materials. And Kate relaxed, because they were still here, still with Roy, in houses they had rebuilt, and with boarders who were like their family. And with Lucia as her friend.

At the end of that year, Rose started at public school, and Lucia came to her bazaars, and Kate to Maria's.

But in 1930, as the year drew on, tension knotted her neck, and headaches nearly burst her head, because Ben talked more and more of Sydney in between cursing the Australian government. 'If we've got to have a Labor government in power at all, they should at least bring in a federal subsidy to raise the price of gold on the Australian market, then we're up and running. It should be staring them in the face, but can we trust them to do that? Why don't they get on with it and help us build things up?

They don't understand business. Or is it building up they're interested in? Is it . . . ?' He stopped and stared at her.

Each time Kate said nothing, just sewed her sampler and prayed the federal government would do as Ben wanted, because the Labor Party was the party of Commies and Catholics, he kept saying, as he pounded the table. She couldn't bear to hear his rage and his half-voiced suspicion, and she couldn't bear to keep swallowing her anger, because her anger shouldn't exist. She was Kate, not Caithleen.

The subsidy was introduced and the revival of the mining could be heard as well as seen, with the cacophony of whistles and sirens, which had multiplied as the mines did. 'Why can't they set their watches and do it together?' She and Roy laughed because the headaches had lifted.

By 1931 the Australian government had been forced to devalue the Australian pound against the English pound. Kalgoorlie expanded again, and as Kate and Roy returned from their picnics with their tours and evening fell, they could see lights for miles around in the bush.

'Lots of new mines, now,' Old Roy wheezed. 'See them poppet heads? They weren't there last year. I knew it was coming. I've got the nose, see.' He tapped it. Kate raised her eyebrows, the tourists laughed.

Two-up games flourished, toys filled the shops. Ben sold corrugated iron and paint in massive quantities.

Letters came from Larry Smith, Ben's Perth hotel contact, who had moved to Sydney, cursing because 'in spite of the defeat of Scullin's Australian Labor government, Jack Lang and his State Labor government still hang on in Sydney, old boy, and while they're still there, no-one's safe. God knows what they're cooking up. We need good firm capitalist management.'

The value of their properties soared as 1932 proceeded but not Kate's spirits because from the depressed East came rumours of the formation and growing strength of militant loyalist groups set up to counter the Labor government. Old Roy's mate confirmed the rumours, but Roy said, 'Now, now. They died down in the Twenties, they'll die down again.'

In the cool of a fine March evening she stood with Ben and toasted Frank's new bride. But as they cut the cake she couldn't push from her mind the thousands who were flocking to the New Guard, and the Old Guard, and the All for Australia League.

Frank looked up and brandished the cake knife. Lamplight flashed across the blade. 'Beaut cake, Kate.'

Had light glinted on the sword of the New Guard member who had galloped up at the opening of the Harbour Bridge, brushing past Premier Jack Lang, slashing at the ribbon? Had triumph surged as he signalled his organization's threat to defend the Establishment? Had he gloried in the hate he brandished – just as the Tans had done? She felt sick.

'Beaut cake,' Frank repeated.

She forced herself to smile, her mind too full to speak. She clutched at the veranda rail for support, while Ben stood beside her, laughing as Frank swung Rose in the air.

Kate felt the wood beneath her hands. It was split. She saw the dust puff up around Frank's feet. She heard the chatter and the laughter of their friends. She fought to keep her voice calm as she asked Ben, 'Why don't we look again at Kalgoorlie hotels? It's so unsettled in the East with these men gathering together.'

He drew on his cigarette and watched the stars through his smoke. 'Who can blame them? The depression's growing deeper, and just today Smith wrote to say Lang's defaulted in his state's loan payments to London bondholders. It's more than a bloody disgrace – it's a declaration. What else will the idiot do – declare a republic? The Australian government should damn well be doing something to sort him out and if they don't, others should. As I said, who can blame them? Who would?'

She tightened her grip on the rail. *She* could blame them. *She* would blame those sabre-wielding Fascists, those Establishment extremists, those . . . Protestants. She looked at him and suddenly she felt cold. It was all back again. The past was back.

He saw her expression and threw his cigarette away and held her. 'I didn't mean that. I'm just frustrated. They're all fools.' He looked over her head at Lucia. No, he hadn't meant it, but he wanted to get on, to get out of here. 'Listen, my darling, when things peak here, we'll buy low again, out there, in the depression areas.' He waved as Bluey piggybacked Rose across the yard.

'Won't you miss all our friends though?' she asked gently, though she wanted to shout it. 'We're comfortable now. We belong, we're established, and yes, they're all fools, and I don't want us to be a part of any of it any more. I just want us to be safe.'

'We'll still see them.' He held her against him, talking into her hair. 'But we're going nowhere yet. Not until it has all passed.' He thought, but didn't say, And then we'll really be where we belong.

Mick wiped his mouth with his hand. 'Cripes, it's hot in here,' he said to Hughie, looking round the suburban town hall.

'It'll be hotter by the time you've finished, with a bit of luck. Now, remember, your job is to drum up moral support for Lang. Some of the party are leaving over this. It's up to you in our area tonight, Mick. This is your chance, there'll be eyes on you. This could be what you've been working towards. You could go high up.'

Mick smiled and stood and listened to the applause. You should hear that Des, he thought. I know you're basking in it in Ireland. Well, now it's my turn. I've raised funds for the party, I've delivered leaflets, and now I'm here, in Sydney, in the spotlight.

'Get on with it,' hissed Hughie.

Mick gripped the lectern and looked along the rows of men gathered in the hall below the stage. He pointed his finger along the rows. There was silence. He raised his hand and brought it down with a wack. 'While we're here, in this hall, Lang has barricaded his treasury to keep out Federal Officers. Why?' He stabbed the air. 'I'll tell you why. He has defaulted on a payment due to the British. Lyons, the right-wing Conservative, has sent in his boys to take money from our coffers to repay interest on the loans that you – you – you.' He stabbed the air again, pointing to the audience, using Des's methods. Well, why not? The bugger had used him often enough. 'You raised for the privilege of fighting for Britain.

'You, who are called Commies and Catholic traitors. You, who fought for them, have had your wages reduced in this capitalist depression, your pensions cut to pay back these loans. Lang said, "No. Our people need every penny." Now our NSW Treasury is about to be raided, and so we must support Lang, now more than ever. We must make our voices heard.'

He stood straight as the cheers resounded round the hall. He had them hooked, they were listening. A voice shouted through the cheers, 'Take to the streets, you mean – kill one another like your mob did in Ireland? Well, we're not in Ireland now, you Catholic fool, so why don't you just grab a ship and get back where you belong, in the bog? Go on, all of you, and take your Commie ideas with you.' The hall fell silent. Heads swivelled to locate the voice.

Hughie whispered from behind, 'New Guard.'

Mick nodded, he could see them now, at the back,

in a bunch. He squared his shoulders, saying conversationally but clearly – and Oh God, if Des could see him now – 'Gentlemen, let me explain something to you. The "voice of reason" shouting from the back is one of those who think that the Catholics are storing arms in convents, are in league with the Italian Mafia and are about to stage a revolution. These are the people who see Lang's stand on the loan as threatening God, King and Empire, and the maintenance of order. They see Justice Truth and Liberty Lang, our leader, as a traitor. Is he? This is a new country. Lang just wants to feed us. He wants to put *us*, the Australians, first. He wants to help *us*.'

Another voice shouted from the back, 'Your Lang's nothing more than a bloody dictator with a gob on him like you – full of hot air.' There was murmuring in the audience, voices raised in anger. Mick felt the sweat rise on his face. He was the star, he must bring them back to him.

He gripped the lectern and smiled, looking along the front row. 'We're talking about the same man, are we, gentlemen? We're talking about the Premier who, when in power in the Twenties, implemented child endowment, widows' pensions and workers' compensation. We're talking about the same man who yes – all right – does things in his own way. But a dictator? Have we seen him drilling on a golf course? Of course not, he's got a Catholic background, he couldn't even get membership to put a silly little ball into a silly little hole.'

There was a burst of laughter. Mick grinned, waited, then continued, 'Has he been stockpiling weapons or slashing his sabre on the harbour bridge? No. I seem to remember he used scissors. Does he substitute force for the democratic process? No—'

Again he was interrupted from the hall. 'What democratic process? He railroads his ideas – look at the members you're losing.'

The hecklers guffawed, the Labor supporters looked uncertain. Mick shouted, 'He has the courage of his convictions. And for me, for us, that's something to be proud of, isn't it? Isn't it?' He was almost chanting now.

The audience were with him again, clapping, shouting, but he'd seen their doubts and now he felt the thrill of possibility. Lang was divisive. Maybe it was time for a new leader, a proper leader.

'Get on with it,' hissed Hughie. 'You'll lose them again.'

Mick raised his voice. 'Yes, we must stay with the party in this crisis, we must not leave as some are doing. We must not leave. We, we, we.'

He had them in the palm of his hand again. They were cheering. The New Guard were jeering. One shouted, 'Bloody Irish. You can never stick together, you'll fight one another if you can't fight someone else.'

Mick felt rage begin to flare. Hughie hissed, 'Steady.'

Mick gripped the lectern again and channelled the rage into his voice, roaring out, 'We are the workers on whom these Prods base their wealth.' Now he was pointing to the back of the room. 'We are the people whom the New Guard will turn their guns on. There are fifty thousand of them. How many more in the Old Guard and the All for Australia League? And does this Holy Trinity frighten us?'

Men in the front row were clapping, nudging one another. Mick screamed out across the hall, 'Do they hell. Think of them out there, in the streets, on the golf courses, training, marching – all in a dither because it looks like we might bite off the hands they thrust in the air like Mussolini's Fascists.'

He walked to the edge of the stage. A man punched the air, others were stamping their feet.

He stared at the New Guard. 'You say we fight – yes we do, when we have cause.' He paused, laughed, scanned the room. God, but they were his. 'And we have a cause. We'll have a Republic like Ireland should have. We'll have a Republic here in Australia, if you just listen to me. Follow me, that's all you have to do.' The room was in uproar. The New Guard were forcing their way through. Laborites were fighting Laborites. Some were shouting, 'Get the fool off the stage.' Others, 'What's he saying?' 'You show the British buggers, Mick – it's Lang we're for.' 'Dump the Prods, you tell 'em.'

Mick punched the air. He'd got them on their feet. He'd done it. Mick O'Brian had done it.

Hughie grabbed him from the back. Mick stumbled, jerked round. Hughie kept going, dragging him off the stage. 'Damn you, Mick, you always go too far. This was about Lang not about you. A republic wasn't the issue. We wanted unity, and this is one area where we won't have it. What are you after, a glorious death or something? You're so damn selfish.'

He was pushing him through the side entrance, and now Mick saw Des and heard him, because he had used those words, and his rage erupted, and he turned on Hughie. 'You've no vision. You've no sense. They wanted to hear me. Damn Lang, damn the lot of you. It's me they'll follow.'

Hughie struck him, once, twice. Mick fell. 'It's in your mind, you fool. They'd not follow you anywhere and if they did, you'd lead them to disaster. You had a chance to talk reason but you don't understand the meaning of the word. You're as extreme as they are, and as useless as they are. Thank God this meeting was only a drop in the ocean and what happened here won't matter. Just like you don't matter.' He walked away.

Chapter Fifteen

In January 1933 Ben travelled to Sydney to meet
Larry Smith. Rose and Kate waved him off at the
station and watched the lines quivering, shimmering
and sinking as the train steamed away. They felt the
flies on their faces, the heat all around them. Kate
smiled at Rose. 'He'll be back soon.'

'Will he bring me a present?'

Kate laughed. 'You gave him a big enough list, so
he won't dare to take no notice, especially as you
sorted out your spellings, in the end.'

Rose pulled a face and dragged at her mother's
hand. 'Come on, it's too hot just to stand and stare.
Let's go to Lucia's for a drink. I wish we could see
Sydney, don't you?'

'We will,' Kate said quietly.

Lang was out of office. Labor were routed. Its
members were bewildered and confused. The militants had subsided, and though the depression was
still rife – except in Kalgoorlie, it seemed – Larry
Smith had written to say that there was a glimmer
of movement in the business arena out East. 'Come
and get a feel. Come and meet some contacts now
the politics are as we want them. Come and make a
killing.'

Kate looked around as they walked. There were
more smokestacks and more poppet heads strad-
dling more mine shafts. The hills of waste were the

same but would not be for long. They were on the point of shrinking and changing as more processing works were established to extract the last farthing's worth of gold. Would they be there to see it?

'Dad will be back in two weeks. He's travelling across the Nullarbor.'

'I'd like to do that, would you?'

No, thought Kate. I want to stay here, where I belong. But she said, 'Yes, if that's what's best.'

Kate didn't sleep that night. The bed was empty without the weight of him, the scent of him, the feel of him, and it became no better as the nights went by. The days were full of cooking for the restaurant and the lodgers, of greeting tourists, of laughing and chatting as they hoisted themselves up into the cart, of talking of the days when there was no water and when Afghans with camel trains carted provisions, talking of the splendour, and the affluence, which had returned to some extent.

Yes, it was the nights that were empty and silent. It was the nights when she longed for him, and for the years that they had enjoyed, the years that she wanted to go on enjoying. Damn Larry Smith.

After two weeks Ben returned, jumping down from the train, his arms full of parcels, laughing as Rose rushed to him and threw her arms around his waist. He said, 'In just two weeks you've grown. I swear you've grown.' But his eyes were on Kate and they were saying, God, how I've missed you. And his lips when he kissed her said the same.

Kate took some of the parcels from him, while Rose jumped up and down, trying to snatch her present from him. Ben held it high above his head, laughing as they left the station. He hailed a cab and Kate wanted to say, Give it to her, and tell me what is going to happen to us. She said nothing. She didn't want to know. Damn Larry Smith.

When they arrived Rose ran up the side of the

house brandishing her new writing-case, dust kicking up with every footfall. Ben and Kate walked behind, their arms full of boxes and packages. 'You've bought up the whole of Sydney, I see,' Kate murmured.

Ben smiled. 'Never. Oh, you should see it. It's just wonderful. It's so huge, established, normal. No dust.' He arched his eyebrows. 'Makes this seem so raw.'

Rose rounded the corner into the yard. Kate said, 'It's home and I'm frightened to leave it.'

Ben stopped her with a touch to her arm. He kissed her mouth. 'Trust me, I wouldn't take you and Rose away if I thought we'd fail. Trust me, I know what's best for us.' He kissed her eyes. 'I've missed you.'

That evening they sat with Old Roy on the veranda and Ben told them of the contacts he had made, of the hotel which would shortly be coming on the market. 'In Canterbury. I just have to decide when to sell here.'

Old Roy tapped his pipe on the arm of his rocking-chair. The kerosene lamp flickered its yellow light. Was he thinking what Kate was thinking? The old man sucked at his empty pipe, then leaned his head back and gazed up at the stars. 'Well, my nose has taken *us* this far. *Us*, Benjamin Williams.'

Yes, he was thinking the same. She pushed her needle through the canvas. Ben reddened, held out his hand. 'I'm sorry, Roy. I'm just so excited. I didn't mean anything.'

She laid down her needle and took his hand. 'We know.'

Old Roy examined his pipe. 'I think we should leave it a while longer to sell up here. Prices are still going down in the East and will go higher here. Look around, see what else is available. Don't go just for the first one you find.'

Kate could have hugged him.

That night she and Ben lay naked in the light from the moon which streamed through the window, and he traced the contours of her breasts with his fingers and the contours of her lips with his. 'I've missed you,' he murmured, and his mouth became fierce on hers, and his hands demanding, but no more than hers.

His body was hard against hers, his legs between hers. He was on her, in her. His eyes looked deep into hers, his love visible, alive, strong. She reared against him, moving with him. 'I love you, I love you,' they both said, together, in time, in tune. 'I love you.'

Later, he talked of his dreams. Of the hotel they would have with its panelled walls, its chandelier in the dining-room, its gleaming cutlery, its pianist, its deep-pile carpets. 'The guests will come again and again. With our joint expertise we'll flourish. We'll sail a yacht, have a beach house. We'll have friends and go to concerts. Mother and Father used to go to the opera in London. We'll do that.'

She breathed in the scent of his body and touched his skin. Now his hands were on her thighs again, and his kisses were hungry. He whispered, 'I'm too tired, but I love you, and I can't have enough of you.' His kisses were fierce again and she relaxed into his love and she knew that she would be happy wherever he was, and her doubts faded.

By mid 1933 Frank's wife, Maisie, was helping to run the boarding-houses. Kate knew that she was grooming her successor and she saw everything about Kalgoorlie and Boulder as though for the first time.

In the bush, as she rode her bike with Rose, Maria and Lucia, she smelt the oily peppercorns and heard the breeze and saw the camp-site in the searing heat. She told the tourists of boiling the kerosene tin on the fire, and felt again the steam. She told them of turning the windlass handle, and felt again the strain.

She told them of the beauty of a starlit night and at this her voice faltered and she fell silent, and each time Old Roy took up the tale, though his voice was hardly steadier.

In June Frank was hurt in an accident and Maisie nursed him in the rooms they had in the end house. Kate basked in the work, in the world which was restored to just her. In July Ben resigned from the mine where he had progressed to a job as wages clerk. 'I need to go to Sydney again. I need to keep my finger on the pulse. I need to try and sort out the details, determine the goodwill, the takings.'

'He's right,' she told Old Roy on the veranda after she had waved Ben off.

'I know,' he agreed sadly. 'It's time to move on.'

'Come with us,' she pleaded as she had done every day.

He shook his head, rocking the chair gently. 'No, this is my place. You must come to me, whenever you want to, whenever you need to.' His gaze was penetrating. 'They'll be different, these Sydney folk. Especially if he sticks with Canterbury. It's a Protestant suburb, you know.'

She hadn't known.

In August and September she, Lucia and Roy took Rose and Maria out into the bush almost every day for picnics. They made damper, and cooked it in the ashes. In October she, Roy and Ben took the children to the camp after Ben had received a letter from Larry Smith confirming that Canterbury was the best deal at the moment. They called in on Chris and Mark to admire the shacks they had built of corrugated iron, with fireplaces and a radio, and shelves. On the way home in the cart Ben laughed, 'God, the bush is so raw. You should just see the houses in Sydney, the dinner parties, the clothes, the stores.'

Kate said, 'We have stores in Kalgoorlie, fine ones.

Ones that rival Sydney. We have race courses, beautiful buildings, wide streets, we have high society here.'

Ben laughed and Roy placed a warning hand on Kate's shoulder. Ben said, 'In Sydney there isn't the dust, there isn't the—'

'I know, the rawness,' Kate interrupted.

Ben flashed a look at her. She smiled, beating the anger down. 'When are you going again, my love?'

He called to Roy, who sat the other side of Kate, 'What's your nose doing, old coot?'

Old Roy said softly, 'I've told you. The time's right. Things are moving behind the scenes in Sydney, and prices are pretty good here.'

In November they sold their share of the properties piecemeal to families who were pouring in. Roy kept his on as a business, and there was even more vividness to the town, and to the yard, and to the laughter over the meals. Bluey's races with Rose seemed faster, and the evenings when she read to Roy on the veranda longer, and the tea and cakes with Lucia more delicious. In December Ben left for Sydney to sign the hotel contract.

It was only now that she grew aware of the raised voices over the meals she served.

'What is the matter with them?' she asked Old Roy at the end of the first week.

'There's tension brewing. When times are bad I can understand it, but not when they're better. Something to do with "sling-backs". Competition's still pretty tough for jobs down the mines. Seems they feel the Italians and Slavs bribe the shift bosses and get taken on.'

Kate dished up the apple pie. 'The miners've always had their own areas, it's always been a question of who knows who. They're being silly.' She slapped the plates down in front of the boarders and they looked at her in surprise. She ignored them.

Two days later she received a cable from Ben, asking Old Roy to join him in Sydney. 'Urgent,' he repeated. 'Good deal stop need your agreement stop.'

Old Roy polished his boots and put on the suit which he had last worn at Frank's wedding. 'Will you be all right without me?' he asked Kate.

She kissed him. 'No, but I'll manage,' she grinned.

All that week Kate was tense. What was so urgent? This thought kept playing in her mind as she cooked and served the food, and took that week's tour to the mine. In the evening she became tenser still because the men seemed to talk of nothing but the sling-backs, about bloody foreigners, about another accident that had occurred down the mine. 'They don't understand orders, they can't read English,' Frank said, cursing as he doused his meal with salt.

'Something wrong with my cooking?' Kate snapped.

Bluey said, 'And they stand all over the pavements so we have to go out in the road. Why do they play bocce when there's cricket?'

She slapped his meal down in front of him, and clipped his ear. 'Watch your mouth. Lucia fed you, or have you forgotten?' The men laughed, but she didn't.

Bluey rubbed his ear. 'Strewth, Kate. I didn't mean them.'

'You meant people like them. That's what you lot of larrikins forget, foreigners are people, not a problem.'

The men concentrated on their plates, swabbing the gravy with their bread. 'And that's a disgusting habit,' she said, as she swept back to the stove.

She walked to Lucia's that night, smiling at the Italians who had gathered on the pavement. They stepped aside to allow her through. She drank tea in the kitchen while Lucia ironed, and Rose and Maria skipped in the yard with ropes Stan had made for them. 'So,' Lucia said, 'great plans are afoot. What is it that is so urgent for your Ben, I wonder? But then I wonder all the time. I wonder what will it be like with you gone from here. What will it be like in Canterbury, amongst strangers, amongst—'

Kate cut in. 'If you say Protestants, I will pour this tea all over that nice clean table-cloth you are folding. It's all gone underground, the militants have dispersed. There are new problems, like the depression – or had you forgotten?'

Lucia sighed, then laughed along with Kate.

Lucia put the table-cloth on the pile, smoothing it with her hands. 'No, I have not forgotten, but I fear for you, out there, away from here. This is your home.'

Kate wouldn't think of it like that, she had made herself promise that she would not, just as she had made herself accept the thought of Canterbury, because she was Ben's wife, she was Kate. She was whatever he wanted because she owed him that.

'Ben is where my home is.' She paused. 'Lucia, can you feel the atmosphere?'

Lucia looked out of the open door at the children who were playing in the light from the windows. 'Yes, it will pass. There are always differences, but they pass, as the years do. So, are you ready for Rose's birthday tomorrow? It's hard to believe she's ten already.'

The next day Ben and Old Roy arrived in the yard as Rose and her party friends played blind man's buff. Rose ran to her father and then to Roy, who swung her round and joined in the game, without speaking to Kate, without looking at her. His face was pale, his eyes cold, his lips tight. She had never seen him like that.

She started towards him, but Ben pulled her back. 'Don't I get a kiss?' His lips were hard, his kiss fierce. She drew back in surprise. He said, 'I've missed you.'

She turned to Roy. His eyes were still cold as he looked at Ben. Ben led her into the kitchen. He dropped his case with a thud.

'Tell me what's going on?' Her voice was firm. Ben removed his hat and wiped his forehead with a handkerchief.

'He's just a stubborn old fool. I met a consortium who're interested in backing us. We've three hotels lined up now, not just Canterbury. If Old Roy puts in some money it will mean more financing from our side. But he won't come in. So I'll just have to take on the role of group hotel manager and work my socks off. But, Kate, it's worth doing. It's just what I've prayed for, you can see that, can't you?' He tilted her head and kissed her lips. 'Trust me. We must go in with them.'

'Isn't it a huge step though? And if Old Roy doesn't—'

He swung away from her and leaned against the kitchen table. He took a cigarette from a new cigarette case. He saw her looking and held it up. 'Celebration present from Larry Smith. He's in the consortium. God, it's our dream – now – Kate. No hanging around, building up from one to two to three. Now, while the time's right, when prices are low. Roy's such a stubborn old fool. His nose is only tuned in to here. I'm the one who understands the East—'

Roy's voice cut in from the doorway. 'Stubborn old fool, am I? Well, what does that make you? It's not right to do this to Kate. Have you told her who this—'

Kate put up her hands and shouted, 'For heaven's sake, stop this. What's the matter with everyone? It's like a taut wire out in the streets, and now you're bringing it in here. Look, Roy, I'm not a fool. This is a Protestant consortium, isn't it?'

Ben looked at Roy, then at her. He nodded.

320

Kate smiled, though with an effort. 'Look at the mines, remember all you've told me. Separation under ground. Peace above. It's obvious the consortium is Protestant. In work, people stick together.' She took a deep breath. 'I'm fine about it. Ben and I love one another. I trust him. He'll do what's best.'

Ben was tracing the grain of the deal table with his finger, looking at that, not at her. Roy was staring at him. She continued. 'Roy, don't worry. The New Guard is finished. It has all died down again. These people must be nice, or they wouldn't be Ben's friends.'

Roy tried to speak. She held up her hand. 'If Ben's happy with it, then we should be. I know why you don't want to back us, and why should you? It's wrong to put all our eggs in one basket. I can help Ben with the work. It'll be good to share it.'

She watched Roy walk out onto the veranda. He was rigid with anger. Why? Was there something else?

Ben gripped her hand. 'I love you. You're wonderful and you won't have to work with me. Wives don't work out there. It's enough that you agree.' He pulled her to him. 'This is our big chance, Kate. This is what we've been struggling for, all these years.' Still she watched Roy through the door, as Ben kissed her hair.

Rose ran up the stairs, pulling at Roy. 'May we have a drink now, Roy? Please.'

Kate pulled away. 'I'll talk to Roy.'

Ben pulled her back. 'No, no, don't do that. I'll talk to him.' His face was dark, and there was ... something? She'd seen it before, but where? Then she realized it was sometimes in his eyes when he looked at Lucia. She looked again. Was it fear? But then it was gone. She was being ridiculous.

Rose called through the door, 'We're thirsty, Mum.'

Kate smiled and poured lemon drinks for the girls, and carried them onto the veranda, murmuring

321

to Roy as she passed, 'Don't worry, my dear. I shall be fine. But you are right to stick to your point of view.'

He nodded, but his face was still fixed. As she took the drinks into the yard she heard him enter the kitchen and shut the door.

Old Roy stood against the door, looking at Ben as he leant against the table.

'You didn't tell her, did you? You didn't tell her that most of the consortium were militants, that Stephens, the head of this brilliant consortium, the one with the contacts and the clout, the one that is going to be steering you, the one you will be beholden to, was a New Guard and, before that, a Tan. You're not going to tell your wife that, are you? Or that he boasted to me about the bog Irish he burnt out in Cork, about the heads he broke in County Limerick, her county. You're going to go ahead. You're going to let greed get in the way of your life. It'll bring you down, Ben. I know it will.'

Ben pushed the table away and knocked over the chair as he stood. 'You know nothing. That's all in the past. Over, forgotten. You heard her.'

Old Roy looked at the man who was clenching and unclenching his fists. 'But you *didn't* tell her he was a Tan?'

Ben glared.

Roy said, 'Good God, man. He might have killed her mother. You know how she feels about it all. She feels just how you or I would feel if they killed our mothers. If we had had to look at her being dragged in the dirt. Give it away, it's not worth it. Go and set up with one of the millions of decent Australians.'

Ben moved a step nearer. 'I've had to forgive and forget too.'

Old Roy clenched his fist now, wanting to hit the man he had loved until this moment. 'Grow up. She lied, she used you – but for her it was war, and she kept you alive, she made sure you were protected, and she fell in love with you. She's done everything she can for you since. She's even sold her damn soul for love of you, and your answer is to betray her.' His voice was little more than a hiss. 'But perhaps that is what you want to do. Tit for tat.' He was looking at Ben closely now. 'Maybe that's it. Maybe you want to rub her nose in it, just to even the score. It's evened, man. It was evened years ago.'

Ben was on him now, gripping his lapels, breathing heavily. 'You know nothing, nothing, do you hear? It's a good deal, that's all. A bloody good deal. It'll set us up. Keep us safe.'

Roy just looked at him.

Ben saw an old man, saw his hands on his lapels and felt disgust at himself. He stepped back. 'Forgive me and believe me. I'm doing this for her, for us. Don't tell her. Please. There is no need for her to ever know. I'll work something out, don't worry.'

Roy dusted himself off. He could feel his legs trembling. He leant on the door. He didn't know what to do. He heard Rose laughing. He looked out into the yard. Kate was chasing her, her hair flying, the boys clapping. What would Maureen do? He didn't know. It was like the cyclone. He didn't know what to do. He hung his head, then said, 'I'll say nothing, because you are life itself to her. But if you hurt her, I will swing for you.'

Ben nodded. 'I love her, you must believe that. It's for her that I'm doing this. I want our family to be safe.'

At Christmas Ben handed the deeds of a farm to Kate. 'It's four hours from Sydney. It's green, with a river. It has a manager who does the hard work. I don't know if it has the sound of wind in the reeds and curlews in the sky, but it is for us. I don't want

323

you in the chaos of Sydney, I want you and Rose in the peace of a farm again. I shall come at weekends. I'm giving you back your past.'

Old Roy turned from them, unable to hide his disgust.

In January Ben returned to Sydney, to sign papers. He would be away for the Australia Day weekend, and the tea that had been planned in the street, but somehow Kate didn't mind, because the days were a blur. They were leaving, and though they were going to the farm, she couldn't bear it.

Each evening she sat with Old Roy whose anger seemed to have disappeared in the face of his sadness at their leaving. She read to Rose in her bedroom and later lay in bed and traced the pictures on the wall, the drapes at the windows, the light from the stars, and wanted to cling to them all, but part of her wanted to be at her farm. Excitement, sadness. It alternated throughout the days.

The heat on 27 January was almost too hot to bear, even for Kalgoorlie, and the jelly ran to water on the trestle-tables in the yard, and the sandwiches curled, but there was laughter, and songs, and Rose sat on the bench, her elbows on the table, her mouth sticky with cake icing, and looked up at Kate as she poured lemon drinks. 'I don't want to leave.'

Kate said, 'We must. It's what Daddy wants.'

'But why can't we do what we want?'

'Just think of the river.'

That night Bluey, Frank and Stan were in Kalgoorlie, drinking in the pubs, toasting Australia, damning foreigners, and she was glad to be free of their grumbling. She cleaned the oven and the cupboards, and washed down the walls, because it must be spotless for Maisie when they left in two weeks' time. The heat had barely died down at all, but it didn't matter. She worked until her shoulders ached, and then she worked a little bit more. Only going to the veranda and sitting with Roy when exhaustion claimed her.

They sat in silence, breathing in the scent of the peppercorns. 'It's been a good day,' she said softly.

Old Roy nodded. 'A very good day.'

They heard shouting then, coming from the street, and the sounds of brawling, then singing and now Kate sighed. 'A good day for them too.'

Bluey and Stan staggered round the corner. 'Shh, shh,' Bluey said to Frank, his finger to his lips, tiptoeing into the yard.

'Not here,' Kate said, moving to the top step. 'Go and kip down in your beds.' She pointed to Roy's house. Stan called to Old Roy. 'Bloody murder, it was.' He nearly fell. 'That Jordan's been stabbed by a bunch of dagos. He's a good bloke, one of us. He's crook, real crook.'

'Go to bed,' Kate shouted.

Bluey staggered further into the yard. 'Bloody foreigners, need kicking out. Gone to hospital, he has. Italian copped him.'

'Naw, it was a Slav,' Bluey slurred.

'Bloody dago which ever way,' Stan grunted.

Old Roy was on his feet now. 'Get to bed.'

By morning rumours were flying because Jordan had died. Bluey and Stan nursed their hangovers and cursed and grumbled over the table in the dining-room. Kate wouldn't listen. On Monday Jordan's death was in the newspapers but there was no clear report of how he'd died, and Kate frowned. The men had to be damped down but they were clustering on corners, convinced it was a stabbing. Tension was sparking in the air, and the heat was growing and growing. Kate longed for Ben to return.

She scrubbed Roy's house, not wanting to be out in the streets. She made Rose stay in the yard. In the late afternoon she hurried to Lucia's. She and Mario were talking in the yard to their boarders. They fell silent as Kate entered, and there were few smiles, few nods, and no *Mamma mia* or the touch of a hand on her long red hair. She and Lucia hugged. 'It will pass,' Lucia said. 'It must. They should say how the boy died.'

Kate left, hurrying home past groups who were cursing and threatening revenge on the foreigners.

Old Roy said, as he hurried to meet her in the street, 'They should shut the boozers. The fools are working themselves into a frenzy.'

She looked back down the street towards the town.

In the evening they heard a roar of voices. They ran towards the town and the roar grew louder. There was the sound of breaking bottles, crashes, shouts. It was like the Tans again. Cars flew past them, men shouting and yelling. Old Roy stopped, bent over, trying to catch his breath. She waited for him. He straightened.

'We must go back,' he panted. 'It's a riot. The fools are rioting.'

She said, 'I must go to Lucia.'

Roy shouted at her, 'You'll go nowhere but home. You have a daughter.' He dragged her away. Men were running past them, away from the town, their shirts bulging with goods. 'Looters,' Roy spat out.

All night long the sound of rioting was carried on the hot air, and then with it came the smoke, as buildings were burned, and it was like Ireland. Kate cowered in her bedroom, a bedroom which had become alien in this strange flickering air which carried the smell of burning wood. 'Ben, Ben,' she whispered, her hand bunched against her mouth, watching the town she loved burn.

In the early hours of the morning Mario, Lucia and Maria limped to her house, carrying what possessions they had been able to save. They had been burnt out, ruined. Their faces were streaked with smoke and sweat and tears. 'They cut the firemen's hoses,' Lucia wept.

Kate held her and remembered the Tans who had done the same.

Rose woke and came to the kitchen, her face puffy with sleep. 'Go to bed. I'll bring in Maria in a moment,' Kate called softly. 'And in the morning, tell no-one that they are here. It is our secret.' Because who could they trust?

'Not even Roy?' Rose asked.

'Of course Roy can be told.'

Mario lifted his daughter and held her close. 'Our friends, many of them, have run to Dingbat Flats. They are making a stand. Others, like us, have friends to take them in.'

When the children slept Kate sat up with Lucia and Mario and they said nothing, just stared at one another, or at the floor.

In the morning when Roy came, it was shame they saw in his face, and disbelief.

All that day they stayed inside. Roy brought them the news that Australian miners were striking until the managements promised that no foreigners would work down the mines.

That night the sound of firing, and home-made bombs punched the air. 'It's Dingbat Flats,' Roy said as he rushed into the kitchen. Kate nodded and touched Lucia's hand. They knew.

In the morning Bluey and Stan bounded up the veranda steps, shouting, 'The dagos are gone, hiding out in the bush. Our lot've razed the Flats. Didn't take many of them either.'

Kate and Roy stood by the kitchen table as Bluey opened the door. 'Get out, get out of here,' Kate raged. 'You bring shame on us. Get out.' She stormed towards them. Her child mustn't hear this triumph, Maria mustn't hear it.

She pushed them out, hitting at them, shoving

until they were on the veranda, then pushing again. Roy watched, leaving her to it, letting her get the rage and fear out of her system.

Bluey fell down the veranda steps, yelling, 'Strewth, Kate.'

'Don't strewth me. Don't even speak to me. Get out, sober up and think about what's been done.' She was shaking. The smell of smoke was in the air. She had fugitives in her house, there was danger all around. Roy was standing beside her now, his arm was around her. Bluey was scrambling to his feet. Stan was helping him.

'Get out,' Kate repeated, turning back into the house.

'Where are the police? Where have they been all this time?' Lucia wept.

Roy said sadly, 'There are too few of them.'

The next day Mario took his family away, to the East, along with their friends. They were ruined. Kate was ashamed and still could barely believe any of it, even when they had walked to the station between walls that were black and misshapen, and over rubble that crunched with every stride.

Mario held Kate's hand as she stood at the train window and said, 'Now I understand you. There are many, many good people still in Kalgoorlie and Boulder, people who hate what has happened, who did their best, like you. But it only takes a few, doesn't it? So Kate, like you, I too will never feel safe again.'

Kate watched the train disappear. But I have Ben now, she thought, and hugged her arms, pushing down the echoes of terror and pain. And I'm leaving to go where there is no firing. There is just a farm and a river, and peace.

The next day, the 'specials' arrived and the day after Ben came home. Kate gripped his hand as they walked to the taxi and stroked it as they travelled past the burnt-out buildings. He said, 'Thank God you weren't involved. You could have been round with that woman.'

Kate looked at him. His voice had been so cold, so . . .

Rose spoke up. 'We weren't round with them, they were round with us. We hid them in our house. We didn't tell Frank and Bluey and Stan. Mum said we mustn't. She said we had to keep it a secret.'

They completed the journey to their house in silence and once in the kitchen he dropped his Gladstone bag, took some sweets from his pocket and handed them to Rose. 'Go and show Roy,' he told her. Kate watched her daughter run out into the sunlight and wanted to follow because her husband's voice had been so full of fury.

Ben shouted at her now. '*You* weren't going to tell me, were you? You were going to do it all behind my back. You were taking a side which wasn't mine – again.'

He was close to her, bending down over her. She backed away. Not this, not after all that had happened these last few days. Not this, after everything. He followed. Then she stopped, drew herself up and shouted back. 'Only a secret from the boys. How could I tell you when you weren't here? I was going to, but Rose got in first. Don't you dare shout at me for doing something you would have done for our friends. Because you would, wouldn't you? Wouldn't you?' She was shaking his arm, her mind in turmoil.

There was a sound on the veranda. They turned. Roy stood there. He stared at Ben, then walked away. They heard only their own breathing as they looked at one another again. At last Ben reached out and pulled her to him. 'I'm sorry, I'm sorry. I was just scared about what might have happened to you. Forgive me. I love you. I just love you.'

She held him, soothing him, because now she heard the note of fear in his voice and was moved by his concern for his family. She made herself forget his accusation. It was the shock of the destruction, it was the worry of the move. She had been clumsy – she should have made sure she told him, and now she berated herself, for, after all, the initial betrayal had been hers.

Ben held her tightly, shutting his eyes against the memories of Ireland, shutting his eyes against the look in Roy's eyes and all he wanted to do was leave this damn place.

Mick slashed at the suckers of the felled gum-tree. His hands were raw, but at least he'd eat at the end of the week. At least he'd not have to ask for a dole docket and go cap in hand for food.

He eased his back. Damn Lang, damn Hughie. The fool wasn't worth the week in clink he'd got for running after him, and giving him a good belting. He'd been riding the rattler ever since. He looked around. Thank God Des couldn't see him now. He could imagine the smirk he'd have on his face. It was a smirk which must be pretty much always in place now that he'd been proved right about the Treaty being a stepping-stone. In Ireland de Valera had been voted into power and was starting to set up the Republic.

Damn politics – it was no job for a proper man. He pushed down his longing for his own land and felt more comfortable with the anger which replaced it.

He kicked the dry earth. He was working his way down from Queensland, trying to get back to Sydney. Why? There were no more jobs there than anywhere else. He didn't know, but he had to have a plan or he'd go mad, like some of his mates had done.

He might pull in some work after this week, down in Newcastle, then again when he got to Sydney, who knew? He slashed again and again. God, he was tired, hungry.

That night he poked the camp-fire and listened to the others who had slogged from town to town just as he was doing. He checked his boots. Still a bit of sole left. The mozzies were at him. He burned cow muck. An old man laughed. 'Works every time.'

'Wish I did,' Mick grumbled.

'Wish we all did,' a lad said. 'I want to go home. I want to cook a steak in me Mum's kitchen, I want to sink a beer.'

The others threw their boots at him. Mick turned the rabbit they had caught. 'Dream on, kid.'

The old man said, 'You should try the hotels in Sydney, Mick. Not just the bars, try the boarding-houses, or the proper hotels. At least you could filch some food from the stores.' He cackled as he pointed to Mick's hands. 'From the state of those they'd be happier washing-up than wrapped round a mattock.'

'It's just the next day I want to get through, mate,' Mick grunted, turning his hands over. But it wasn't such a bad idea at that.

Chapter Sixteen

A month later, in February 1934, a Kalgoorlie news-paper carried the Coroner's report on Jordan, ex-plaining that he had died after striking his head on the ground, after being pushed. His skull was found to be abnormally thin.

Ben punted the boat towards the landing stage, pushing, withdrawing, water trickling from the pole. The wood-framed house came into view. It was set back about fifty feet from the bank. Rose scrambled forward for a better look. 'Steady,' Ben warned. 'You'll have us, and the luggage, in. I'm a novice at this, remember. So, what do you think of it?'

His arms were tanned against his rolled-up sleeves, his eyes were alight with laughter. Kate looked from him to the house, and all the days of strain, all the years of struggle, were forgotten. 'I love you, Ben Williams,' she shouted, and again, and again, until Rose put her hand across her mother's mouth. 'Shh, they'll think you're mad.' But she was laughing too.

'Who'll think I'm mad?' Kate said, pulling her daughter's hand away from her mouth. 'There's no-one here, just us. I love you, Ben Williams,' she shouted again. 'You've given me this, and I love you.'

Ben was doubled up with laughter as the punt glided into the landing stage. 'There's only the man-ager, and he's waiting for us – just there.' A man in a brown shirt and thick patched trousers emerged.

Kate clapped a hand to her mouth. She'd forgotten. The punt drifted up to the landing stage. Rose rolled in the bottom of the punt now, unable to speak, unable to move, laughter making her ribs ache. She felt her father's hands on her arm, pulling her up, and his own face was creased, his lips were clamped shut, fighting, but it was no good. Laughter burst from him again, and Rose flung her arms round him, feeling his warmth beneath his shirt, as his laughter shook her body too.

The manager tied up the boat. Kate took the hand he offered and stepped out onto the jetty. The man grinned. She said, 'What can I say? It's just that I'm so happy to be here.'

He touched the brim of his hat. 'Glad to hear it, and hear it we did.'

Kate laughed and held out her hand. 'I'm Kate Williams, and Rose is the one who finds the whole thing hysterical.'

Ben was turfing Rose up and out of the boat, towards the hand the manager now held out to her. The manager called over his shoulder to Kate, 'I'm Charlie Best. Please, go on to the house. I'll help Mr Williams with the bags.'

Kate walked while Rose ran towards the house, her auburn hair streaming, calling, 'Mum, come and see, there's a veranda with a bed. Just like Roy's.' Kate watched her daughter stop, turn, all laughter gone. 'Wouldn't Old Roy love this? And Maria and Lucia.' There was aching loss on her face and it found an echo in Kate.

But then she heard the scraping of the punt against the landing stage and heard Ben's laughter, and she hurried to her daughter. They walked on together, arm in arm, and talked of Old Roy standing on the platform, waving as the train left, flanked by Bluey, Stan and Frank, whose shame about the riots had at last surfaced. 'We'll meet again soon,' she said to Rose. 'He'll write too.'

His letters would be full of the harsh sun, and the winds, and the dust, and the boys, and Sydney Bailey, who had given her an orchid for good luck. Roy's letter would also be full of love, for whatever had caused yet another row between Ben and Roy before they left, just after the riot, did not extend to Kate and Rose. Though neither would say what it was.

They rounded the house and saw fruit trees stretching as far as the fence, and there were wattles growing either side of a track which curved and disappeared behind gum-trees. Cows grazed in the paddocks, and chooks scratched in the yard behind the house.

Rose pulled at her arm. 'So that's the same, at least,' Rose murmured pointing to the chooks. 'But it's so green. Old Roy wouldn't believe his eyes. There's no dust. Mum, we must get him to come soon. We really must.' Rose was running now, swooping in amongst the fruit trees which had been pruned.

That evening, as Kate and Ben washed the dishes in the sink and looked out onto the veranda where Rose slept beneath the mosquito-net, she asked again, 'But why has Roy become so angry?'

Ben dried the cup and put it in the cupboard. 'I've already told you. He thinks we should be patient and start with just one hotel.'

Kate gazed down to the river, seeing the moon reflected in the water. 'And I've already said, perhaps it's his nose. Perhaps we should have listened.'

Ben's arms were round her waist now, pulling her back against him, kissing her neck. 'Everything I've done is for us. I have to trust my judgement, and I do. Now is the time to take that gamble. He'll come round. When he sees it's all right, he'll come round.'

He cupped her breasts, kissed her hair, ran his hands down her body, then dragged her away from the sink. She threw the tea towel onto the table as he pulled her through the kitchen and into the bedroom, and when they lay together later, and heard the breeze outside the house and the mosquitoes outside the net, he thought of how he loved her. 'This is a fresh beginning,' he murmured, loving her weight in his arms. Kate nodded.

Yes, it must be and she must not ever think of Dingbat Flats again, or his voice when he . . . No. She wouldn't think of it.

Kate woke early, and crept out into the long dew-drenched grass, her nightdress clinging to her legs. She walked down to the creek, but heavens, it was more of a river. She stood, her hand on a red gum, gazing down into the clear water. She lay down in the grass. The dew was soft and cool. She dangled her hand in the water. The current tugged.

She rolled on her back, and looked up at the sky through the gum leaves. They moved in the breeze and flickered shadows across her face. Insects stirred, clicked, buzzed. 'Oh Roy,' she whispered, 'what's happened? You should be here with us, breathing in the scent of hay.'

'Mum, Mum,' Rose called. Kate ran through the grass, her nightgown tangling in her legs, the breeze lifting her hair, the sun beginning to warm her, and scooped up her daughter from the step, swinging her round, joining in with her laughter. Inside she heard the rattle of the shovel as Ben cleaned out last night's ashes. 'Come on, Rose,' she panted, grabbing her daughter's hand and leaping up the steps. 'Let's help Dad.'

Ben looked up and grinned at them as they came in. 'Come on, Rose,' he said as he threw the newspaper at her. 'Crumple that up and then fetch the chips over from the box. You, Kate, stop running around like a fairy at the bottom of the garden and put the kettle on.'

'Yes, sir,' Kate said, saluting. Rose giggled. Ben laughed. He allowed Rose to strike the match which lit the fire. The paper glowed, then flared.

'You're ten now, so when I'm away in the week, this is your job. You must help your mother, darling.'

Kate grinned at Rose and arched her eyebrows. Rose said, 'Yes, Dad, but I've done that for months at home, and for Old Roy too.' She paused, then continued, her voice subdued. 'Who will be doing it for him now?'

The smile left Ben's face. He threw the spent match onto the flames and squatted before the blaze, saying coldly, 'He's perfectly capable of looking after himself, for God's sake.'

Kate turned away quickly, stirring the porridge. She said, 'Fetch the milk in from the veranda, Rose. Charlie said he'd leave some.'

Rose brought in a galvanised bucket. Muslin cloth covered it. Rose heaved it onto the table and said, 'There's butter out there too, in a dish.' Her voice trembled, her eyes were full of tears.

Kate touched her shoulder and said softly, 'Bring it in then, darling.'

As Rose left she looked across at Ben.

He shouted, 'Just don't say anything. I'm sick of the whole damn "Roy" business. This is a new start, let's keep it at that.' He turned on his heel and left the room. She heard him rummaging in the bedroom.

She stirred the porridge faster and faster. The steam soaked into her hair. Rose brought in the butter and placed it beside the stove. Moisture glistened on the ridged yellow surface. 'It looks like it's crying, Mum,' she said.

'Yes,' Kate said. 'So it does.'

At breakfast they ate bread thick with the butter and Rose asked Ben, 'So you're going to live at a hotel and the waiters will serve you? You'll ride in the lifts. You'll read papers in the big leather chairs that hotels have.'

Her father laughed, throwing back his head, catching Kate's hand as she walked behind him, kissing it. She stopped and stroked his hair. This is how it had been since they had left Kalgoorlie – sunlight and shadows. Tension and laughter.

Ben said, 'Not quite, Rose. I actually have to work. I have three to look after. If we'd been able to put more money in, as we planned with Roy,' his voice tightened, 'we would have had the back-up to put a manager in each, but now I have to handle them all. It's part of the deal.'

Kate had stopped stroking his hair. She handed jam to Rose. 'Hurry up. We've a picnic to prepare, and Dad is going to teach us to swim.' Her voice was a careful monotone.

'When are we coming to live in the hotel with you, Dad?'

He shook his head, his eyes on the bread he was buttering. 'You're not. This is your home. This is my sanctuary. This is where you and your mother will be happiest.'

During the morning he made a float out of empty treacle tins and an old board, as Charlie suggested. Kate used an old dress to wrap around both and as they worked quietly together in the shade of the veranda they were happy, and his lips were gentle as they kissed her fingers, one by one, and then her mouth. 'I love you, don't ever forget that,' he murmured.

At midday Kate and Rose put on the swimming-costumes that Ben had asked the hotel housekeeper to buy. They were woollen and itched, but so did Ben's and the faces they pulled made laughter spring from them. It was as though there had never been tension, and as they walked to the river Kate said, 'I love you. I always have and I always will. We're so very lucky.'

He watched Rose running through the grass. Yes, they were lucky. Yes, it would be all right. So, tell her. He couldn't.

He ran on ahead of Kate, scooping up Rose. She shrieked. Her arms were warm and soft around his neck. He carried her to the edge of the river, then eased himself into the cold flowing current, sinking, floating on his back, moving his arms, drifting beneath the sky, the pale hot sky. 'Watch me, Rose. It's easy.' He swam back to the bank, his arms out to his daughter. Stephens was just a source of money. That's what he'd say, when he said anything.

He swam on his back, dragging Rose with him. She panicked, struggled.

'Trust Dad,' Kate called from the bank. 'Trust him.' Rose relaxed.

They stayed in the water until lunch-time, then ate their picnic under the shade of the gum-tree while flies buzzed and boats passed. Rose waved, the bargees waved back. Kate peeled the hard-boiled eggs, sprinkled salt, handed them out. They ate tomatoes and freshly baked bread which Mrs Best had sent across with Charlie.

In the afternoon the sun beat down and again they slid into the water. Ben held Rose, swam with her, coaxed her, cajoled her, until it was Kate's turn, and she felt his hands beneath her shoulders, his legs working in the water. 'Relax,' he murmured, swimming out with her. 'Move your legs up and down.'

She did.

'Move your hands.'

She did, feeling the water resist then give way, feeling the sun on her face. Ben felt her hair drift across his chest, felt her body so close to him, saw her face, sun splashed and beautiful, and turned her over until she lay on his moving body, her face lifted from the water. He kissed her open mouth. 'I love you. Remember, all I'm doing is for us.' He hurt with love for her and could not look into her blue eyes, in case she saw inside his head. He guided her to the shallows, then swam away.

She watched him, then edged towards the bank, feeling for stones, the current pulling at her. She lost balance, fell forward, water covered her, she couldn't breathe, she thrashed, pushed herself up, gasped, staggered to her feet, brushing the water from her eyes, grabbed for the bank, and suddenly she remembered Des.

That evening they all stirred their hot cocoa until the bubbles raced, and laughed at the brown moustaches it had given them. They talked until they could barely keep their eyes open then Kate watched as Ben lifted Rose and carried her to her bed. She watched as he kissed his daughter, and the love was tangible.

He walked with Kate to their room, and slowly he undressed her, and in the moonlight he kissed her shoulders, her breasts, belly, thighs, and her fingers gripped his hair and brought him up, and now she kissed his mouth, his neck, his chest, his belly. His hands were in her hair, pulling her to him. He carried her to the rug by the fireplace and knelt beside her, tracing her curves in the moonlight. Love was in every gesture, in every breath he took, just as it was in every part of her, and she pulled him to her and kissed him, needing to block her mouth because she must ask again about Roy, but not yet, not now. Now was their time.

By lunch-time of the next day Rose had learned to swim, and Kate too, after a fashion. Ben said, as he dried himself on the bank, 'Now I shall relax when I'm on that train, knowing that I've done everything to make you safe.' Water dripped from his hair to his chest and rolled down to his belly. Kate stroked it away. His skin was hot from the sun already. He gripped her hand. 'Everything.'

339

Kate said, 'You are so good to us.' She couldn't ask why? Not today.

On Sunday night the house seemed so quiet without him, but he would be home the next Friday. 'When we hear the train whistle', Kate said, as she and Rose sat in the kitchen before the fireplace, 'we'll row down and meet the punt on the bend. Remember, he's only four hours away by train, and that doesn't seem so far, does it? Maybe Mr Best will let you milk the cows, and there's the Clydesdale too. You can go and groom him and then collect the eggs.'

Rose leaned against her mother's knees. 'I just wish Old Roy was here too. You didn't ask Dad what's happened.'

'I will.'

They rose with the sun, raked out the ash, lit the fire, stirred the porridge, hunted for eggs, then helped Charlie bring in the cows, chasing them through the slip-rails into the yard, urging them into their stalls, fixing the chain as they stuck their heads into the feed-boxes.

Charlie kicked the stool into place in one stall. 'Watch me with Daisy, then see if you can milk Clara next door,' he said to Kate. Charlie washed the udders, patted them dry, slung the towel back round his neck, balanced the stool between his knees, leaning his forehead against the cow. 'Easy now, Daisy, easy now.' It was what her father used to say.

Jets of milk rang against the sides of the bucket until the bottom was covered, and then it was just a swish, swish.

'You, young Rose, take this bucket.' Charlie sat on the stool and held a steaming pail he had just filled with milk from Daisy. 'Get on over there, and make sure that calf has some.'

Kate watched as the calf snuffled at the pail and as her daughter dipped her fingers into the milk, and as the calf's tongue licked at her hand.

She knew it would be rough, and rasping. Like . . . She milked Clara now, feeling the heat of the cow against her forehead, smelling the sweet grassy smell of the milk.

She and Charlie moved along the bails, milking silently. Rose patted the calf, then took the enamel mug that Charlie gave her, drank some, wiped her hand across her mouth, then dawdled out past the dairy, down the bank where clover and grass grew. The dew had dried now, the flies and insects were buzzing. She sat and watched the river meander. She shouted back to Kate, 'I'll write to Old Roy and draw this for him.'

Charlie and Kate released the cows into the paddock, and poured the milk into the churns. 'A cart'll come and take them to the creamery in the township down the track,' Charlie said as he put down the bucket. The handle clanked as it dropped.

'You've done this before,' Charlie stated, as they washed out the milking pails.

She nodded. 'In a past life.'

He looked puzzled. She said nothing more.

That afternoon she and Rose walked out down the track, through the wattles and the gums, seeking their shade, their eyes peeled for snakes. They came to a shack. Mrs Best came out and waved. 'A cup of tea?'

They nodded. 'We've come to thank you for the milk and butter.'

They sat on the veranda with her, drinking tea and eating scones. The shack was grey and weathered, and the bark roof sagged. Light blazed in through the gaps. The cane chairs creaked, the breeze rustled in the gum-trees.

'D'you like your new house?' Sylvia Best asked.

'It's wonderful,' Rose said. 'And I sleep on the veranda like Old Roy, and I'm going to write to him, and I'm going to draw it for him, and I miss

341

him, and there's a big gap just here, because of it.'
She pointed to her chest.

Mrs Best smiled. 'A picture would be beaut. And it'd fill the ache in his chest, cos I bet he's got one too. There's paper in the shack, in the kitchen drawer, and pencils. Go and get a start on now, and draw me with me hair all pretty.' She patted her grey, stringy hair.

Rose did, and the women sat gazing out onto the heat-drenched quiet of the day. 'Old Roy is a friend, well more than a friend,' Kate said finally.

'You left him behind? Well, we all leave things behind. That's what life does to us.' Sylvia sounded weary suddenly, her face seemed drawn.

'He was annoyed at a business decision of my husband's. He's a partner, but didn't put in as much money as my husband hoped. Or I think that's the problem . . .' She trailed off.

Mrs Best said nothing, and now Kate couldn't stop talking. 'I think it's because he's worried. We have a mixed marriage. He thinks my husband is upsetting me because one hotel is in a Protestant suburb. He thinks I will mind because all his friends are Protestants. He loves me, you see. He's like a father to me. Yes, that's what it must be.' She stopped.

Mrs Best smiled gently, not understanding, and why should she? She said, 'An old man's fears I 'spect. You're right, he's thinking of it how it was, and the spot of bother in the war, and of those fools who sprang up when Lang was in. Now they've got him out they've stopped being so daft. There are other problems. There's the depression.'

Kate asked, 'What have you left behind?'

Mrs Best smiled gently. 'Our home.' Kate looked at the shack. Mrs Best said, 'We were real grateful when your husband bought our farm and gave us the job. It meant we could stay on the land.' She waved her hand towards the farm. 'The bank was calling in our loan.

342

We'd have been turfed off. They weren't allowing our fruit into Sydney. They were throwing it into the sea off the Heads to keep the prices up. We got nothing, of course. Fish don't pay you, do they? It was the last straw. You had camels in Kalgoorlie? Well, our fruit going for a swim is what broke this camel's back.'

That evening as Kate lay beneath the mosquito-net, smelling its mustiness, feeling the heat, hearing the mosquitoes, she thought of Mrs Best's words as she and Rose left the shack. 'What I don't understand is why you're here and your husband's there. Seems strange to me.' Kate rolled onto her side aching for his touch. She turned onto her other side. She turned again. Was he missing her, as she was missing him? Would there be tension when he came, because she must ask him, just once more, about Roy?

Ben clung to her on Friday evening as they lay in bed. 'God, I've missed you.' His kisses were fierce, his hands and body urgent, and she said nothing, because all his talk had been of the hotel and their future, and his excitement at it all was too precious to disturb.

As summer ended and autumn cooled the days, Rose settled into her correspondence lessons, and Kate into the rhythm of the farm. She helped Charlie with the ploughing, she herded in the cows, she plucked the chooks they killed for the weekends, and, because Ben was not here, it was soon all too much like Ireland. As she cleaned the house and baked bread and scones and heard the animals, and the breeze in the trees, that too became too much like Ireland. And the river became too much like 'their' river, and too much like the river that had dragged Des to Widow Murphy's.

And the nights, because she was alone, gave her too much time to think, and she wondered again why Ben and Roy had fought. And as winter came, and the chooks beneath the gums scratched, she began

343

to wonder who was baking her father's bread, who was tending her mother's grave. And sometimes the noise of the Dingbat Flats riot merged into that of the battles fought around the farm, and the snarls of the Tans, and the sound of the halls they broke up, and the fires they lit.

And it was on a night before Ben came home that she saw in her mind, for the first time since it had happened, the face of the Tan who had murdered her mother, and it seemed that the past was flowing all over her and around her.

Mrs Best said, 'It's because you've stopped working so hard, and because you are alone, everything is coming to the surface, and from there, it'll go into the air, and float up and out of sight.'

'When?'

Mrs Best shrugged. 'The days are still good, aren't they? Talk to your husband about it.'

She could not and so she worked harder.

She cleaned out the dairy, she groomed the horse, she gathered up the branches of the apple, orange and lemon trees as Mr Best pruned, and the wind was heavy with the scent of blossom. In the evenings she sat with Rose in the soft flickering light of the hurricane lamp and sewed a quilt and darned socks and reread *Wuthering Heights* and *Jane Eyre*, while her daughter read *Tom Sawyer* and imagined that the creek was the Mississippi.

They wrote to Old Roy, or to Lucia and Mario who had bought a greengrocer's in Melbourne. 'We are saving to go home,' Lucia wrote.

At the weekends she clung to Ben, holding his hand when they walked, pulling her chair up close to him when they sat, lying awake beside him when he slept, listening to his breathing, feeling his warmth, kissing his skin lightly, feeling as though her heart was being torn out as he left in the punt for the station on Sunday. 'Don't leave me,' she called after

344

him. 'Don't leave me here.' He didn't hear. He just smiled and waved.

Rose said, slipping her hand in her mother's, 'I'm here, Mum.'

As winter reached a climax in July she told Ben when he came home that she wanted to come back with him to Sydney. 'It's lovely, but it's not home without you. I need to be with you.'

He stormed from the veranda, his shoulders tense. 'Isn't it enough that I have so much work to do? I bought you this for your happiness. Are you throwing it back in my face? I have to keep the shareholders happy, the customers, and the damn staff. But the staff are hopeless. There are so many mistakes. I just don't understand it. Dirty plates are brought from the kitchen. Customers have started complaining. It's just started this week. For God's sake, Kate, stay where you are. I can't cope with you at the moment.'

She was rooted to the spot for a moment, then ran down the steps after him.

'Cope with me, what do you mean, cope with me? I'm your wife, you don't have to *cope* with me. If you say you're having trouble at work, let me help.'

'What do you mean when you say – if you say? Are you doubting my word?'

The wind was whistling through the gums, plucking at her hair, the leaves were scudding across the yard. She caught at the strands which were blowing in her face. She shook her head. 'Ben. Let's talk about it. Please.'

'There's nothing to talk about.' He strode off across the yard and down the track.

She shouted after him, 'Like there's nothing to talk about with you and Roy? Like that, d'you mean?'

That night they slept side by side, not touching, and it was only as dawn broke that he moved and stroked her hair. 'Please stay here. I've had a bad week. I've no time there for you whilst we're building up, and it helps to think of you and Rose here, amongst the river and the fruit trees.' He kissed her cheek, and then her lips, saying, 'I can't bear it when we fight.'

His arms were round her, his warmth all over her, wiping away the anger, the worry, the tiredness.

'Promise me you'll stay,' he murmured, holding her face between his hands, looking deep into her eyes. His face was so fine, his eyes so grey, his lashes so long, and it was the face of the man she loved more each day.

'I promise,' she breathed as he lowered himself onto and into her.

She stayed, but he only came twice more in July, and each time he was more tense, the frown lines greater. On the first weekend in August she held him in bed while he talked and grappled with dirty linen put back on the beds, with dirty towels in the bathroom, with disgruntled customers, and with the consortium who wanted results. 'Let me help,' she pleaded again as he left.

'You can't help. Women don't work. It's not done.' His voice was clipped and cold. 'Don't you know anything?' He did not wave from the punt, and neither did she call, 'Don't go.' Though she wanted to pull the boat back and shake him until they had talked to one another.

As August drew on, the westerlies blew apples from the trees, and she and Rose gathered them in a wicker basket on Saturday morning, when Ben had not come again. They carried them between them to the veranda. 'Do we have to, Mum?'

'Yes.' It was better to be busy.

They washed them, then tipped them into the big kerosene tin she had cut and beaten, and simmered them on the stove. Kate smiled when Rose tasted the mixture, and shuddered. 'It's sour.'

By evening the apples were soft.

Rose stoked the fire, then Kate allowed her to tip in the sugar. Kate stirred, breathing in the rich smell. Then she put the spoon into Rose's hand. 'You stir.' She took a spoonful from the pan, tested it on the plate. It formed a skin. She put the frame she had made over the big enamel dish and poured great jugfuls of the apples into the gauze she suspended between the frame.

'Let's leave it now, until morning,' Kate said.

Rose shook her as dawn broke. 'Come on, Mum. The dish is full and it's still warm.'

They poured the apple jelly cup by cup into jelly jars, and then they sat by the warmth of the stove and cut squares of paper and lengths of string. They covered the jars with the paper, squeezing them tightly over the rim. Kate tied the strings. They labelled them: *Endersley Farm, August 1934.*

'Did your mum teach you to do this?' Rose asked.

Kate ran her hand through her hair, and sat down. 'Yes.'

'Did you have a farm?'

'Not then. We stayed on someone else's. He let us pick the apples and then my mother made jelly.'

She saw Mick's face as he scrumped, and then as he fell, and she heard his laughter. Her mother had bathed his knee. Ben had never met her mother. She'd never met his.

Rose said, 'Whose farm was it?'

Kate looked at her. Her daughter did not know that she had a grandfather in Ireland. She did not know that Kate had fought for the cause, that her father had been an Auxie. She heard her father's voice: 'No better than a Tan.' There was so much she didn't know, and so much she mustn't know, because it was in the past. Damn it, Caithleen Healy, it's in the past, so shut your mind up.

She walked out onto the veranda and looked at the full, sluggish, wind-whipped river. They should

347

never have come here, to a place where a river ran by, where wind breathed in the long grass, where memories drifted in as the mist in Ireland had done. She should have known they shouldn't have come.

Summer came, and the wheat ripened, and on Christmas Day Ben lay in bed, listening to Kate raking the ash, to Rose chattering, and he turned on his side. God, it was a mess. The trouble had spread to the Bondi Beach hotel and to the city, where he now had his apartment. It was spasmodic. He never knew when the service would deteriorate. It was crazy.

Once the presents had been given out in the morning he worked on the pricing for the new contract. He barely noticed the decorations Rose and Kate had made, except to curse when a paper streamer fell and tangled in his hair.

Kate shouted at him when Rose was in bed, 'It's Christmas, we have a child.'

He shouted back, 'It's because I have a child, and a wife, that I'm working so hard. I've told you until I'm sick that all this is for you.'

'But I didn't want three hotels in the first place. Neither did Roy.'

He slammed his hand down on the table. 'Well, we've got them, and I don't give a tinker's cuss what Roy wanted. As well as shoddy service, stores have gone missing. I'll sack the lot of them.'

Now she slammed her hand on the table. 'Don't be so sanctimonious. People are starving out there. We're in depression or rather we're not, just people like the Bests, like those who pound the streets. So what if a few stores are missing? Think of the big mines and the gold you all filtered out. That was all right, when it was your perk. Ben, be reasonable.'

'I'm sick of being reasonable. I work all hours and am being squashed in the middle. Oh go to bed, Kate, and let me get on.'

As she left the room, she saw the firelight glinting on the decorations they had made. They looked sad and limp, and she wanted to tear their mocking glitter down.

Ben came to bed at midnight and slipped between the sheets, taking her in his arms, dragging off her nightgown, kissing her, stroking her, loving her. 'I'm sorry,' he whispered, and he moved inside her. 'I'm so sorry. You're right. Poor buggers.'

In February 1935 they rowed out to meet his punt. He was leaning forward as Mr Best pushed in the pole and dragged it out, and Rose put her hand in her mother's as she saw her father's face beneath his hat.

He raged all evening about the contract they had lost because the representative of the travel firm had found a dirty towel in his room and his fork had been encrusted with egg.

'The laundry denies all responsibility. They say it's checked before it leaves them. The housekeeper says they're reliable. I've changed them anyway. But if it isn't them, it has to be someone in the hotel. Why are they doing it? For God's sake, they're lucky to be employed. Are they blind? Haven't they seen the dole queues, the shanty towns?'

Kate fanned herself as she sat in the chair by the fly door, looking out onto the river. At least he was talking to her. She said, 'It seems so stupid – and a dirty fork. It can't have been deliberate, can it? What possible grounds? I mean, you're paying the legal wage, of course.'

Ben flung down his pen. 'I'm paying as much as they deserve. They can't be choosy, you know, Kate. We could get a dozen in tomorrow.'

She said nothing, just looked at him, and, for the first time, she wondered about Charlie and Sylvia Best in their shack. 'And is it the same for Charlie, Ben?'

Her voice was cold. 'How does it work? Does he slave away for a pittance too?'

Ben pushed past her. She pulled him back. 'Rose is sleeping out there. Don't you dare storm out, don't you dare present your back to me.'

He pulled away from her. 'And don't you dare speak to me in this way, when all this is for you. Keep your nose out when you don't understand something, Kate. This is business. It's above you.'

He was tapping out a cigarette, standing by the stove, drumming on the mantel.

'I understood it well enough to get the boarding-houses off the ground, to build up our reputation for honesty, for fair dealing.' Her voice was low. Rose must not be disturbed. 'Who is this consortium? Who are they that your budget is so tight?'

He flung his cigarette packet at her. 'Ah, this is what I've been waiting for. My Catholic wife rearing up against my friends.'

The cigarette packet hit her, dropped to the ground. She tried to grasp his words. She stared for a long moment then said, 'I thought all that was finished?'

He came to her, held her. 'Oh God, Kate. I didn't mean it. You just don't understand. It's so hard. I'm so tired. I'm trying to please everyone. Help me, you must help me. It's all such a mess.' Stephens had shouted and ranted, showing him the figures, cursing him for losing the consortium money, threatening to withdraw, and if he did that, they'd be on the street with the rest of the no-hopers.

She held him, and now he was weeping, and she couldn't bear it, and his tears swept his words away. 'We'll write to Old Roy. You must bury whatever your differences are. He'll know.'

He pushed her away. 'You're like a dog with a bloody bone. Leave him out of it. I must do it myself.'

'You're not alone. You have me.' She tried to keep her voice calm. 'And you could have Roy too. He loves you, I know he does, and this quarrel, whatever it is, has gone on too long.'

Ben stormed from her. 'I must do this myself,' he shouted. 'I don't need any clapped-out old fool.'

He left as usual on Sunday afternoon. On Tuesday Rose and Kate were packed, and Mr Best took them to the station in the punt. Kate shook his hand.

'From now on, you receive your wages plus any profits, is that clear. However we are still responsible for maintenance.' Mr Best looked puzzled. She continued, 'And you might as well move back into the house. That way maintenance costs will be reduced for us.' She grinned.

'But Mr Williams said nothing of this to me.'

'Mr Williams has a great deal on his mind, that's why we're going to Sydney. He needs us there. If we do come back for a holiday, we can sort out the arrangements beforehand. Just look after our apple jelly for us.' She walked to the landing stage with Rose. She must join Ben, whatever he said, or the rift would grow too great, even for the love she knew they both held for one another.

Mick drank down his beer and smiled. They'd lost the contract, had they? Well, let's have another drink, Michael O'Brian. He called the barman. 'C'mon, Tom, get 'em in.'

The beer was warm, too damn warm. The kitchens of Ben high-and-mighty Williams were too warm, and now the seat of the Auxie's breeches would be too warm from that consortium's boots. He swallowed and grinned. He'd close them down if it killed him. He'd close them down, and then what would that Proddy consortium say? What would Caithleen Williams say?

He hadn't put two and two together at first. Up to his elbows in greasy suds, he hadn't cared who his boss was. It was only when the chef was grouching about Ben Williams's low wages that he'd twigged, and then he'd nearly choked.

He slammed the glass down on the bar. 'Another, and quick.'

How could she have swung the Auxie round? How the hell could she do that? And now she was living on the fat of the land, out at some farm. How dare she have a farm, when he was banned from his own, when Des was sitting there, with his feet under his father's table?

Cait, the Tan and their child. Well, it wouldn't last. He'd make sure it didn't. Soon they'd be out there, tramping the roads, living in the shacks in the Happy Valley shanty towns, scrabbling for food, for life, just like he'd had to do.

Chapter Seventeen

The porter showed her up to the apartment and together she and Rose waited, longing for the sound of Ben's footsteps, but fearing them also. They sat opposite one another in the immaculate armchairs.

'Leather,' Rose whispered, touching the arms.

'We can talk aloud,' Kate replied, but realized she was whispering too. She clenched her hands on her handbag.

'The lady at the desk said she'd page him,' Rose continued to whisper.

'Yes.'

'What does that mean?'

'Find him.'

'Then he'll come?' Rose asked.

'Yes.' Kate's voice was loud. She looked around as though she feared she had disturbed the pictures on the walls, the dark red flocked wallpaper, and austere fireplace, the wooden clock on the mantelpiece, the dust-free mahogany tables beside each of their chairs, and the sofa. There was nothing of Ben here, it was just like any other hotel apartment.

'He'll let us stay?' Rose asked, fingering the colouring-book Mrs Best had given her.

'We won't budge so he'll have to.' Kate smiled at Rose, but her shoulders were rigid.

At last, as they sat in the soft light from the lamps they had lit as the afternoon sun died, they recognized his footsteps approaching. He stopped, the doorknob turned. Kate clutched her handbag tighter still. Would he let them stay?

He came in and stood there, looking from one to the other, and Kate saw that his face was eager and loving, but tired, so tired. He held out his arms and they both ran to him, and they were all laughing and talking, and he took them down to the dining-room for a meal and she hardly dared to look at the cutlery, or the table-cloth but Rose did and said, 'They look nice and clean to me. This is a good day, is it, Dad?'

Kate stiffened and glanced at Ben who was staring at Rose. Then he smiled, reached out and touched his daughter's cheek. 'A very good day. The Williams family is together, and the forks are clean. Who could ask for anything more?'

That night they lay together in a room that had no sense of her in it, and barely any sense of him. 'I'll make this a home for us, my darling,' she'd whispered after they had made love.

He held her tightly. 'Yes, you can do that. Make it a home, be my wife, Rose's mother, concentrate on that, nothing else.' There was desperation in his eyes. 'I've missed you. God, how I've missed you. I need you here, behind me. Do you understand? Here, creating a home for me. Here, separate from my work. Here, just here.' His voice was urgent, his fingers gripped her arms. 'Do you understand?'

The next day she began to scour the shops for cheap material, which she made into curtains and bedspreads, and cheerful pictures which she hung in the sombre frames. As the months passed the bed-room had a sense of them both in it, the sitting-room too, and Rose's bedroom had the essence of a young girl.

Autumn came, and winter, and as it drew to a close

354

there was hardly a shop that Kate had not been into, a tram she hadn't boarded, a street she had not been down, with empty cicada cases crunching beneath her feet. She was always alone, so she talked within her head and heard the traffic noise with every step she took, and echoes of Ben's voice which was terse and clipped and now too busy for words of love, or the trivia with which lovers built bridges; too busy for questions about Old Roy.

In the evenings, after Rose was in bed, Kate tried to tell him of the books she had discovered in the library, and of the progress of their daughter. He usually said, 'Not now, I'm too busy.' When she asked about his friends, and about the consortium and the possibility that they should all meet, he said, 'Not now. I'm too busy.'

In the mornings she checked Rose's school uniform and waved her goodbye as the lift descended. It was a Protestant school the consortium wives had recommended to Ben, of course. Every morning she bit back the anger and told herself, Why not, you stupid woman? Why not? This is who you are.

She walked around the hotel, along the carpeted corridors, touching the mock-antique tables, smelling the fresh flowers. Ben had said, 'I listened to you, you see. It is as you would have wished.' It was.

'Let me help?' she pleaded again one night. 'You look so tired. I understand the business of hotels. I worked at Joe's, remember.'

'Do you wish to shame me? No-one in our set works. I told you I need you here, making a life for me, here.' His shout reverberated around their apartment. From the windows she could see the harbour, and the city lights. 'Isn't it enough that I have arranged to live in the city hotel to spare your sensibilities? Would I have ever heard the end of it if we had lived in Canterbury? What do you want from me, blood?'

355

'I want nothing from you, but to help you. I've never mentioned Canterbury. What's the matter with you?'

'Why do you always have to argue? Isn't it enough that I have to deal with the staff? Go for a walk, for God's sake.'

'No, the parks are too full of men without work, the pavements too full of men queuing at food stations. They walk along, Ben, holding up their handkerchief to dry. There are refugees in leather coats and worn briefcases who stand lost and confused.'

'Oh, for heaven's sake. Is it tears you want from me now?' He slammed his hand down on the table.

'No, I just wanted to share it with you.'

'I'm too—'

She interrupted. 'Busy, yes, I know.'

So she walked to the library again and sat in the downstairs hall, reading, losing herself in books, pushing down the confusion which was tearing at her, grasping at some sort of safety, because everything was different, and she didn't know what she should be doing. She only knew that she must not complain, because it had been her decision to leave the farm and to come to him.

On the second Friday in September, as she ate breakfast and checked through Rose's homework, Ben phoned through from his office. 'Be ready at 8.00 p.m. Brenda and Harold Sinclair are insisting we all meet at their house for dinner. I might as well tell you that I have refused all invitations so far. For your own sake. The housekeeper will stay in with Rose. It's all a great nuisance. There's trouble brewing again with the staff. I really need to be here.'

'What sort of trouble?'

'Wages trouble, but nothing to concern you.'

She packed Rose off to school. She walked to the library, she read, she pushed aside his words. Why had he refused all invitations for her own sake? Mrs

Best said that everything had calmed down. It didn't really matter what you were these days. Was it because he was ashamed of her? Was that it?

That evening, as Ben fixed his cuff-links he felt the tension clawing at his back, neck and head. Would Stephens be there? He'd known he couldn't go on refusing, and tonight Sinclair had insisted.

Kate came up behind him. 'Why have you refused all invitations?'

He slipped on his jacket, looking at her in the mirror. 'They're a lot to take on. I wanted to introduce you gradually. You will have to be careful in what you say. They're pretty snobbish, you see.'

She smiled gently. 'I can cope. I want to help.'

'You do see, though, what I mean? Follow my lead. Weigh your words. We need to keep in with them.' His voice was harsh. His head ached. It always ached these days.

Her smile faded. 'Yes, I see what you mean.'

His hands were trembling. God, he was so tired. There was so much to do. Damn Roy for not coming in with the money. Should they have gone for just the one hotel? No, damn it. He had to make good, and he could, if only the staff would come to heel. If only he could sleep, but he couldn't. He tossed and turned, and rose more tired than when he went to bed.

Brenda Sinclair smelt of roses. Her hair was as cropped as her voice. She was plump and blond, with fair skin which was almost untouched by the sun. How did she do it? Kate wondered, looking across the table at her hostess. Kate touched her own hair nervously. Were there any loose strands? She caught sight of herself in the antique mirror which hung at one end of the dining-room. No, it was neat enough in its pleat, the long loose curls hidden, but she looked older than her thirty-four years.

She smiled at Ben who sat opposite. His smile

was tight, preoccupied. Brenda drank wine from a crystal goblet. Her lips barely touched the glass. She looked so young but she must have been the same age as Kate.

Kate started as Brenda's husband laughed out loud. She knew he was only Ben's age. Ben looked older, worn down with worry. Love for him twisted inside her, and helplessness. He should let her help, but it was as though he trusted no-one. It was as though everyone was his enemy, not just the workers.

Larry Smith patted the table. 'Quite right, Harold,' he guffawed. 'A few of that bowler Larwood's body-liners wouldn't go amiss in the kitchens, eh Ben?'

Ben smiled. 'There are certainly no Don Bradmans in there to counter the balls, just a load of trouble-makers.'

Kate heard herself speak. 'I always felt Larwood behaved disgracefully. His bowling was dangerous.'

Ben froze.

Brenda laughed. 'My dear, we won.'

'We?'

'Why the British.'

'But didn't you support Australia?'

Brenda laughed again. 'My dear, we must support the Empire. That's why we've all sent our boys home to Eton. You must think yourself lucky that you have a daughter. One does miss them so much. But then again, one does get home to England more often – to see them.' She laughed lightly. 'But come along, let us hear more about you.'

Brenda turned to Ben. 'You've kept your delight-ful wife to yourself for far too long, Ben. Too much work, my dear boy.'

The glass was cool in her hand, the wine too as she drank, and her lips were on the glass. Larry Smith raised his eyebrows. 'They need a good thrashing, that's what they need, damn unionists. They would have got one too, if Lang and his lot hadn't gone.'

The others were talking now, the women's jewellery glittered, the men's bow-ties were sombre, clear cut. Ben's mouth was set in a smile, his eyes were wary. Kate cut up her duck, piece by piece, smaller and smaller.

Brenda spoke again. 'So, tell me, my dear, where is your home?'

Kate looked up at Brenda. She took a deep breath. 'Where Ben is,' she replied quietly. Be careful, he had said.

Brenda laughed, and touched Ben's arm. 'How sweet.'

Ben flushed and looked into Kate's violet eyes, the colour of an Irish sky, and saw the love in them, and wanted to take her away from here.

Brenda persisted. 'But where really?'

Kate's eyes were steady on Ben's and he couldn't let her answer, in spite of the love. There was no way he could let her spoil it for them. He blurted, 'Manchester.'

Kate looked down at her plate and cut, and cut again, and now the potato, as Ben told Brenda of the accountancy firm her father had owned, the small summer house at the side of a lake, the long lazy days, the picnics she had had on its banks.

She put her knife and fork down as he redrew her past. And why this anger? Why the pain? Isn't this what she had done to herself? It was she who should have prepared these lies. She barely touched dessert and she talked little when the women withdrew for coffee, but she smiled as they sat in the deep comfortable chairs and talked of the school bazaar, and the problems with servants, and the heat, and the next trip home.

The men joined them as the clock struck eleven, but Ben was not with them. Larry Smith said, 'Phone call, I'm afraid, Kate. Trouble, a strike is threatened. I took the liberty of saying that you would join us in

359

the car when the party breaks up. Shame to end a perfect evening early, eh?'

Kate smiled and nodded and counted the seconds, and the minutes, and listened to the clipped voices, and the golf talk, and the girl talk, and agreed to meet for lunch at the David Jones store next week. Because she was Kate Williams, and her husband had created a past for her, and a future for her, and it was one she wanted. She just had to remember that.

In the car on the way to the hotel, Larry shook his head. 'Poor old Ben. He's having a few problems. It must be good to have you with him. I'm glad you feel fully recovered and able to join us here. He has warned us that you tire easily, but do try and come to a few of our soirées. You simply must meet Stephens. What a man.'

She rode up in the lift, smiling at the lift boy, who looked at his feet. 'Has it been a busy night, Nigel?' she asked. 'Are you tired? Is your mother any better? Did she go to the doctor? I hope so, and there should have been no bill.'

Nigel looked up at her now. 'Yes, and thank you. There was no bill.' He smiled now, but briefly.

She said, 'There's more trouble, isn't there?'

He shrugged.

The lift stopped. He pulled open the folding guard. She looked at him. 'Is there someone behind this? What's going on?'

He wouldn't meet her eyes. He just waited, his finger poised over the button. She said, 'Good night, Nigel.'

Ben was still in his office, shouting on the phone. 'I don't know, Harold. I just don't know. I'll report to Stephens in the morning. He won't like it. We'll have to give in.' He paused, listened. 'Fine, so we have our hotels picketed, and scare away the last of our customers . . . All right, all right. But we have to give in, that's what I'm telling you. And yes, I know

360

there must be someone behind it. It's all too focused. It's one damn thing after another ... Yes, I know it's my job to handle it, and that's what I'm doing.' He paused again, rubbing his eyes with his trembling hands, listening to the voice which was ranting on. It ceased. 'All right, but I haven't got a sabre to run through them, if that's what you want.' His laugh was harsh. 'These people are human beings, God damn it.'

She moved to him, then lay her gloved hand on his shoulder, the pain and the confusion swept away by this the real Ben. He slammed the phone down, and rested his head in his hands. 'Oh God, I'm so tired, Kate. So damn tired.'

'I love you,' she said tentatively, not knowing if he would shout and rage at her, or need her comfort.

He just shook his head again and again. 'I've wanted to give them the minimum wage for months, but the consortium have baulked me. So now we've another crisis. They're threatening to picket unless we give in. It'll look like weakness to give it to them now. It'll be as though we've been pushed into it, as though we've been defeated. Why didn't they offer it to them when I wanted to?'

He slammed his hand down on the table, then leaned against her. She relaxed. Just for once he was hers again. Just for once he was not pushing her aside.

Her mind raced, grappling with ideas and thoughts until it came to her. She said, 'Think of Roy's mine. You were shareholders. You cared if it did well. The consortium are shareholders because they've put up the money. You're having to work because we couldn't put up anything like the same but you'll have a share in the profit in the long run, so you think it's worth it. The workers would think the same if they had a stake. Give them one. Regain the initiative. Give them the minimum wage and offer a small share in the profits.

Offer them it as a package, Ben. Explain to them that you've been discussing the best deal for them, trying to find ways and that's why it's taken this long.' She crouched beside him, looking up into his face.

He rubbed his eyes, mulling it over. The clock ticked on his desk. He watched the pendulum. Could it work? It would need Stephens's approval. He should see it was a sound proposition, or would he? If it got the business booming of course he would. The rest of the consortium would then come into line. He took the pen from his pocket, unscrewing it as he pulled paper towards him.

Kate stood, and touched his hair. He nodded. 'Yes, it might work. I'll get Stephens over. I'll present it to him properly. I'll stall the workers until I've seen him.'

She knew he was talking to himself, that she was forgotten. But it didn't matter. She had helped, and she had seen the old Ben, and soon he would see that they had drawn their inspiration from Roy. It would all come good. She bent and kissed his hair and hoped that he would hold her when he came to bed. He did not. He was too tired, as usual, and just rolled onto his side, away from her.

The next morning Ben was even more drawn and tired, but he called through to Kate, 'I've booked the driver to take you and Rose out to Bondi Beach. He'll pick Alice, Brenda's daughter, up on the way. Thought it might be a good idea, get you into their good books.'

Kate swallowed her retort. What about putting them into my good books?

He called again. 'Hurry up, the car will be here in five minutes.'

Rose rushed for her swimsuit and towel. Kate shook her head. She wouldn't be swimming. Since the farm, swimming reminded her of Des.

Ben listened for the door, then the lift, then breathed a sigh of relief. He didn't want her to be here when Stephens came. She mustn't know who he was.

The driver drove through Sydney, dodging the trams, and out towards Bondi Beach. Kate watched the sharp shadows on the pavements and roads, the cars, the horse-drawn cabs, the men walking to and from the shanty towns. Well, at least Ben's workers would have something to celebrate tonight.

The girls were chattering about their friends. Rose wound down the window. It was hot. The traffic was heavy and grew heavier still as they approached. The road surface was rough. Men worked behind barriers ahead of them. Kate could smell the tar. The traffic slowed to a halt, then crawled. Some boys whistled as they wove their bikes in between the cars, one rode no hands. The girls laughed. Housewives stood at their front gates, their arms folded across their breasts, talking, frowning, smiling. Kate ached to be one of them, in a normal house, with her husband doing a normal job, even no job.

They passed the workmen and the steamroller and the chaos, and picked up speed, and Kate wondered if Stephens had arrived. They crested the hill, and the bay spread out before them, glistening and blue, and clean. The girls pointed. 'I'm going straight in to paddle,' Alice said.

'My dad taught me to swim at Endersley Farm,' Rose said.

Alice pouted. 'I can't swim. My father hasn't time to do things like that.'

Rose looked at her mother, and they smiled together. I love him so much, Kate thought, and it no longer mattered that she wasn't a housewife at a picket fence.

They passed lantana shrubs and castor oil trees. The girls pointed to a cockatoo on a fence. And then they were there. The driver waved. 'I'll be back in three hours.'

The girls raced down the beach, then stopped, yelling for Kate. She ran and held towels for them to change behind. 'But only paddle, the waves are huge.'

She watched Rose chasing the froth, laughing and leaping with Alice, and felt the sun on her own legs as she sat on the deck-chair she had hired from the attendant. Boys rode the waves on boards or bellies. Fishing boats crossed the bay. Children dug sandcastles. Mothers licked handkerchiefs and wiped faces. Ice-creams melted over hands. Fathers read newspapers.

She missed Ben with a sharp ache. Was he all right? He had supported the workers, shouted that they were human beings. He wasn't like Brenda and Harold and Larry and the others. He wasn't. He was her Ben. He was just tired, frayed. They would survive, they would make it all work, then they could leave these people behind and find Roy again. Somehow they would do that when she and Ben had time to sit down and talk.

The girls were running up now, flicking their hands all over her. The water was cool and sticky with salt. They bought buckets and spades from the shop and built great castles, although they had at first said they were too old at eleven. They grew hungry and ate the cut lunch Kate had thrown together as they left.

'No boiled eggs, I'm afraid. Can't quite produce miracles.'

There was sand in the sandwiches. It crunched. Kate brushed the crumbs from her dress, and screwed up the paper, throwing it from one hand to another.

Rose said, 'Do you remember the cyclone, all the sand in our mouths?'

Kate said, 'It was the same in the sandstorm

at the mine. It shredded my tent.'

Alice looked up scornfully. 'You didn't live in a tent?'

Kate looked out to sea. Be careful, Ben had said. 'Let's buy a ball,' she suggested.

They did, but first they had to blow it up, and then Kate played with them and ran with them, and when the wind whipped the ball from them, she chased it along the beach with them, laughing and panting, falling on it in desperation, bursting it, and laughing again.

They carried it back and hung it on the umbrella as a trophy. Then they lay in the shade, all three of them, and dozed, then talked, and dozed again and were careful not to talk of tents.

At two-thirty they packed up and walked along to the pavilion, with its ballrooms, dining-room, restaurants, indoor swimming-pool, and open-air theatre. How was Ben getting on?

They walked along the promenade, and the wind plucked their hair from beneath their hats and blew it across their faces as they passed tea rooms and shop fronts. At a Greek milk bar Kate and Rose chose caramel milkshakes. Alice wanted chocolate.

The swarthy owner smiled. He had a gold tooth. Kalgoorlie gold? Kate wondered and smiled. He smiled back and flipped open the lid of the refrigerated milk container, dipped in the long-handled ladle and poured the foaming milk into the container. Then he flipped the lid closed and grinned at them. He flipped open the ice-cream container, scooped one, two, three balls of ice-cream and grinned again.

'He's like Mario,' Rose exclaimed. 'His smile's the same. Have they gone home to Italy?'

Kate shook her head. 'They're still here. They hope to leave next year.'

'We'll bring Roy, if he comes. He will come, won't he?'

Kate said, 'I hope so.'

The caramel was being dripped into the container, and then the malt. The man put it onto the electric mixer. The buzzing startled them. They laughed.

'Roy would love one,' Rose sighed.

'Yes, he would indeed,' Kate agreed.

'Did he live in the tent with you?' Alice asked.

Rose said, 'Certainly not. That wouldn't be proper. I'm surprised at you.' She caught her mother's eye and grinned. Kate laughed. Yes, they'd be all right.

They were late for the driver but he didn't mind. Their skin glowed from the wind and the sun, their limbs were heavy. Their lids too. The girls dozed until they had left Bondi, and then they woke, looking out of the window, beginning to sing, their voices soaring, and Kate's spirits soared even higher with them.

They turned left, then right, past the Catholic school, and now the girls were chanting:

> Catholics, Catholics make me sick.
> Ring the doctor quick, quick, quick.
> If the doctor doesn't come,
> Then kick the Catholics up the bum.

Rose shrieked with laughter and they chanted it again and now Kate moved, slapping Rose, glaring at them both. 'Don't you dare sing that. What's the matter with you? How dare you?'

Rose fell back against the door. Shocked, speechless. Alice looked from one to the other and began to cry.

Kate looked up and saw the driver's startled eyes in the mirror, startled then bemused.

She pulled Rose to her, and Alice. Both were stiff against her. 'I'm sorry, but that's a very rude song. I'm sure your mother wouldn't like to hear it, Alice. You should know, both of you, that people have a right to be different.'

Alice pulled away. 'The Catholics sing songs about us as well.' They were approaching Alice's house.

'Well, neither of you should.' Kate wished she'd said nothing.

The car pulled up. The driver opened the door. Alice ran up the path and rang the bell. Kate followed. Rose wouldn't come. Brenda Sinclair answered the door. Kate smiled. 'We've had a lovely day, but I'm afraid I became rather cross. They were singing a foolish song.'

Alice tugged at her mother's skirt. 'It's only one of the ones I sing when you take me to school.'

Kate fumbled with her bag. 'Well, you see, we were in Kalgoorlie, for the race riots. It seems unnecessary somehow, after that.'

Brenda was smiling at her and patting Alice, but there was no understanding in her eyes, just boredom. 'That's quite all right and we must meet for coffee. These rhymes are just childish nonsense, you know.'

Kate nodded and walked back to the car. Rose sat in the corner and wouldn't speak. Kate's anger was white hot, and it was at herself. Why didn't she just accept? Had she learned nothing? She pulled her daughter to her. 'I'm so sorry. Just so sorry.'

There was no picket outside the hotel. He hadn't sacked them. Relief made her footsteps feel light. They hurried across the foyer, treading sand.

Nigel smiled at Rose in the lift, but not at Kate. Her heart sank. So there may not be pickets, but neither had good news been announced.

When Nigel opened the lift gates Rose ran towards their apartment, but Kate waited for the lift to descend and then listened at Ben's office door.

She heard raised voices. She pressed closer. A man was shouting, 'Just get your house in order, sir.

367

Just get it in order and start bringing the customers back, and less of your damned Commie ideas. Shares indeed.' The voice was growing louder. The man, it must be Stephens, was approaching the door. But he should have come hours ago. He continued, 'Why don't you just join Lang and his mob? But then you'd have to withdraw from the golf club, and you wouldn't like that.' Kate backed to the lift door. She stopped as the office door opened, then walked towards Stephens.

Stephens saw her. He stopped. 'My dear Mrs Williams, where has Ben been hiding you all this time?'

He shook her hand. His was large. His voice and skin were coarse.

'I've been a little unwell.' Her eyes travelled to Ben, searching for approval. There was only chagrin and fury.

Stephens said, 'One day, when this mess is sorted, we must dine, just the three of us.'

The lift pinged, the doors opened. He was gone.

Ben stood in the doorway of his office, watching her. 'I should never have listened to you,' he ranted. 'What do you, or that old fool Roy, know about business? And whose side are you on anyway?'

Mick sat in his room. The bugs were at it again. He scratched himself and stirred the mince on the one ring. The news was worth a pint or two for Nigel tonight. A minimum wage for the lads, but no share offer. Thank God for that. If that had gone through there'd have been no way he could have got them to niggle at Ben Williams. No way would they have responded to his words.

He tasted the mince and shook more salt onto the meat, and a bit of flour. His fingers smelt of onions, the dry skins were still on the chopping-board. Now who was this Stephens who'd put the mockers on?

And who'd have thought Ben Williams would come up with something like that? Mick stopped stirring and looked up at the ceiling.

Ted was shouting the odds at his missis in the room above, and the lavatory was blocked again down the hall. The mince bubbled and burst through the layer of fat which shone in the dim light.

Was it Caithleen who'd led him on to offer shares? Now why would she do that, the tart? What was she after? It couldn't have been out of the good of her heart. She didn't have a heart, not to do what she had done to him.

He tasted the mince again, draining the fat first. Yes, he must find out more about this Stephens. He must be a right stupid sod to have stopped the share offer, because if he, Mick, were running the business he'd have agreed. It made sense, anyone could see that. Nigel said it was the big boss who'd put paid to it.

Amazing what you heard in the lift, like a husband shouting at a wife, like noticing strain lines around a red-haired woman's face.

He grinned.

Chapter Eighteen

The housekeeper passed Kate and Rose in the lobby and grimaced, whispering to Kate, 'Only half the staff turned up to wait on table at the dinner in Bondi Beach last night. That particular firm won't be using us again. We're almost on our knees. Is Mr Williams back from the hotel?'

Kate shook her head. 'Off you go, and have a good day, Rose. Don't forget your violin lesson after school.'

Rose kissed her. Kate smiled. Mrs Burnett walked on. Rose ran through the revolving doors and was gone, merging with the pedestrians hurrying to work. 'Mrs Burnett.' Kate joined the older woman, walking with her to the stairs. 'What's happening? It's only a week since Ben gave them the minimum wage. They seemed happy.'

Mrs Burnett touched the keys dangling from her belt. 'And so they were, but after last night's performance the consortium brought in this new system. They're sick of all the sabotage but they won't talk to them about it. They've decided to sack the workers at the end of the week and re-employ them at the beginning of the next. Lots of firms are doing it. It's designed to save paying a week's severance pay should they have to sack people. It's also to make sure the workers behave themselves – or they're not re-employed.'

Mrs Burnett swept on up the stairs.

Kate began to follow, then walked across to the lift instead.

Nigel closed the doors behind her and pressed the button for the top floor. He didn't smile, he didn't talk. She watched the numbers lighting up. One. Two. Three. In between Four and Five she reached across and pressed the emergency stop.

He swung round. 'What the . . . ?'

Kate stared at him, her hand protecting the button. 'I could ask you the same. What *is* going on?' Her voice was cold, and her eyes reflected the raging anger she felt. Anger at the consortium for inflaming the situation. Anger at the workers for jeopardizing their own positions. Anger at them all for making Ben's position intolerable. 'Don't you realize that there are queues of unemployed out there? Don't you realize that they've stitched you up? They *will* sack you all if this goes on. For heaven's sake, forget who's right and who's wrong, just stay in the job. Tell whoever's behind it that. Tell them if the consortium goes down, so do their jobs.'

Nigel tried to reach the buttons. She pushed him away. 'Are you mad, all of you?' He shook his head as he slumped back against the wall. He looked so young, but then he was only sixteen, she thought. Only sixteen, with a sick mother. Kate shouted again, 'Are you mad, all of you? Why are you doing this? We'll fold. The consortium are doing nothing that a lot of other firms aren't doing also. It's not ideal, in fact, it's outrageous, but you're all digging yourself into positions you can't get out of.'

Nigel pushed himself off the wall, and shouted at her, 'Tell your husband that.'

'Do you think I haven't tried? But he's tried too. God, this is all so stupid.' Kate dropped her hand from in front of the button. 'Go on, then. Take me up.' Her voice was flat, defeated.

Nigel pressed for the top floor. The lift moved. The boy remained by the buttons, his finger poised, white gloved. He said quietly, without looking at her, 'I don't know what's right or wrong any more. He stirs us up, and the consortium don't help.'

Kate moved closer, touched his arm. He looked at her hand, then into her face. 'Who? Why?' she asked quietly. 'Tell me, Nigel.'

He shook his head. 'I don't know why. Because he's trying to help us, I suppose.' The lift juddered to a stop. Nigel moved towards the doors. She stopped him.

'Tell me who he is.'

'I don't know his name. Some Irish bloke.'

Kate stepped to one side. Nigel opened the lift doors. She looked out onto the carpeted corridor. The door to their apartment was ajar. She could see the chambermaid sweeping the hearth. It had been cool last night. She and Rose had lit a fire while Ben had been at the Bondi Beach Hotel. She touched her lips. She wore no gloves. What would Brenda say? But no, she had not been out, she had only been to wave Rose off to school.

She didn't want to think about the words Nigel had spoken, anything but that. She said, at last, as the light flashed on Nigel's board, summoning the lift to floor three, 'What does he look like, this Irishman?'

Nigel looked at his lights, and then, pointedly, to her apartment door. She grabbed his arm. 'Tell me what he looks like.'

Nigel shrugged. 'I dunno really. Like anyone else.'

'Dark hair, light hair? Tall, short? Come on, Nigel, and damn floor three.'

Nigel pulled away. 'I dunno I said. Dark hair, sort of curly. Blue eyes, but not as dark as yours. Talks about the fight in Ireland a lot. Talks about a brother on the other side.'

It couldn't be. Mick would have gone back. It

372

couldn't be. 'Where does he live? Come on, Nigel. I helped your mother. Come on.' She'd use anything she had to.

'I told you, I don't know his name, but I know where he lives. You won't tell anyone I told you?' Nigel asked, his finger poised above the buttons.

She shook her head. 'Just tell me.'

'You see, I took my report there. He's been paying me for news.' Nigel looked at the floor.

Kate shook his arm. 'Just tell me where he lives.'

He did.

Kate grabbed her hat and coat from the apartment. The phone rang. It was Brenda. 'Last meeting for the school bazaar this morning, Kate, so do, please, be prompt. And luncheon afterwards, with the other wives.'

The phone clicked. Kate looked around the room. She'd have to go. It would look strange if she didn't, and it wouldn't be Mick, it couldn't be. The man she would find in the room would be a stranger, and it was with this stranger that she would have to deal, because she had to do something to help Ben. But no-one must know, so she must go out this morning as though nothing had happened. Damn it.

At Brenda's they sat around the table examining the hall plan, and then the rota, and then the crafts. Brenda held up a sample of patchwork between two fingers. 'My dears, handmade is one thing. This is simply nasty.'

Kate nodded along with the others, not seeing it. She checked the clock. Ben hadn't returned by the time she left. He'd be worn out, distressed, angry. Why had he let the consortium talk him into this last move? Why hadn't he talked to the workers as Roy would have done?

Lunch was three courses and interminable. The conversation equally so.

373

'You seem a little quiet today, Kate,' Brenda queried as coffee was served in the sitting-room.

Kate stirred her coffee. The spoon clicked against the sides of her cup, bubbles formed. She looked at Brenda and smiled. 'Such a headache.'

Mary Parkes reached for another chocolate, unwrapping it with white soft hands. 'I would imagine that Ben has one too, today.' Her voice was harsh. 'It seems to be getting away from him.'

Kate rose. 'I simply must go. Do you mind, Brenda? I need to lie down, have a little silence, some fresh air.' Her voice was harsh too, her eyes piercing.

Brenda put down her cup, her mouth still open. She glanced around at the other women, then back to Kate, who was leaving. She hurried after her. 'I think we've sorted out the bazaar, and it's so good of you to give up your valuable time.' She helped Kate on with her jacket, and watched her stride down the steps, and along the pavement. 'It should be a great success,' she called after her.

Kate didn't acknowledge her, she merely increased her stride and jumped on a tram. She checked the address. What valuable time? What had she done since she'd been here? Nothing. Nothing.

Ben waited until he reached his office, and only then did he open the note which had been left at reception for him, sinking onto his swivel chair, holding it up to the window, the blinds of which he'd pulled up. The private detective had been working on the case since last week, trying to discover if the trouble with the staff was being orchestrated, and if so, by whom.

Ben was so tired that he had had to fight to bring the closely typed letter into focus. He should get spectacles, but there was never any time. He rubbed his eyes, narrowed them. That was better. He read the report once, then again, and the paper fell from his hands onto the desk. Mick O'Brian.

374

He scrabbled for the phone. It was picked up on the first ring. 'Evans? Ben Williams. I've your report. There's no address.'

Evans replied. 'That's cos there's a lot of tight mouths. Got the name off an operative who drinks with him. Mick O'Brian's changed his room recently. We'll have the new address by morning.'

Ben slammed the receiver on the cradle. Mick O'Brian. He couldn't breathe. Mick O'Brian.

He tore up to the apartment. 'Kate, Kate.' His voice was rough. He checked all the rooms. He ran back to his office. Mick O'Brian.

His secretary pressed the intercom. 'Mrs Sinclair on the telephone, Mr Williams.'

He pressed the reply button. 'Tell her to wait. Have you seen my wife, Miss Hill?'

'Not since she left this morning for a meeting with Mrs Sinclair to discuss the bazaar. She was to stay for luncheon.'

Ben said, 'Fine, put the woman on.'

Brenda said, 'Dear Ben, how is Kate? She left in such a hurry, such a headache. Thought I'd better check up on her, though she often leaves our meetings early.'

Ben clenched the phone, looking out of the window, across the roofs of Sydney. She often leaves our meetings early . . . She often leaves . . . Mick O'Brian. Caithleen Healy. No, it couldn't be. It mustn't be. He'd brought her here so that they were safe.

'Ben, Ben?' Brenda said. 'Are you there?'

Ben looked at the letter, then at the photograph of Kate on the desk. He said, 'When did she leave?'

'An hour ago.'

'Then she's been asleep for a nice long time,' Ben lied. He replaced the receiver carefully, and walked to the window, carefully. Out there was the library where she said she read. Out there were the streets which she said she walked, and the parks, and the

375

shops. Out there was Mick O'Brian. Out there was Kate Williams, or was it Caithleen Healy? Out there, not here, lying down, as she should have been. How many times had that happened? How many? How damn many? His head was pounding. He thought it would burst.

Kate stepped from the tram and walked along the lanes and the alleyways, stopping to ask directions from a woman who was leaning on her rusty corrugated-iron fence. 'Down that way, dearie, left at the grog shop.'

She walked on past the school. Ahead, refuse-men emptied bins out onto a sheet of hessian. She stepped into the road, trying not to breathe in the stink of the rotting rubbish. A dog yelped as one of the men saw it off. The man winked at her, wiping his hands on his filthy hessian apron. Blowflies crawled, buzzed and seemed to chase her down the street. A child ran up, pinched a pumpkin from the pile.

'You little devil,' a man called.

'Go chase yourself,' the lad yelled back.

Brownstone houses edged the road, their paint peeling, their windows rotting, their doors ajar. Trucks roared past. Children dodged between them carrying billies. A brewery truck hooted as she crossed the road and turned left after the grog shop.

She smelt and saw poverty and shadows. She looked up to the sky, the pale hot sky. She asked a child who was picking through a rubbish bin the way to Sandford Street. He eyed her clothes, her hat, her shoes. 'What's it worth?'

Everything, she thought. But gave him a shilling. 'For that, I'll take ya.'

She followed him. He had no soles in his shoes. He had holes in his trousers and jumper. A man shambled towards them wearing an old army coat, hair grease staining his hat. Two boys were roaring along on a billycart.

'Why aren't you at school?' she asked the lad.

'I'm fifteen. Got no job.' He nodded at the other lads. 'They're skiving, waiting for their mates to get out of school.'

She checked her watch. She must be back for Rose. She stopped. The lad stopped. It was three o'clock. Then she relaxed. It was violin, she had time. She must have time to speak to this man, to do what she could. It would be a stranger. It must be a stranger.

They walked down an alleyway. The lad pointed to a house. It was three storeys high, the paint was peeling, the wrought-iron balconies were draped with poorly washed clothes. 'Get up them steps, into the house. Someone will tell you where whoever you want to see has his room.' He ran off.

She climbed the stairs, walked into the lobby. She knew which room, Nigel had told her. She searched until she found Room 9. She knocked. There was shouting from upstairs, a door banged downstairs in the lobby. A chair scraped in the room, the handle turned. The door opened.

Mick stood there, his curly hair long, his pale blue eyes cold and unsurprised, his face thinner, older, with bitter lines to his mouth. It couldn't be. But it was. And she had known it would be. Of course she had known, and now she just shook her head again and again.

He said, 'Well, Caithleen, I've been waiting for you. I knew you'd find me, just as I found you.'

He stood to one side sweeping her a bow. 'Come on in to my home. Not as fine as you would be used to, but mine own – for this week at least. Next week it could be a shack in the shanty town, or a park bench, but you wouldn't be knowing about that sort of thing now, would you?' He was smiling, but his eyes were angry. 'Come on in now, Caithleen. Don't let the neighbours be after hearing every little word two old friends speak to one another.'

With his voice came the scent and sounds of Ireland, of Caithleen Healy, of her father, her past.

He took her arm and guided her in, slamming the door behind her. He led her to one of the two chairs which were set at a small table. There were two wire beds, and a penny-in-the-slot gas stove. She sat, clutching her handbag. Her gloves were sticky and stained from the banister. She rubbed at them.

'The feel of poverty isn't pleasant, is it, my Caithleen?'

He sat opposite her, leaning forward on his elbows. 'Not what you're used to, is it, my Caithleen Healy?'

She said, clutching her handbag in her lap, 'Why have you done this to us?'

'Now don't be flattering yourself, my dear Caithleen. I work from the purest of motives.' He pulled out his cigarettes, threw one across to her. She ignored it. He lit his own, blowing smoke up into the air. 'I work to destroy injustice. I've seen the other side. I've worked where men have died because of bosses who wouldn't take care of their safety. I've worked for wages which were an insult to a grown man.' His voice was conversational, but his eyes were narrowed in anger. 'You and your consortium are an insult to humanity.'

She slammed her hand on the table. 'Rubbish. This isn't for anyone other than you. If you cared for the workers you'd let them be. It's us you're trying to destroy, no matter how many you hurt in the process. You're disgusting. You're totally disgusting, and you should have gone home.'

'With what, you stupid Irish bitch?' She could smell the nicotine on his breath as he shouted across the table at her. 'This is it. This is my life, the life you and damn Des gave me. You've got three hotels, and I eat from your dustbins.'

He flung his cigarette into a cold mug of tea by the cooker. It hissed. He laughed. It was a harsh, cruel sound. He stormed to the window. 'I look out of here into a yard. You, you must look across the whole of Sydney, like bloody kings. I came for a job and was turned away. Then I got a job there for one day. Standing there up to me elbows in suds, I heard the boss's name and the name of his wife who was basking on her farm.'

He leaned back against the window frame, looking at her now. 'You and my brother took my farm from me. You sit in your penthouse and look out over the peasants while I bet my brother sits with de Valera, his hands on the reins. He'll have changed his allegiance just like that, and it could have been me there instead.'

He stabbed the air with his finger. She tried to speak. He shouted, 'Shut up. I could have been something. He didn't want that, he wanted me out. I was a challenge. He got you to take me away. He knew I could never go back. I'd be known as a deserter, Caithleen. I'd be known as the O'Brian who ran while there was still a war to be fought. But you, what did you want? I've never been able to sort it out.'

His voice was uncertain now, and he came across and touched her hair. 'You've forgotten who you were, Caithleen. But me, I've never forgotten who you were.' God, but she was still so beautiful, her eyes so blue, her hair the colour of copper.

She jerked away. 'Mick, you should have cabled home. I thought you'd do that. I told you to.'

He laughed. 'So the queen speaks. We should do as you tell us, is that it? All the Irish peasants should do what you, the Proddy bosses, say.'

She shouted at him, 'You haven't changed, you haven't grown up.' She stood, pushed him away, walked to the door. 'I'm telling Ben it's you. Now we know who it is, we can fight, and we will, and let me tell you, Mick O'Brian, you are not worth the death of your brother.' Her voice broke. 'He loved you so much. He knew if you stayed you'd not know when to stop. He knew you'd destroy yourself. Well, look at you. You have, and you're not taking my family with you.'

She ran down the stairs, out of the house, down the street. She could hear him following. She ran faster. She must get to Ben.

There was a cold wind now, lifting litter, blowing crisp leaves into the air. More children were on the street, playing tag, throwing balls against a wall. She dodged between them, on and on. Was it the right way? Yes, there was the grog shop. The brewery truck had gone. On and on to the tramstop. She leapt on, paid her fare, the breath rasping in her chest. She could see him, running along the pavement as the tram snaked along its lines.

He boarded at the next stop, his hair damp with sweat. He stood in front of her. 'What do you mean, the death of my brother?'

People stared. Two old ladies stopped talking to listen.

'What do you mean?' he shouted.

The conductor approached. 'Less of that. Is he annoying you, missis?'

They were approaching another stop. Kate pushed Mick back and jumped off. He came too. She rushed along the street which was now full of people hurrying home from work. He grabbed her again, swung her round. 'What do you mean, the death of my brother?' His eyes were disbelieving, shocked, wounded. He looked as he had done when he had fallen from the apple tree.

She whispered, 'He loved you. He wanted you safe. He wanted a life for you, so he led his own troops away from us. They must have shot him. He crawled from the river at Widow Murphy's. He was riddled with bullets. If you had cabled, you would have known. But he had no time to send you money.' She pulled away from him gently in the face of his pain. 'He wanted you to survive, to make something of your life. And what have you done with it, Mick?'

He gripped her hard again, hanging on to her, as though his life depended on it. Des, dead. All this time he'd been dead, shot by his own men. Not even by the British or the Republicans.

People were pushing past them. She wrenched herself from his grasp. 'Make something of your life for Des's sake, and leave us alone.' She walked away. He followed, caught up, grabbed her again. 'For heaven's sake, Mick, leave us alone.'

'Us?' he shouted. 'Us? You think you're so perfect, with your English voice, your Tan's name, your life, but what would Des have thought of you, consorting with Tans, living off them?'

She shook him off again. The street was crowded. She turned into the stream, but he was there, grabbing at her again, pulling her into a shop doorway. She said, 'Don't be stupid. Des knew I loved a Tan. That's why he made me take you. He said I would be responsible for your death if I didn't go. I loved you then, like the old friend you were. Des made it impossible for me to stay because he knew my father would come and find us putting you in the cart. Des told him about the Tan, about Ben. Ben isn't like the others were. He's a fine man. He wanted to leave them. I made him stay – you remember.'

Mick laughed, right in her face. 'Leave them? You must be joking. You're right in the middle of them. Your hotels are funded by Stephens and his cronies. Stephens was a Tan, he's New Guard, so are most of the others. He wanted to leave them, did he? You stupid woman.'

Kate looked at him with horror, no longer aware of the people pushing past them, or the trucks, or the trams, or the cold wind.

Rose was sitting on the tram, hugging her violin case. She hated music lessons, they were so boring. She was hungry. What would mum make for tea? She looked at the lady sitting next to her, she looked at the conductor. She looked out of the window at the people striding, slowing, swirling. The crowd parted. She saw her mother. A man was kissing her. The crowd closed. She leapt up, looked again. She could still see her mother's hat. Yes, it had been her.

The conductor asked, 'You getting off or just cluttering the place up?'

She sat down and all she could see was that man's face, his hair. He hadn't been wearing a hat. Everyone wore hats. His hair had been so curly, next to the red of her mother's, and the green of her small hat.

This was her stop. She must get off. Her legs seemed leaden. The lobby seemed too big, the lift so slow. Her father wasn't in his office. His secretary said, 'He's in your apartment.'

'Why?' Rose asked. It didn't sound like her voice.

'He's waiting for your mother,' Miss Hill said, returning to her typing.

The door into the apartment was heavy. The room was dark, the drapes were drawn. Her father sat in the chair by the fire, which wasn't lit. She and her mother had lit it last night when it had been cool. She felt like that now. She walked to her father. He was staring at her, then shifted his gaze to the corridor. 'Have you seen your mother?' he said, and his voice sounded a mixture of anger and sorrow.

She stood before him. The violin case slipped from her hands. The violin inside it banged when it hit the carpet. 'Yes,' she said. 'She was kissing a man on the pavement. Why, Dad? Why?'

Kate pushed Mick away from her, wiping his kiss from her mouth with her hand, hitting him again and again. A man said, 'Are you all right, madam?' He was raising his hat, his eyes concerned.

She looked around. What was she doing here? Why was she here? She must get back to Ben. She pushed past the man, out into the road. She hailed a cab. She turned. Mick was standing in the gutter, shaking his head and laughing. She flopped back on the seat. Stephens, a Tan. Ben can't have known. New Guard. Most of them New Guard. He wouldn't do that to her.

She hunched forward now, her head in her hands dredging Old Roy's anger from the back of her mind, and Ben's pleas. *Remember I do everything for you. Remember I love you.*

She heard the wind in the reeds, the curlews crying, her father's disgust at her, her mother's cries, the mud, the sudden silence, the Tans' laughter. She sat back. The cabby's eyes were on her in the mirror. She nodded. 'I'm all right, just tired.' Her voice was a whisper.

A Tan, a Tan. She shut her eyes, and saw Ben, the lines of strain, the struggle, the overwork, and love filled her. What did it matter who funded them? What did it matter if Stephens was a Tan? What did it matter if Mick said he had helped burn Cork? What did it matter if he had been stationed in Limerick when her mother was killed? He wasn't her murderer. He was part of a war that had gone. But hate was raging. She would never see Stephens again. She would tell Ben that. She must tell Ben that.

But he had known how she hated them, hadn't he?

It didn't matter. She loved him. She must tell him that his betrayal didn't hurt, that nothing was changed. That they could stop Mick. Old Roy would come back to them, everything would be all right. She rubbed at her chest because, Holy Mother of God, it hurt, but it would pass, just as his pain at her lies had passed.

She could still taste Mick's kiss. 'I'll take one from your Tan,' he'd said, grabbing her, forcing her.

She paid off the cabby at the hotel. She climbed the stairs to their floor, not wanting to meet Nigel. She wiped her mouth again as she approached the apartment door. How dare he claim they belonged together, that he could not bear to be alone?

She pushed open the door. Ben was there, in the evening gloom, standing by the fireplace, facing her.

He watched her walk towards him, and smile with those lips that had kissed Mick O'Brian. How many times? He looked into her eyes, those eyes which had looked at Mick O'Brian's body – how many times? That's where she'd been, not the library. No. It all made sense now. A long-term plan. No wonder she had hidden Lucia – she hadn't left her past behind at all. His head was bursting. He pushed past her. He couldn't bear it.

She called, 'Ben.'

He stopped by the occasional table, far enough away so that he could not smell her perfume, so that he could not touch that skin, which he had always feared had been known by Mick, and which he now knew, deep in his heart, had. Far enough from her to remember clearly the Irish river, the kisses which Mick had laughed at, the barracks which had been burned after information she had gleaned from him.

He had worked it all out, sitting here in the dark alone, uninterrupted, except for the message that Miss Hill had brought in. She had said, 'A Mr O'Brian has just rung for Mrs Williams. He wouldn't leave a message.' How many times had he rung before? How many?

He said, 'All this time you've been working with him, haven't you? All this time when you were lying with me, whispering your filthy love, it was a game, just a game. Still fighting the cause are you, you two? Still destroying your Auxie?'

Kate felt for the chair. Her legs were weak. His face was so full of hate. 'Ben, what are you talking about?'

'You've been with him. Don't deny it.'

· She said, 'I'm not going to. I was with him. I found out where the man causing the trouble lived. I went to see him, to make him stop.' She struggled to keep her voice calm. 'It was Mick.'

Ben laughed. 'How well you lie, but then you always did. You were seen, Kate, or is it Caithleen? You were seen kissing in the street. How bold. Were you so certain of your victory? Were you so certain you would bring me down?'

'Ben, I love you. I wouldn't bring you down. I was trying to help. Yes, Mick kissed me. I pushed him away.'

Again Ben laughed. He picked up Rose's photograph from the table, held it up to the fading light. 'So like you. But I expect she's his. Did you sneak off to meet in the bush? Did you copulate in the dust, where you both belong? Did you laugh together after you hid Lucia, after you took sides against me – again?'

He dropped the photograph onto the floor. 'She's his bastard, isn't she?'

Kate couldn't believe what she was hearing. 'Rose is your daughter, she's the child you taught to swim. I'm not lying. You are the one who's lied. Stephens was a Tan. You know how I feel, but I can live with it, because I love you.'

Ben pointed to the cases in the corner and his

385

voice was little more than a hiss. 'Well, that's very big of you. Take those and get out. I'm scraping you off my shoe, I'm freeing myself from you. Just as you planned to free yourself from me, right from the start. I've been sitting here in the darkness, thinking. A civil service wedding, so that, in the eyes of your God, you were never married. Mornings in the library, afternoons walking? I can just imagine, but spare me the details.'

Kate stepped towards him. 'Stop it, Ben. Don't say any more. You're tired, more than tired, you're exhausted and yes, it was my fault if you like. I brought out Mick. If he wasn't here this wouldn't have happened. Just don't say any more.'

He shouted, 'It's too late, Caithleen — far too late. You can't lie yourself out of this. You were seen. Do I have to spell it out? You were seen kissing your lover, in this city, on the street. Your lover has been destroying my job. He knew every move. He had someone inside. I just never thought it was you. Now get out, go to him, or go to hell. I can't stand the sight of you, or the sound of you.'

He walked away, calling, 'I'm going to my office. I shall expect you to be gone when I return.'

She shouted, 'How could it be me? I was at the farm. You're mad, you're not thinking clearly.'

He spun round and advanced, his hand up to strike her. He stopped, turned away, saying, 'You must think I'm a complete fool. There are cables, there are letters. No wonder you wanted to come to Sydney, and I thought it was because of me. Get out of my life. You soil everything you touch.'

Chapter Nineteen

Ben sat in his armchair at the apartment and drank again from the whisky bottle as dawn broke the next morning. He held up the bottle, peering at it in the weak light. One more swallow left and he still wasn't drunk. Nothing was blurred, nothing had disappeared; he could still hear her voice, see her face, and her pain. He let the bottle drop from his hands onto the carpet. Well good, she deserved pain because she had brought all of this back, as he had always known she would. It was bred in her. Up the Volunteers!

He washed, shaved. His face was haggard – just as soon, please God, hers would be. There were clean shirts in the drawer. Oh yes, she'd looked after those parts of him. She'd adjusted his cuff-links, bought with his money. How many had she bought her lover?

He strode to the door. He heard the crunch of glass beneath his foot, stooped and picked up the photograph of Rose, splintered, damaged. Oh God. He hurled it at the wall. Damn you, Kate. He slammed from the apartment, and pressed the button for the lift.

Nigel rode up, pulling at his gold-braided blue jacket, brushing off fluff, straightening his hat in the polished brass of the button plate. They all knew. The housekeeper had heard the shouting, then the desk had seen Mrs Williams and Rose carry their own bags across the lobby. They'd hailed a cab. 'White and drawn they were. Good woman that,' the housekeeper had said.

Mrs Williams hadn't travelled in the lift, she'd taken the stairs, and now Nigel swallowed nervously as the lift reached the top floor. He opened the doors. Mr Williams stepped in, nodding, his face as white as Nigel's mother's, but she was ill.

'Morning, sir,' Nigel said.

Ben nodded. 'The lobby.' He had the workers to deal with, names to take. Some would not be re-employed next week, and it was their own damn fault. It would teach them to spoil any more functions. Damn them, damn her, and he heard her voice and saw her face again, and wanted to beat her, hold her, kill her, love her. How could she? How the hell could she? In the street too. She must have wanted to be seen.

The lift stopped between the fourth and fifth floors. The lift boy was looking at him – what was his name? Damned if he knew. Ben straightened. 'What's the problem? Has it stuck?'

Nigel cleared his throat. 'It's just, well, you see, I just wanted to say that I'd never have given her the address yesterday if I'd known it would end in a blue between you.'

Ben just looked at him, the words floating, whirling, not settling. Nigel continued. 'She was worried, she wanted to help you. She kept on at me until I told her there was someone stirring. I didn't know his name, but I knew where he lived. I'd had to run a message, you see. She said she'd go out to see him. But said she'd keep me out of it.'

The words were in Ben's head now, blurred, moving, dancing around the image of her face and the sound of her voice. He tasted the sourness of stale whisky. The lift began again, stopped at the lobby.

Nigel opened the doors, and pressed Mick's address into Ben's hand. 'Am I sacked, sir?'

Ben didn't answer, he didn't even hear, as he ran through the lobby, out of the doors, past the doorman, hailing a cab. 'The library.'

When he arrived it wasn't open. It wouldn't be for another hour. He walked the streets which she said she had walked. He walked the parks where she said she had walked. God, but she was clever. That was it, she was clever, getting that lift boy involved. What was his damn name?

He checked his watch, and back-tracked to the library. His shoes clicked in the silence of the hall. It was like his old school had been. He grabbed a librarian by the arm. She withdrew, offended. He apologized, 'Forgive me, this is urgent. A woman, red hair, blue eyes, says she came and read, sat in the window, or some such rubbish.'

The librarian smiled. 'Kate Williams. Oh yes, we had many a chat. I gave her a book list.'

He hailed a cab, thrusting the address Nigel had given him into the cabby's hand. 'There, and hurry.'

'In this traffic, mate. You must be joking.'

Ben sat back as they raced and weaved between trucks and trams, rage snatching and pulling at him. Worked it out neatly, hadn't they? Covered themselves. That's what it was, like they did in Ireland. Yes, like Ireland. He'd been right to send her away. He'd been right to bundle her clothes, and those of her child, into bags.

His head was cracking open. He couldn't think straight. Everyone was fighting him, everyone. Wherever he turned it was coming apart, and only now did he know why, only now, when Rose had told him of the kiss. He tried to rub the image away. All this time. God damn it, all this time.

They were in narrow dingy streets, leaves and paper blew in the road and on the pavements. They were forced to stop for a truck laden with milk cans taking up too much of the road. He saw Kate's red hair blowing beneath the Irish sky, the churn rattling as she left the roadblock, ready to haul him in with her lies. He saw Mick in Fremantle, telling him.

The cab pulled around a stalled truck and now Ben looked out at the rusted corrugated fencing, the narrow back alleys scattered with garbage tins. But why did Mick tell him on the docks then, if they were working to a plan? He shook his head. God, if only he could think.

'Down here, then, mate?' The cabby was turning left by a grog shop.

They crawled along the gutter, checking the numbers. 'Twelve,' Ben barked. 'That's it.' He paid the cabby off, then turned to the house with its peeling paint, its rotten windows, and began to climb the steps.

In the backyard Mick prodded the sheets which were boiling in the copper. He added more wood chips, then turned to the wooden frame of his bed, swamping it with a solution of caustic soda and hot water, stamping on the bugs that scuttled away, grinding them into the dirt, and another, and another. He kicked at the frame. More scuttled out. He stamped on those. He wished it was himself. Des was dead. Des had died for him.

He gripped his head between his hands. The fumes rose. He backed away, choking. Cait had brought him here for his own sake, and he'd done everything to hurt her. He leaned on the wall, rocking backwards and forwards. He'd tried to ring, to say he was sorry. She had not been there. He'd left no message, but why had he left his name? Would it hurt her? Why hadn't he thought? When did he ever think?

Bugs were pouring out of the old mattress he had slung at the bottom of the yard but now he didn't move to stamp on them. Instead he shut his eyes and there was Des, as he had been all night, talking to the men in the glade, strong and clean and good, turning to him, putting his arm round his shoulder, walking with him, saving him – again – telling him to operate as his back-up.

Mick brushed his eyes with his arm, his sleeve was filthy. He looked down at his clothes as though for the first time. He was disgusting. Why hadn't he seen it before? Why hadn't anyone told him?

He heard Hughie with the New Guard baying behind them in the meeting hall. 'You're a stupid bloody fool.' He tasted his own blood again, felt the pain in his split lip as Hughie had punched him. Felt the bruising of his own knuckles after he'd beaten Hughie, taking him from behind.

Hughie had tried to tell him. Hughie had been his friend. Had been, just as Des had been, just as Cait had been. Had been. *Had been.* His head was throbbing. He grasped at the tumbling images of Des hammering at the roof of their father's barn, Des laughing up at the stars, Des heaving him onto his shoulders to reach the best apples.

Hughie came again and he felt the weight of the fist which had burst his lip.

More bugs were rushing from the mattress and the frame. Now he stamped on them, crushing them, ignoring the stench, wanting them all dead. All of them, because now he was remembering the blood from Cait's lip after he had hit her on the ship. Oh God, Oh Des, help me. What have I done? Where's it all gone? Was I always so stupid?

The sun was beating down, the stench of the bugs clogged the air, the breath hammered in his chest. The copper was bubbling. He stopped and stared at the hard-baked earth. The bugs were dead, but even as he thought that, more came from the mattress. Des would never come back. Des had crawled from the river, to die at Widow Murphy's feet. Des was dead and could never answer him any more. He could never look after him – any more. Des was dead. He was alone.

He ran at the wooden frame and kicked it again, sending it hurtling across the yard. Des was dead. He had been saying those words all night, sitting in his room or pacing the floor until Ted had hammered from above telling him to 'shut it'. Des was dead. He'd died saving Mick bloody O'Brian.

All the time Cait had told the truth. All the time. All the damn time, and for none of those hours, days, months had he been worth it. He kicked the bed, shook it, splinters tore into his hands. 'But I never bloody asked you to. Either of you.' He screamed into the air.

Another voice answered him. 'But then you never ask, do you? You're like her, you just take. So, where's the woman you took – upstairs, is she?' Mick spun round. Ben stood at the back door. 'My word, how she's come down in the world. My word, how powerful the cause must be. It can't be this she finds irresistible.' Ben flung his arm out, encompassing the copper, the mattress.

Mick started forward. 'Why are you here?' His voice was as full of rage as Ben's. 'Get out of my yard.'

'I just wanted to see where *my* family were to be living.' Ben had to force the words out. 'My family,' he raged again, 'which never was mine. And it could have been my business as well.'

'Look. I was crazy. I know I've messed you up. I know I've worked against you. I was just crazy.' Mick stood in full sunlight, the heat beat down.

Ben laughed. 'What, you were crazy when you kissed her? She wouldn't like to hear you say that.' His head was bursting. His wife had gone, his daughter too, but she wasn't his daughter. Mick was reaching

392

out. He'd slap him on his arm and laugh in a minute, just like he'd laughed in Fremantle, just like he had laughed as he watched them by the willow.

'Where is she?' Ben snarled. 'Up there, in your bed?'

Mick flung out his arm towards the frame. 'Here's my bed, and it won't be like your great soft treasure house of a one and I don't see anyone in it, except bugs, but then you wouldn't know anything about that side of life. Get away from here. Just get away. Go back to her. Pick up your life. I'm finished with you. Yes, I kissed her. But she didn't kiss me, you fool.' He squared up to Ben, seeing the Tan by the river, seeing Des dying, hating Ben, hating himself, hating Cait and Des, everyone . . .

Ben grabbed his lapels, and thrust his face into Mick's. 'What do you mean, she didn't kiss you? Why did you phone?' Desperation was mixed with the anger, the fear, and the agony. 'Where is she?' he screamed at Mick, shaking him harder and harder.

Mick brought up his hands, breaking Ben's grip, pushing him back. 'What do you mean, where is she? She's your wife. You're the one who should know where she is. Surely not even you would throw her out because of a kiss she didn't want, a message that was left. I was only trying to apologize.' His face was appalled.

Ben came at him again. 'You don't expect me to believe any of that. She can't just have found you. It's been going on for ever, hasn't it? It's never stopped, has it? Has it?' His hands were on Mick's lapels again, his breath was whisky-laden, his eyes bloodshot. Words were roaring in his head, images were flashing.

Mick flared. 'You know it all then – you, the great Tan – know it all? OK then, if you say it's been going on for years, then it has. Is that what you want to hear?'

Ben thought he'd faint with the pain.

Mick shook his head. 'You stupid fool. You don't know a good thing when it's dropped in your bloody lap.' He shoved Ben away again. 'Of course it's not been going on for years. Nothing's gone on. She only found me yesterday. Now let me get on with my life.'

He turned his back and Ben couldn't grasp his words. He'd been wrong. Oh God, he'd been wrong. No. No. He couldn't have done that to her. No, this man had to be lying. But he didn't want him to be lying.

Mick turned. 'You still here, you double-crossing pom – getting the Tans into her life. We should have killed you when we could.'

Ben flew at him, his fists working, thumping into Mick's body. Mick kicked his legs from under him. Ben fell to the ground. He punched Mick's legs from under him. They rolled over, punching, cursing, kicking, and it was at the pain, it was at the past, it was at themselves that they were really aiming, thrashing, hurting, tearing.

Again and again they grunted out curses. Again and again their fists lashed into ribs, faces, bellies, until they both had the taste of blood in their mouths, and dust in their wounds, and until, at last, there was no more strength, no more will.

They fell apart then, their breathing louder than the boiling of the copper, the stench of the crushed bugs all around them, the light of the morning in their eyes. The heat of it beating on their bruised faces. They both hauled themselves up to sitting positions and eased themselves back against the rusted fence.

Mick drew out his cigarettes with sore and trembling fingers. He took one, gingerly placed it between his lips. He looked across at the Tan, whose eyes were glued to his face. He tossed one to Ben, lit his own, threw the matches across.

'I'll tell you once more,' Mick said softly, 'she's not here. She never came until yesterday.'

Ben drew on his cigarette and tasted the nicotine. His heart was racing as he dragged the smoke deep into his lungs. He rested his arms on his knees, letting his hands hang limp. 'I know. I think I knew in the lift this morning.' His voice was quiet and defeated, filled with disgust and shame. 'I've always known, but I've never really dared to believe it. I love her, you see, but I couldn't bring myself to trust her. Deep down, that's what it was. I couldn't forget the agony of thinking she hadn't loved me.'

Mick crushed a bug with his thumbnail. 'So what'd you do? Get in with a Tan to pay her back?'

'No, not that. He had money. I could give her a future. I could give her everything she wanted. That way I'd be sure she stayed.'

Mick just looked at him, his lip swelling, his eye blackening. Then he said, 'Don't make me puke.'

Ben looked away. Had he wanted to hurt her too? Oh God, he didn't know anything any more, only that he loved her. Only that he was face to face, here in a stinking yard, with her past, and that he'd made something out of it that hadn't existed. He had weaved complicity where there was none.

'But there *was* before,' he groaned aloud.

Mick looked confused. Ben said, 'There was complicity before.'

Mick said, 'There was a war before. Look, my brother gave his life for me, and Caithleen gave hers to you. She became what you wanted, a little English miss. Love shone out of her. Once more I'll say it. Yes, I kissed her. She fought me off. She loved you, even though you'd brought a Tan into her life, and Fascists too. I couldn't bear to see such love. I kissed her. I was crazy. I wanted to take something from you.' His voice broke. 'I never thought you'd send her packing. I never really thought that. But then I don't think. My brother knew that.'

Ben watched the ash lengthen on his cigarette

and felt more weary than he had ever done in his life before. 'What the hell have I done?' he murmured.

'What have we both done?' Mick replied, and together they sat as the shadows shortened and lengthened again, and by then, the fire beneath the copper had long since died.

Kate sat in the back room of Lucia's vegetable shop in Melbourne, drinking tea, clasping the cup with both hands. Rose was in bed, worn out, confused, distraught, asleep at last.

'You must go back,' Lucia said. 'He can't have meant it.'

There were sacks of potatoes at one end of the room, and carrots in netting. There was a smell of earth. It was like Ireland.

'I loved him. I would have died for him. He must have had me followed to know where I was. Me, his wife.' She wiped her mouth with the back of her hand. 'How could he trust me so little, after all the years we had together, after everything we've been through?' She thought of the heat of Kalgoorlie, the work, the fun, the struggles.

She looked at Lucia. 'Mick forced the kiss on me. Why didn't the detective wait, see me push him away? How could Ben believe it, just like that? How could he think that it was a plan? But, of course, he could, with my past.' She was sobbing now. Lucia came to her.

Mario came into the room, his apron dirty from the potatoes he had lugged from the truck. Lucia shook her head at him, and he carried the sack back into the shop.

Kate put down her mug. The enamel was chipped where she had been drinking. It was stained brown. She said, 'Stephens is a Tan, one of the New Guard. Most of the others are too. My husband has these friends, but I could have lived with even that because

I love him so much.' She turned to Lucia. 'But how he must hate me, to accuse me of such things, and to say that our daughter isn't his.' Her voice shook again, and now the sobs racked her body.

Lucia let her cry, whispering, 'You were never truly married to him. It was not before the altar.'

But Kate cried, 'Oh yes, in spite of that, I was, and I always will be, because I love him. I always have, and I always will, not even this will change that.'

'So, my dear Kate, you must go back.'

'No, there has to be an end to it. I can't go on any more. Somehow, I'll return to Ireland.' She wiped her face with the handkerchief Lucia offered.

Lucia said, 'You will take the money we have saved, and you will go now. You will take your child to meet your father. You gave us refuge when we needed it, and now we will do the same.' She folded her hands on her ample lap, her plump face determined.

Kate shook her head, her voice firm. 'No. You are half packed. Good heavens, you leave next week. I'll work for it, save up. I'm not taking anything from anyone again. I've got to be my own person. The lies have all got to stop, all of them.'

That night she sat on Rose's bed, comforting her, soothing away the nightmare her daughter had woken from. 'I am his child, aren't I, Mum?'

Kate held her close, stroking her hair. 'You shouldn't listen at doors, but of course you are. It's me he hates. He thinks I love someone else.'

'But, Mum, all those things he said.'

'He was wrong. He must have had me followed. A friend from Ireland kissed me. I didn't want him to. I pushed him away. Your father's detective didn't see that.'

Rose fell silent. What had she done?

But her mother was talking, holding her away

from her, her voice very low, very steady, very strong. She told her of the man she had visited yesterday, of the boyfriend he had once been, of the role she had played in Ireland.

Rose tried to follow, but why Ireland? Her mother was from Manchester?

She said, 'I don't understand.'

Kate's voice rose. 'You've got to try. The time for being someone other than I am, is at an end. Perhaps if I'd been myself, perhaps if I hadn't been what I thought your father wanted he'd not have hated me. Perhaps . . .' She stopped. Perhaps what? It was all so confused, so difficult. She took a deep breath. 'I've lied about myself, and therefore about you, for long enough. You deserve to know who you are.'

She told Rose about the struggles in Ireland, about her father, about Des. She told her everything, and they sat quietly together looking through the window at the Melbourne skyline and for Rose there was no security any more.

She'd sung songs and sneered at the Catholics – and she was one. She had a grandfather, when she thought she'd only Roy. But to her grandfather she was dead, as her mother was dead to him. But one day they were going there, leaving Australia. 'Going home,' her mother whispered.

She wanted to shout, 'Australia is my home, that's all I'm certain of any more.' But how could she? Her father hated them because of something she had told him. It had broken her mother's heart and nothing must ever hurt her again.

For three days and nights Ben sat in his armchair and drank whisky, gin, anything. He locked the door and wouldn't answer to anyone. He let the phone ring. He'd been wrong, so wrong. And she'd gone, vanished.

On the fourth day the master-key turned in the lock.

He picked up a glass from the floor by the armchair and threw it at the door. It smashed and fell to the ground. Mick came in with Old Roy. They shut the door, Mick leaned on it. Roy came to Ben.

Ben yelled, 'What the hell are you two doing here together? Get the hell out, both of you. Leave me alone. Have you come to gloat?' He fumbled for the bottle. Old Roy yanked it out of his hand. Ben grabbed it back, yelling, 'I said, what the hell are you doing here? You, you damned old man, should be out digging in the dust.'

Old Roy slapped him round the face. Ben fell back, his mouth slack, then started forward. 'You damned—'

Mick moved quickly, coming to Roy's side. Roy held up his hand to Mick. 'Even *he* wouldn't do that.'

Ben looked from one to the other, then fell back again, and put his head into his hands, and now he cried aloud because that is what he had been doing silently ever since he had thrown her out.

Roy and Mick waited, standing quite still. There was only the sound of the clock, and Ben. Finally Old Roy nodded to the small kitchen. 'See if you can rustle up some coffee – strong and black.'

Mick nodded. His walk was crisp, his clothes clean, his hair cut short. His movements were decisive as he hunted through cupboards. He listened for the sound of trouble from the sitting-room. There was none. He found the coffee, tipped the beans into the grinder. Enough for three. He searched for cups, found them, just as Old Roy had done when he'd come to his room last night.

Mick waited for the water to boil, feeling it with his hands. Just as Roy had done. He shook his head. What an old devil the man was, but he was right. He owed Ben and Cait something. He poured the boiling

399

water through the ground coffee he'd heaped into the tea strainer. Probably wasn't how it should be done, but one day he'd learn to do it properly. He sipped. It tasted good but not as good as the tea Old Roy had made him, before walking him round the room until he was sober.

He loaded the tray with the cups and carried it through to the sitting-room. Roy was pulling Ben to his feet, saying, 'That's enough of that. You brought it on yourself. You were a bloody fool.'

Ben leaned on the old man, then struggled free, supporting himself on the back of his chair. 'Why are you here? You and him together?' He nodded as Mick put the tray on the polished table. 'And mind my table, you Irish fool.'

Roy said, 'Kate cabled me. Your marriage might be over, but she still cares. I arrived last night, talked to that boy Nigel, went to see Mick. I know what happened. Now I want to know what you're both going to do about it?'

'I'm doing nothing with him.' Ben gripped the back of the chair even tighter.

Mick stared at him and said, 'I've lost my brother. I haven't got a family, just like Roy said last night – said all through the damn night, in fact. You see, he said all the things I hoped the booze would drown out. He said I've wasted what life I've had. I've made nothing of it. I've built nothing up. I've destroyed it all and helped you destroy yours. But only helped. You did a lot of it.' Mick stabbed his finger at Ben now. 'And them's my words. Cait's my oldest friend. I've been a pig to her. But you've been a right bastard too.' He moved across and picked up the bottle of Scotch. 'This doesn't help. It's like Roy says. It's doing something that'll help.' He stood turning the bottle round and round in his hands.

400

Ben watched this man whose face looked as haggard as his but whose shoulders were straight. 'Another trick?' he ground out.

Old Roy called out as he lowered himself into the chair opposite Ben, 'I'll have that coffee now, Mick, though maybe whisky would be better.' He beckoned to Mick, smiling slightly. Mick tipped a little whisky into Roy's cup and carried it across.

Ben shouted, 'All right, you've helped, you've taken an old man his coffee. Now get out and leave me to sort out my life.'

Mick turned now, anger boiling inside him. He controlled it. For the first time in his life, he thought with surprise, he'd controlled himself. He said, 'Sure, I nearly brought your hotel down. I've been away talking to the staff, trying to sort it out. We can swing it, it won't take long. *We* – because you need me to undo the damage. *We* – need to find Cait, all three of us. There's no room for pride.' He turned to Roy. 'That's right, isn't it, old man? It's like you said last night. We all need to find her, 'cause we've all let her down.'

Ben stared at Roy then said quietly, 'You've never let her down.'

Roy smiled to himself. Ben was talking so he'd be all right. And Mick would make good. He was less of a fool with every minute, now that he was facing up to himself. Then the smile faded. He said softly, 'I let her come, knowing what she was coming to. Oh yes, I think you could say we've all let her down.'

Ben pushed himself away from the chair, and walked towards the coffee. Mick moved, reached for the tray.

Ben snarled, 'I'll get my own damn coffee.'

His head was hammering. He reached carefully for the cup and saucer, and drank. It was weak. 'Don't you even know how to make a decent cup of coffee?' he grunted.

'I'll learn over the next few weeks. Then I'll go, when I've done as much as I can.' Mick's voice was neutral.

Ben drank the coffee to the dregs, then looked at Roy, then round the room, then at last, at Mick. He recognized the same sense of desperation in all their eyes.

'A few weeks, that's all,' he said.

Mick nodded.

Cait and Rose flew to Darwin, and then took the train to the small town along the Stuart Highway where Lucia's friend, Mr Villas, needed a manager in the run-down hotel he had bought for his son, but the son had preferred Darwin.

They stood in the dust, running with sweat in the humid heat. There was no platform, just baked red earth. Cicadas clicked. Apart from that, there was silence.

Rose said, 'We can't stay here. There are only a few shacks.'

Cait said, 'We must, until we have the money to go home.' They picked up their bags and walked, their heels rubbing in their shoes, sweat streaming down their legs, flies crawling on their faces, their clothes. The street ran alongside the railway line. There were a few houses. A woman on a veranda shaded her eyes. Aboriginals sat in the shade of a gum, motionless. Soon it would be dark.

There were the ruins of buildings. In the distance there were the ruins of gold-mining windlasses. Soon it would be the wet season Lucia had said the morning after they arrived in Melbourne. 'Please go to Ireland instead. We can wait for Italy.'

Cait had refused. 'I mustn't stay here for more than another day. He might try and find me, accuse me of something more.' Her laugh had been bitter. 'I've thought it all out. You have a friend in the shipping line, the one you're travelling with?'

Lucia had nodded. Cait had continued, 'Could he add our names to the passenger list? It's a lot to ask, I know, and I've written this letter. Could he, or you, send it from wherever he lands next? Then, as far as Ben, or any detective knows, we have left the country, and in the letter I will tell him that we'll never return.'

Lucia nodded again. 'But are you sure, quite sure?'

'Never more so.'

Mr Villas had also agreed to employ a certain Katherine Adams and her daughter Shirley Rose, in case any enquiries were made by Ben. That same night Cait had written a letter telling Ben that she would never return to Australia. That she was seeking a home in Europe. That he had hurt her beyond endurance. That Rose was his child, but she did not expect him to believe her. That she could no longer live a lie. That there finally had to be an end.

Rose had begged her mother to plead with him to take them back. Cait had refused. 'We don't need men in our lives, they just bring pain, make sure you remember that. We're going home, away from this place.' Her voice had been hard.

Lucia had taken Rose to one side. 'Your mother is hurting. She is bitter, and she is frightened, and she is trying to survive. She loves you, never doubt it, and this hatred will pass.'

Now they walked on in the heat until they came to the hotel at the end of the street. It was built of corrugated iron and wood. The veranda rail was broken. There was a sleep-out at one end. Dust clung to their damp skin. It was in their mouths and eyes, it stained their clothes. Rose wanted to kick and scream and yell, 'I won't stay, not here. I won't, I won't.'

Her mother said, dropping her bags, 'We can make something of this, you and I.' She put her arm around her daughter's shoulder. 'We'll make this our home while we wait. We'll be safe here.'

Rose leaned against her mother, slipping her arm round her waist, smiling but thinking that this would never be home, and that she'd never feel safe again.

They dragged their cases up the steps. A fat, cheerful woman came to the door, holding back the fly door. 'Get yourselves inside. The mozzies will be out soon.' Her voice was thick and warm, her blond hair wild and free. Her roots were black. Rose was shocked. It was dyed. Only loose women dyed their hair. She looked up at her mother, who smiled wearily.

It was dark inside. They stood in the corridor which ran down the centre. On the right was the bar and the billiards room. The walls stopped before they reached the ceiling. The heat was stifling. There was a steady murmur from the bar, and the smell of beer.

On the left was the coffee-room, and the dining-room, and, at the back, the kitchen. Rose and Cait followed the vast bulk of the woman into the kitchen. A stove was burning, stew bubbled on the top. The woman stopped and thrust out her hand first to Kate, and then to Rose. Her nails were varnished. Rose drew back quickly, wiping her hand on her skirt. This woman was common.

'I'm Mrs Harvey. Been running it for that old skinflint Villas. Me and Sam, that is. Sam's got the shakes – oh my, how he has – but he'll fetch the stores from the train, no worries. Best to keep him away from the grog though. He gets his malaria too. Gawd, he gets a right shake on then, I'm telling you.'

Cait laughed. Rose was appalled.

'C'mon then, sit yer down. Got tea on the go.' Mrs Harvey pulled out two chairs. They were greasy to the touch. Rose sat on the edge of hers, but Cait leaned back. 'Are you staying to help me, Mrs Harvey?'

Rose shot her mother a look. It wasn't proper. This woman was just not proper.

'If you want me, be glad to. Mrs Adams, is it?'

'Yes, and I do want you.' Cait smiled. 'I want you very much.'

Mrs Harvey showed them the hotel accommodation which was in a long shack at the back of the hotel. Had Roy gone to look after Ben? Cait thought. She couldn't bear to think of her husband, of his eyes, his mouth, his body, his voice which she missed more with every second that passed.

Rose said, 'You said we shouldn't lie about ourselves again, so I hate this name business.'

'Not as much as I do, darling, but you can be known as Rose. It would make sense.'

She and Rose slept in separate back veranda sleep-outs, beneath mosquito-nets, fighting for breath in the heat, cringing at the noise of the dry thunderstorm. Mrs Harvey lived in her own home, along the main road. Old Sam lived who knew where, or so Mrs Harvey told them. 'Don't like being tied down. Don't like noses in his business, or that's what he tells me.' Yes, Cait could understand that.

They rose to a day even hotter. Mrs Harvey was stirring the porridge, and sweat was trickling down her fleshy arm. She said, 'Get's hot here, just before the wet. Then it's just wet and hot.' She cackled. Cait laughed. Rose watched the sweat drip into the porridge and felt sick.

Mrs Harvey said, as she dished up two bowls and slapped them before Rose and Cait, 'Busy time, the wet. The ringers'll set up camp on the outskirts. No work you see on the stations. They'll be in for tucker, booze, girls. Better lock up your daughter, missis.'

Cait didn't laugh. She just said, 'We're not interested in men. We're saving to go home to Ireland.'

After breakfast, which Rose refused to eat, Cait said, 'School tomorrow. Today we'll start on the bedrooms.'

'But, Mum.'

'But Mum nothing.' Her mother's voice was hard again. 'Sometimes the train stays overnight, so we'll have visitors. If we build up the business, we'll earn more, so come along.' Didn't the child understand that they were alone? They had to do this themselves.

They worked all morning in the humid heat, stripping the beds, cleaning the kerosene lamps, washing the jug and bowl on the dresser. They squashed the big grey cattle ticks that crawled over the cement floors, they topped up the tins of water that the bed legs stood in, and flicked out the few dead ants. Rose said, 'Stupid things, they should learn to swim.'

They looked at one another, and Cait hugged her. 'It'll be all right, darling. I promise.'

How can you promise? Rose thought, wanting to stay in her mother's arms for ever. You couldn't stop what happened from happening. Nothing's safe.

In the afternoon Cait ironed on the veranda, loving the smell of the beeswax, carefully folding the sheets and the table-cloths, looking out at the frangipanis, the paw-paw trees and the neglected lawn, trying not to think of her daughter's haunted eyes.

Perhaps she should go back and try to talk to Ben. But no. It was pointless. His hate was so vivid, and if distrust had lasted this long, it would last for ever.

She braved the heat of the kitchen to change the flat iron for one which contained red-hot coals. Mrs Harvey had just stoked up the stove, and her hair was hanging limp as she sprinkled water onto bread and put it into the oven. Cait said, 'Doesn't anyone mind stale bread?'

Mrs Harvey shook her head. 'Naw, the ringers don't know the difference, and until we get down to baking our own we'll just have to freshen up the stuff the train brings in.'

Cait nodded. 'I'll do some baking this afternoon.' She called through to the wash-house, 'Rose, how's the starching coming along?'

'I don't see why I have to do it?' Rose grumbled.

Cait raised her eyebrows at Mrs Harvey who said, 'Seems to me you're working both of you a little too hard. The bread can wait, and the starching too.'

Cait ignored her, changed the irons and continued ironing on the veranda. They had to work, they had to earn money, and, besides, it kept them both from thinking.

She made the bread as clouds gathered, layer upon layer, and the humidity soared. 'Will it rain?' Rose asked Mrs Harvey, slumping on a cane chair on the front veranda, looking down the road at the school.

'Not yet. This is just the build-up to the wet. Set your clock by it, you can.'

Rose looked down the road. Nothing stirred except the flies, not even the aboriginals who were still sitting motionless. 'It's so big, and empty, and damp, and hot, and lonely,' she complained.

Mrs Harvey slapped at a fly on her arm. She sang, conducting with her hands. 'Give it a day or two, get a friend or two, you'll soon forget whatever it is that's troubling you, then you can sing along with me.'

Rose cringed with embarrassment.

Mrs Harvey broke into peals of laughter. 'I'll take you out tonight to meet young Shirley. She'll be your classmate but it'll be difficult with you being a Shirley too. Nice kid, she is. Her father works on the railway.'

Rose looked back along the road. Dad, come and get us. But of course he wouldn't. He thought he wasn't her father. He was horrid and foul and she hated him. Her mother was right: they must manage on their own. They must be themselves. But who was she? 'Call me Rose,' she said. 'It's my second name.'

Cait served behind the bar while Mrs Harvey took Rose to meet Shirley. The heat was still stifling, the beer was warm, the carbide lights cast a dim glow. The billiard balls clicked. The men leaned on the bar, drinking beer without seeming to swallow, watching her as she took the tops off bottles, watching as she tipped the glass as Mrs Harvey had showed her, watching as she poured. Did they guess at her relief when the froth lay in a thin band on the top?

There was a dull murmur of conversation, a loud laugh from the corner of the room. Sam came in, carrying a crate of beer, putting it down gently as though it was ambrosia, pursing his lips as he saw her pour another beer.

'Not yours, Sam,' a young ringer called, laughing at him.

Sam's eyes were bloodshot, the bags beneath them sagged, his mouth was slack. He rubbed his chin. 'Go on, give him one, missis. And where's your bloke?'

She shot the young ringer a look.

'I don't have a bloke.'

The man standing beside the ringer said, 'Give us another beer.' He pushed the glass towards her, his eyes on her breasts. There were deep sun-scored lines round his eyes and mouth.

She could feel her hands trembling. She wanted to hide.

He said again, 'Give us what I want.' His eyes were still on her breasts.

The other men had fallen silent. Some shifted uncomfortably. The young ringer flushed. 'Leave it, Len,' he muttered. 'No call for that.'

Another man called from the end, 'Another beer up here, missis.'

Now she felt the rage erupt. She picked up the broom from behind her, walked out from the bar, holding it up at Len. 'Get out. Go on, get out until you can keep a civil tongue in your head, and your dirty little eyes in their sockets. Get on, or by the Holy Mother, I'll sweep you out.' She was shouting, and she could hear her Irish brogue again.

She poked him with the broom. 'Go! Out! And only be coming back in here when you're ready to say please and thank you, and that goes for the lot of you.'

She glared at the man down the end. There was not even the click of the billiard balls to disturb the air, only the humming of the mozzies.

She said, 'By tomorrow evening I'll have made some fans. That should cool the lot of you down, so I don't want this ever again.' She went back behind the bar. Sam was staring at her, his mouth open. 'Go and hold open the door for the gentleman, Sam.' She stared at Len. 'No-one gets a drink until you go out and come back in again with a different face on you. No-one, and the wet is coming, so I hope you like the taste of rain.'

She glared at Len, her hands on her hips. He glared back at her, then at the others. A man shouted from the corner, 'For God's sake, do as she says, I'm not spending three months paddling like a duck with nothing to wet my whistle.'

Len was pushed and shoved to the door. Cait turned to the man at the end. 'Did you say something earlier?'

He nodded. 'Please can I have a beer, missis?'

She smiled as though nothing out of the ordinary had happened. 'Certainly.' They watched as she took off the bottle cap, watched as she tilted the glass, watched as she poured it. 'There we are.' She pushed it across the counter to him, smiling. He paid her. 'Thank you,' she said.

He said, 'Ta,' and grinned.

The front door slammed. Len returned. He stood at the bar and dropped his money on the table. A coin spun, fell. He said, 'A beer please, missis.' But there was no pleasantness in his tone.

*   *   *

At the end of the evening Mrs Harvey said, 'You could have had a riot on your hands.' She was tense. 'Sam told me about it. That bloke Len's a bad 'un. Be careful.'

Cait shrugged and grinned. For a moment Ben had been forgotten. She had coped. She had won. She had been herself. This was her pub, her life, and she would work all the hours God sent to get home with her daughter. Nothing would stop her and she didn't need anyone to help her. D'you hear that, Ben? Your daughter and I don't need anyone.

Ben stood in front of the consortium who were gathered around the huge shining table in the board-room. Oil paintings hung on the walls, paintings of British hunting scenes, British sailing ships, British cricket matches. 'So there you have it. I want out. I want to take the Bondi Beach Hotel off your hands. You are welcome to the other two.'

Stephens looked around, then leaned back in his chair. His black hair was brilliantined back from his face, his moustache was neatly trimmed. He touched it. 'I wonder if the recent exodus of your wife has affected your mental health, my dear Ben. You want to leave us, when there are those who would give their right arms to have our backing? You want to leave us, though you have sorted out the staff discontent? Doesn't make sense.'

Ben nodded. 'For the first time, I am making sense. Now, as I said, I have my own consortium. I've told you the terms. They're generous. You will all make a profit.'

Stephens nodded. 'One can't dispute that. But forgive our curiosity – you still haven't told us why.'

'I have my reasons. You see, my wife is not English, she is Irish. The Black and Tans murdered her mother and I have broken her heart and flung everything she is, and everything she has done for me, back in her face. I am going into business with a Kalgoorlie miner and a former member of the Irish Volunteers who is both a Catholic and a Socialist. I will find my wife one day, and I want to be free of all taint when that moment comes.'

He picked up his hat. He looked around the table. Larry Smith stared at him, his kunckles white as he gripped the blotter in front of him. Into the stunned silence Ben said, 'I assume I have your agreement?' The men nodded dumbly. He looked at the paintings. 'Try hanging Australian paintings. Hans Heysen's "Droving into the Light" is one of my wife's favourites. You're Australians, after all.'

That evening he and Mick and Old Roy raised their glasses to the Bondi Beach Hotel, and to Caithleen Healy and Rose, wherever they were. There was still the same sense of desperation in all their eyes. It was right that they should stay together while they searched for her. Mick could tolerate Ben until then, and Ben could just about tolerate Mick, they'd agreed.

Chapter Twenty

Rose had hated her first year: the humidity of the wet season, the dust of the dry. She'd hated the hotel, hated the malaria, hated Mrs Harvey's peroxided hair, her black hair roots; she'd hated school, hated Shirley, hated everything. Had her mother? She didn't know. They didn't speak of what they liked and didn't like, only of how they could save more money for Ireland.

Now, as she lolled on her bed in the sleep-out one late afternoon in February 1939 she threw aside the poetry book her mother had given her for Christmas. A poetry book for a fifteen year old, for heaven's sake. And anyway, what relevance did nodding daffodils have to her? Australia was her land, her country. The Lake District was nothing to her. Ireland was nothing.

She picked up her pen and tried to concentrate on the list for Shirley's party tonight but she couldn't. She flung her pen aside and hugged her knees, flicking her tumbling red hair back from her face. It was slightly paler than her mother's, but so were her eyes.

The wet this year had been as wonderful as ever, with tumbling skies slashed by lightning, rain like sheets, children running out into it, glorying in it. Rose had run out into it too, because Mrs Harvey was right: she had grown to love it. She had grown to love the small one-class school and had almost forgotten the neatness and precision, and religion, of the school in Sydney. This year she had been going in to help the teacher in return for some extra tuition.

She attended neither the Catholic nor Protestant Church in the township, though her mother had said she could choose which she preferred.

Rose had attended neither because her mother would not, but said her own God was out there, in the sky, and the wind, and the bush. For Rose would do everything that her mother did, she would do everything her mother said, because it was she, Rose, who had caused all this, she, who had misconstrued a kiss.

She rested her chin on her knees. Tonight she would dance at Shirley's farewell party, and smile and laugh, and not mind that the last of her friends was leaving for college in Darwin.

She eased her shoulders. Who would she go swimming in the pools with? Who would she laugh and giggle with at the parties they held when a train stayed overnight?

'Rose, come on, me darlin', time to sort out the food and the tables,' Mrs Harvey called.

Rose grinned and called, 'Only if you dance a tango with me tonight, and come swimming in the pool next week. No crocs, so you can't give them indigestion.'

'You come out here and say that.' Mrs Harvey roared with laughter.

Rose tied back her hair as she left. Mrs Harvey was baking in the kitchen, sweat was rolling off her, but then it always did. Rose smiled, picked up the table-cloths and walked through the hotel – no longer noticing the smell of last night's beer, or the flies – and out onto the front veranda. Old Sam was dragging the trestles across from the store. Red dust rose in his wake.

The township looked as it had done that first day,

but it was not dead, it was not dull or isolated, after all. Here there was warmth, friendliness, here was the Australia of their farm by the river, of Kalgoorlie, not the stiffness of their friends in Sydney. Here there was poetry in every season, in every sound, in the black of the aboriginals, in the feel of the pool as you slid into its coolness, in the laughter of your friends in the truck on the journey home. There would be the same poetry in Darwin, there would be college, there would be a career.

Mrs Harvey called, 'Those table-cloths aren't going to put themselves on the tables.'

Rose laughed. 'Well neither am I right now. Sam's still at the trestle stage.'

Her mother called from the bar, her voice crisp and hard, 'He'll have to go. He's getting worse and worse. It's a waste of my money.'

Mrs Harvey walked down the passage towards the front veranda, wiping her hands on her apron, her tread heavy. She stood beside Rose. 'Have you asked her again whether you can go with Shirley?'

Rose shook her head. 'There's no point, she needs me here.'

Mrs Harvey nodded, and for once there was no laughter in her eyes. She looked back towards the bar and said quietly, 'Let's help Sam. He'll think I'm one of his pink elephants, and heaven alone knows what he'll think you are – a skeleton at the feast, with that face on you. Come on, something will turn up.'

Rose grinned, but she knew it wouldn't. She knew nothing would change her mother, but Ireland.

That evening the ringers, the children, the priest, the parents, everyone of the township, came, as they always did. Rose hurried to and from the Coolgardie safes set up on the veranda, bringing back raspberry drinks for the children. Her mother served beer on one of the trestle-tables for the men. Mrs Harvey manned the tea urn.

Shirley's father played the accordion, and his friend, Fred Smith, the mouth organ. Sam stoked the fires that were burning cow manure around the yard to ward away the mosquitoes. Rose smiled at the thought of Alice Sinclair and her mother dancing here as she and her mother had done. She glanced at her mother. Would she dance tonight? It depended on her mood.

The priest was beckoning to Mrs Harvey, who shrieked with pleasure and left the urn to dance the two step. Sam had damped down the earth to settle the dust, but the air was thick with it anyway.

A ringer was dancing with Shirley, whirling her round and round. A young man came to Rose. He tried to take her tray from her. She shook her head. 'I'm working.' His hands were tanned and strong. What would it feel like if hers were in his?

'Aw c'mon, one little dance won't hurt.'

Rose looked across at her mother. Yes, she was watching. Rose gripped the tray tighter. 'No really, I can't, but thank you.' His face was young and thin, and his eyes were blue, his lips full. What would it feel like to be kissed? Shirley knew. Rose didn't.

The ringer flashed a look at Cait. 'So she still thinks you'll turn into a wombat if you touch one of us?' His voice was angry.

Rose shrugged. 'No, but if you didn't get your beer, you'd turn into a riot, so I have to look after the raspberry drinks. She can't do both.'

The ringer touched his hat. 'Got your point.'

He drifted off, as they always did. Her mother smiled. Rose smiled back, but she wanted to scream and shout and rage. Soon the priest would come and dance with her and she would die of embarrassment and humiliation. Rose put down the tray, her hands were trembling. She should be grateful though – at least he was a man, but a safe one. One who wouldn't snatch her away into marriage – away from the dream of Ireland.

Mrs Harvey was panting as the music ended, and so was Shirley, who came across and draped herself over Rose. 'Oh Rose, I'm going to miss all this.' Shirley's dark brown eyes were bright with laughter, and tears. 'And you.'

Cait called, 'Take a break now, Rose.'

Rose grimaced. Now, when the ringer was gone.

Shirley and she sat on the veranda steps, thigh to thigh, arm in arm. 'Have you asked her again?' Shirley breathed. 'For heaven's sake, Rose, you're fifteen. We could go together, meet up with Deirdre and Felicity, share the same landlady. There are places on the shorthand and typing course, I know there are. I checked.'

Rose knew, she'd also checked. 'No, I haven't asked again. She said no, she meant no.'

Shirley flung herself from Rose, her hands flailing the air. 'For heaven's sake, you should stick up for yourself. Make a scene.'

'I can't.'

'You can, you just won't. Why? She needs someone to tell her to back off. You've got to fight for yourself, you've got to make a life. Tell me, now I'm going, what happened in Sydney?'

Rose watched Mrs Harvey whirling round the young ringer whose hat flew off, and whose friends were laughing, whistling, whooping.

'Nothing happened in Sydney except that my dad sent us away. He hates us. It seems like he always did, but we didn't know it. It was all over his face, in his voice. It's because my mother's Irish. That's why.'

But it was also because she had told him about the kiss. If she hadn't done her mother would not have the lines, the hardness, that covered the heartache which Rose shared, but which neither talked about.

*   *   *

Mrs Harvey slumped down on the bench next to
Cait, fanning herself with her handkerchief. 'You
could do to have a whirl,' she said, nudging Cait.
'Nice old ringer over there, and there's a couple of
miners in tonight. Good for business if more mines
pick up.'

Cait watched the miners smoking in the shadows
of the kerosene lamps, cupping their cigarettes in
their hands as the ten o'clock breeze blew up. The
table-cloths flapped, the accordion played. She looked
away. Had Ben hated her in Kalgoorlie too? She
rubbed her forehead.

'Sam,' she called. 'Put another boy on the fans.
Danny's tired.'

Mrs Harvey pushed at the cuticles of her scarlet
nails. 'Good idea of yours, those fans.'

'Not good enough to bring the punters in.'

Mrs Harvey put her hands on her knees, breathing
heavily still. 'You've picked up the business no end.
Villas is pleased.'

'But not enough. I thought we'd be gone by now.'
Cait paused and turned to her. 'And how did you
know he said he was pleased?'

Mrs Harvey roared with laughter. 'We know everything, it's a party line, remember. Joyce loves to listen.'

Cait clicked with annoyance. Mrs Harvey examined her nails again and said, 'Since you are still
here, wouldn't it be right to let Rose loose?'

Cait watched Sam pay Danny off, and put Trevor
on the rope. Sam was staggering, sipping from something. Oh God, not drunk again. She started to rise
but Mrs Harvey held her down. 'No, I've got to say
this, Mrs Adams. You have become a hard, selfish
woman. You've had pain, we've all had pain, but that
girl deserves a future.'

Cait looked down at the fat hand that held her.
'Take your hand from my arm.' Her voice was cold

417

with fury. 'Take your hand off me, and your nose out of my business. My daughter wants to come back to Ireland with me, that's all that matters to us. She doesn't want to go off gallivanting with men, or wasting our savings on courses. All that's important is to go home, together.'

Mrs Harvey maintained her grip. 'That's what you think she wants, because that's what *you* want.'

Cait pulled away. 'Go back to your dancing. If Rose wanted that, she'd have told me.'

'She did.'

'She mentioned it, but she said it's not important to her. Has she mentioned it again? No, she's needed here, to help in the hotel. She's got a job, she's got a life. It's enough. It's not for long. Soon we'll be going.' She was striding towards Sam now, grabbing his arm. 'You've been drinking.'

He was skeletal beneath her hand. She could smell the booze, feel the shake of his body. 'How many times have I told you to stop boozing when I need you? What am I paying you for, you stupid old man? This is it. You're off the payroll, you're worse than useless.'

Rose came running then, pulling her mother away from Sam, who was jibbering, staggering. 'Leave him alone. Just leave him alone, Mother. How can you be so cruel?'

Rose stood between her mother and Sam, her blue eyes angry, her hair flowing in the breeze. She was the same height, their eyes were on a level. Cait had not noticed that before.

Rose led Sam away, the music played in the background, Shirley danced with a ringer, another danced with Shirley's mother, holding her, talking, laughing, as Ben had once done with her. She must go home.

Mick kissed his wife in their apartment at the Manly Hotel. 'I love you, Sylvie.'

She touched his hair, curling it round her finger. 'I know you do. When will Ben be back? You've been working such long hours.'

'That's the price of success. With this new hotel it puts an extra load on. But young Nigel is working out very well. Good thing Ben pulled him out from the Tans' hotel; he's trained up good. Old Roy's appointed him assistant manager under him at the Beach.'

'But when is Ben back?' she insisted, the sun lighting her blond hair as they sat in the window overlooking the sea. 'What does he say in his letter? Europe's about to go up in flames from the look of it and he'll be stuck there. This is the second time he's been to Europe. It's crazy, there are no leads, and the Vincenzis can't be found. All we know is that Caithleen Healy and Rose travelled out on the same ship, then everyone has faded. We've advertised, we've had detectives on the case. If only the Vincenzis hadn't left Melbourne before he reached them.'

Mick held her to him. Where was Cait? Ben loved her and knew he'd made a mess of it, and all he wanted was the chance to tell her that, but there was no sense in chasing round and round that particular tree. He said, 'He says he'll be home when he can.'

Sylvie spoke again. 'Will there be war?'

Mick kissed her hair. 'Who knows.'

'If there is, will you fight?'

Mick shook his head. 'Not for the Empire.'

Sylvie groaned. 'Dad won't like that.'

Mick laughed softly. 'He and Ben can grouch about it together.'

Sylvie pulled back in alarm. 'Oh no, you won't be going back to those days. You haven't quarrelled for – oh I don't know – I suppose since Old Roy sat you down and told you the business wouldn't grow if you kept it up.'

Mick laughed again. 'He was right, we could both see that, and Ben's not that bad. Anyway until we find Cait, I'm not moving on. And don't worry about your father. He didn't like his telephonist daughter marrying a Catholic, but he agreed, and he's happy that you're happy, and so we'll cross that bridge when we come to it.'

'What will Ireland do if there's a war?' she asked.

He didn't know. Would they fight for England? He had asked his father that, when he returned in 1937, and even now, he couldn't believe how green it had been as he had travelled towards his home, how purple the hills, how damp the air, how cool even in the height of summer.

He had dismissed the taxi outside the town and waited beside the stone wall, breathing in the fragrance of its honeysuckle, remembering how much Caithleen had loved it, how it had spilled from her vases. Where are you, Cait? Here, with your father? Here, where Ben can't come because he's a Tan? Is this where you feel safe?

He had slipped through the small town after dark, unsure of his welcome. The taxi-driver had said that in some families the legacy of the civil war still lingered; brother still hated brother. He walked out of the town, stopping at the crossroads, looking back at the lights, at the skyline against the moon-drenched sky. It was the same as it had been when he was a boy. The billiard hall had been rebuilt, as had the shops, the burnt-out houses. Lights had shone from their windows too, as he had passed through.

He walked on up the lane, the blackthorn still grew, the owls still hooted. To the right should be the lights of Widow Murphy's farm. There was none, and he could see the ruins of her croft. The track was as rutted as ever. He stuck to the side, where the dew-drenched grass soaked his trousers. Did the carts still come down every day, their churns rattling? Should he have written to his father? But no, he might not have allowed him to come.

He saw Cait's farm in the distance on the right, and his father's over on the left. He cut across the fields towards his own farm. He had wanted to come this way, rather than take the track at the crossroads because this was the path he and Cait had used when they were children, and life had been so simple.

He had thought he might have forgotten the way across the fields, but it was as though he'd never left. He was drawing close. Oil lamps were in the kitchen window, lighting up the yard. He vaulted the fence which he had mended with Des before civil war broke out. He touched the post, shifted the bag over his shoulder, pulled down his cap, and walked across the Home Meadow towards the house.

The cows lifted their heads as he passed; he could hear them chewing. He approached the barn, seeing Des with a hammer in his hand, taking nails from him, their fingers touching, and his eyes filled. He blinked the tears away, but not the ache. Daddy, will you speak to me? Daddy, I had to come to find Cait, see if the detectives had missed something. And I had to come to make peace with you, as well.

There was the sweet smell of hay from the barn, there was the stirring of the hens from the yard, the yap of Barney, the dog. 'Come here then, boy.'

The yap continued. The dog was tied to his kennel. Mick went across. It wasn't Barney. Of course it damn well wasn't. The great Mick O'Brian had left over fifteen years ago. The dog's yap was louder now. 'Shh,' Mick whispered, backing away.

He heard the door open, light fell across the swept concrete. His father stood there, a lamp in his hand. 'Who's that? Come on away into the light, where I can be seeing you.'

Mick stood still, seeing his grey-haired, much older father as though for the first time. Des had been made in his image. Why hadn't he realized that? He stepped forward into the light. 'Daddy, I'm back.' He said it quietly. Would his father send him away? Would he shout, berate him?

For a moment his father said nothing, did nothing. Then he set down the lamp on the covered water butt, his hand trembling. He held out his arms. 'At last you're home. At last one of my boys is home.'

Mick walked into his arms. His father was thin and old, but the arms that came round and held him were as strong as ever, and as gentle as ever as they stroked his hair. 'At last you're home,' his father whispered. His voice was so full of love that Mick wept.

'Daddy,' he sobbed. 'Daddy, I'm so sorry. I'm so sorry about it all.'

Mrs Murphy appeared from the kitchen. 'Don't be standing out there, the two of you. You come along in, Liam, and let's see how much my stepson has changed.'

They sat up until late, around the kitchen table, and now Mick understood why Mrs Murphy's house had not been rebuilt. She said, her strong arms crossed on the table, her fingers nervously plucking at the tanned skin, 'I couldn't go back, you see, not after Des. Every time I went to bring up the cows from the river meadow I could see and hear him.'

She stopped at Mick's father's signal. Mick made her go on. 'He was dripping blood and water onto the bank. His beautiful eyes were clouded, his poor body was full of bullet after bullet. He said, "Tell Caithleen I'm sorry." He kept saying it. He was in so much pain, but that's all he kept saying. So I kept telling him I would tell her. I hope it brought him peace.'

Now that she had said this, she relaxed. Mick told them then what Des had done, and why he had done it. 'Ben told me that Cait said Des promised to go back and see her father, explain everything again, and make sure he understood. He didn't do that, so he was sorry.' Mick's voice broke. He swallowed, recovered.

His father said, 'And what have you done with the life Des gave you?'

Mick was able to tell him of the hotels, and of Ben. His father went rigid. Mick said, 'He's not so bad, and Cait loved him.'

Mrs Murphy nodded. 'Des said to me once that he thought they could be friends. Des loved Cait, you know.'

Mick nodded. It was the only thing that would explain all that had happened.

'Cait wrote to her father to tell him of the child, to beg the man's understanding.'

Mick leaned forward. 'She's not here then? She hasn't been back?'

His father shifted in his chair. 'Now why should you be after asking us that? Sure, it's you who should know all about Cait, if you're working with her husband.'

Mrs Murphy held up her hand to Liam. 'Shh.' She crossed her arms again. 'Where is Cait? What's happened?'

Mick told them everything. As he finished he said, 'Ben and I are sticking together until we find her. It seems right, somehow.'

Mrs Murphy said, 'By all that's holy, what did the Tan think he was doing?'

'That's in the past. Now he's going through hell.'

The next day he walked across the fields to Cait's farm. 'He'll not want to see you,' Mrs Murphy had warned. 'He's a grand man for a grudge, though you'd have thought he'd have learned sense after the feud with his own father.'

When Mick entered the Healys' yard Cait's father stared at him, then reached for the pitchfork against the dairy wall. 'You bastard. You come back here, after your brother betrays his side, after my daughter runs off with you in her cart, courtesy of the Tan.' He advanced. 'Get off my land.'

Mick held up his hands. 'In a minute I'll be doing just that. But she's gone. We can't find her, and she's taken her daughter with her. Have you heard from her?'

Paul Healy hesitated, then stiffened. 'And why would she think of writing to me? She knows I have no interest in her, not now, not ever.'

Mick let his arms drop. 'You're a hard man, Paul Healy. You'll listen to me now, and you'll listen good.'

Mick told him all that Des would have said.

Paul Healy just gripped the pitchfork tighter. 'So, you're telling me the story that was in the letter. What does it matter why things happened? She's gone, she loves a Tan, one of those murdering swine, and she lied about it. That's the thing, Michael. She lied to me.'

Mick laughed bitterly. 'Would you look at yourself? And why wouldn't she lie to a father like you? Why shouldn't a daughter have love, as you had love?'

Paul shook the pitchfork at him. 'You shut your mouth. And wasn't I right, after all? Why's she run away, if this Tan was so wonderful?'

Mick controlled his anger. His voice was cold, clipped. 'She ran away because I couldn't keep my mouth shut and my sticky fingers out of their lives. Ben thought she'd done something she hadn't – harsh words were said. She's all alone with her daughter.' Mick swept his arm in an arc. 'She's all alone, thinking that the man she's given her life to hates her, mistrusts her. She's your daughter, man. Have you no pity?'

Paul Healy brandished the pitchfork again. 'Get off my land. I care nothing for you, except to spit on you, as there are many who will, if you show your face in town.'

Mick brought out his wallet from his inside pocket, searching through it, saying, 'I've a photo of your daughter, and your granddaughter.'

Paul threw the pitchfork into the corner of the yard. The hens scattered. 'Get off my land.' He walked into the dairy.

Mick followed, and stood in the doorway. Paul ignored him. Mick held out the photograph. 'From Ben, your son-in-law.'

Paul didn't turn. Mick placed the photograph on the top of an empty churn. He walked out of the yard and headed towards the town.

Paul Healy continued to scrub the pails, then the sink, then anything he could find. He stripped off his milking coat, hung it on the peg, not looking at the churn as he left. He started to kick off his boots at the back door, then cursed, retraced his steps. He picked up the photograph, his hands trembling as he saw Cait, with her blue eyes and red hair, and Rose. He took it to the compost and tore it into small pieces. How dare they look like his murdered wife?

Now Mick felt Sylvie stir against him. 'If there's war, will it pull Ireland together, as your father thought?'

'Something's got to heal the past. Civil war is a terrible thing, my darling. I didn't realize it then, but the scars don't heal. A common goal, my daddy said. Neutrality in the war, that'll bring them together.'

The next week Ben arrived back from Germany, taking a cab to the Bondi Beach Hotel, which was his home. He spoke to Roy and Mick, and to both of them he said the same thing: 'If she's there, then I dread the coming years. There'll be war. Chamberlain has bought nothing but time.'

Chapter Twenty-One

At the outbreak of war, Ben joined up. Roy and Mick stood on the platform with him. Roy looked at the men in uniform surging all around them, and the women who hugged them, children who tugged at their trousers. 'I'm too damn old. I was for the last one too.'

Mick grinned. 'You'll never be too old.'

Ben checked his watch and searched the seething platform. 'Where's Nigel? If he's late at this stage, God help him on the parade ground.' He turned to Mick. 'Now, you two will be all right holding the fort? Don't let Roy take on too much.'

Mick said, 'I'm training some of the girls up, and Sylvie is taking to management like a duck to water. Now don't be fretting, you'll have enough to do, showing the squaddies how to work the Bren guns you keep talking about.' Mick paused. 'Ben . . .'

Ben nodded. 'I know. Ireland's neutral, so are you. Well, that's your decision.' His voice was crisp. Doors were slamming, men were climbing aboard, women were crying, the smell of sulphur pervaded everything.

Ben hugged Roy. 'Take care. If you hear anything—'

Roy and Mick said together, 'We'll let you know.'

He started to climb aboard but then they heard Nigel call. He was running along the platform. 'Ben,

426

hang on.'

Ben raised his eyebrows, jumped back down onto the platform, and shoved the boy on first. 'Get on.'

The first few weeks at Ingleburn were spent marching, tending blisters, cursing the sergeants. 'You should go for a commission, with your experience,' an officer said to Ben.

He refused. 'I'm too old for that sort of responsibility.' Instead he was given the rank of sergeant and trained the soldiers in the use of the Vickers gun. On Saturday evenings he went out with Nigel and the others and the young men kissed the girls, and drank too much beer, but Ben thought of Caithleen and Rose, and prayed that they were safe.

Within two months Mick joined him, shrugging when Ben looked at him in surprise, saying, 'Decided I was Australian, and this is a world war, after all. Why should you British buggers get all the fun?'

Now it was the three of them that drank, but only Nigel kissed the girls. They sailed for the Middle East and joined the camp at Gaza, and in the heat and the dust they were given Bren guns. 'Lighter and more useful,' Ben said.

Nigel looked at Mick. 'I guess we gathered that ourselves, oh Lord and master.'

Ben cuffed him, and they all laughed, then Ben said quietly to Mick, 'Sorry you've been assigned to me. Shall I get you transferred?'

Mick took a drag on his cigarette. 'No, better the devil you know. Leave it be.'

They were assigned to a three-man, tracked, armoured vehicle. Mick was the gunner, Nigel the driver. Day after day they trained in the blazing heat, with the dust choking them as the tracks hurled up the dust. At sunrise and sunset they sat around fires and talked, or read, or watched the Arabs labouring their laden donkeys. Ben and Mick thought of the

427

donkey carts and rattling churns, and the county of Limerick.

In September 1940 Japan joined the Axis. Japan accepted hegemony of Germany and Italy in Europe, and these two nations recognized Japan's right to organize the Greater East-Asia Co-Prosperity Sphere. Ben and Mick wondered if the Japs would turn towards Australia, but everyone laughed. No way would they ever dare set foot on Australian soil. But they heard of troops being sent to reinforce Darwin, and set up a listening post, none the less.

In November Mick and Ben and their company were on readiness for the push through the Western Desert, and now Ben looked with pride on the men who had been transformed from the mob of a year ago, to a disciplined army. He wrote of this to Roy from their camp near Alexandria whilst Mick wrote to Sylvie, and Nigel to his three girlfriends. 'You'll be fried alive if you put the letters in the wrong envelopes,' Mick warned.

'Trust me,' Nigel said, licking the envelope. Ben sat across from them. Trust me. *Trust me*, echoed in his mind. Today, with Christmas coming, it was Rose's birthday. She would be seventeen.

On December 9 General Wavell's attack began, and now the men were eager, ready, but they didn't move out until the end of December. When they did they ate their own dust as their carriers churned up the dirt, and their women were forgotten as they took Bardia, Tobruk, Derna and Benghazi, amid noise and fear and a sense of excitement.

From Derna they were ordered to chase through Barce to the main Benghazi and Tripoli highway after the Italians, but the rains came down and the red dirt roads became bogged and impassable, and the men cursed and shouted as they had to get out and push the vehicles. Mick groaned, 'God, it's like being back in the mining-camp south of Darwin. God, the wet there. The ringers used to come in to the broken-down hotel. Owned by an Italian bloke. Name of Villas. Wonder if he's in that mob we're chasing.'

Nigel called from the carrier, 'Get your backs into it, or do you want a young 'un there with you?'

'Shut up,' Mick and Ben called, wiping the mud from their faces.

They reached Derna too late for the action but the British tanks had arrived in time, and now there was only desolation to greet the Australians. There were only burnt-out tanks, the smell of death. Nigel fell quiet, Ben remembered the trenches, and Mick said, 'Did I tell you the billiard hall had been rebuilt?'

Ben nodded.

The battalion regrouped and returned to the camp near Alexandria. They set up their tent, brewed tea on the billy, cooked up stew on the saucepan and breathed in the smell of the canvas at night.

Within a few weeks they were on a rusty old freighter bound for Greece, and Ben and Mick groaned as the ship lurched and tossed on the fourth night in a storm that wiped even the smile off Nigel's face. But it kept away the bombers which had bombarded them every night since they had sailed, and for once there were no funerals, no bodies to be consigned to the deep at sunrise, no bugle notes to float across the waters.

They landed at Piraeus and were ordered to a staging camp set amongst pine trees at Daphne. 'It's just like the hills around Perth,' Mick said. 'Just look at the flowers. Sylvie would love them.'

Ben remembered the geraniums Cait had grown, the sweet-smelling stocks. The flowers in the hotel. He turned away from the beauty and the scent, and instead looked at the sky, and breathed in the scent of the pines.

Within a few days they had loaded their carriers

onto flat rail cars and travelled north through the hills, and the flowers were vibrant and alive. 'How many of us will be left when this is over?' Nigel murmured.

'All of us,' Mick insisted, punching him lightly on his arm. 'Or I'll murder the lot of you.'

The troops unloaded the carriers and drove them to HQ at the foot of Mount Olympus, but at dawn the alarm sounded and they moved out, hurrying, shouting, clinging to the carriers as they tore down the track, following one another, coughing as the dust caught them. 'Why don't we ever get used to it?' Nigel groaned.

The *Luftwaffe* bombed the village where they had been, they bombed them wherever they went. Their heads ached with the noise, and with the fear, and with the rage. They were pushed back through Larisa and Lamia. The Stukas dive bombed them at Thermopylae-Thermplylae Pass. The ground shuddered, shrapnel flew.

'Keep going,' the officer ordered, waving their carrier forward. 'We're evacuating. Follow the others. There'll be ships.' Nigel hunched over the wheel, his head down, dodging the potholes, cursing.

'Your mother wouldn't care for that language.' Ben laughed, ducking as a bomb exploded.

'I don't care for this,' Nigel retorted.

They were over the pass. They were ordered to sweep the area. The Bren gun seemed heavy to Ben, the webbing strap dug into his shoulder. 'I'm too old for this,' he murmured to Mick at his side.

'I'm just deciding I'm Irish and therefore neutral after all,' Mick replied. They laughed softly.

The Company forced their carriers up and down the narrow road, not looking at those burnt out at the side of the track. The Germans were close behind, the bombers were over them. The ships evacuating them were a mile away. 'Come on, come on,' urged Nigel.

They made it, but only set off for the ships and climbed up the rope nets slung over the side after they had destroyed the engine of their carrier. Nigel sat slumped next to them on the corner of the deck. 'It was like shooting a horse,' he said quietly.

Mick sat back against the bulkhead, looking at his hands. 'We ran away, our tails between our legs.'

Ben eased his neck. 'To fight another day.' But defeat tasted sour.

The Stukas found them and screamed into the dive. The Royal Navy destroyers fired back. Defeat was replaced by fear again. They survived and landed at Suda Bay, in Crete.

'What's the point?' Mick said quietly to Ben. 'We'll only destroy this too.'

Ben jerked his head towards the officer. 'They think the Germans are coming in by parachute. We're here to stop them.'

Nigel said, 'We're here to march, from what I heard.'

They did march, all day, until their heels were raw, and they cursed the Germans, and the tracks, and the whole God-damned world, and that night they crushed leaves from the Eucalyptus trees which grew all around, and lay on them, but sleep still didn't come. 'Just for once you're right, Ben,' Mick groaned as dawn came. 'We're too damned old.'

They marched all day until they reached the airstrip they were to defend, lying on their bellies beneath the olive trees, and it was from here they saw the paratroopers dropping from the sky miles to their left, then more to their right, and some far distant.

They marched again, hearing the firing, finding their men, supporting them, helping to hold back the Germans. 'There's no damn front line,' Ben panted, reloading. 'They're all over the place.' He fired until his Bren was hot.

There were cries and shouts and screams. Nigel flung him more ammunition, then reloaded his own Bren. 'You all right?' Ben shouted over the firing.

Nigel was white, he looked to his left where Sid Burrows lay. Flies buzzed. He threw stones at them. Ben shouted over his shoulder. 'Leave it. Get firing.'

It was hot, they were thirsty. There was no time to drink, no time to think, to feel fear, even when the Germans broke through, and they fled across the boulders, leaping, running, skidding. 'We've left Sid,' Nigel shouted at Ben.

'We had to.'

Nigel said, 'Don't leave me if . . .'

Ben grinned. 'We won't have to. You've got those girls to think of.'

They ran on, regrouped under an officer, stood their ground, acting as rearguard for the rest. Then retreating as others acted as rearguard for them.

They toiled across the island in the heat and the noise, their ammunition gone, but their Brens still in their hands. 'No bloody German's getting this,' Mick panted.

The firing behind them had stopped. 'Keep going,' the officer called. 'Ships are at Sfakia to take us off.'

'This is getting to be a habit,' Ben muttered.

The bombers came then, firing from the rear turrets, the bullets kicking up the dust, tearing into the rocks, the dirt, the trees and shrubs. Nigel screamed. Ben turned, and then bullets tore into his own leg. He groaned and fell. He lay, his face in the dirt, seeing sparks, as bullets struck the boulder ahead, hearing Nigel. He tried to crawl. He couldn't. Nigel stopped screaming.

Ben lifted his head slowly. It was so heavy. He dragged his gaze around. Where was the boy? There, by the rocks. Motionless. Flies buzzed. Ben dug down with his elbows, trying to heave himself forward again, but Mick was already crawling across the space. He

432

reached out, touched Nigel's neck, feeling for the pulse. He looked at Ben and shook his head.

The planes were still firing, their shadows huge as they crossed and recrossed between the sun and the earth, their engines tearing and roaring, bullets were still striking sparks off the rocks, and the dirt from the ground, and blood from bodies. Ben watched as Mick closed Nigel's eyes, stroked his hair, straightened his jacket, and lay with him, beating off the flies, until they were ordered to move out.

Mick came to Ben then and began to strap his leg. 'Leave me,' Ben ordered. 'I can't walk. Leave me.'

Men straggled past them, some supporting others. 'Leave me,' Ben insisted, pain tearing at him. Mick ignored him, finished, then hacked at a branch of a sapling and thrust it into Ben's hand. He collected Nigel's identity disc and his Bren, throwing it to a Corporal who was shouting, 'Come on, get going. D'you want the Krauts to get you?'

Mick shouted, 'Take this, don't let the lad's gun be taken by the buggers.' He hauled Ben to his feet. 'And you stop being so bloody noble. You're coming back with me.' Mick's face was set.

Ben struggled. 'I'll stay. You can't take me. Just do as you're told for once. That's an order.' He fell to the ground and groaned with pain. His bandages were bloodstained already.

Mick wrenched Ben's Bren off his shoulder, and smashed it on the rocks. 'Now you're a few pounds lighter, and you'll be ten pounds lighter than that in a moment, when I knock your block off. You should know better than to give me orders. Now give us your hand.'

He hauled Ben up, and together they stumbled on, hour after hour, beneath a beating sun until they arrived at Sfakia. They ignored the assembly point for the evacuation in the valley, and struggled to the beachhead, and neither man knew how he could still

433

put one foot in front of the other.

Men were embarking silently, their shoulders slumped. There were the clinks of guns on water canteens, the shuffle of boots on the pebbles.

Mick found a medic and pulled him round to face Ben. 'He needs a stretcher. Get him sorted *now*.' His voice was cracked, his lips barely moved. The medic called for a stretcher. Mick eased Ben down onto it, and all Ben could hear was the roaring in his head which had grown louder with every step, and all he could feel was the pain, and all he could see was Nigel.

Mick crouched beside him and poured what was left of his water into Ben's mouth, a trickle at a time. Ben looked at him, then gripped his hand. He whispered, 'Damn fool, that's what you are.' He tailed off, his eyes closed. A sergeant shouted at Mick to back off. Mick tried to withdraw his hand. Ben opened his eyes and held him, saying, 'You were right, better the devil you know – so you'd better come home safely.' Their eyes met. They smiled at one another, and both of them nodded.

'I'll be back, you old bugger,' Mick said softly.

'Make sure you are,' Ben murmured.

Mick didn't join the ship with Ben, he trudged back to the assembly point and waited to be ordered forward to the beachhead. Two days later the Germans landed mortar shells at each end of the valley and sealed off the troops. In June 1941 the senior British officer surrendered.

Cait sponged Sam as he lay in the hotel room at the back of the main building. He shook uncontrollably. Mrs Harvey asked, 'What did the doc say?'

Cait wrung the flannel out, and tucked the sheets around the old man. She shook her head. 'He's too weak, and the malaria won't break.'

Mrs Harvey leaned back against the door post.

'Rose will wish she'd been here.'

'It's as well she isn't,' Cait said crisply. 'Death is never pleasant.'

They heard the phone ringing. Mrs Harvey said, 'I'll take over, you answer that. You've been here since closing-time last night, you've not even come out for lunch.'

'I'll stay. You see to the phone, and if it's Villas again, tell him I will not come to Darwin and run his damn hostel, even if it is June and the weather is lovely. Tell him it's lovely here too.'

Mrs Harvey looked at her. 'It would be good for Rose. She could go to college.'

Cait shouted at her, 'I've told you before. She doesn't need college. If it wasn't for this damn war we'd be in Ireland by now. She can train there. Until then I need her here, do you understand?' Her voice was almost a scream. Sam groaned. Mrs Harvey left, slopping across the yard, shaking her hair. 'And get your roots done,' Cait yelled, then pressed her hand to her mouth. Oh God, when was she ever going to get home.

She moved to the doorway, folding her arms across her chest. It was years since she had seen Ben. He was probably married by now. Could he remarry without finding her? What did it matter? All she knew was that he would be living his life, glad that he was free of them.

At the end of the day Rose cycled back from the picnic, with Mrs Fail's children racing ahead, their hair streaming out behind them. 'Put your hats on,' she called, as they swept out from the bush, past the aboriginals who were selling pegs. 'Try the hotel,' she called to them. The children braked to a stop in front of their house, their bikes skidding and slewing, their laughter ringing out in the still, dense heat.

Mrs Fail came out onto her veranda as the children

ran up the path. The fly-door banged behind her. She waved at Rose as she dismounted from her bike, shading her eyes with her hand. 'You'd better get straight on back, Rose. But you'll have missed the funeral. Sam died at two this afternoon. He'll be well under by now, 'cause of the heat. Pauper's burial, I suspect.'

Rose didn't understand for a moment, she just looked at Mrs Fail, who smiled kindly. 'Poor old devil, he didn't have much of a life, not much of a death either.'

Rose pumped the pedals, heedless of the heat, towards the hotel, leaping off the bike, throwing it down, running up the path, pounding up the steps of the veranda. Her mother sat in the rocking-chair she had rescued from the dump and done up. She was hemming napkins. Rose snatched the napkin from her, throwing it to the floor. The needle flashed as it fell. Cait threw out her hands, then looked in amazement at Rose.

'What on earth is the matter with you?'

Rose pointed at the chair. 'That's what's the matter with me. You'll spend money on that, and books of poetry, and stories about Ireland, but you won't spend money on an old man's funeral. I suppose he was alone when he died and when he was buried because I wasn't here, because I was taking some stupid kids on a picnic. Which was because you told their mother I would. We've all got to do as you say, haven't we? None of us can choose what we want. We can only have it, if it satisfies you.' She was gasping for breath, her fists were clenched, she wanted to hit her mother, pound her body with these hands.

The priest spoke from the doorway then. 'Come now, Rose. Your mother made sure he had a proper box, and that there was a proper service. You're overwrought. It's the heat. Come now.' He tried to lead her to the kitchen.

She wrenched away from him, and ran off to the

cemetery, dodging beneath the leaves of the gum, the stripped bark crackling beneath her feet. There was a new grave at the back, the red earth heaped high. There was a wooden cross, and wild flowers in a tin.

Rose stooped and picked up some of the earth, crumbling it, watching it fall. 'I haven't got much of a life either, Sam, and I can't tell her, like you told me I should. I can't tell her I want to go to Darwin. I can't tell her I don't want to go to Ireland.'

When she trailed back to the hotel the sun was down, the mosquitoes were biting. She slapped at them as she climbed the back veranda steps. Fred was pulling at the punkah rope. Her mother was at the stove. Rose stood by the table, enjoying the breeze. Insects fluttered at the lights. She said, 'I'm sorry, Mother. I know you were up with him all last night. I just forgot.'

Cait spun round. She wanted to hold her daughter, to tell her that she loved her, but Rose was so distant, so aloof, and had been for so long now, that she hesitated. Then Rose asked, nodding at the saucepan which was bubbling with chilli, a dish her mother cooked when travellers stayed, 'Who's in tonight?'

The moment passed, and Cait whipped a tea towel off the airer. 'A boy, Luke, and his father, Mr Patrick Prover. They had a lift up from Alice Springs and are waiting for the train to take them on to Darwin. I've explained that they'll have to wait a couple of nights, but they're happy with that. The boy's got work with one of the contracts to up-grade the port facilities. It's the war panic.' She lowered her voice. 'I'll dish up, then would you take in the chilli? There's something wrong with the boy. I think he's deaf.'

Rose picked up the plates heaped with rice and chilli. Steam rose.

Cait said, as she walked from the room, 'I stayed with him until he died. He wasn't alone.'

Rose continued to walk. 'Thank you, Mother.' How civilized they both were.

In the corridor the breeze was still pleasant, the punkahs were flapping, the low walls allowed the breeze to circulate. The men in the bar were talking and laughing. Mrs Harvey waved at her. Rose smiled back. A young ringer grinned. His name was Pete. He wanted to go into the Army but one leg was shorter than the other, though that didn't affect his dancing. She had danced with him at the last party, but her mother had called her to help with the scones. Rose sighed, and entered the dining-room.

In the centre of the room sat a grey-haired, dark-eyed man, with deep lines running from his eyes. He was leaning forward, talking to his son. Rose stopped. This was no boy. He was the most beautiful blond man, with wide shoulders and blue eyes the same colour as her mother's, and therefore darker than hers.

The son looked up and smiled, and she no longer heard the insects, or noticed the heat, or the breeze, or anything but him. The father turned. 'Excellent. We're so hungry we could eat a horse.'

Rose blushed and became aware of the food cooling on the plates.

The distance to the table seemed immense. The boy smiled. The breath caught in her throat. She placed the food before them. 'I'm sorry, I hope it's still hot,' she shouted at them.

Mr Prover laughed as Luke wrote something on a pad. He held it up. *Save your voice, I'm unable to speak, but I can hear perfectly.*

Rose blushed again. 'I'm sorry.'

Luke wrote. She heard the pen scratching on the paper. He held it up. His fingers were long, his hands strong. *Please, do me a favour, and stop apologizing.*

She blushed even more, smiled, and turned away. Mr Prover called her back.

'What is there to do around here? We're having a look around the country before Luke begins in Darwin. He's got some labouring contract work on the defences – there's a bit of a flap on about the Japs and how far they intend to go. But don't get me on to that. It's all too worrying. He's seventeen and it seems a bit young. Anyway, he feels he wants to do his bit, even if it is only helping to build up the harbour. He really wants to fight, but they won't have him.'

She spoke to Mr Prover, but was only aware of Luke. 'There are the mines, there's the creek, a mile or so out. It's got a pool you can swim in. There's the bush for picnics. You'll see Katherine on your way to Darwin, so don't bother with that. And don't bother about the Japs. They won't come to Australia. And I'm seventeen too. I've just had my birthday. It was in December.'

Luke was signing to his father. Mr Prover watched, nodded, and signed back, then smiled, his face warm, one eyebrow lifted. He said to Rose, 'In this heat all this young man wants to do is slip into water, and eat a picnic in the shade of gum-trees. And he's a month older than you.'

Rose laughed. 'We'll make you up a cut lunch, and point you in the right direction.'

Mr Prover shook his head. 'Two lads from the bush could easily get lost, get hot and tired, and never even find the pool. How about taking us? Would your mother mind? Luke's just about sick, sore and tired of listening to my voice.'

Cait waved them off from the veranda, laughing as Mr Prover wobbled on the bicycle, then gathered speed. Rose was over her sulk, and it was an excellent idea to take the Provers out. It would take the girl's mind off Darwin and settle her down again. After all, the war wouldn't last for ever.

As they rode away she thought again of the bombing raids on Dublin. Didn't neutrality mean anything to the Germans? Was anyone she knew hurt? She'd find out when they went back.

Rose led the way down the steep incline to the pool. The creek had been dammed. The two men slipped and slid behind her. 'Careful with the lunch,' Mr Prover called to Luke.

'D'you like cheese sandwiches?' she called back to Luke. Then put her hand to her mouth. 'Oh, I'm sorry.' She had forgotten he couldn't answer.

Mr Prover caught up with her. 'Don't be. It takes time to get used to it. It took us a while when we found out – he has a malformed larynx – but it worked out all right.'

The pool was glistening beneath the gums at the base of the hill. It was shadowed by the rocks which rose around it. 'Oh, that looks so good,' Mr Prover panted. 'It's so humid here, much worse than Margaret River.'

'Where's that?' Rose asked as she climbed over the boulders leading up to the pool. They were on flat ground now, and out of the direct sun. It was a place she loved to come.

'South of Perth. We're farmers there.'

Rose put her towel down on a flat rock. 'I usually change over there.' She pointed to an overhang and blushed. She'd never blushed so much in her life as she had done this past few hours. She felt clumsy as she walked towards the shelter. She'd have to come out in her swimsuit, in front of Luke. He'd see her bare arms and legs. Only her girlfriends had seen her swim, or her mother, or her mother's friends.

Her fingers felt stiff as she removed her clothes, and pulled on her swimsuit, and then she heard a splash, and then another, and then the echoing voice of Mr Prover. Relief swamped her. They were in, they wouldn't be looking as she came to the water. She ran down to the creek and waded in.

They swam together, ducking and diving, but it was only her voice and Mr Prover's whooping and laughing and shouting, and suddenly the strangeness of Luke's silence overwhelmed her, and she swam off alone.

Luke started to chase her, but Pat Prover called him back. 'Leave her, for now.'

He saw a shadow sweep over his son's face, and felt sorrow turn his heart. It was a familiar ache for him, and Deborah his wife, and one which twisted and stabbed even more now, as they thought of Luke's manhood.

Rose swam to the edge and clambered out, balancing on the submerged stones, which hurt her feet. 'Ouch.'

Could he say 'ouch'?

She wished he would say, 'Come and walk with me.'

She stood on the edge, drying her hair. It lifted in the breeze. She heard Mr Prover shout to Luke, 'Time we were getting out, I'm hungry.' She fled to the overhang and dressed, taking her time, waiting until she heard them leave the water and dress. Only then did she emerge, and lay out the lunch.

They ate in the shade, gazing at the water, talking a little. She poured tea from the flask. Milk floated in blobs on the surface. She tipped her cup backwards and forwards, watching them move. She heard snores and looked across. Mr Prover was lying on the ground, his hat over his face. Luke smiled at her, and she smiled back, and all the awkwardness disappeared as their eyes held for what seemed like a lifetime.

They turned away and gazed out over the pool. The water trickled through the dam. Luke wrote. *I*

441

learned to swim in a pool like this, with my father, and my friend Jimmie.

She said, 'My father taught my mother and me in a river.' Her voice broke. 'I'm sorry, I haven't talked of him for so long.'

She heard the scratch of his pen again. *Is he dead?*

'Sort of.' She looked back at the pool.

That night, after the train had arrived, Shirley's father played his accordion at the party, and Rose handed out raspberry drinks to the children, and everything was as it had always been, but everything was different, because Luke sat on the veranda steps, and his eyes were on her, and then he rose, walked towards her, took the tray from her and danced with her. This time her mother did not call her over.

Cait had said earlier, 'Be kind to the boy, he's handicapped.'

As Rose danced there was, to her, no handicap. There were just his fine eyes, his firm lips, his hair which gleamed golden in the light. There was just the feel of her hand in his, the strength of his body next to hers. It didn't matter that he had no voice to murmur to her, because his eyes said everything.

When the music ended, they walked back to the steps, side by side, their hands touching, separating, touching. They sat, and she felt the warmth of his arm against hers. She said, 'You are lucky to be going to Darwin. It's not very far away though.'

He nodded, and signed to her. She couldn't understand. He wrote.

Perhaps one day you can come to see me. You said at the pool you wanted to learn shorthand and typing.

Her laugh was bitter. 'The only place I will be going to is Ireland.'

His face clouded. *Is that what you want?*

'No, I want a job. I want to go to Darwin, now

more than ever.' She blushed again. He touched her arm with his finger, so lightly, so gently.

Well, learn to sign. I did. Learn shorthand from a book. Learn to type.

The accordion was playing again. Mrs Fail's children were calling to her.

'How can I? I need a typewriter.'

How can you not? Find a machine. Someone must have one.

She watched them leave the next day, though she didn't go to the station to see them off. It would have been too much. That night she lay in the sleep-out and kissed her hand, where he had touched it. She kissed her arm which his finger had stroked.

When the train came at the end of the week, she and Mrs Harvey took the cart to the station to collect the large bottles of beer which were packed in wooden cases. The guard dumped them at their feet, and she and Mrs Harvey heaved them into the cart.

'Does wonders for my figure,' Mrs Harvey said.

The guard came up to them as they heaved up the last one. 'Good timing, Joe,' Mrs Harvey laughed.

'Just you get those back and get them covered with wet bags. I want a cool drink when I'm done with this lot.' He pushed back his cap. 'Seems to me we'll all need a drink soon, if them Japs get a mite more restless out Indochina way. We're sitting ducks, you know. Darwin's too damn close. Mark you,' he nodded at Rose, 'your mum should be thinking of taking up Villas' offer to run the boarding-house in Darwin. It's brimming with workers, let alone soldiers. And while I think of it, some dumb kid gave me this to give to you.' He pressed a shorthand book into Rose's hand. 'And here's another.' It was a typing book.

She took it, and said coldly, 'Don't call him dumb. He just can't speak.' She clambered onto the cart.

443

Mrs Harvey pulled a face at Joe, and climbed up beside Rose, who flicked the reins. As the cart started moving, Rose asked, 'How long has my mother known she could have a job in Darwin?'

Mrs Harvey thought for a moment, but what was the good of pretending? She said, 'Two years.'

That evening Rose asked the vicar if she could use his typewriter every evening to practise on. He agreed. When she had finished on the typewriter she returned to the sleep-out and learned shorthand signs.

At the next party she danced with the young ringer who limped, and with Len, the ringer her mother hated. She danced and danced until her mother sent Mrs Harvey over. Then Rose whispered to Len, and pressed her body against him. And when she had finished handing out the raspberry drinks and scones, and was supposed to be washing the dishes, she slipped out to the stables.

Len was there, in the shadows, and now the party and the lights seemed far away as she stood near the bridle rack. He said, 'I'm glad you wanted to meet me here. I like your hair. You should wear it loose. It'd look good falling down against your skin.' He pointed to her breasts.

Suddenly her rage at her mother evaporated and fear took its place. He was so old, his lips were wet, he was rubbing his crotch. She backed into the door-frame. What was she doing here? Was she mad?

She said, 'I was stupid. I was using you. I wanted to make her mad. I'm sorry. I want to go now.'

She turned. He moved quickly, catching her hand. His breath was heavy with beer. 'One kiss, that's all I want. One kiss from the bitch's daughter. One kiss, and I'll die happy.'

He was pulling her towards him, his hand was in her hair. She pushed away. He caught her again, pulling her close. She could feel his paunch against

444

her. 'Please,' she said. 'Please let me go. I'm sorry. I shouldn't have asked you here. Please.'

His face was close. 'Little girls shouldn't try and use big boys.' His breath was all over her face, in her nose. She fought, he laughed.

Then she heard her mother's voice, loud and fierce. 'Take your hands off my daughter.' He stepped back. Cait rushed at him, hitting him with the broom, and again. He grabbed it, threw it away, advancing on both women. Rose shrank against the stable door. Cait shielded her. 'Get away, go and sober up.'

They heard the sound of running. The young ringer limped past Rose, knocking her out of the way. He grabbed the older man, holding him in a bear hug. Len was shouting, 'Let me at the silly bitches.'

The young ringer dragged Len out of the stable, cursing Rose as he did so. 'You stupid kid. You don't play games, not out here.'

Straw and hay were flying about. She heard her mother's breathing. Her legs were trembling. Her mother pulled her away from the wall. Rose flinched. Cait dropped her arms. 'Why?'

Rose said, 'Because I'm lonely. I want to learn. I want to go to Darwin, and we could, but you won't, and it's not fair to ask you to.'

Cait whispered, 'But why this? Why Len?'

Rose shook her head. She was trembling from head to foot. 'I wanted to hurt you because we could have gone two years ago. But I love you too. Oh Mum. I don't know what's wrong with me. I should be happy here, but I'm not, and you're not, and I don't know what I want, and there's this great gap, and this darkness, and this longing.'

Cait held her now, stroking her daughter's hair, and that night she rang Villas in Darwin. After all, the extra money could go towards a farm in Killarney if her father refused to have them back.

Chapter Twenty-Two

Ben struggled across the sitting-room of Old Roy's apartment at the Bondi Beach Hotel and winced as the crutches rubbed his armpits. 'Damn things,' he muttered, but then he caught sight of Mick's letter and grinned. Thank God he was safe, for now at any rate. He'd escaped from Crete with a couple of other men, and was in Syria, but he was champing to be home. They were all anxious about Australia, Mick had written, with the Japs on the move in the Far East.

Ben reached the veranda, and felt the blast of the hot sea breeze as he looked out across the bay. The light was so vivid. He lowered himself into the creaking cane chair. Old Roy came into the apartment and across the room, carrying a tray of coffee. Ben said as Roy settled himself into the other chair and poured the coffee, 'He's worried about the Japs.'

Roy passed him his coffee. 'He's not the only one.' He picked up his paper and shook it out. 'War's not going well for anyone, except the Axis. We need the US in the war, but there's no way they'll get involved unless they're attacked, and who's going to be daft enough to do that.'

Ben rested his head back against the chair, and gazed across to the horizon. The sea was a deep blue, almost the colour of an Irish summer sky.

Roy said, 'They're sending some of your mob up to Darwin, aren't they?'

Ben nodded and pointed to his leg. 'When this is better that's where they'll send me.'

Mr Villas led Cait and Rose towards the bamboo house on stilts. He mopped his brow and his sweat-rotted shirt tore beneath the arm. Cait and Rose exchanged a look. Mr Villas called as they followed him along the path, 'I am dirty and hot. Forgive me. We have been busy packing all yesterday and all today. Then I came here to dust and I am not so good with a duster.'

He laughed, waved his hands, his handkerchief fluttered. They laughed as they followed him up the steps. He moved heavily and slumped into a chair on the veranda, gesturing to them to do the same. They did, and gazed out across the palms in the garden and then up to the bright sky over the sea.

'You will find this more comfortable than those.' He pointed to the houses in the street which were at ground level. 'This is built of a pine which leaves the termites scratching their heads and feeling hungry, and angry.' He rubbed his huge stomach. 'But then, that is how I feel when my wife does not let me have my puddings.' He laughed again and his stomach wobbled.

'Now, Mrs Adams. I have lodgers in the buildings at the back, and there are more coming on Monday. This alarm over the Japanese has been good for business. The Government bring in workers to help sort out the defences and to build housing for the troops, and housing for the workers, and so it goes on, so pouff – we are in big business. The Japs will not come here, but we shall not tell the Government. We shall just count our money.' He laughed again.

'You are leaving this morning?'

Mr Villas nodded. 'My wife, she insists. It is the dengue fever. I have lost a stone in two months. I

447

say, "I must drink a pint of beer a day to stop it." She says, "Over my dead body." So she takes me away instead.' He shrugged his shoulders and Cait looked at his stomach and wondered how big it had once been. Rose caught her eye, and they grinned.

His face was running with sweat as he gestured to the bamboo hoppers propped open with rods of timber. 'You will find these windows are very good. You can close them quickly in the rain, but keep them open otherwise and let the air circulate. The huts at the back are of corrugated iron and are hotter. But this is war, Mrs Adams.' He spread his hands.

Cait said, 'And the other matter?'

He was panting, his stomach was straining against his shirt which was stained with sweat all over now. 'Yes, I have checked out the shorthand and typing teacher. You start the course tomorrow, young lady.'

Rose looked at him, confused. He said, 'This teacher is very good. She will have you good enough to go out to work by December.'

Rose shook her head in amazement. 'Oh, Mr Villas, you are so kind. How did you know?'

He shrugged, and smiled. 'Your mother, of course. She found out the name of this lady from a friend, and I fix the rest.'

Rose swung round to Cait. 'A friend – Shirley?'

'Shirley's just this minute moved to Sydney, like the others did. No, I cabled Luke. He found her for me. Mr Villas did the rest. There were no intensive courses so Mrs Halliday will teach you. Then you're out in an office, doing your bit.' Cait smiled as Rose kissed her cheek. 'Luke will be round later, to show us the town, but first we have to clean this house, and the rooms, madam.'

Her daughter glowed, and Cait knew that it was of Luke that she was thinking. Well, let it be. There could be no future in that match. With his handicap the excitement would soon wear off for Rose, but it would keep her out of harm's way in the mean time.

Mr Villas wagged his finger at them both. 'You must be careful and not go out alone after dusk. There are a great many soldiers, and fewer and fewer women. They are worried, so they leave, it is so silly.' He winked at Rose. 'If you are looking for a husband, you have come to the right place.'

Cait said coldly, 'She is not looking for a husband.'

Rose heard neither of them because she was thinking of Luke, his blond hair, his blue eyes, his kindness. His body.

That afternoon they mopped the polished floor of the house, damped down the dust, shook out the linen, and Rose hummed as she did so, and counted the minutes until he would come. She couldn't eat her meal but instead pushed her salad round and round the plate. She said, 'I'm too hot. I'll go onto the veranda.'

She sat on the bamboo chair, looking at the frangipani, and the bougainvillaea. Soon there would be a sunset which would roar across the sky, slashing red and orange in great sweeps, or so Mr Villas had said as he left, suddenly ashen. 'I love the Northern Territory. It is my home. I do not want to leave for Perth.'

Her mother had said, 'Ireland is our home.'

Rose looked back down the road again. What should Luke's voice be like? Like Mr Prover's perhaps. She wished she could hear him call as he ran along the street towards her when he came this evening. She wished she could hear the joy in his voice. Would there be joy? She looked at her hands. They were so rough from the cleaning. She checked the road again. She had time.

She ran inside, put cream on her hands, rubbing them together as she ran back out, and there he was, coming up the path. She rushed down the steps. 'Luke, Luke.'

449

He smiled and mouthed, 'Hallo.' He signed, 'Hallo.' There was joy in the gesture, and in his face, and what need was there of words? He reached for her hands. They slid from his grasp. She blushed, stepped back, hiding them behind her back. 'Oh, I'm sorry. It's just cream, not sweat.'

He shook his head, and his eyes creased in mock annoyance. He reached out, pulled her hands from behind her back, held them, kissed them, looking into her eyes, then he dropped her hands, took out his pad and wrote. *When will you stop saying sorry?*

Cait watched them from the doorway, and her heart twisted at the love in Luke's eyes. Poor boy, he couldn't expect any girl to marry him – he must know it couldn't last. She picked up Rose's hat from the chair.

She came down the steps, handing the hat to Rose, holding out her hand to Luke. 'I'm so glad to see you, and thank you for finding Mrs Halliday, and now you're going to show us Darwin. You're very kind to give us your time.'

Luke and Rose exchanged glances and smiled at one another. Rose knew that he was thinking, as she was, that it was love, not kindness, for both of them.

They walked along the esplanade and saw the ships in the harbour, and the defences around it, and as the sun sank they saw the sunset that Mr Villas had promised, and stood silently as the sky caught fire over the limpid sea. The ships – so many of them – seemed aglow.

The breeze clutched at Cait's dress, and the beauty at her heart. Rose stood beside her, with Luke. His fingers touched hers. She put her hand in his and felt the warmth of him. She could hardly breathe because he was so close. She felt weak with love, and longing.

When darkness had come they walked further, past sweet-scented gardens and, in time, a library, and then the stilted Returned Soldiers and Sailors League Clubroom. They laughed at the mountain of empty bottles beneath, but Cait was conscious only of hearing the sound of her daughter's laugh, and her own.

He pointed out the Don Hotel and wrote beneath the moonlight, *Where Asiatics and wharfies go to protect themselves against dengue fever!* Again there was laughter.

He showed them the Hotel Darwin: *The posh hotel for the tourists and overseas visitors, and the local public servants' watering hole.* This time Rose and Cait just looked at one another and remembered other hotels, other nightmares, and for them the fun was gone, as surely as the day was gone.

He showed them the Chinese quarter. *You must get dresses made for your journey away from here. Because the Japanese might come, and you should go.*

Rose said, 'We won't go, will we, Mum? Because they won't come. Mr Villas said so.'

He pointed out the street they must not go down. *It is for the ladies of the night.*

Now Cait fell silent because Kalgoorlie was here again, and the memory of Ben, and of Roy, and the smell of the tent as he tended her, and she longed to write to her old friend, but dare not.

They began to walk back to the house with Luke, who refused to allow them to walk alone, nodding at the troops.

At the house, in the dim light of the sitting-room he wrote, *In the morning shall I show you where your teacher, Mrs Halliday, lives? We could have sandwiches on the esplanade at lunch-time. I could walk you home afterwards. It would be safer with all the soldiers about.*

Cait nodded to Rose. 'That would be a good idea.' Yes, it would keep her safe from temptation.

Rose worked hard all the next morning, and her hand smudged the pencil all over the paper, because of the heat.

Old Mrs Halliday sat across from her at the table, her half-moon glasses sliding down her nose, fanning herself as she dictated. 'You can tell why they call these the suicide months.'

Rose could.

Mrs Halliday corrected her transcription and praised her. 'My dear, you've done so well whilst working on your own that you could find employment in November, I'm quite sure.'

At lunch-time, as she sat on a wall looking out over the esplanade with Luke, she told him this. He put down his sandwiches and wrote, *A clerk in the boss's office is leaving soon. As you should. But if you don't I'll see if you can take the job. They're desperate for staff.*

She put down her sandwiches, wiping her hand on her handkerchief saying, 'Sign that. I want to hear you talk to me. Make me understand you.'

He smiled at her and put out his hand and touched her cheek, her lips. She pressed his hand to her mouth and kissed it, then leaned forward and pressed her lips to his, and she didn't care that the troops and the workers whistled and catcalled. All she knew was that his lips were soft, and her body was on fire, and she wanted to merge into him, and be him.

Luke returned her kiss again and again, and her lips were sweet, and her hair, which he wound round his hands, was thick and red, and his body was on fire, and he wanted to merge into her, and be her.

She pulled away and traced the line of his mouth. 'Now talk to me,' she insisted.

He put up his hand. 'Wait,' he mouthed, and also signed. He wrote out for her the etiquette of signing, the starting of a conversation, keeping it going, taking your turn, interrupting and ending, showing her as he did so. He wrote, at the end, *Soon you will be able to paint pictures in the air.*

He began to teach her, and the sandwiches were forgotten, and work too nearly, but a mate called out, 'Come on, Luke. You'll get the sack.'

She ran back to Mrs Halliday's in spite of the heat, and all afternoon she pounded on the typewriter until her fingers were sore, and then worked on her shorthand in the evening, and on her signing. Cait watched as she knitted, and her hands sweated on the wool, and it stuck to the needles until she cast them aside.

'That's enough,' she shouted at last.

Rose looked up in surprise.

Cait said more gently, 'We're both tired. Time for bed.'

Cait fed the lodgers out on the back veranda, and the heat soared as October became November and the clerk left for Adelaide. Mrs Halliday wrote Rose a reference which she showed Cait that night.

'I can work now, Mum. I can help with the money. Luke's got me a job at the wharf. The sub-contractor needs help.'

Cait looked out of the window at the glazed sky. 'We should leave.'

'We're needed here. We're both earning money too. Besides, where would we go? We have no home.'

'We have Ireland,' Cait murmured almost in a whisper.

'Oh Mum, we can't travel there in the war.'

Cait shook herself, then pointed towards the harbour. 'They're digging trenches in the town. More troops are piling in.'

'No-one's telling us to go, so I'm not, that's that.'

'There's talk of a Japanese fleet sailing south of Formosa,' Cait snapped.

'There's always talk.'

'We'll stay for a while longer then,' Cait agreed, because Rose was right. Where could they go?

Rose began work and now she saw Luke every morning and every lunch-time, and he walked her home after work, and it was as though no-one else existed. It was as though there had never been another time for them, never any other place. As November wore on, and the heat became almost unbearable, her understanding of signing improved, and she heard him tell of his life in the South-West of Western Australia, of his farm, of the Group Settlers who had been conned into coming from Britain by advertisements placed by the West Australian government which told of the land of milk and honey, and dairy farms, only to find they did not exist.

'They were our neighbours. There are hardly any left. There were no farms, just forests, sour earth, poor equipment, debt, illness. The British government would not help them return home. They left them here. There was fun too, though. They were very brave. There were dances at the school house, and I learned to track with Jimmie.'

He told her of Jimmie, the half aboriginal who had returned from Broome to his tribal area on which the Prover farm rested. He told of how Jimmie had worked with the Provers, how he had guided them, how he had called himself a mute, because he was the last of his tribe, and how, as Luke was also a mute, Luke was the only one who could share in his tribal lore. 'He made me feel special. He made me feel as though it did not matter, to have no voice. He has his own farm now.'

He told her how Jimmie had shown Deborah, his mother, the boronia valley. 'Boronia flowers smell so sweet. I will show you one day.'

He told of his grandmother, old Mrs Prover, who had refused to see them after his father left Lenora, his family's sheep station in Victoria, to build up his own farm in Margaret River. 'She never wrote, she would never visit. She said we were dead to her. Now she's dead, and we have a sheep station in Victoria which has a manager.'

She pointed to the wharf. 'Why didn't you go there, instead of here?'

He shrugged and signed, 'Because I must do something for my country.'

She looked at the ships which seemed to grow in number every day. Today there was one with blacked-out portholes, which was to take women and children to other parts of Australia. She said, holding his hand, not wanting him to interrupt her, 'I have a grandfather who will not speak to us. That's something we share. I have a father who will not speak to us, and the reason he won't is my fault and I've never told anyone.'

He pulled away from her in order to use his hands. 'Perhaps you would like to tell me?' he signed.

She nodded. Their eyes held. He took her hands while she told him of the day she saw her mother with the other man. Of her father who had accused her mother of a lifelong affair after Rose had reported it to him, of their bags which had been packed by him. She told him that her name was Williams, not Adams.

He signed, 'I can understand that it was not, truly, your fault. You should tell her. It is hanging over you.'

'I can't,' she replied. 'She is all I have.'

'You have me,' he signed.

'It's not the same,' she said.

That evening Luke came to eat with them, and Rose asked her mother if he could have the spare room in the lodgers' building. Cait agreed, though anger stirred. Later she said, 'How could I refuse when you asked in front of him?'

Rose shook her head. 'Why would you want to

refuse? It's more money for your fund, isn't it?' The anger was back between them, and Rose didn't know why because, up to now, her mother had welcomed Luke. It must be the weather.

The next week, as November became December, the air was bursting with pre-wet heat, and tension, and Cait prayed that the wet would come, and that the Japanese would not.

The lodgers were bad-tempered. They drank at the Don, they fought in the streets with the soldiers. More trenches were dug, more sandbags were set up round gun emplacements. Planes flew over, taking off from the RAF base outside Darwin. There seemed to be nothing to talk about, other than the Japanese. Nothing to think about, other than invasion.

On 1 December Cait bought vegetables from the Chinese trader, and ordered two dresses, and took a dress of Rose's with her to be copied, because soon they must leave.

She prepared a meal for the men, laying out the places in the kitchen, making sure that no light showed through the blackout curtains. The men came when she rang the bell, and sat round the table. Cait served, making Rose sit down and eat. 'You've been working as hard as they have.'

The men picked at the food. They poured beer they had bought themselves. It was too hot to speak, too hot to eat. Luke signed for the salt. A new lodger, Ted, said, 'For God's sake, give the dummy the salt.'

The men fell silent. Rose turned to speak. Luke gripped her arm, shaking his head. The men looked at Ted. Cait said, 'Luke Prover is my guest, my friend. If anyone is the dummy it's you, Ted Atkins. Any more of that talk and you are out of here.'

There was silence. Ted flung down his knife and fork. 'Then I'm out. I'm going for a beer.'

He stormed off, slamming the fly door shut. Cait picked up his plate, rushed to the door, and threw it out after him. 'And don't come back,' she shouted over the sound of breaking crockery. She was surprised at her anger. It was the heat. The damned heat.

She walked round the veranda and sat at the front of the house, the bamboo creaking.

The rains came, and the tension faded a little, but only a little, and Ted was still not allowed back, because of the rage that lingered in Cait and Rose. 'Luke's a nice boy,' Cait explained to herself and Rose. 'No-one should poke fun at handicapped people.'

Rose walked away, too angry to speak.

On 5 December the Australian government cancelled all Australian leave. On 10 December Japan took Guam, and sank the *Prince of Wales* and the battle cruiser *Repulse*. In Darwin there was talk of air raid practices. Cait, Rose and the men dug a slit trench across Mr Villas' garden.

'Won't he mind?' Rose panted, her hands sore. The men were cursing at the mosquitoes.

'He won't know, will he? But soon we *must* go,' Cait said, throwing out another spadeful.

Luke nodded, unable to talk because he was digging, and Cait felt irritated. For God's sake, what sort of a person couldn't talk because they were digging?

On 8 December the Japanese had bombed Pearl Harbor, and a few evenings later Cait sat in the sitting-room listening to the wireless. Australia had declared war on Japan. She thought of Darwin harbour full of Allied shipping. She thought of Mr Villas saying that war would never come to Darwin. It might. Holy Mother, it might.

Rose was talking with Luke, and now Cait could understand sign language, or some of it, enough of it, and she watched for words of love. But Luke was saying, 'You should go.'

Rose replied, 'Someone has to work.'

That night Cait lay in the humidity of the wet

457

beneath the mosquito-net, wanting sleep, wanting oblivion but then a screaming siren split the air, wailing and shrieking. She couldn't think what to do. She rushed to the window. The Japanese. Bombs. The trench was only half dug. People were streaming from their houses, running towards the beach, mothers were scooping their children up.

She flung on her shoes, grabbed a wrap. Rose burst into the room. 'Mum, Mum, what shall we do?' The noise was still there, reverberating, screaming. She couldn't think. She still couldn't think. She pulled Rose towards the door. They were out of the house, rushing down the steps. 'Run, get to the beach. Follow the others.'

'Luke's on night shift.'

'For God's sake, forget about Luke, get to the beach,' Cait screamed, running along the road, dragging Rose. Rose began to run with her now, faster, faster. The siren was rising and falling. There were others with them, searching the sky, the heat forgotten. They hurried down the esplanade cliffs. There was no moon, it was so dark. Cait stumbled. Rose pulled her to her feet. People were pushing past. Down they went to the sand below.

They crouched. Cait took off her wrap, put her arm around Rose, and tossed the wrap over them, but still the sandflies bit, and the mosquitoes too. A child near them cried. They gave him the wrap and Rose wept with fear, but it was fear for Luke.

Cait soothed her. 'Don't be frightened. It'll be all right. I'll make sure you're all right. No-one will hurt you. I won't let them.' She searched the clouded skies listening, but all she could hear were the mosquitoes droning and the sounds of fear all around them. Again and again she spoke these words, because her fear was all for her child.

Rose felt her mother's arm, heard her words of love, and though she was not safe, she felt so, just as she had done when her mother had stood between her and the ringer. But there was another time too. She tried to think as one hour passed, digging her hands into the sand, letting it fall through her fingers. There had been darkness, and fear, and then her mother had . . . What had she done?

After some hours, the all-clear sounded. The mother of the child handed back the wrap. 'I'm leaving Darwin,' the woman blurted out to Cait. 'We should all leave.'

Rose hung back because she had remembered being under the house when the cyclone came, and the weight of that veranda on her mother's back, and the calmness of her mother's voice, and the bruising and the cuts which had bled through her blouse as she cajoled Ben into rebuilding. She called, 'Mum.'

Cait stopped. Sand was in her shoes and her hair. 'Do you remember how the sand got into our picnic at Bondi?' she asked Rose, then wondered why she had dragged up the past.

Rose nodded impatiently. There was something more important she had to say. Something she owed her mother, because her mother had held up the veranda, she had made her father rebuild. She had always kept her safe. 'Do you remember too, Mum, how Dad said he knew that man had kissed you?'

People were passing them, kicking sand up, slapping at the mosquitoes. Cait could hear the waves lapping on the shore. She could smell the brine. She waited.

Rose said, 'I told him I saw you. I'm sorry, Mum. It's all been my fault.'

Cait relived that day as they stood there while the beach emptied. She could barely see her daughter in the darkness. Eventually she smiled tiredly and said, 'None of it was your fault. It was the fault of your parents, nobody else. Now come along.'

They trudged up the beach not speaking, just thinking. They climbed up the cliffs onto the esplanade. The breeze caught them, cooled them. They were too tired to hurry, and their minds too full to speak. At last Cait looked at her daughter as they turned into their garden. She said quietly, 'Would you like me to try and find your father?'

Rose had expected her to ask this and hadn't known what she would say. She did now. 'No. He rejected us once. I couldn't bear it a second time. We don't need him. We have each other.' And Luke, she thought.

Cait climbed the veranda steps and looked out across Darwin, breathing in deeply. Ben had not had her followed, and the knowledge released something in her, and she wished that Rose's answer had been different, but she was also glad that it was not, because there were still his words, so clear in her head – why should his feelings have changed?

As Christmas approached, women and children were evacuated and the few who refused to leave were cautioned that they stayed at their own risk. Rose wouldn't leave. 'I have a necessary job and you have the boarding-house, and Villas fixed it so that's essential work too.'

Luke, however, persuaded Cait to buy a second-hand Dodge from a family who were leaving, and then to buy cans of fuel wherever and however they could, as others were doing. 'Then you can escape to Mrs Harvey even if the train's knocked out, and go on from there.'

'You've forgotten one thing. I can't drive.'

Luke grinned. 'It's a straight road.'

Cait shook her head. 'But I've still got to get going, and keep going.'

The weekend before Christmas he drove with Rose and Cait along the Stuart Highway. 'Watch me,' he had signed before he started the car. Cait had watched his feet on the pedals, and his hands on the wheel, shouting at him as he took his hands away to sign, shouting at Rose when she laughed, until she herself was forced to laugh.

Luke stopped, changed places with Cait, and now her shoulders were rigid and her feet clumsy, and as they drove back towards Darwin and she looked at the gear lever instead of the road yet again, Luke's hands jabbed the air, and jabbed them again, until Cait and Rose yelled at him, 'Just stop shouting, so we can think.'

Backwards and forwards along the road they drove until at last Cait was sitting more easily in the seat, and Luke's gestures were calmer, and Rose had taken her hands from her eyes.

After Hong Kong fell at Christmas he insisted that they pack bags and leave them by the door, ready to flee at a moment's notice. He shoved the three cans of fuel in the boot. 'So you can refuel along the way.'

Now, at lunch-time Rose and he watched the troops training on the beaches at low tide, hearing their screams as they charged at sandbags. Screaming and yelling and sweating in the high humidity of the wet. The troops dug rows of slit trenches above the high-water mark. 'To protect against tanks?' Rose asked. Luke nodded.

He signed, 'You must go, my darling.'

'Not without you,' she whispered.

'What does your mother say to that?' he signed, his eyes serious and sad.

'I don't tell her. She doesn't want me to get fond of anyone because we have to go back to Ireland.'

They sat quite still, then she smiled. 'But we can't, until after the war, and that's why I'm happy.'

He kissed her. 'I love you,' he signed. She signed the same, and it was the first time that words of love had been spoken, but they had read it in one another's eyes, almost from the moment they had met.

* * *

On 12 January Kuala Lumpur fell, and a few days later Singapore was threatened. On 24 January the Rising Sun flew over Australian Territory after the Japanese landed in Australian New Guinea. In early February Singapore was invaded, and one night, over supper, after the men had come in from working on the jetty, one of them said, 'A mate of mine got out of there. They were strafed and bombed. They'd rather have died than be taken prisoner. They were told if they did surrender to head for the Japanese Navy, not the Army. Their infantry don't take prisoners, they use you for bayonet practice . . .'

Cait slammed her hand down on the table. 'That's more than enough.'

That night she said the same to Rose, knocking on her door, lifting the mosquito-net, looking down at her daughter, with her hair spread out on the pillow. 'This is more than enough. I'm your mother. I must know that you're safe. You must go.'

Rose shook her head. 'I won't go without you.'

'Then I'll come too.'

'I can't go without Luke.'

Cait burst out, 'There's a war on. Men stay and women go, or more correctly, have already gone.'

'Wait a little longer, Mum. Just a little longer. Mrs Halliday is still here, and a few others.'

Her mother left the room, and Rose lay in bed, her mother's words playing in her mind. No, she couldn't go.

Cait tossed and turned. They'd have to go. Rose was so stubborn, she wouldn't listen. She wouldn't do as she was told, and now her father's voice played in her mind because he had said the same to her, when she had insisted on using Ben. She rolled onto her stomach and buried her face in the pillow, feeling like a child again, not knowing what to do about anything.

Chapter Twenty-Three

Ben telephoned Old Roy from the base when he heard that Singapore had surrendered. 'I'm stuck here like a useless piece of wood. I've go to do something, but my Darwin posting still hasn't come through and the leg's better, for God's sake.'

Old Roy had to listen hard because the line was crackling. 'Just keep your hair on. You'll go when you're needed, and how's that Mick? Sylvie says to tell him the baby's kicking well.'

Ben laughed. 'Mick's good, but he's getting mad too, stuck here.'

Old Roy chuckled. 'It's as well you've got one another then, isn't it?'

There was a pause before Ben replied. 'Yes, I suppose it is.'

Luke eased his back in the harbour workshop. Sweat dripped onto the wood he had just jointed, flies droned heavily in the heat, vivid light shafted in through the door. Rain, damn you. Rain, he thought, wiping his face with a handkerchief which was rough with sawdust.

'Come on, Luke. Stop messing about in there and come on out. Cait'll give us the ladle across our ears if we're late for tea,' Martin called, banging on the side of the shed.

Then there was a shout from Roger. 'Strewth,

look at that mob coming back.'

'Aw, bloody hell,' Martin groaned.

Luke stuffed his handkerchief into his back pocket. What now? He slung his tools into the box, but the shouts and calls from outside drowned the noise they made. He hurried out. There, in the brilliant sun, he saw the convoy which had left a few days earlier returning to harbour. They'd been hit. The soldiers were still on board, clearly visible. Roger said, 'Well, talk about a load of sitting ducks. With that lot back in harbour, and the remains of the Pearl Harbor ships 'n' all . . .' They all gazed nervously up into the sky.

Martin said with a harsh laugh, 'Well, slit-eyes or not, they'll be bloody blind if they don't spot that this lot are ripe for a few bombs.'

'They wouldn't dare,' Roger said. 'No worries.'

They hurried back to Cait's. The esplanade seemed to hold more patrolling soldiers every day. Luke counted the machine-gun posts. There was another one since this morning, wasn't there? They skirted the barbed-wire entanglements in the streets. The sandbags smelt of cat's pee.

Martin groaned, 'God, the smell of that'll scare the buggers away, if nothing else does.'

Luke grinned, Roger laughed, but no amusement reached their eyes.

They ate tea quickly, and no-one spoke. The air was electric with tension, and Cait's frown was deeper than ever. The other men hurried to the Don. Luke exchanged a glance with Cait. She nodded. He took Rose's arm and led her to the veranda. Cait hauled out the boxes of provisions from the pantry, checking the water, the dried milk, tea, sugar, the . . . She stopped. Put her hands to her face. They had to get out.

She slipped down the back steps, past the boarders' rooms, hurrying along the street to Mrs Halliday, hearing the constable yelling at someone who was showing a chink of light. She banged on the door. 'Come on, come on,' she breathed.

She heard the tap of Mrs Halliday's walking-stick, and her frail voice calling, 'In a minute. I'll be there in a minute.'

Cait called, 'It's only me, Mrs Halliday.'

'Then why didn't you say so before. Come along in, my dear. It'll save me coming all the way.'

Cait pushed open the fly door, and slipped past the curtain quickly, letting a minimum of light escape. Mrs Halliday was standing in the room, leaning on her stick, her black clothes hanging loosely. How could anyone wear black in this heat?

Cait said, 'Luke is talking to Rose now. We're trying to get her to leave. I've stocked up on provisions. The convoy's returned and the harbour's chock-a-block. The Japs are bound to find out.'

Mrs Halliday was smiling gently, and nodding her head.

'Don't you see, Mrs Halliday? We must leave. If the Japanese cut off the sea lanes Darwin would be so vulnerable. If they bomb the harbour you could be killed. I want to be able to say to Rose that you are ready to leave. I want you to come with us, in the car. I don't know how you've managed to talk the authorities into letting you stay as it is.'

The old lady shook her head. 'But as I told the man, this is my home. I'm too old to go gallivanting around the countryside. I told him my plans were in hand and he went off, saying he'd send someone else. He hasn't, yet.' She pointed to the chair near Cait. 'Do sit down, my dear. I'll make us some tea.'

Cait came across the room to her, trying to keep calm. She kept her voice level as she said, 'I really don't want any tea, Mrs Halliday. Now when we go, I would like you to come with us. Please think about it. I can't leave you here, and I can't stay, not with Rose to think of.'

Mrs Halliday limped towards the kitchen, the insects were buzzing and banging into the lights, her walking-stick was tapping on the floor. 'Now shall we have a cup of tea?'

Cait sighed, looking around at the photos. When she came for Mrs Halliday she must remember to bring a bag, put the photos in and try to find out tonight which possessions were of importance to her. She checked her watch. Was Luke persuading Rose?

On the veranda Rose shouted, 'I'm not going. So what if there are a few more ships in the harbour? That's what harbours are for, you stupid boy.'

Luke signed violently, 'You are the stupid one. Soon you'll be the dead one. Most of the others have been evacuated. Why won't you?'

Rose shouted even louder, 'Because I'm needed in the office. That's why we were allowed to stay in the first place. Mrs Halliday is still here, what's everyone panicking about?'

'War,' Luke signed. 'That's what we're panicking about. There are forty or so ships in that harbour. Cruisers, destroyers, troop carriers, all sorts. The Japs bombed the convoy and they'll have tracked it to here.'

'They haven't bombed us yet, so why should they start doing it now? I can't go. I have a job. I have you.'

He started to sign again. She grabbed his hands. 'Shut up. Just be quiet. I don't want to hear any more. You and Mum are just two old women. Go and get drunk if you're that scared.'

He pulled his hands from her, stuck them deep into his pockets and glared at her, before storming off down the steps. She shouted after him, 'No-one likes a sulker.' But he didn't reply.

When Cait came in, Rose was in bed. She knocked on the door and entered. Rose was on her side, feigning sleep. Cait shut the door as she left. She waited up for Luke, sitting in the dark of the kitchen, listening, always listening, for the bombers, as she had done for days now.

They must have had a row, or they would still be together, looking up at the stars, or sheltering from the rain, listening to it drumming on the roof, and finding enchantment even in that. How the young could love. But it wouldn't last, not with the boy as he was, and again she felt that pang when she thought of the love in Luke's eyes.

She heard the voices of the men as they sang and catcalled up the street. She waited at the kitchen door for them to come into the yard. Luke was with them. She called to him softly. He came to the bottom of the steps. He was drunk. His signing was clumsy. Cait tried to follow.

'Say it again,' she demanded.

He did. 'She won't listen. She called me stupid.'

He stumbled back to his room.

Cait watched. No. It couldn't last, and so they would leave here, and when it was all over they would go home. That night she slept better than she had done for months.

In the morning, Rose sat at her desk typing. Her head ached because she had not slept at all. Luke, I'm so sorry. Luke, forgive me, she thought as she typed the words and figures, and made up pay-slips, and felt the sweat trickle down her back, her arms, her legs.

Her boss, Mr Miller, said, 'Strewth, if only it would rain.'

She thought, If only I could talk to him, say I'm sorry. Say I love him. She looked up. 9.30 a.m. on 19 February 1942. She felt light-headed with tiredness, her fingers trembled as she opened her drawer.

'We need stamps, Mr Miller.'

He looked up from the plans he was studying.

467

'Nip out and get some then, and for goodness sake, see Luke on your way back – he's down on the wharf today. Maybe then we'll get some work from you. You look just like I feel after a blue with the wife.' He smiled briefly, then looked down again.

She grabbed her bag and hurried out into the town, to the Post Office.

Cait dragged out the bags she had packed that morning and checked through them once again in the sitting-room. They would go tomorrow morning. She had decided over breakfast, and relief gave her an energy which drove her on, in spite of the heat. She loaded the bags into the car, leaving space for Mrs Halliday and her bag. She picked up the box of provisions. She'd packed too much. She emptied some. She carried it out to the car. She sat in the driver's seat, practising the gear changes.

She'd arranged for Chang, the Chinese cook from Cavanagh Street, to come up and feed the men. She leaned back and looked up at the sky. At last they were going.

Luke sawed through the wood. The blade stuck. He wished he could curse. He wished he could go and see her. He wished he could shout across Darwin of his love for her, of his sorrow at their harsh words. Martin called, 'Come on, Luke. Take a break.'

He wrenched the saw free and threw it down. I don't damn well want to, he wished he could shout. But he went outside and joined them. They watched the small boats ferrying supplies as they walked along the wharf. 'Bet there are a few packs of smokes on that lot,' Martin grumbled. 'I've got to give up this boozing if I want to be able to see in the morning. How's your head, Luke?' Martin and Roger nudged one another and laughed.

It was thudding, and Luke didn't need to sign, he

just grimaced. The men laughed louder. Luke smiled. They were all right. They accepted him. Some people didn't. Rose had, and he'd blown it.

Men were unloading supplies on the wharf. Troops were repairing and making good their ships. Roger said, pointing to an oil tanker and munitions ship, 'Look at that lot ferrying out supplies. Look like a load of flies round a honey pot.'

Frank, another boarder, joined them. 'There's talk that there was a Jap plane over earlier, having a look-see.'

The men looked at one another, then shrugged. 'Not for the first time,' Roger said. 'Rumour has it that they're sending Yank planes across to keep an eye on this lot. Or maybe our own will come out and take a shifty.'

They heard a drumming of aircraft engines then. They shaded their eyes and looked around. 'Can't be the Yanks yet. Anyone want to take a bet on it being ours instead?' Martin murmured, craning round. No-one would. 'Can't see anything,' Martin said. 'Go on, there's still time – a quid, that's all. A lousy quid. I could be a rich man by tonight.'

Luke looked up into the sun, squinting. There they were. He pulled at Martin's shirt, and signed, 'Coming out of the sun. Ours or the Yanks?'

They stood looking and watching, and then some-one further down the wharf screamed, 'It's Zeros. It's the Japs.' Now the sirens were sounding, drowning out the thudding in Luke's head. They began to run. Men were jostling, pushing, running along the wharf. Rose, get down, get out. Rose, Luke thought.

The bombers came on, so huge, so dark, so loud, drumming in the air, so low. Wave after wave, coming in level, blotting out the sun, darkening the sky. The men weren't looking any more, they were running, and the noise of the aircraft was drowning them, pulverizing them, and the bombs were whistling, screaming, crashing, and the wharf was juddering, and men were crying out. The breath was being sucked from Luke's body, and panic was tearing at him. The world was blowing up around them all, hurling them into the air, blasting at them, searing them.

Martin was blown out into the water. Debris smacked into Luke as he was hurled up, and then down onto the deck, and pain would have forced a scream but he couldn't scream Rose. I can't scream; but in his mind he did as the air burned in his lungs, and the air filled with smoke and oil from the bombed tanker, and there was still the sound of men running. And now there was another wave of bombers, and somewhere the wharf creaked and groaned, and crashed into the water. But not his part, not yet.

He crawled on arms that were broken and hands that were torn and bleeding and crushed, and a leg that dragged. Now the dive-bombers were screaming down, the ships were sinking beneath the bombs. The planes were peeling away. Luke was beyond pain. He was just moving an inch at a time, dragging in deep, burning breaths. Rose, Rose, his mind screamed. Get out, Rose.

Rose had watched the bombers coming in as she came back towards the harbour from the Post Office. There you are, you see – she was rehearsing in her mind the words she would say to her mother and Luke. There you are, there are women still working at the Post Office.

'About time the Yanks arrived,' a man muttered as he passed her. 'What use is the handful of RAAF planes we've been given? Damn stupid.'

She'd stood and watched and smiled, but then the siren had soared, and the smile had become fixed, and her feet were rooted to the ground as the bombers came in, drumming and throbbing, and humming, so low, so level, and as the bombs had dropped, she had screamed, 'Luke. Luke.'

She had run towards the bombs and the noise, pushing past those who screamed and cowered, and dived into slit trenches. 'Luke,' she screamed again and again as the bombs fell and exploded, and shoots of water and debris and flames burst into the air.

But then a man grabbed her and pushed her down into a trench. 'Get in there, you stupid bitch.' He jumped in beside her, pushing her right down. She peered up. A dive-bomber passed, banked, returned, and screamed as it dived. They could see the pilot's face, and now he was firing, strafing across the trench, and another came and she tasted the dirt which fell into the trench, and the stones, and the fear. And now others came and the ground shuddered, jolted, and earth stuck to their sweat, and they saw the sky in strips, and the man who had saved her, saw his death come, in strips.

Cait crouched beneath the house, seeing and hearing the bombing and the anti-aircraft guns. She felt the ground shake. She saw the flames, the dust, the waves of Betty bombers, the waves of dive-bombers, and the debris hurled into the air, and the Zeros strafing. Again they were here, again the bullets tore and kicked up the earth, tore fronds from the palms, smashed into the house.

She screamed, lying low, her hands over her head, her throat hoarse as she screamed again and again, and again. A beetle crawled beneath her hands and she smashed it, smashed it, smashed it, and then wept and screamed and wept again because her daughter was out there and she was too frightened to move.

As the Zeros left, Rose listened to the cries of anguish, and to the sound of her own heart, and the trickle of earth which was still falling into the trench. She felt the weight of the man who was slumped on her legs, and the wetness of his blood. The ack-ack battery on the oval had stopped firing. A woman in the trench was saying again and again, 'He's dead. He's dead.'

'Shut up. Shut up,' Rose screamed as she tried to get up. The weight of the dead man was too great. 'Help me, help me,' she moaned to the soldier who was peering into the trench.

He reached down and dragged her up, his face grimy, his eyes bloodshot. He was coughing. She was coughing. There were bodies in the street, there was wreckage all around, there were branches strewn as though a cyclone had been through. They breathed smoke, thick oily smoke.

There was blood on her skirt, and her legs. 'It's not mine. It's not mine,' she told the soldier. 'It's not mine.' She couldn't stop herself from saying it. Others were scrambling from the trench. Her limbs were stiff, her mouth dry. Her throat was sore, and all around was acrid oil-drenched smoke. She looked towards the harbour and the raging fires.

She began to run, on legs which seemed to belong to someone else, and it was as though she was wading through sand. The town was ablaze. Nothing familiar surrounded her. There were dazed people stumbling to the left and right of her. There were others crouching by the wounded, and soldiers rushing around, and Jeeps storming up the roads, and Red Cross trucks revving their gears.

On she ran across the esplanade.

'Rose, Rose.'

Rose stopped. Her mother ran up and held her. 'Thank the Lord you're all right.'

She saw the blood on Rose's dress and paled. Rose said, 'It was a man. He died on top of me. He saved me. I'm trying to find Luke.' She ran on.

The harbour was full of damaged and sunk, or sinking, ships, and the cries of men, and the noise of flames, and sudden blasts as something else blew up. It was dark from the smoke, it was hot. The rocks around the harbour shore were black from the oil, bodies were floating, medics were attending stretchers. Rose's office was smashed to smithereens. They picked over the debris. 'Mr Miller's dead,' a man called.

They searched for Luke, calling, but knowing he couldn't call back.

They ran back to the car, seeing the provost pointing guns at a Japanese family, forcing them into the back of a truck. A soldier said, 'Internment for them, and good riddance.'

A patrol stopped them as they ran down their street. 'Get ready to evacuate. Got to get you all out. The Japs are probably on their way right now.'

Cait nodded. 'We've got to find a relative.'

They ran to the house. Cait made Rose strip off her dress and sluiced the blood away. They drove to Mrs Halliday who was sitting on the veranda with a bag by her side. Cait ran up the path, kicking aside the broken branches, coughing in the smoke.

Mrs Halliday smiled. 'Just packed a few things, dear. I popped my photographs in too. I knew you'd be here.' Cait suddenly felt as though everything had slowed, as though, for a moment, the world made sense again, because Mrs Halliday was spotless, unmoved. Her hat sat on her well-groomed white hair, and her black dress was without a mark. They drove on to the hospital, which had been bombed, in spite of the Red Cross markings on the roof. No-one recognized Luke's name.

A soldier spoke to them, pointing in the direction of the mass grave which was being prepared. It was Cait who went to the officer and waited while he checked his list but finally shook his head.

473

Cait slammed the car door shut. 'We must go.'

Rose said, 'No, not without Luke.'

Cait turned on her, shouting, 'Yes, without Luke. He's probably already on the road somewhere. Or in the train, waiting to move. It will be of no help to him if you are stuck here and he has escaped.'

Rose couldn't speak, she just nodded, and her mother started the car, and they drove, but then another wave of bombers came, but this time it was the RAAF airfield they were after, and so, when silence fell again, they drove on. Refugees were trailing along the road. They picked up a woman with two children, and the children were silent too.

'What's the Army doing? Why didn't our planes fight off the Japs?' the woman called from the back seat.

'What are you doing, still here? You should have got out weeks ago,' Cait said.

The woman replied, 'Me mum was dying. I couldn't leave. She died last Tuesday. I was on me way, soon as I could.'

'Where are we going?' asked Rose, her voice hoarse.

Mrs Halliday said, her voice croaky from the smoke she had inhaled, 'The Army is probably waiting for the Japanese to come, my dear. They will hold them while we escape. We had so few planes, and now we probably have none. Who knows where they were the first time, saving themselves for the invasion, if they had any sense.'

Everyone fell silent again.

There were people, trucks, motor cycles, horses, all moving south.

They crammed in another old woman. Rose took the two children on her lap. Her sweat mingled with theirs. She could hardly breathe in the heat, she could hardly think, all she could do was look out at the magnetic termite hills that soared out of the high grass which had not yet been knocked down by

474

the rains, and the wind, but which would have been by the end of the wet. Or would they be knocked down by the Japanese with their bombs? Or by their marching feet?

As she looked she heard the bombs in her mind, saw the flames, the wounded ships, the oil-drenched skies and sea, and wanted to scream out for Luke, because there was a pain as violent as though a bullet had torn her apart. Where was he?

A man jumped on the running-board. 'My mate's sprained his ankle. Take him, can ya?'

'How?' shouted Cait, braking.

Mrs Halliday said, 'With difficulty, but we can manage.'

They all moved up, their bodies squashed together in the heat. The man opened the door and pushed his friend in. 'No,' he mumbled.

'Don't be absurd,' Mrs Halliday chided, pulling him down beside her.

Rose looked at her mother and Cait touched Rose's hair. 'He'll be all right.' Her voice was a bare whisper, and still dry and scratchy.

She drove on, past wattle bushes with their large heavy yellow blossoms. On and on, and now the gauge was flickering just above empty. Cait cursed the running about they had done before leaving Darwin, and now they had such a load in the car.

'We'll need to pull off. If we stop on the road we'll be swamped and we can't take any more.'

Rose grabbed her arm and pointed. 'Up that track, Mum. Stop by the two gums and the wattle.'

She turned off the road and the car lurched down the track. She switched off the engine, and grabbed the cans from the boot. The children on Rose's lap were asleep. 'Stay there,' Cait yelled. 'Don't wake them.'

She could smell the wattle. She could feel the heat, and the flies on her eyes, and arms. She unscrewed the cap, petrol wafted.

Rose called, 'Don't let it spill, use the funnel we put in the boot.'

Cait was already doing so. 'Teach your grandmother to suck eggs, why don't you?' she called. Everyone laughed, too much.

As she poured she searched the sky for planes, listening for firing. There was none. She used all the cans, and chucked them, empty, into the bush. They didn't need any more weight than they already had.

'Will we get to Mrs Harvey's?' Rose called.

'Should do. We'll get the train there.' But would there be one?

She climbed back into the car, started the engine, turned the car round, and headed back to the road.

That night they camped in the bush. There were fires all around, and mosquitoes. She cooked damper and picked out the ashes before cutting it up and handing it round. She and Rose looked at one another again. Rose said, 'I wonder if Old Roy is still alive?'

Cait shrugged and looked out into the bush. Where was Ben? And Mick, and Bluey, and Stan, and Frank, and Nigel? Where was Luke? How was her father? Too many open-ended questions.

Mrs Halliday and Mrs Simson, the other old lady, slept in the car, along with the children. The others rolled up in sheets and tried to sleep, but all Rose could think of, and hear, were the bombs, and the man she loved. It was the same for the others.

As dawn broke the wattle blossom glistened and birds filled the air with their song. A kookaburra laughed.

'Doesn't it know what's happened?' Rose murmured.

They drove back out onto Stuart Highway as the gums cast their shadows, and the acacia bloomed.

The air was not yet steaming hot.

So far the roads had been passable, Cait thought. Would they continue to be so, in this, the wet season? A season of bogs, of mud, of breakdowns.

After an hour she saw soldiers across the road, looming out of the shimmering heat, their shapes fragmented, solidifying, growing larger and clearer, just as the Tans at the roadblock had. They were almost at the roadblock and she could hear the wind in the reeds, see the greenness of Ireland, hear the coarseness of the Tan's voice, the kindness of Ben's.

'Mum,' Rose snapped. 'Stop the car.'

Cait jerked and came back to the moment. The soldier was standing, pointing down a track. 'Road's bogged. Get off it, and take this piece of paper with you.' He handed the sheet to Cait. 'We're requisitioning the car. This is a receipt. Follow those others.' He pointed to the people walking, and the cars and trucks disappearing down the track. 'You'll give up the car at the station. We're transporting you by train to Alice Springs, and then on to Adelaide, but don't ask me details.'

The paper was fluttering in her hand. 'Get on then,' the soldier barked.

She drove down the track towards the township.

Rose said, 'Luke might be here.' She craned forward as they reached the disused gravel pit where the Army had set up an open-air soup kitchen.

Mrs Halliday said drily, 'Of course, all is quite clear now. The Army have been making soup.' There was more laughter, but this time it was genuine.

They stayed together, around their own fire, amongst the other refugees, who started at every loud noise, who looked up as every truck came in. Was it the Japs?

Rose and Cait trailed round the site, asking for Luke. They talked to the nurses, who shook their heads, and the doctors who did likewise. 'He might still be in Darwin and be coming out on one of the trains.'

They peered into the sheds, choking on the dust. No, he wasn't here. They found Mrs Halliday and the others. 'Any sign of the train?'

It came towards the end of the second day, after too many hours of heat and flies and anxiety.

Soldiers tried to control the crowd who pushed and jostled to get in close.

'Come on, everyone. Let the stretcher cases on first,' a sergeant bellowed.

The crowd moved back, and Rose strained to see, strained to recognize, slipping to the side, searching as the stretchers passed her, but there were so many, and now she was weeping. Her mother pulled her into her arms.

'They've already said he isn't here. Wait until Alice Springs now, darling.'

The train took on water, the firemen stoked the engine. There was no room for Cait's party in the passenger carriages, and instead they clambered into the covered wagons. A soldier called to Mrs Halliday, 'We'll make room in one of the coaches.'

She shook her head and smiled at Cait. 'I'm staying with my friends.'

Cait made Mrs Halliday and Mrs Simson sit on the blanket she had taken from the car. The train lurched, jerked. They were on their way. They felt every rattle, every jolt, but they were leaving danger, and at last they slept.

They travelled for hours, then stopped at their old township to refuel, and take on water. They were fed by the townspeople, and Mrs Harvey was one, but she didn't know of Luke's whereabouts either. Neither would she leave with them. 'You go on. You find that boy.' The women gave them dampers, scones and tins for the journey, and water, lots of water.

They continued on towards the centre of Australia. They stopped at the end of the line in Larrimah and were transferred to trucks. The rain pounded on the covers, and the cold made Mrs Halliday shake. Cait covered her with whatever clothes they could find in their cases. She made Rose read to the children. Anything to keep her mind away from Luke, and her eyes from looking dark, and desperate.

Now there were only browns, yellows and reds, and gone were the grasses that would be knocked down by the wind and rain, and gone were the gums, and the wattle. There was only stillness, and daytime heat and night-time chill, and inside the truck there was quietness because no-one could think of anything to say any more.

At Alice Springs the trucks braked and stopped. Cait and the others eased their aching limbs, and scrambled to the ground. They were safe. For now they were safe.

An officer used a loud hailer to order them to a nearby hall where there was tea and sandwiches, and Red Cross and CWA women whose eyes were gentle and curious and sad. They handed cigarettes to the men, and to any woman who needed them. Rose wouldn't stay. She pushed back through the crowd and back to the stretchers which were being carried to a collection point. Cait ran after her, and together they searched one by one.

A nurse came up. 'If he sees you, he'll call.'

Rose turned on her, shouting, her voice still hoarse and sore. 'How can he call? He has no voice. He's mute.'

A doctor passed and stopped. 'What did you say?'

Rose repeated it. The doctor said, 'Come with me. We thought it was shock.'

Rose and Cait followed the man whose stethoscope dangled from his pocket. He hurried to a sergeant who was ticking names on a sheet. The doctor called, 'Sergeant, that young lad with shock.'

'No identity, sir? Got pulled out of the water? Won't speak? Was put on the train at Darwin?'

The doctor nodded. 'That's the one.'

The sergeant scratched his head, checked his board, then pointed to a nurse checking the pulse of one of the patients.

Rose ran, skirting the stretcher patients, and Cait followed. She watched her daughter reach the nurse. Saw the nurse point to the left. Rose ran, stopped, knelt, and touched the hair of the boy, and Cait saw it was dark with oil, and she saw Rose bend and kiss his lips, and his hands which were bandaged. Rose turned, and tears were coursing down her cheeks as she cried out to Cait, 'He can't talk. They've bandaged his hands. Oh, Mum. He can't talk.'

Cait walked to the nurse. But her daughter reached the woman before she did. She heard Rose say, 'Please, can you just bandage the fingers that are hurt, and release at least a thumb and finger, and more if possible. You see, he needs to talk. He really does need to be able to talk. Just like you or I.'

The nurse smiled and replied, 'Let's see what we can do.'

Rose knelt at Luke's side again. 'There you are, darling. Now you can tell me what happened, and where it hurts.' Tears were sliding from the corners of Luke's eyes, and falling onto the stretcher, and his face was drawn, but now two fingers and a thumb were free, and his face was relaxing, as Rose kissed him again.

Still Cait stood and watched and knew that her bigotry had been as great as any that Stephens had exhibited, or the Tans, or Ben, or the rioters in Kalgoorlie, and that Luke was a fine boy, and that her daughter's love was mature, true and accepting, and the only person to diminish it had been Cait.

Ben and Mick were ordered to Darwin two days after the bombing.

Patrick and Deborah Prover heard of the bombing of Darwin on the radio, the day after the raid. The newscaster said that damage had been slight and there had been very few civilian casualties, and they relaxed, knowing that Luke would cable them as soon as he could.

The cable they received was from Caithleen Williams, who said she had run the hotel in the Northern Territory. She told them that their son was in hospital in Adelaide with severe injuries to both arms and one leg. His hands were affected but he could still sign.

As they travelled across the Nullarbor on the train to Adelaide, Deborah thought of Luke's hands, only his hands, whilst Patrick Prover wondered who Caithleen Williams was, because he could only recollect a Katherine Adams at the hotel.

Chapter Twenty-Four

When Ben arrived in Darwin with Mick and the other men they stared in horror. 'The bloody radio said slight damage and hardly any deaths,' Ben muttered.

Lieutenant Morton said, 'Bad for morale, don't want to panic the rest of the country.'

Ben shook his head at Mick. 'Tough for those who had to put up with it. What must they be thinking now? No-one will believe them, no-one will understand their shock.'

The sergeant was shouting orders. Ben hurried towards the truck with the others. Thank heavens no-one he knew had been here.

The sergeant shouted again, 'Come on, I said. Come on. The way you lot are strolling about the Japs'd have time to sit down and have a smoko before marching through the rest of the country. There's a siege on here, bombing raids whenever you damn well blink, so sort yourselves out, will you. This isn't going to be any picnic. Water's on for two hours a day, but don't worry, the sweat you work up under me will be better than a shower.'

In the back of the truck Cait hung on to the sides and looked up at the jarrah trees, the branches of which almost met above them. They had travelled for a mile and a half now, since arriving at Margaret

River Station, and she heard Patrick Prover yell from the cab, 'Nearly there. Everyone all right?'

Luke and Rose, who sat opposite Cait, looked at one another and Rose shouted, while Luke signed, 'Everyone's fine.' They laughed.

The truck lurched down and out of a pothole. Luke winced and signed, 'Nothing's changed.'

But everything had, thought Cait. My daughter loves you and I have accepted that, and I don't know what it means where Ireland is concerned. And I don't care, for the moment, because Rose is safe and alive, and you are too, Luke.

She smiled at Rose, who pointed to a wooden house in the middle of acres of cleared parched land. It had a veranda on which hung washing, and there were bags of super stacked against the house. 'That house is the same as the others we have passed.'

Luke signed, 'It is a Group Settlement house. The Taylors came over with the scheme. He was a clerk, but farm training had been promised. It never materialized. God, it was hard for them. It was bad enough for Mum and Dad, but they had experience and their own money.' Luke's face contorted with rage. He gesticulated at the trees. 'These were the farms they had been promised. Acres and acres of trees they had to ringbark, fell, grub, with just a mattock, saw and axe. They had to fight bushfires, live in shacks, lose sight of their dreams. They had every little thing they were allocated, from the saw, to the seed, put against their debt. The Groupies had to sow what the Board told them, and pay for the mistakes the Board made. If a crop was unsuitable, the cost of the seed still went against the farmer.'

His hands were flying. 'The Taylors were like so many others. The price for produce was so low, and the yield too, that they never produced enough to live on. The Taylors had to walk off, leaving their son in the graveyard – he drowned in one of the drainage ditches. Last year, Dad managed to buy it. They've done it up for you.' He pointed to the jarrahs. 'Your Churchill talked of blood, sweat and tears, well, there was enough shed here to last a lifetime.' He spread his hands wide. 'We have this beautiful country cleared, and a road and rail network, thanks to the efforts of the Groupies, who were used as cheap labour by people who should have known better.'

His hands lay still at last, and now he smiled ruefully at them. Then signed once more, 'Lecture over.'

Cait and Rose looked back at the house as it disappeared from view behind the trees that lined the track.

Cait felt the ghosts all around. She looked again at the trees they passed. She thought of the washing flapping on the veranda, the cleared paddocks, the silence of it all, beyond the snarling and lurching of the truck. Could she farm this land even now, as Deborah had asked her to?

She'd have to. It meant that Rose could be with Luke and that she, Cait, would be useful while she was here – Patrick had joined the Voluntary Defence Corps so another pair of hands was needed. 'It will save getting a couple of land-girls,' Deborah had insisted.

Cait looked out at the paddocks. She was a farmer's daughter, for heaven's sake. So, yes, if the Settlers had struggled with virgin forest, she must be able to manage this cleared land.

They turned left, down a track, and soon Rose pointed to the house which they were approaching. A sign proclaimed it as Stoke Farm. This was the Provers' house. A woman ran out onto the veranda, wiping her hands on her apron, then waving. It must be Sarah who lived on the next farm up and had been caring for both farms, with her husband Ernie.

She was running towards the truck, which drew

484

to a halt beside the corrugated-iron milkshed, and to the right of the pig-pens.

'Hallo, hallo. Are we glad you're back, and safe and sound too. And with Caithleen and Rose. How wonderful.'

Deborah jumped from the cab and hugged Sarah, and together they hurried to the tailboard. Sarah called to Cait, 'Welcome. It will be so good to have you here. And you, young man. Do you never stop getting yourself into trouble?' Sarah was signing as she spoke, and laughing as Luke replied, 'Nice trouble though, and her name's Rose.'

He tried to stand, but shook his head. Cait and Rose put their arms around him and helped him to his feet. He limped to the end of the truck, and looked down at the ground which seemed too far.

His father came round to the back of the truck with an aboriginal who had appeared from nowhere. Patrick and the aboriginal stood with their hands on their hips, shaking their heads at Luke, then at one another. Patrick said, 'This is the boy who helped repair Darwin wharf, and he can't even work out how to get out of a truck. Where did we go wrong, Jimmie?'

The aboriginal laughed. 'Back in that pool, where we taught him to swim. Thought everything was easy after that. Maybe he's looking for some water wings.'

Patrick laughed. 'Just wings maybe.'

Cait and Rose were giggling as they lowered Luke into a sitting position. He swung his legs over the end, and eased himself to the ground, wincing, falling back against the tailboard in his pain. Instantly the men were at his side.

Cait looked at them, and at the land which stretched for acres to the trees in the distance, and the cows which grazed. Deborah had said that soon it would rain, and the land would grow green again. Cait felt

485

peace steal over her in the midst of the love all around her, and the beauty too.

That evening they ate on the veranda with the Provers and Jimmie, who talked of his people, the Bibbulmen, who no longer existed, but whose spirits still roamed the land. He said to Cait, 'Tomorrow I will take you to your land. Tomorrow I will show you the milking shed, the water tank, the house which Sarah and Claire cleaned for you today.'

He nodded towards Luke's sixteen-year-old sister.

Cait smiled at her. 'That was good of you.'

Claire shook her head. 'No, you're the one who has been good. You found him, undid his hands, stayed with him until we could come. He told us.'

'No, it was Rose,' Cait said firmly.

The next morning they walked with Jimmie across the cleared paddocks of Stoke Farm, and through the trees, following the blazed trail. Jimmie said, 'Wherever you go, you must make sure you mark the trees or you could get lost. But I think this trail will be well used by a certain girl.' He nodded towards Rose, who grinned. Jimmie added, 'Until Luke returns to the war.' The smile faded from Rose's eyes.

As April became May, and the paddocks became tinged with green from the heavy rain, Rose milked the fifteen cows with her mother, pulling and squeezing at the teats, remembering the farm by the river four hours from Sydney, whilst her mother remembered not only that farm, but also the one by the river in Ireland. Neither spoke of their thoughts.

Each evening Rose walked through the trees, a cape slung over her head and shoulders, her feet slurping in the mud, to sit with Luke in the warmth of the Provers' kitchen, and she read to him from *Wuthering Heights*, a book which her mother had handed her the day after they arrived.

Together, in their minds, they walked the moors, and felt the wind, and the pain, and the rage of thwarted love, and knew that theirs was honest and true, and would last until the day they died. But then their hands gripped tighter still, for the war wasn't over, and Luke would return to it, and they must not think of death.

Cait milked each morning and evening and carted the churn to the bottom of the track in the spring cart, and each time she thought of Ireland. She brushed the horse down, gave him fodder, smelt the hay and remembered the willow.

In June, with Patrick and Jimmie, she cleared the drainage channels, slicing in the spade, heaving the mud up, and remembered the slane, and the peat, and the purple hills, and the soft mellow air.

She washed clothes and hung them on the veranda to dry while the rain poured down over the paddocks, and remembered the heat of Kalgoorlie, and the heat of Ben's body, and the love they had shared. As she watched the same love between her daughter and Luke, she felt loneliness tugging at her.

She grubbed around the roots of saplings in July, in the cold and the rain, exposing the roots, cutting them, levering them out from the ground.

'Don't work so hard,' Deborah urged.

'I like to,' Cait smiled. 'It helps me to sleep.' Everywhere she worked, she imagined the Taylors working beside her, and she did it for them, as well as herself.

In August Luke could put his leg to the ground. The gouges on his arms had healed, and the bones too, and there were only scars on his hands. To celebrate they gathered at the Provers' to eat pork, which Deborah had roasted, and pumpkin pie, which Cait had baked.

'Sarah is coming, and bringing Mollie,' Deborah said when she greeted Rose and Cait, shaking out their capes, and hanging them on the veranda, and bustling them into the warmth of the kitchen.

'Mollie?' queried Rose.

'Luke grew up with her. He's picking them up in the cart. She's a nurse in Perth. He's missed her. They're very close.' Deborah was shaking out a table-cloth. Patrick was banging his pipe on the stove. Just as Old Roy had done, thought Cait, as she saw the joy fade from her daughter's face.

She laid out the cutlery as Rose stood by the window, watching for the cart, which came as the roast was crisping. Cait heard the light laughter of Sarah, the deeper laughter of Sarah's sixteen-year-old son, Bob. His voice rose and fell as they ran from the barn. They burst into the room, bringing the cold with them, slamming the door shut behind them.

'Luke and Mollie are taking the horse round to the stable. They've so much to talk about. How are you, Cait? And Rose?'

Cait said, 'We're fine.' Answering for her daughter, because Rose was staring out into the darkness.

'Is Ernie with them?' Rose asked, not turning round.

Sarah took the bowl of vegetables from Deborah. 'No, he's stuck in doing his books, and his leg's aching. Always does in this weather. Did you hear about that, Cait? He hurt his leg, and Jimmie worked our farm for us, or we'd have had to leave. The Group Board didn't pay the sustenance allowance if you didn't work.'

Cait answered but she was watching Rose, appalled at the stark fear. But why? Luke loved her.

Rose could see the dim kerosene lamp in the stable, she could see shapes. Were they too close? She couldn't see, the rain was sheeting down. She'd been a fool. She'd read love in his eyes, but she could have been wrong, just as her mother had been wrong. Men sent you away. They promised love, but meant none of it.

She felt a touch on her arm. Her mother said

quietly, 'Not every man rejects love. Trust him. You must, you know.'

Rose wanted to fall into the arms of this woman who had left her hardness behind, who had allowed her to love. She wanted to plead with her, 'Does he love me?'

Her mother touched her daughter's cheek, reading the unspoken question. 'Luke loves you. There is no past to destroy that.'

They heard footsteps on the veranda, the sound of capes being shaken, the sound of a girl's laughter, and Cait forced herself not to tense as her daughter was doing. She turned as the door banged open.

Deborah Prover said, 'At last, you two. Now come on in, Mollie, and meet Rose.'

A dark-haired girl, with her mother's brown eyes, came towards Rose, her hand outstretched. 'So this is the girl Luke's been telling me about. What was it, Luke?' She turned back to Luke, holding out her hand. Luke grasped it, grinning at Rose and Cait. 'Oh yes, hair like copper, eyes like a spring sky.' Rose was smiling now, and her eyes met her mother's.

Luke signed, 'Rose, this is my life-long friend, Mollie. Mollie, this is the girl I love.'

In September, Cait top-dressed the oats, and planted pie melons, pumpkins, tomatoes. She sprinkled ash as Deborah had advised. She planted strawberry runners, cucumbers and rhubarb and, as the sun warmed the earth and dried the sodden ground to a rich green, she listened to the robins and the thrushes, and watched the parrots, the rosellas, and though the world was at war, she was at peace. Here, the seasons unfolded in a way in which they had done in Ireland.

In mid-September, as she did at least once a week, Deborah brought scones and they drank tea on the veranda. Deborah said, as they heard the screech of the squeakers, 'When Luke was born and the months went by I denied that he was a mute. I would take him out into the bush and say, "Listen to that, my child. You listen. It's not silent after all." Because I had thought this land was silent, and it was not. And therefore he would not be.'

'It must have been hard for you both, though you had your love to sustain you,' Cait said, flapping her hands at the flies, then sipping her tea.

Deborah fingered her greying hair. There were deep lines at the corners of her brown eyes. 'No, my dear, we didn't. We had only distance and suspicion. I met Patrick in Somerset. He asked me to marry him. I didn't love him at the time, but I knew I could. He returned before me. I travelled out to meet him and fell in love with him, as we stayed on his mother's sheep station in Victoria. I thought I had found a family I could be part of. He, though, had only seen me as a farm girl he could use over here.' Her voice was a monotone. 'He wanted to leave his past behind, you see. He wanted to leave his mother, who was possessive and jealous, and start again. He broke my heart, because he used me.'

Cait placed her cup carefully on the saucer. Just as she had used Ben.

'But you forgave him and love grew?'

'Where love is involved it's not a question of forgiveness, is it? It is love, or it isn't. Our marriage survived – in spite of Patrick's betrayal, and my own, and out of it grew a deep and enduring love.'

Cait watched Deborah as she poured more tea. What betrayal of yours? she wanted to ask, but did not.

Instead, as Claire came trotting towards them on her pony, she said, 'It must have been a relief to you, when Claire was born, and could speak.'

Deborah flushed. Cait looked away. She should not have said it, but she must. 'It isn't in either your family or Patrick's? It won't repeat itself?'

Deborah leaned forward. 'You are right. It isn't in either of our families. But it is in Luke's father's.'

Cait didn't understand. 'But what do you mean?'

'Patrick is not Luke's father. That was my betrayal. When I knew of Patrick's plans for me, and his lack of love, I left Lenora, the sheep station. I went to Melbourne, to Edward, an English friend I had made on the journey out. He had blue eyes and blond hair. In my desperation he was everything I thought I wanted. He was English, he was familiar. I thought he loved me. We made love.' Deborah shook her head. 'No, that is not the right word. There was no love, there was lust born out of loneliness. Luke was conceived. He knows, but he forgets because Patrick is so much his father.'

Claire was cantering now and was almost within earshot.

Deborah looked anxiously at Cait. 'That's why I came over today, because soon Luke will be leaving and in Adelaide you were honest enough to tell us that you had changed your name to Adams to avoid being found by your husband, though the reasons are entirely your own. Marriage between our children could be spoken of. You must tell Rose, if he has not. You see, Edward's uncle was a mute. It is a congenital defect of the vocal chords. It could appear in Luke's child also.'

Claire was here, reining in her pony. 'Thought I'd find you supping tea,' she panted. She dismounted and leaned against the veranda post. 'I'm bored. Rose and Luke have gone to the boronia valley, and Luke said go away and play. I'm sixteen and he says that.'

Deborah laughed. 'You should be bringing in the cows or doing the washing, not roaring about like a mad woman.' She rose. 'Well, I'll walk back, and you can lead the pony and talk to me. I've pounded Cait's ears long enough as it is.' She looked at Cait, and though she was smiling her eyes were serious. 'He's a wonderful boy,' she said.

Cait nodded. 'I know.'

That evening she said to Rose, as they ate their meal, 'Did you know that Luke is not Patrick's child, and that his father's uncle was mute?'

Rose nodded, not looking at her mother, but cutting up her meat.

Cait said, 'Does it make a difference? You do understand don't you, that your children could be mute too?'

Rose nodded again and now she did look up. 'It bothered me to begin with, in Darwin, before the bombing, but I can't change the person I love to satisfy myself, any more than I could, or should, change to satisfy him. I'm me. Luke is Luke. Anyway, why are we talking about children? He hasn't asked me to marry him yet.'

All that night Cait sat up in the chair on the veranda, thinking of Deborah and Patrick, of the betrayals and the love. Of her daughter and Luke, and the wisdom of this child who was not even in her twenties but seemed more like eighty, and Cait knew that Rose was right. One should not change to satisfy another. And that is what Old Roy had tried to tell her so long ago.

In October Luke could walk without limping, and wield an axe to fell the trees of the paddock his father was clearing, and soon he must go, they all knew that, though it was only when the boronia scent was filling the valley, and wisteria was growing on the shrubs and logs, and the coral creeper on the bushes, that he took Rose to the pool where he had been taught to swim, and kissed her. He signed, 'Soon I must leave for Darwin. It will be lonely. I love you. Please marry me? Stay with Mrs Harvey. I can see you then. But remember that our children could be mute. It is a lot to ask of you.'

His eyes were anxious, tender, loving. His hands were still. She gripped them. 'It is nothing to ask of me,' she said. 'I will follow you anywhere.'

Rose decided on a Protestant wedding. 'I'm sorry, Mum,' she said when she was confirmed just after Christmas.

Cait smiled gently. 'You are right to decide for yourself. You are who you are.'

Evening after evening Cait sewed the wedding dress, fitting it, turning her daughter round, her mouth full of pins, signing at her to stand still. It was finished at the end of January when the heat was intense.

Now, evening after evening, Rose grew more silent when Deborah and Cait discussed the food they would prepare, and the numbers of guests until she said to Cait, as they walked back to the farm through the trees whose leaves hung limp in the heat, 'They are all the Provers' friends.'

Cait stepped over a branch. 'Shall we ask Mrs Harvey?'

Rose shrugged, and walked on, kicking at the dried bark on the track, and the twigs. She said, 'I need someone to give me away. Mr Prover has offered. It's usually the father.'

Cait looked at the wisteria which was heat dried and parched. Leaves and bark cracked beneath her feet.

'Then perhaps we should find your father, and ask him,' Cait said.

The words hung between them in the still hot air. They stopped walking.

'We could try,' Rose said, and her voice was small and quiet.

'Yes, we could try,' Cait agreed. She smoothed

493

her dress, and looked up at the trees, seeing the sky through their branches.

Old Roy read the envelope which had been forwarded from the Canterbury Hotel. He recognized the writing and tore it open, though it was not addressed to him. He read.

Dear Ben,
Forgive me for writing to you, but Rose marries in Margaret River, South West of Western Australia, on 30 January. They are both very young, only nineteen, but in many ways much older. It is the wish of us both that you should give your daughter away. We realize that your life might have moved on. That you might still believe that she is not your child. I say again – she is, and she is beautiful, and she is honest and true, and very much in love with a boy, Luke Prover, who can't speak, but who deserves everyone's respect and love and admiration.

Please, if you can dredge up any feeling for her, and ignore any distaste for me, come. You may cable Mr Patrick Prover at Stoke Farm, Margaret River, and we will meet you at the station.

I realize I might be writing to no-one. I have no idea where you are. I am also writing to Old Roy in Kalgoorlie since to have you both here, and all the mining boys, on this most happy of days, would bring such pleasure to Rose, and much gratitude from me.

Caithleen

Old Roy cabled Ben, who was stationed in Northam, near Perth. He then caught the next train across the Nullarbor, and his heart was breaking to think that Cait imagined that her husband might look with distaste upon the finest woman who ever walked the earth.

494

Chapter Twenty-Five

Ben and Old Roy sat opposite one another, gazing out of the train window. They had left Perth at midnight, with Bluey, Stan and Frank who were now snoring beside them.

There was only darkness out there, miles of impenetrable darkness, but the stars were vivid. Was Cait watching them too? Ben closed his eyes. At last he was going to her. Distaste – how could he think of her with distaste? How could she not have sensed how his feelings had changed? How could she not sense that every day since she had gone, she had been in his thoughts? Because it was probably her own distaste that she was mirroring, he told himself.

Old Roy murmured, 'I can't believe Rose is to be married. She was such a child. Is she really nineteen? Have so many years passed?' His voice faded, he pressed his lips together. He looked at Ben, whose hair was so grey that it matched his eyes, and whose face was more lined than a man in his forties should be. Ben had changed, thank God. He was mellow, tolerant. He had learned to love, but was it too late? Had Cait found another life? She had signed herself Caithleen. Now Old Roy sighed.

As dawn broke they stopped in Busselton and drank tea on the station and bought sandwiches and pastries, along with the other passengers. Old Roy pulled at his suit, the others at their uniforms. They talked only of the war and the invasion of Darwin that had not come, and the battles that were being fought in New Guinea, though all their thoughts were really with Cait and Rose.

'Mick's on stand-by, lucky devil,' Bluey said. 'I want to get in it too.'

'You'll get your turn, lad,' Old Roy said quietly. 'There's plenty of time, it'll not be over in a hurry.'

They boarded the train as the whistle blew and settled again, checking their watches as they passed through Vasse and Yelverton, and now the timber was thicker and larger. Soon, Ben thought. Soon I'll see her and I don't know what to say.

He leaned forward and clenched his hands together, his khaki rough on his wrists. He whispered to Old Roy, 'What can I say?'

Old Roy leaned forward. 'That's up to you. I won't say anything. It's just up to the pair of you now.'

Cait and Rose waited at the station. Patrick stayed on the cart. It was a fine, hot day. Cait tucked her arm through her daughter's and said, 'It's such a dry heat here. There's not the humidity of the Northern Territory.' But she was thinking of his telegram: *Arriving 11 a.m. With Roy, Bluey, Stan and Frank. Have to report back at depot same day. Ben.* Nothing more. Oh God, nothing more, but what was she feeling? She didn't know.

Rose replied, 'It's not as humid as the East either. It's very beautiful here. I feel it's home.' But she was thinking that she should tell her father that she was wrong, that Mum hadn't loved that man, but her mother had forbidden her, saying, 'Leave well alone. This is your day, the start of your new life, and by coming he is acknowledging you and that gives me all the happiness I need.'

Cait said, 'I'm glad you feel that it is home here.

Now you understand why I must still go to Ireland, though I will return to Australia because you are here. I shall travel between the two, somehow.'

Rose squeezed her arm. 'I know, Mum. But you'll be alone.'

Cait smiled. 'I've grown up at last. I don't mind being alone.'

The railway lines were quivering, and sinking as they had done in Kalgoorlie. When the war was over she would write to Lucia in Italy. She would travel to see her, somehow. She thought of that, not of the train which was now shimmering in the distance, fragmenting in the heat, consolidating, emerging, roaring into the station.

She felt the pressure of Rose's arm. Would he be cold? Would his eyes be full of contempt, rage? She looked back to where Patrick sat. He smiled and nodded to her, signing, 'It will be all right.' She smiled back, glad that at last she had told them everything. He wore his suit. They were going straight to the church. Time was short.

Doors were opening, people were emerging. Ben was there, at an open door, and for a moment there was no noise, no movement, just him, so lean, so tanned, so familiar, and Cait felt her love for him consume her, weaken her, shorten her breath just as it had always done. It was more than she could bear. She looked away.

Rose clutched her arm. 'Mum, he's grown older.'

Cait said, 'We all have. It's been a long time.' She looked towards Ben again. He was on the platform. He moved in the same way, but for a stiffness in one leg. Anxiety pulled at her, then she thrust it aside. Stupid, stupid woman. It was not her place any more to care for him.

Then Old Roy climbed down onto the platform, and Bluey and Frank, and now Rose was running, her arms outstretched. 'Roy, Roy! Bluey, Stan, Frank.'

Her arms were round Roy, who was smaller and frailer, but still Roy. 'My darling little girl,' he whispered. 'Now go and say hallo to your dad.' He pushed her from him. Rose turned to her father. He was gazing from her to Cait, who was walking towards them. He looked back at Rose.

His daughter was as her mother had been on the cart in Ireland. Her hair was wafting in the breeze, her eyes were almost as blue, but her lips were his. He had no right to be here. He had no right to be invited back into their lives, and the guilt of it all, and the shame, and the love which filled him, took any words from him.

He held out his hands to his daughter who was a woman. All those years wasted. He nodded to her. She said, 'You came. Thank you.'

He said, 'Thank you for asking me.' His voice was low and formal.

Rose turned to Cait who had reached them, and Cait saw the disappointment in her daughter's eyes, and now it was in her own heart though there should be no surprise in that. She saw the rigidity of her husband's shoulders, and the thinness of his lips as he pressed them together. She held out her hand, and fought to keep her voice level as he shook it.

'I'm glad you could come,' she said coolly and marvelled at her tone. 'We need to be at the church in twenty minutes. Perhaps you would like to ride in the front with Patrick, and he can brief you.'

He wanted to hold onto her hand, kiss it, pull her to him, ask her forgiveness, plead for love to which he had no right. Instead he said, 'Very well.'

They rode to the church, and Rose sat in the back of the cart, on a covered box, as Bluey swore her to a dance at the reception, and Old Roy held Cait's hand, and wouldn't let it go, even as they walked down the aisle and stood together in the bride's pew.

Cait introduced him to Luke and to Jimmie, who was the best man.

The piano struck up, and heads craned as Rose walked down the aisle on her father's arm, carrying the bouquet of white roses set against the myrtle which Deborah had cut from the bush she had planted from a Somerset cutting. 'For worthiness and constancy,' Deborah had murmured. 'And you will plant a cutting from this, and it will grow for your own daughter, Rose.'

Rose's face was so beautiful behind the veil, and Ben was so beautiful, and Cait wept with wonder at her child, and with regret for all that could have been.

Luke stood with Jimmie but looked only at Rose as she approached, and Ben saw the clear uncomplicated love on both their faces, though theirs would not be an uncomplicated life. Ben wished that he could turn the clock back and begin again with Cait, imbued with this young couple's wisdom and courage.

He stood beside the daughter he barely knew but loved so deeply. And as the vicar asked who gave Rose Williams to Luke Prover, he handed his daughter to Luke, and slipped into the pew, next to Caithleen. There were tears running down her face. He handed her his handkerchief, as he had done before, so very long ago when the Irish mists hung over hills.

Their hands touched as, this time, she took it. 'Thank you,' she whispered.

He was conscious of her close to him and wanted to hold her against him, and never let her go. He wanted to be able to stand at the reception and talk of the daughter they had borne, as Patrick had just asked him to do. But she was a daughter he barely knew. 'I can't,' he had said.

'You won't,' Patrick had accused as the cart lurched in a rut.

'I can't. I don't know her any more, and I have no right.'

499

Patrick had muttered low, so that those in the back of the cart couldn't hear, 'My mother refused to speak to me, or to my family, once I had moved here. She never saw her grandson or granddaughter. It was a loss for us all. You, as Rose's father, should speak for her.'

'I can't,' he whispered aloud again, as the music began, and his daughter, Mrs Luke Prover, walked back down the aisle.

They all travelled to Stoke Farm in a convoy of carts, and Deborah sat with Ben and talked of the heat, and the rain of the winter, and the bombing in Darwin, and the care that Cait and Rose had taken of her son, and Ben needed to do nothing but nod and smile – and think. God, how he thought.

Trestle-tables had been set out on the buffalo grass, in front of the farm house, and jellies hung down the wells, and Coolgardie safes lined the veranda, borrowed from neighbours. Cait helped Old Roy down from the cart, and though they had talked non-stop – about Kalgoorlie, and Bluey, Stan and Frank, and Darwin, and the world – they had said nothing, not really.

Patrick sat the bride and groom at the table in front of the veranda, with their families, and the other guests were sitting at tables which ran down from either end at right angles. Bluey and Frank poured wine and beer that Ben had donated, and they all ate the food that everyone had provided.

Patrick and Jimmie had set up sheets as awnings, and a soft shadowed breeze blew. The talk was spasmodic between Ben and Deborah, and between Cait and Patrick, and non-existent between Ben and Cait. Whatever can we say? thought Cait, fingering her bread roll. And the effort of smiling continued.

At the close of the meal Luke rose and toasted his bride, using his hands. His father spoke Luke's words, telling their friends of his love for Rose, and of the care she and her mother had taken of him. Of his thanks to her father, and to her friends, for travelling from the East, and from Northam, to be with them today. He asked them to raise their glasses to Rose.

They did. Then Luke signed again, and again Patrick interpreted, 'My father would now like to say a few words about the bride.'

But now Ben rose, and looked at Patrick. 'Perhaps you would allow me?'

Patrick grinned. 'I'd be more than delighted.'

Rose looked at her mother, her face flushing, anxiety in her eyes. What would her father say?

Cait clenched her hands, and half rose. Old Roy pulled her down. 'Let him. He won't hurt either of you ever again.'

Bluey, Stan and Frank had stiffened. What was the stupid bugger going to do now? Hadn't he already done enough?

The breeze was rising, the awning flapped.

Ben cleared his throat. He said, 'I haven't known Luke for more than a few hours, if that, but all I need to do is to look at my daughter's face to know what sort of a man he is.' His voice was unsteady. He swallowed and spoke again and his voice was stronger now, and Cait could hardly bear to watch his beautiful face, to see him smooth down his tunic with hands which had once stroked her. They were trembling, just as she was. How strange.

Ben said, 'He is a worthy partner to a beautiful woman. But there is more to Rose than physical beauty. She has a depth of caring and compassion, and an honesty and love of life, as we can see today. Together she and her mother helped Luke, just as he helped them in Darwin, by ensuring that they could escape, when they needed to escape.' Cait smiled gently at the joy in her daughter's face.

Old Roy touched Cait's arm. She laid her hand over his. His veins stood out, his hand was thin, that of the eighty-year-old man he now was. 'Thank you for bringing him,' she murmured.

He squeezed her hand. 'He brought himself,' he replied. 'He's been looking for you since the day you left.'

She stared at him, her grip tightened. Why? Why? she wanted to shout, but she turned instead to Ben whose voice was strong as he said, 'My daughter was born in Kalgoorlie in the midst of the sound of stampers and mine whistles. She picnicked in the bush. She danced with Bluey and Frank and Stan. She sat on Old Roy's lap in the rocking-chair. She survived the cyclone because my wife took the weight of the veranda and the wall that had fallen on it, while Rose crawled to safety. We all survived the ruination of our hopes, because Caithleen Healy would not allow us to give up.'

Bluey and Frank were smiling now. Old Roy was gripping Cait's hand tightly, and his lips were trembling.

Cait had almost stopped breathing. She dared not move. She couldn't bear his kind words. Not for herself. Not here. Not now. It was too cruel.

Ben continued, 'We left Kalgoorlie, and in my greed and my arrogance I formed a partnership which both Caithleen and I know was an insult to her, and to her mother's memory. I was filled with justification because I felt that I had been used on an earlier occasion. Seeing my daughter today, consumed with the love she feels for Luke, makes me realize that I was never truly used. I was instead truly loved by a woman in just that way. A woman who dared, in the face of bigotry, to love me. I destroyed that, and I ask both her forgiveness and that of my daughter. And I offer them my love. Particularly I offer my wife my undying love.' He reached for his glass. 'Now, I propose a toast to Rose and Luke.'

There was utter silence, not even the birds called. No-one stirred, but then Patrick lifted his glass and repeated, 'To Rose and Luke.'

Everyone stood, everyone toasted, everyone drank, and all the time Rose and Cait looked at one another. Ben stared down at his glass, his face drawn, his hands shaking, and then Rose looked at her father. But Cait could not. All she could do was listen to the echo of those words. Words she had never dared hope to hear. Words she could not believe she had heard. Words which shouldn't have been spoken unless they were true, and how could she ever again believe that they were? She stared at her napkin. No. It had ended in Sydney.

Luke touched his father-in-law's arm. Ben straightened. Luke held out his hand and smiled and nodded. Patrick clapped Ben on the back. 'Come on, everyone. Clear the tables. We've dancing to do.'

The women carried food into the house. Men shifted tables and benches. Rose went to her father, took his hands. He said, 'Little Rose, I love you. I always have. Forgive me. I'm such a stupid fool.' At last she felt his arms around her.

'Daddy, we've missed you,' she said.

The music started, and Luke dragged Rose from her father, and together they danced, and his lips were on her hair, and his body against hers, and they were husband and wife, and tonight they would know one another's bodies, though they already knew one another's souls.

Now others danced and laughed and talked, and Old Roy watched the distance between Cait and Ben who were left on either side of the garden, and wanted to drag one to the other, but he turned away. No. This must be their choice.

Ben watched Bluey drag Rose from Luke, and dance as they had once danced in the dust of the

Kalgoorlie yard, and now his daughter was laughing, throwing back her head, her white dress swirling across the grass. Now it was Frank, then Stan, who dragged her from Bluey, and their laughter rang across the years and at the memory he turned to Cait.

He started towards her, then stopped when she made no move to join him. She looked at Roy, then back at Ben. No, she could take no more pain from him.

He called to her, 'I tried to find you. You were booked on a ship to Italy. We advertised. I hired detectives. Mick went to Ireland to look. He's my partner now, along with Roy. I left the consortium, but not until I told them to chuck out all their prints of English scenes and put up a Hans Heysen. I love you, Caithleen Healy.'

His face was eager, desperate, and it was the face of the young man by the river in Ireland on the day he had come to say goodbye, and it was full of love.

'You really told them to put up a Hans Heysen?' she whispered, watching the movement of his body as he began to walk towards her again, and when he nodded, she at last moved towards him. They met where the myrtle bush grew, its leaves glossy and cool in the heat. They stood, not quite touching.

He said, 'I love you. I always have. Forgive me. I understand myself now.' His voice was soft, the music loud, but she heard every word, just as she saw the truth in his eyes.

She said, 'You work with Mick?'

'He's my friend. We've looked for you together. We fought in Crete together. He saved my life. I love you. I always have. Forgive me.'

Ben took her hands, lifted them to his lips. She asked again, 'You told the Tan to buy a Hans Heysen? You really told him that?'

She could feel his lips on her hands. He smiled

at her. 'I really told him that, Caithleen Healy.' She heard the sound of the wind in the reeds, and the curlews crying, and then they were dancing, alone, by the myrtle bush, and his arms were round her, and his lips were on her hair, and his body was against hers.

That night he did not return with Old Roy and the boys. He stayed in the Taylors' house once they had waved goodbye to Luke and Rose who were staying in Busselton before travelling on to Mrs Harvey's hotel.

They lay together in the starlight, quietly, and at peace, though the war still raged. 'You'll be in trouble from the sergeant,' she whispered.

He kissed her hair. 'That's a small price to pay for the return of my life.'

Chapter Twenty-Six

In June 1947 Mick and Sylvie lifted up their son, Des, and waved farewell to Ben and Cait from Fremantle quay. Rose and Luke lifted their son also, and he shouted, 'Bye, Grandma.'

Cait called as she threw out streamers. 'Goodbye, Roy. Be good for Mummy.' Old Roy had died in 1945, in Mrs Taylor's house, where he had come to be nursed by Cait.

Patrick and Deborah Prover were waving. 'See you in six months.'

'Yes. Yes.'

But not Bluey and Frank. They were dead, killed in Europe, and would never dance again, but Stan was back at Old Roy's mine.

The voyage was calm. Cait and Ben sat in deck-chairs, or played quoits, and worked out the figures on the Perth hotel which Mick and Ben had bought with the money they had made from the sale of the Bondi Beach and Manly hotels when peace broke out.

In the evenings they leaned on the rail and breathed in the salted air, and traced the stars, and watched the flying fish, and Cait pictured the mist-shrouded land they were approaching, and her father who did not know they were coming.

They hired a taxi to drive them to his farm, but as they drove alongside the green summer fields, watching clouds which tumbled above them and slanted shadows over the ripening wheat, Cait leaned forward.

'Please, drop us on the far side of the town. We'd like to walk up the lane.'

She glanced at Ben, who nodded his agreement. He reached for her hand and held it.

She said, 'Thank you for coming back with me.'

He smiled. 'I'll come as many times as you want. It's your home, Cait.'

The taxi drove through the town, and it was just the same. The billiards hall had been rebuilt, the convent was there. Straw from market day blew in the wind. Sunlight struck the shop fronts. She looked into the faces they passed. Was that her friend Rose? Was that Patricia? She'd find out, but not now.

The taxi drew to a halt. They paid him, and watched him drive away. She said, 'I'm going to the cemetery.'

He knew she would. She was silent as she walked down the street, into the cemetery. She prayed at her mother's grave first, and he listened to the Latin prayers and saw again the Catholic he had fallen in love with, and the Catholic she had become again.

Cait searched. 'Where did Mick say?'

Together they found Des's grave. She touched the headstone. 'You would have liked him. He said he wanted to meet you, he said he knew he'd like you.'

The trees were shuddering in the wind, the sky was darkening as clouds hid the sun. Ben looked across to the hills. There was no menace now, there was no fear in him, but there was anxiety. Would her father see her? If not, what would it do to her?

They left the churchyard and now they turned towards the farm. They passed through the crossroads which was alive with memories. They clasped hands. The lane was still rutted, honeysuckle still grew. The blackthorn remained.

507

Cait murmured, 'We were so young. It's a million years ago.'

Widow Murphy's farm still lay, dishevelled and roofless. 'It's so strange to think of her as Mrs O'Brian. Should I have written to Dada, Ben? But Mick's father said that he would still not hear my name mentioned.'

Ben urged her on. 'You can only try.'

The farm was a hundred yards ahead, over to the right, behind the laurel. The creeper had grown; it was half covering her bedroom window. They stopped. She leaned on the wall, straining to see the willow. All she could see was a stump. It had been cut down. She leaned into Ben. He said, 'Come on. Don't give up now. You have to see him.'

They walked on until they reached the gate. The hinge creaked as Cait pushed it open. Ben asked, 'Shall I stay here?'

'Please come.' They walked into the drive down which she had driven the pony trap, and then into the yard. The Home Field was the same, and the cow byres. The kitchen door was open. She peered in. It was dusty, dirty, but it was the same. She heard noises from the dairy and looked at Ben. He raised his eyebrows.

'Are you sure you want me to stay?' he asked.

Cait looked from the dairy to Ben. 'I'm sure. Once he meets you it will wipe out the past.' Her voice was nervous, she was rubbing her thumb with her forefinger.

'Relax,' Ben whispered.

She walked to the dairy but stopped a yard from the open doorway.

'Dada,' she called. 'It's Caithleen. I'm home.'

The clattering of the scrubbing brush on the pail stopped. Cait waited. She called again. 'Dada, I'm home.'

He came to the opening then, his tan overalls torn, his shoulders stooped. His face was thin and old. She started towards him, her hands outstretched. He put up his arm as though to ward her off. She stopped at the look on his face. He said, 'This is not your home. Now get off my land.'

The shock of his words made her reel. Ben started towards her. She held out her hand and stopped him. Her father looked at Ben. 'So this is the Tan you took up with. I thought you'd left him. Ran back to him, did you?'

She stretched out her hand. 'Dada, please. I love you. I miss you. Please. Remember Grandpa. You came home. I've come home.'

He shook his head. 'This is not your home. You chose the Tan.'

Cait shook her head. 'But that was so long ago. So much has happened.'

Her father pushed past her and walked to the back door, steadying himself as he wrenched off his left boot, and then his right. There were holes in his socks. He straightened and looked at her. 'Not to me. I've been alone. My wife is dead, my daughter gone with one of her mother's murderers.'

Ben spoke. 'Please, Mr Healy. She loves you. She misses you. Please. I know your wife is dead. I know that you blame me and I can understand that, but I also know you loved your wife. Well, that's how Cait loves me, and I love her. Would you deny her her happiness?'

Her father flushed. 'Like you and your scum denied mine, you mean?'

He stepped back inside the kitchen and shut the door.

'Dada,' Cait called. They heard the sound of the key turning in the lock. 'Dada.'

Her father called, 'There is too much to remember, Caithleen Healy. Too much has happened to start again. There is too much in the past to ever forget or forgive.'

*   *   *

Paul Healy leaned against the door until they had gone, and all the time he looked at the photograph of Caithleen and Rose that he had recovered from the compost heap, and stuck back together again. He pressed his head back against the door as he heard her shut the gate. Too much had happened. How could he be expected to forget? How? How?

Caithleen and Ben walked away from the farm, down the track, looking to neither left nor right, clasping one another's hands. Then Cait stopped, swung round, stared back at her father's house. She said fiercely to Ben, 'I'm going back.'

She started to run down the road, her hair flying. Her ankle twisted, she nearly fell. Ben started after her. She recovered. He stopped and let her run on alone and he could hardly breathe with the agony of it all.

Just then, her father appeared, stumbling out of the gate, onto the track, his jacket flapping in the wind. He started along the road to his daughter, his arms reaching out, calling, 'Cait, don't go. Please don't go.'

Ben watched as his wife slowed, then ran on, into the arms of her father and he heard her say, 'Oh Dada.'

He stood quite still and smiled as the clouds cleared above the hills, and the sun burst through.

THE END

LOOK WITHIN YOUR HEART
Margaret Graham

Returning from the First World War driven by torment and a misguided sense of guilt, the Reverend Walter Symmonds uproots his family from the tranquillity of Rempton vicarage to the urban sprawl of Newcastle, where he works tirelessly with his beautiful wife Belle to establish a shelter for ex-servicemen. Through this desire to help the needy, the Symmonds family encounter again young Binnie Rogers, an unmarried mother, who was forced from Rempton in disgrace. But neither Binnie nor her daughter Dora are the innocent victims they appear.

As the years pass and Walter's beloved daughter Connie grows into womanhood, she takes up fresh challenges that lead her from Newcastle to India and, eventually, a family of her own. Yet with each step she takes, the vengeful and manipulating influence of the Rogers women is always close on her heels. But Connie never forgets the beauty and peace of Rempton, or her idyllic childhood there. It is only at Rempton she will discover true happiness and find herself, once more, longing for a family reunion at the vicarage.

'Wonderfully evocative romantic saga . . . A moving family drama that spans three generations'
Chic Magazine

A Bantam Paperback

0 553 40817 8

A SELECTION OF FINE NOVELS
AVAILABLE FROM BANTAM BOOKS

THE PRICES SHOWN BELOW WERE CORRECT AT THE TIME OF
GOING TO PRESS. HOWEVER TRANSWORLD PUBLISHERS
RESERVE THE RIGHT TO SHOW NEW RETAIL PRICES ON COVERS
WHICH MAY DIFFER FROM THOSE PREVIOUSLY ADVERTISED IN
THE TEXT OR ELSEWHERE.

17632 3	DARK ANGEL	Sally Beauman	£4.99
17352 9	DESTINY	Sally Beauman	£5.99
40727 9	LOVERS AND LIARS	Sally Beauman	£5.99
40803 8	SACRED AND PROFANE	Marcelle Bernstein	£5.99
40429 6	AT HOME	Charlotte Bingham	£3.99
40427 X	BELGRAVIA	Charlotte Bingham	£3.99
40497 0	CHANGE OF HEART	Charlotte Bingham	£4.99
40428 8	COUNTRY LIFE	Charlotte Bingham	£3.99
40890 9	DEBUTANTES	Charlotte Bingham	£4.99
40296 X	IN SUNSHINE OR IN SHADOW		
		Charlotte Bingham	£4.99
40496 2	NANNY	Charlotte Bingham	£4.99
40171 8	STARDUST	Charlotte Bingham	£4.99
40163 7	THE BUSINESS	Charlotte Bingham	£5.99
17635 8	TO HEAR A NIGHTINGALE		
		Charlotte Bingham	£5.99
40820 8	LILY'S WAR	June Francis	£4.99
40996 4	GOING HOME TO LIVERPOOL		
		June Francis	£4.99
40817 8	LOOK WITHIN YOUR HEART		
		Margaret Graham	£4.99
17504 1	DAZZLE	Judith Krantz	£5.99
17242 5	I'LL TAKE MANHATTAN	Judith Krantz	£5.99
40730 9	LOVERS	Judith Krantz	£5.99
17174 7	MISTRAL'S DAUGHTER	Judith Krantz	£5.99
17389 8	PRINCESS DAISY	Judith Krantz	£5.99
17505 X	SCRUPLES TWO	Judith Krantz	£5.99
17503 3	TILL WE MEET AGAIN	Judith Krantz	£5.99
40206 4	FAST FRIENDS	Jill Mansell	£4.99
40361 3	KISS	Jill Mansell	£4.99
40612 4	OPEN HOUSE	Jill Mansell	£4.99
40611 6	SHEER MISCHIEF	Jill Mansell	£4.99
40938 7	TWO'S COMPANY	Jill Mansell	£4.99
40884 4	FAST FORWARD	Judy Mercer	£4.99
40947 6	FOREIGN AFFAIRS	Patricia Scanlan	£4.99
40945 X	FINISHING TOUCHES	Patricia Scanlan	£4.99
40483 0	SINS OF THE MOTHER	Arabella Seymour	£4.99